DRAGON
RIDER

DRAGON RIDER

TARAN MATHARU

HARPER Voyager
An Imprint of HarperCollins*Publishers*

DRAGON RIDER. Copyright © 2024 by Taran Matharu Ltd. All rights reserved. Printed in the United States of America. No part of this book may be used or reproduced in any manner whatsoever without written permission except in the case of brief quotations embodied in critical articles and reviews. For information, address HarperCollins Publishers, 195 Broadway, New York, NY 10007.

HarperCollins books may be purchased for educational, business, or sales promotional use. For information, please email the Special Markets Department at SPsales@harpercollins.com.

Harper Voyager and design are trademarks of HarperCollins Publishers LLC.

FIRST EDITION

Map credit © Nicolette Caven 2024

Library of Congress Cataloging-in-Publication Data has been applied for.

ISBN 978-0-06-322757-6

24 25 26 27 28 LBC 5 4 3 2 1

To my mother, Liege,
with all the love and gratitude my heart can hold.

FROSTWEALD

YALTAI MOUNTAINS

PETRUS MOUNTAINS

PORTICUS

GREAT
STEPPE

HUDDITE LANDS

KIDARAN LANDS

PETRUS MOUNTAINS

RUFUS'
HIDEAWAY

THE
HOENIX

KENNA'S
GALLIPOT

EMPIRE

NAMBIAN DESERT

SHAMBALAI

RN LANDS

Chapter 1

They served candies before the battle started. Men sweated beneath their armour in the fields while the royals of the Sabine Empire popped sugared cherries in their mouths, laughing and pointing from their raised thrones.

Jai's belly rumbled at the sickly-sweet scent wafting through the grand pavilion. The open-ended tent was built upon a platform, one so tall that, even kneeling as he was, he could see the entire Sabine legion arrayed at its front and the enemy massing on the low, grassy ridge at the horizon.

Jai turned his head and went back to rubbing the feet of the man who had killed his father. The feet of the old emperor. The wizened shell of a once-great ruler, swaddled in silk and kashmere. A man who had founded the Sabine dynasty, and an empire that stretched from the Silver Sea to the Great Steppe.

Leonid the Great. The Lion of the Sabines. He had handed his rule on to his son years ago, for now he, the elder, was half-blind and senile. Leonid sat apart from his descendants here, no more than an afterthought, brought to the battle out of obligation. His progeny owed him everything yet treated the man as a relic. If Jai did not hate him so, he might have pitied the old man.

'Jai.'

Jai looked up and saw a skeletal finger crook. He let the wrinkled feet fall into the perfumed water of the bowl, bowing his head as he stood beside the smallest of the three thrones. The old man within was hunched and stared ahead with unseeing eyes. Those once-great hands were knotted with arthritis such that they could hardly brush his long, threadbare hair from his deep-lined face.

'Tell me what your young eyes see,' Leonid said, in the half-croak Jai had come to know so well.

It was the croak that instructed him when he washed the man's back. Chided him when he was slow. Or droned on and on as the old man recounted former glories. Jai was Leonid's constant companion and had been for almost ten of his seventeen years.

'They're gathering now,' Jai whispered, gazing beyond the arrayed legion. 'There's nowhere left for them to run.'

The old man let out a grunt of acknowledgement, one that turned into a hacking cough. Jai was swift to crouch and rub Leonid's back, feeling the knuckles of the old man's spine beneath the soft kashmere of his gown.

It would not be long before the old man passed on to the Beyond. Until then, Jai would be a dutiful servant. Not that he had any choice in the matter.

'These barbarians were fools not to surrender,' Leonid sighed once he had settled again. 'We face them with only one of our eight legions today and still they have no chance.'

'What was their alternative?' Jai asked, measuring each word with care. 'To lose their ancestral lands and be subjects to a foreign empire?'

He asked it not impertinently, but in the way Leonid preferred: as a student might question his teacher.

'To live,' Leonid replied. 'And live free. Now . . .'

A horn rang out, reverberating through the great tent, and silenced even the voices of the emperor and his son, who had been chattering above on their thrones as if at the amphitheatre.

It was the horn of the enemy upon the hillside. The last of the Huddites.

Even from leagues away, the day was clear enough for Jai to make them out, hastily preparing for battle. Children clutching at the legs of their parents, even as they were pushed back to what Jai knew would be the grasping hands of the elderly and frail.

Swarthy men and women gathered at the front ranks, clutching what weapons they had. There were blades enough, but scattered among them were pitchforks, scythes, even makeshift clubs. These were farmers' tools. Not a jot of armour to be seen. This was no army, but the remains of a civilisation. One that had been chased from their homelands to the very edge of the Silver Seas; the waters just out of sight beyond the hillside. The Huddite army had been slaughtered in battle but a month before, and the survivors taken as fettered, as was custom.

Now, all that was left was the civilians. Those who had refused to be subsumed by the Sabine Empire, preferring migration than to be under the yoke. But the Sabines were insatiable and would not allow them to escape.

This was the Huddites' last stand. The end of a culture. Of a way of life. There was something so brave in their refusal to accept defeat. Brave, yet utterly foolish, for any who took up arms against the Sabines were fair game to be claimed as spoils.

Fools, just like Jai's father.

'Speak,' Leonid croaked.

'They gather for a charge,' Jai whispered. 'There are many of them. More than the legion's five thousand. Perhaps ten times more.'

Leonid waved away Jai's words with a blue-veined hand.

'No army can defeat a Sabine legion, let alone this untrained rabble.'

Jai resisted the urge to retort that his father's army *had*, once. Instead, he watched the royals, who leaned forward, excited for the upcoming entertainment. There was a nonchalance to the way they were draped over their thrones, with servants surrounding them, fanning their brows, rubbing their bejewelled fingers. It was no more than a show for them. Like the baiting of a cave bear, or the rhyming of a bard.

Then the roar of the charge and the thunder of feet. Jai did not want to watch, but his eyes belonged to Leonid and so he turned them to the battle.

The Sabine legion seemed to hardly move. A dark, fragmented wave of Huddites broke upon the bulwark of their gleaming front line. Even at almost a mile away, he could hear the clash of steel and the wails of pain and fury. The sound rose and fell with the breeze, but never quieted.

Beyond the front line's clash Jai could see little of the horror, just the backs of men pressing forward. He could only imagine, drawing on what he had read in Leonid's diaries, or overheard from drunken soldiers when boasting had ended and the lament of lost friends began.

Inside the pavilion it was strangely silent and a full minute ticked by as they all listened to the barrage of battle before the chatter of the royals and nobility returned. All the while, Jai willed the Huddites to break the line.

Finally, a twitch of Leonid's impatient hand stirred Jai's lips as well.

'They fight,' was all he said. 'The First Legion stands strong.'

'A poor tactic,' Leonid grunted. 'Where is the encirclement? Why no cavalry? My son has grown complacent.'

He leaned forward, as if his cataracted eyes could somehow see better that way.

'Do the men fight well?'

Jai had no answer for him. His eyes had been drawn elsewhere.

A great shadow now swept across the arrayed legion such that, almost as one, thousands paused, their faces turned to the heavens.

And then, a roar. Deep and guttural, reverberating in Jai's stomach. Fear overtook him. A visceral, animal instinct that froze his body, his heart hammering, despite every thought telling him to run.

Yet somehow old Leonid showed no fear. Instead, he spoke mildly, barely audible over the excited cries of the pavilion's occupants.

'Ah. My future granddaughter is here.'

Chapter 2

It landed at the pavilion's front not with a thud, but with such grace that Jai barely heard anything. Yet he did feel the gust of its great wings, billowing the fabric ceiling and clouding dust.

This was the first dragon he had ever seen. Indeed, it was likely the first dragon any Sabine had ever seen, even Leonid himself. This must be – if the stories held true – one of the last of its kind.

At first he only saw its shape, surrounded by a dust-haze of its own making. A serpentine neck and languorous wings that folded into its back like a cloak. A tail, curling beneath itself in the tight space between the back ranks of the legion and the platform of the tent. The dragon was as large as three warhorses nose to tail.

Jai took in its colour. Emerald scales that gleamed like burnished armour, smooth but for the row of spikes that studded its back down to the spur at its tail's tip. A horned head completed the sight, one with a long snout and a hint of sharp teeth at the edges of its mouth, its lips curling wolfishly.

It was all so much to take in that Jai hardly noticed the rider straddling the beast's back. Only when they leaped onto the platform of the tent did he tear his eyes away.

The figure was lithe, clad in a white muslin dress that clung to her legs as she stalked closer to the thrones. Her face and hair were covered by a thin veil, and though Jai might have guessed the visitor was a she by the grace of her movements – a curl of waist-length golden hair that had come loose from behind the gauze confirmed it.

A bejewelled hand tucked the strand away as she approached the emperor's throne. The seat of Constantine the Blessed. Or, as most knew him . . . Constantine the Cruel.

She came to a stop before the two thrones of the emperor and prince, silent as the cries of battle drifted on the wind.

Beside the emperor, guards twitched hands closer to their hilts, and murmuring began when she did not kneel. Even Prince Titus had to bow before his own father, yet the girl stood unabashed, her head slowly turning in curiosity at the spectacle of the raised thrones before her.

'We bring you a gift, Emperor Constantine,' she called out.

Her voice was loud and hard, accented with what Jai knew to be the lilt of the Dansk. The people of the Northern Tundra; a kingdom unconquered by the Sabines. Apparently they had chosen to marry into the dynasty rather than fight it.

Constantine motioned with his hands to the guards on either side of him and the tension in the room eased with the emperor's sudden smile.

'What gift is that, Princess Erica?' Constantine replied, leaning forward to look closer. 'Perhaps the early pleasure of your company? We had not expected you for some weeks yet.'

'Victory,' was the girl's reply.

As if by some unseen command, the dragon lifted its head to the sky. The great mouth opened, revealing a tooth-filled maw that could swallow a man whole. The sight stoppered Jai's throat.

Then, a roar.

The sound tore through the tent and up into the sky. Even above the din of battle it echoed across the plain. It went on and on, the great beast's chest heaving with the effort. With every passing second Jai had to resist the urge to run.

Silence in the tent followed, but for the distant clash of arms and the wails of the dying in the field. And then, an answer: another roar, far away. Jai could now see another dragon in the sky, soaring above the ridge beyond. But it was not this that drew his eye, but the darkening wave forming where the ridge met the horizon. One that glimmered in the sunlight, above the morass of the Huddite horde.

An army had arrived, but a hundred feet behind the back ranks of the Huddites. Thousands of men, axes clashing on shields, chanting a guttural warsong in tandem with the beat. Now, the exhausted Huddites turned to face the new threat, their wails of horror just audible above the clamour.

Constantine stood on his throne for a better look, then clapped his hands in delight.

'You have your work cut out for you, my boy,' he laughed, leaning over and slapping his son's shoulder. 'Your bride will have you for breakfast if you're not careful. If her dragon doesn't first.'

Constantine laughed again at his own joke as he sat once more, as did the entourage that stood behind him. Titus, sitting beside his father on his own throne, only scowled at the words, turning to whisper to his personal guard.

As always, Jai was struck by how unassuming the emperor looked, with his clipped goatee and thin moustache. He shared the same upturned nose as his son, who glowered at his father from beneath a mop of blond hair. The prince's sharp face twisted, his lip curling. He did not greet his future bride.

Beside Jai, Leonid tutted beneath his breath, peering at the scene through bleary eyes. At a dozen paces away, the old man could just about see the interaction between dragon rider and emperor. It was a relief for Jai that he did not ask for a description, for he did not wish to break the relative silence of the tent. When Constantine spoke, few dared do anything but listen.

The girl stood alone, almost awkward in her stance, until she turned her back on the royals. Her dragon let out a low rumble, stretching its graceful neck towards her from where it sat beside the platform.

At this rudeness, even Constantine frowned, but the reason for the girl's movement was soon revealed. Jai could hardly believe the speed at which the other dragon traversed the maelstrom of battle, but in moments the second beast landed beside the first, and Jai ducked his head as dust billowed once more.

This dragon looked older than Erica's, for its black scales did not shine with the same brilliance and some of its teeth were missing. Scars crisscrossed its back, testament to a lifetime of battles against the empire's gryphons. By now Jai knew who to expect leaping onto the platform, clad in all the finery that the Northern Tundra had to offer.

King Ivar, Erica's father. He wore the white furs of a cave bear across his shoulders, with its upper jaw resting upon his head. A circlet of silver could be seen across his craggy brow and torques jingled up his arms – arms that were still muscled despite the king's advanced age.

The Dansk king lifted his chin, his face as inscrutable as Erica's beneath her veil. Only his eyes hinted at his thoughts, flicking between the faces of the emperor and his son.

Compared to the emperor, Ivar was almost savage in

appearance, the effect made more so by the yellow of his teeth and the tattoos that traced in whorls across his exposed chest and neck – though these were half-obscured by a tawny beard. In contrast, Constantine was resplendent in pressed robes of purple and an elaborate golden crown.

Ivar spread his arms wide, his weathered face breaking into a smile.

'We apologise for our expeditious arrival, Constantine,' he said, and even from a stone's throw away Jai could smell the beer on Ivar's breath. 'The winds of the Silver Sea were kind to our ships as we travelled down the coast.'

He too refused to bow, instead nodding to the emperor and his son. To Leonid, he gave the most deference, his roguish smile fading as he inclined his head at the old man. Then he wrapped an arm around his daughter and winked at Titus. Again the prince grimaced and shifted uncomfortably in his throne. Erica tugged at her father's arm until he released her with a grunt.

'How can we not forgive your untimeliness?' Constantine asked, 'When you bring such a generous gift.'

He swept his hand up at the Dansk army.

'Our legion does not need your help, but we welcome it. Still, I must point out you have rather given away the element of surprise.'

Ivar laughed a deep, booming laugh.

'We have no quarrel with the Huddites,' he said, shaking his head. 'It is . . . shall we say . . . a demonstration of what our new alliance *might* bring. That should be enough for today. For we are not allies yet. Not until the marriage bed is blooded, eh Titus?'

The bear-like king nudged his daughter and laughed again. The girl remained silent behind her veil, but Jai could not miss her gloved hand ball into a fist.

Constantine's lips pursed, but if Ivar noticed, he did not let on. Instead, he rubbed his not-insubstantial belly and gestured at the battle behind.

'Come now, let us feast,' Ivar said. 'Allow this rabble to surrender. See, they already begin to lay down their arms.'

A flick to Jai's ear from Leonid's finger turned Jai's head back to the battle. Indeed, the sounds of combat were receding, leaving only the rattle and chant of the Dansk warriors. The Huddites had retreated from the ordered legion ranks, their tens of thousands milling between the hammer of the Dansk and the anvil of the Sabines.

'He's right,' was all Jai dared to whisper in Leonid's ear.

Not all the weapons had fallen, but the Huddites had to know that now there was no glorious last stand to be had. Just slaughter, or subjugation as the fettered – forced to work for the empire until the end of their days. Prisoners of war were fair game under imperial law.

Even from afar Jai saw men and women fall to their knees in supplication. A few hundred remained defiant, yanking at those kneeling, trying to convince them to stand. These few would fight to the bitter end, but the rest might be spared to live on as fettered. If such a thing could be considered living.

Constantine cleared his throat and stood from his throne. He approached Ivar, the portly little man looking up at the six-foot, battle-hardened king. Until now, the two men had been rivals. Enemies even, though rarely in direct conflict.

Then, Constantine swept out his arms and clasped Ivar in a hug.

'Blessed mercy, then!' he announced, stepping away. 'To celebrate the union of our two great dynasties. Mercy!'

Leonid grunted with approval and pulled Jai's ear to his mouth.

'Keep an eye on these Dansk,' he hissed. 'This alliance isn't sealed yet.'

Chapter 3

The journey back to the imperial palace was one of jostling cushions and cracking whips, as Jai and Leonid travelled the Kashmere Road in the old emperor's carriage. To Jai's dismay Leonid had chosen again to keep the curtains of their padded interior closed, and he could do little more than stare at the old man as he snored through the two-day journey from the coast back to Latium.

Jai longed for his books. For real food, rather than the thin but easily consumed gruel that Leonid subsisted on when he travelled – which Jai had to share. But more than anything, Jai longed for a view of the outside.

Almost his entire life had been spent in the Sabine court. In the decade since he had arrived there he had hardly left the grounds of the imperial palace. It was as if he were a prisoner there. And in a way, he supposed, he was.

Jai was a glorified hostage.

When Jai was a child his father, Rohan, king of the Kidara tribe, had allied with the other peoples of the Great Steppe against the Sabine Empire. Rohan became High Khan of the Steppefolk, and he had led his people in a bloody campaign of resistance that ended in a stalemate, with great suffering on both sides. In the end it had come to a final battle. One that Jai's father had lost. Following his capture Leonid had executed the High Khan personally.

But Leonid was already an old man by then, made more so by the year-long war. Exhausted, he had handed his son Constantine the emperor's crown on the very same day as Rohan's execution. Constantine had harboured no desire to invade the seemingly endless grasslands; not with unrest from the many civilisations his empire had subsumed springing up – inspired by Jai's father's example.

So, a peace agreement emerged. One where the tribes' leaders paid a yearly tribute to the Sabines and the warriors already captured would remain fettered.

The leaders also sent their children to be raised in the Sabine court until they reached twenty years of age. Should the khans of the various tribes break the peace or refuse to pay their tribute . . . their children would be slain.

As the third son of his father's lineage, and born of a nameless courtesan, Jai was as unimportant at the court as he would have been back home. While his two older brothers were treated with a modicum of respect, serving as Prince Titus's hunting guides and companions, Jai's lot had been to wipe drool from Leonid's wispy beard and other even more ignoble responsibilities. His nickname, "arsewipe", was a cruel one, but not inaccurate.

He had no purpose, both in this court and back in the Great Steppe. He was a footnote in the annals of history. And Jai liked that just fine. He just wanted a peaceful existence in a place he could call home . . . though sometimes he wondered if he could even call the Great Steppe his homeland when he did not remember it.

'Do we near home?'

Leonid's question disturbed Jai from his thoughts. The old man lifted his head, and Jai was swift to support the old man's neck and bring a gourd of water to Leonid's lips.

'Soon, I hope,' Jai said. 'If I could look outside, I might give you a better answer.'

Leonid looked up at Jai, searching his face. Did he see Jai's mixed heritage there? That paler skin from his mother that stood him apart from the other Steppefolk. Or did Leonid just see the Steppeman, like his father, in the black of his shoulder-cut hair and the hazel of his eyes? Certainly everyone else did.

After a moment he grunted his approval and Jai grinned as he gently pulled open a chink in the curtains, careful not to blind the elder with the new light.

He pressed his face against the glass, watching the rolling hills of the Sabine heartlands. To another, it might have appeared boring, for there was little to see but dense fields of wheat stalks waving in the afternoon sun. But to Jai it was a sight unseen, one he'd only read of in Leonid's extensive library, or heard about when the old man reminisced. He wondered how different his homelands might look from these hills and searched his memory.

His memory of where he came from was all a blur. After all, he had been four years old – hardly weaned from his wet nurse's breast – when he had been sent away. Though he had flashes of memory.

Of men and women, sitting in circles, oiling and braiding each other's hair. Of food that burned his mouth yet left him feeling warm and *alive*. And, most galling, scents he could not name and tastes he only savoured in dreams.

Poor roots for a prince of the steppe.

Were it not for Balbir, the woman sent to care for him and

his brothers, he might not have had any knowledge of his people at all.

Even *she* was kept from him now, working for a noble family in Latium's merchant district. On the rare occasions he was allowed to leave the palace, Jai would do his best to see her, but it was rare she could do much more than exchange a few words as she scrubbed the front steps, before Balbir was shooed inside by her mistress.

'Well?' Leonid asked.

Jai sighed and let the curtain fall back.

'I see only fields.'

Leonid nodded wryly and nestled deeper into the cushions.

'We are close,' he said. 'The city has always been surrounded by fields. Any attackers could be seen long before they reach its walls.'

'Raiders?' Jai asked. 'This far south?'

Leonid chuckled.

'In the old days we had many enemies. And rebellions, uprisings. It's not a problem anymore. Now, only the Dansk remain.'

Jai shuffled closer.

'Remain? Still? You asked me to watch them for you. Why?'

Leonid sighed and rubbed his eyes.

'For decades they've raided our coasts and the northern reaches of our empire. Ask me, Jai, why I have not crushed them like all my other enemies?'

'The dragons, obviously,' Jai said.

Leonid cackled and the laughter turned into a hacking cough. Jai lifted him upright and rubbed the old man's back until it was over.

Dragons. Even in a land like the Sabine Empire, where the wilds were populated by many dangerous creatures, the very word struck fear and awe into all who heard it. Legends still told of when these predators haunted every sky across the world. Now, but a few dozen remained, flying where they willed but returning each year to breed in the icy mountains of the Northern Tundra, hunting narwhals and seals in the Silver Seas.

Leonid's cough came to a shuddering stop, and he gulped down some more water.

'Dragons. *Pah*! The Dansk would like to think so,' Leonid rasped. 'But our Gryphon Guard would match their dragons if it came to it. Numbers, my boy. We've a hundred or more gryphons to fight their dozen dragons. A fair fight.'

Jai's heart pumped a little faster at the thought of the emperor's personal protectors, riders of their own great beasts. Gryphons were smaller and weaker than dragons, true, but Leonid was right that there were more of them – and all bonded to a military guard. Dragons, as far as he knew, were only soulbound with the upper echelons of Dansk society.

'So why, then?' Jai asked.

Leonid pulled a fur across his legs and winced as the bones of his shoulder clicked at the motion.

'The cold,' he said simply. 'The Dansk live in near-perpetual winter and their kingdom is scattered across hundreds of remote villages. Not to mention their warriors excel at ambushes – ask any of our border militia. We'd bleed our armies and supply lines dry to invade and then pay a pound of flesh to hold it. And for what? A hardscrabble land where crops hardly grow? *Pah*!'

He spat with annoyance once more.

As always, Jai listened with care, learning all he could. It still amazed him that Leonid deigned to speak with him in this way. It amazed him even more that Leonid's relatives, and indeed even the nobility of the Sabine court, ignored their elder. The old man had outlived all his peers. The man had seen almost a hundred harvests.

Leonid's son, Constantine, hardly saw his own father, preferring to carouse with his entourage of sycophants. As for his grandson, Titus had a fascination with the ex-emperor's legacy, but hardly ever visited him, taking after his father. The palace was grand enough that months could go by without any of the royals crossing paths.

'Do you agree with this marriage?' Jai asked. 'I didn't even know it was happening.'

Leonid cackled.

'I was not consulted, but I knew it was coming. It's a clever move by Constantine. He is a peace-time emperor, but not without his own wiles. The marriage will allow us to stand down our legions on the northern borders, which in turn bolsters our coffers. But most importantly of all, when Titus's future son takes the throne, the Northern Tundra will become part of our empire.'

Jai nodded along, but he'd known the old man long enough to tell Leonid was not speaking the whole truth. He kept his voice light. 'But they cannot be trusted?'

Leonid arched an eyebrow. This was more conversation than Leonid usually indulged Jai with, for the retired emperor was more often interested in recounting past glories. Now Jai was straying into the politics of today's court. But finally, the old man inclined his head.

'They landed a hundred longships on our coast and marched an army across our sovereign lands. Had the Gryphon Guard not caught sight of their approach and warned our coastal defences to not engage them, fighting might have broken out on their arrival. It was reckless of them, and all for a petty show of force. A reckless enemy is a dangerous one. Unpredictable. It was why Rohan gave me so much trouble.'

He caught sight of Jai's downcast expression at the mention

of his father and cleared his throat. Even after a decade, the topic was one they avoided.

Thankfully, the thud of their carriage driver's fist upon the roof interrupted the awkward silence.

'Five minutes!' the muffled voice called.

Jai twitched back the curtains of the window once more, eliciting a tut from Leonid. He was willing to risk Leonid's displeasure for this. Now, for the first time, he saw Latium from the outside.

A cliff jutted from the countryside – a giant ramped incline ending in a sharp drop on its opposite side. But this oddity of geography was overshadowed by the sprawling marble palace built upon its slopes, punctuated by bronze-capped domes and ziggurats. Pleasure gardens were interspersed throughout the white buildings, yet Jai's eyes were drawn to the high spire of the Gryphon Guard's eyrie, as he sought out a glimpse of the greatest warriors of the empire returning to their roost. None could be seen. They were likely in the air behind them, keeping an eye on the Dansk army, which was marching some miles behind the royal train.

'Seen enough?' Leonid asked with an edge.

Jai let the curtain fall, returning to darkness once again.

'I don't know how you expect me to watch the Dansk,' Jai muttered. 'You hardly ever leave your quarters.'

Leonid chuckled drily.

'Titus and his new bride Erica will be hunting in the morning. I will join them . . . and so will you.'

Chapter 4

U pon their arrival, Jai had hurried Leonid back through the palace, dodging frantic servants as they rushed to arrange a feast, one that had not yet been planned due to the Dansk's early arrival. Even though they had all night and the morrow to prepare, they would be hard pressed to have everything finished on time.

Leonid tutted impatiently each time Jai slowed his wheelchair to weave around a harried servant, until they were finally through the great doors to Leonid's chamber.

Jai was swift to tug a small rope beside Leonid's bed, summoning attendants with buckets of hot water. The old man wished to wash away the dust of the road before bed and, despite the onset of dusk, Jai found himself going through the motions of his morning routine.

Every morning, the old man had to be washed, groomed and dressed, which meant drawing him a bath, combing his hair and the long process of picking out robes he would find acceptable. Never mind that Leonid almost never left his chambers and hardly anyone would see him.

Next Jai set the fire in the crackling hearth that he often h

to maintain at all hours – Leonid liked it to be warm, such that
he might be reminded of the years he campaigned in the tropical
south, carving out the bulk of his empire.

Jai had a wiry strength to him now, after so many years of
hauling logs from the palace sculleries. A silver lining, or he'd
likely have run to fat long ago.

The constant carrying and reorganising of books contributed
to Jai's build too: Leonid's room might have been confused for
a library were it not for the enormous bed at the room's centre.
Every wall was lined with books, and the old man's favourite
pastime was sitting by the fire reading over his old journals,
often making amendments and additions in the margins.

Though Jai would never admit it, it was one of his favourite
pastimes too. The life stories of not just Leonid but every other
military mind through history were contained within this room.
It was, Leonid told him, the source of his success.

Many a night had Jai fantasised about leading his own men
into battle, even riding a gryphon at their front. It was a joy to
daydream, trapped in the confines of that dusty room. While he
remained, his mind could soar with any flight of fancy that took
him.

He had read most books in these rooms at least once, but
one section remained untouched, gathering dust upon a low shelf
in the corner. The ragged journal of Leonid's wars with Jai's
father. He could not bring himself to read that tome.

It wasn't because Jai held some deep love for his father –
though by all accounts Rohan had been a good ruler, who had
loved his people and fought with honour. Indeed that was all
he was to Jai, for he did not truly remember what the man
looked like. His mother too was but a fleeting memory – a pale
face that stroked his hair and hummed lullabies. Even Balbir
did not know what had become of her.

No, it was the shame of it. For within those pages lay the reason men spat at him in the streets or cursed the colour of his skin. He needed no reminder of his people's supposed inferiority beyond the fact that Steppefolk made up almost half of the fettered in the empire. He did not need another reason to hate the old emperor. It was hard enough serving him as it was.

'A game of tablus,' Leonid called, clapping his thin hands. 'While I bathe.'

Jai grimaced. It was not that he did not enjoy the game. Indeed, on the rare occasions that Jai was able to leave the palace he'd always stop by the city's main plaza to play a few games with the old men there, winning most.

No, he liked the game well enough. He was just sick of losing to Leonid, who he had never beaten. The man's eyes might be clouded but his mind certainly was not.

Jai only wished there was someone else in the palace that might play it with him. But few servants would even meet his gaze, let alone strike up conversation. He was, and always would be, a savage oddity. A royal and a servant. A Sabine Steppeman. An enemy and an ally. A contradiction best avoided. He was trouble and certainly most considered his friendship not worth the ire of the many who hated Steppefolk. Rohan's raids on their border towns were not yet forgiven.

Jai sighed, the truth of this made more apparent by the servants who avoided his eye as they hauled buckets to fill the gold-clawed bath in the chamber's centre.

'Thank you,' Jai said.

They hardly met his gaze and were soon gone, leaving Jai to remove Leonid's robe and lift his frail body from his wheeled chair into the steaming water.

The old man groaned and Jai set up the chequered board and a stool beside the bath, staring at the pieces. It was not dissimilar to the battlefield they had seen that morning. Infantry pieces on the front row, with horsemen on the edges. And behind, the more useful pieces, made up of the rare beasts of whatever land the board originated from. As it was a Sabine board the pieces were gryphons, chamroshes, manticores and the like. In the Northern Tundra, Jai knew the pieces included cave bears and dragons, while his own folk used mammoths and khiroi. Still, whatever the creature, the pieces moved in the same way.

'Come now, I'll let you make the first move,' Leonid wheezed, settling deeper into the steaming water.

Jai shrugged and moved the first piece. A common opening gambit: a tentative foray from a shielded legionary. Leonid still managed to find fault in it, tutting beneath his breath.

'Tell me, Jai,' Leonid said, moving a gryphon forward to meet the legionary, 'what should my son's generals have done in the battle with the Huddites?'

Jai did not even need to think of a reply. He'd had plenty of time to mull it over on their long journey. He'd read enough of Leonid's journals to know what he'd observed from the Huddites had been the tactics of an infant.

Jai cocked his head, bringing a second legionary forward to cover the one the gryphon threatened.

'They allowed the enemy to pick the battlefield,' Jai said. 'The ridge gave the Huddites the high ground, and their leaders a view of their surroundings.'

'Surrounding,' Leonid muttered. 'There's a good word.'

He brought his next piece forward along a diagonal, a chamrosh. The creature, carved from bone, was a perfect replica of the real thing, a hawk-headed and winged canine favoured as a bonded beast by the apprentice warriors, squires, of the Gryphon Guard. Already Jai could see his mistake, his two legionaries vulnerable and encircled in the middle of the board. Surrounded indeed.

'How are battles won?' Leonid asked, idly.

'The battle is won not when the last enemy is dead, but when the first enemy is routed,' Jai said, repeating the words Leonid had drummed into him over the years.

With an ironic smile, Jai shifted back the foremost legionary, tucking it behind the first. Leonid had always been an aggressive player and Jai's defensive position rarely withstood the old man's attacks for long.

'I've fought battles where the enemy ran before they lost a single man. A battle is not a meat grinder, much as my son seems to think it is. What should he have done today, Jai?'

Jai chose his words with care. Leonid loved his son, cruel though the emperor could be.

'Sire, a single legion would have seemed outnumbered, giving the enemy confidence they had a chance. Three would have demonstrated the futility of resistance and forced a surrender.'

He did not mention that a surrender would have yielded more fettered, though undoubtably it was one of the reasons Constantine had chased the horde of Huddites in the first place. With the vast farmlands of the Huddites suddenly his, the Sabines needed new fettered to work the fields.

Leonid raised a thin finger.

'What else?'

Jai thought for a moment. Then:

'With their backs to the sea, they had nowhere to run. So their choices were to fight to the death or surrender. But if they'd had a way out . . .'

Leonid interrupted him, as Jai lost steam.

'A battle is won in the heart of the common soldier,' he said. 'It is convincing your own soldiers that to fight is better than to run, and your opponents' that the reverse is true. Never trap an enemy without giving them a path to retreat. More foes of mine have been slain or captured in retreat than ever were in battle.'

Leonid shifted out a cavalryman and Jai had no choice but to move his legionary back again. Already, the board was a disaster. Leonid had brought many of his best troops forward, threatening his entire line. Meanwhile, Jai was practically back to square one, with a single legionary alone in the centre of the board.

'Your father . . .' Leonid muttered, knocking over the lonely legionary with his gryphon. 'He knew this well enough. Gave me my first ever real defeat.'

Jai frowned. This was the second time today Leonid had brought up his father. That was twice more than he had in the last year. Clearly, something was on the old man's mind.

'Oh?' was all Jai allowed. It was all he could say without betraying the tightening of his throat.

Leonid surveyed the board, his jowls tucked into his neck. 'Our first battle, he baited me. Sent his army forward and then had them run away in supposed panic within minutes. And when my men broke their formations to give chase, and my cavalry charged ahead of the infantry lines to cut them down . . . they reformed. Turned, and met us head on, a perfect line of thundering khiroi, swallowing up my scattered horsemen like they were nothing. It was all I could do to reform what was left of the infantry and retreat to our camp. Your father's army slaughtered more Sabines in one day than any foe had my entire life.'

Jai stared at Leonid. He knew about this battle. Everyone did, really. But the details of *how* Jai's father had defeated Leonid had been muddied by rumour of betrayal, to save the Sabines' face.

Jai felt something rare, especially when it came to his family and folk. Pride.

He noticed he was smiling and wiped the expression from his face. If Leonid had noticed the shift in Jai's mood he gave no sign of it. Instead, he became silent, mulling over the board a while. He sniffed.

'Four or five moves and I have you.'

Leonid nodded at the emperor figurine at the centre of Jai's formation, one that bore a striking resemblance to a younger Constantine, and Jai dutifully knocked it over, admitting defeat.

Leonid sniffed and scattered the pieces to the floor with a sweep of his gnarled hand.

'You are too timid. Too scared to make a mistake, to take a risk. You are your father's son. *Act* like it.'

Chapter 5

Jai lay on his back listening to the morning calls of the peacocks in the pleasure gardens. It was dark in his room, for there was no window. Indeed, he could hardly call it a room at all, but rather a wardrobe that had been masquerading as his dorm since he had entered the ex-emperor's service. It was located in the corner of Leonid's own bedchamber so that the old man could call out to him if he needed.

Today was different. Today was not a day of grooming or of transcribing Leonid's dictation, of scratching quill and drying ink. Nor was it one of reading books aloud or rubbing the old man's aching back.

Today . . . he would hunt.

Or rather, observe a hunt, if the invitation that had come for Leonid the prior evening gave any indication. He hoped it was only to observe – riding horses had always put him on edge.

Jai's name, for whatever reason, had been on the invitation too. Perhaps it was to seem more hospitable to the Dansk, who might disapprove of the Sabine policy of holding the children of their defeated enemies hostage, and indeed kept no fettered of their own.

Either way, Jai was overjoyed to be leaving the walled city of Latium *again*. And so soon after the last time – a rare treat that set his heart beating.

Indeed, he would see the city's outskirts for the first time since he was a child, back when Balbir was still allowed to take him and his brothers beyond the city limits and had taught him the Steppefolk names and uses for the plants that grew there.

Balbir. His heart twisted a little at the thought of her weathered face and soft brown eyes. It had been so many years since he'd done more than exchange a few words with her. And she, worked to the bone. He should stop by again soon. Make sure she was well cared for.

And when he came of age . . . he'd take her home with him. That . . . that was what he was waiting for. She'd finally be free from backbreaking service and would tell him how to be a Steppeman on their long journey home. She'd teach him their ways so that he would not be a stranger among them, as he was here, when he arrived.

They would live off the fat of the land, welcomed by his tribe. He'd find a wife, a role in the tribe. Perhaps finally, he'd feel welcomed. He'd *belong*.

Jai sighed and forced himself to rise.

Leonid's old robes were what Jai usually wore while pottering around the dusty interior of Leonid's boudoir, but they would not do for this occasion. Nor would the day-to-day uniform of the kitchen boys – which he wore whenever he went on errands.

Somewhere in the mess of his room the ceremonial attire of a palace servant was gathering lint. He discovered it beneath his cot, brushed off the dust and changed into it with a grimace. It was too small – too short in the leg and arm, tight across the chest. It would have to do.

A cracked mirror allowed him to examine his travel-worn

appearance as he frantically dunked his mop of thick dark hair in cold water and scrubbed at his face with the soapy rag. An old razor, resharpened on the cobbles outside, allowed him to scrape away the fledgling whiskers above his lip. He only wished that he could do something about the dark rings beneath his slightly sunken eyes.

He was grateful, at least, for the sharp cheekbones his mother must have given him, and the strong jaw that came from his father. His skin, darker than that of the olive-skinned Sabines, but lighter than the brown tones of the Steppefolk, came from both parents. All he knew of his mother was that she had been fair, but he knew almost nothing else about her. Even Balbir had never met her, though she'd seen her from afar.

He cared about his appearance more than usual that day, not least because he would be in a formal setting . . . emerging from the ex-emperor's room into the public was rare enough. And though he hated to admit it, it was also because he would be in the presence of Erica. The dragon-riding princess of the Northern Tundra.

Though he had little idea of what she looked like, the courage she had shown in the face of the Sabines had already won him over.

Like him, she would be dragged from her homelands to the court of the Sabines in the name of peace. Her lot was likely much more comfortable than his, true, but somehow he did not imagine she would find much joy in the petty gossip and intrigues of palace life. She seemed a girl of action, gliding on the wind.

He only wished he could say the same about himself. Though he fantasised about someday soul-bonding with a gryphon, perhaps even joining the Gryphon Guard, he was not cut out for such adventure – nor capable of soul-bonding with more than a flea, most like.

He would have to stick to reading about their exploits in Leonid's journals, in the quiet peace of his chamber.

'Boy, if you are not out here in the next ten seconds, my riding crop will find a new purpose.'

Leonid's voice snapped him away from the mirror and he emerged to find the ex-emperor alone in his wheelchair, fumbling with the dress uniform that Jai had picked out the evening before.

'I doubt you'll be doing much riding today, sire,' Jai retorted. 'Didn't you say your . . . seat . . . can't handle it anymore?'

Leonid flashed him a glare that told Jai that the ex-emperor's buttocks were not an acceptable topic of conversation this morning.

It was but a few minutes before Jai was trundling Leonid's wheelchair down the long corridor bordering the principal court-yard of the imperial palace. The corridor was hardly used by anyone other than Jai and occasionally Leonid. The man had become a recluse in his old age, rarely leaving the comfort of his room.

Something was different today though. The palace was busier with anticipation of the feast, true, but that was not all that had changed. No . . . it was also the legionaries stationed at every doorway, and the others marching back and forth in the court-yard below. The palace soldiers were in their dress uniform, all cloaks, tassels and horsehair helms, but the blades at their sides were as deadly as ever. Stranger still, many of them were armed with ugly looking crossbows, which did not often form part of the legion's armaments.

'A show of strength,' Leonid muttered, tilting his head at the arrayed guards. 'In case this wedding was all a ruse to get their army into our capital.'

Considering the Dansk army was camped with a legion between them and the palace, it seemed unnecessary. But Jai supposed if the Dansk had made a show of strength that morning, Constantine wished to return the favour several times over.

As they neared the palace's entrance, two servants walked by, carrying a large pewter amphora. Neither servant even glanced at him. He recognised one – Ava. A maid with big eyes that had pressed him up against the palace wall one night after last harvest feast and reached between his legs. She had led him away from the hall with a laugh, taking him to a shadowed corner where he'd had his first kiss. He still remembered her breath in his ear, the taste of wine on her lips and her contented sigh. But then a voice had called from the kitchen, and she had been whisked away, grinning over her shoulder.

Jai tried to meet Ava's eye. It had been months ago. He searched for a way to speak to her, to communicate something and have her look at him. Instead, she averted her gaze, her head bowed in deference to the old man.

Jai swallowed his disappointment as they reached the palace's front steps and pushed the chair down the long sloping ramp that had been carved there just for Leonid.

Jai took in the plaza below where a half-dozen horse-drawn carriages were waiting. Among them Jai could see Dansk and Sabine alike, the two groups ostentatiously avoiding each other.

It was strange to see the vibrant garments of the servants and Sabine nobility alongside those of the Dansk. Even the lowliest kitchen boy looked better dressed when contrasted with the muted greys, whites and fawns of the Dansk. They seemed to exclusively wear rough-spun flaxcloth, furs and leathers, though their jewellery, such as it was, was on full display.

But this was not the delicate filigree and cut jewels that adorned the fingers of the Sabines. Instead, simpler rune-stamped brooches and twisting torques of gold and silver gleamed on chests and necks. Even Ivar, standing tall above all the rest, looked more like a wild and magical hermit unearthed from the forest rather than the king of an unconquerable land.

At the sight of Leonid's arrival servants hurried forward, lifting the chair in the air as if he weighed nothing at all and inserting him into the foremost carriage, where Jai imagined Constantine and Titus were waiting for him.

Jai stood there, somewhat at a loss. It was only when a trumpet sounded and the waiting rivals were bundling into their carriages that he realised he was about to be left behind.

Already, the drivers were cracking their whips, and it was all Jai could do to leap onto the footplate of the last Dansk vehicle before they were rattling down the main avenue that bisected the city.

Jai sucked in a breath, revelling in the open sky above and the hustle and bustle of a living city. He leaned out over the rushing cobbles, stretching up his face to catch the breeze. The sun was bright and clear and it seemed his duties to Leonid would be taken care of by Constantine's servants that day. Jai grinned even as grizzled Dansk faces peered out at their strange passenger through the glass.

Jai waved and clambered up to sit beside the grizzled driver. The fresh air had never smelled so sweet.

Chapter 6

J ai spent much of the journey building the courage to introduce himself to the driver, who had taken Jai's joining him in his stride. But it seemed the caravan had hardly wheeled out of the city gates and down a road before the carriages were rolling to a stop. They had hardly gone a mile.

In fact, their destination was so close that an area of refreshments had already been set up, along with a cold feast arrayed on long, rustic tables.

Jai's belly grumbled at the sight, for he had not eaten all morning and the sun was now high. But food was forgotten when he saw his brothers leaping from their carriages, laughing uproariously at some joke of Titus's.

The young future emperor was dressed in full military regalia, though he'd never taken part in any battle. He was an excellent swordsman by all accounts, trained by the best of the best, and had even taken part in fencing tournaments in Latium's Colosseum. But even Jai knew that the ornate chest armour Titus bore was carved with rippling musculature that did not exist beneath.

Jai's brothers had not worn servants' uniforms for years, and both wore fine hunting jodhpurs of stitched, green-dyed moleskin. Their eyes seemed to pass by him, even as Jai waved.

'Arjun!' Jai called. 'Samar!'

Arjun looked up in surprise and as usual the sight of his face jolted Jai with warmth and a brief, uncomfortable flash of jealousy. Rohan's son in almost every way, or so the rumours said. Tall, handsome, and heir apparent, he would soon return to the Great Steppe to rule their father's tribe. Even Titus's sycophants were jealous of Arjun's long dark lashes and chiselled jaw.

Despite being a supposed savage, his popularity among the upper crust's young ladies was well known – a touch of the exotic for them to lust after before they settled down with parent-approved husbands.

But it was hard to hate Arjun. The burden of future rule lay heavy on his shoulders and he ran towards it rather than shirked it. He balanced this weight with an easy geniality and teased Jai fondly in the few moments they spent together each year, as any brother would.

'Jai?' Samar cried out, striding up to Arjun's side, a smile splitting his round face. 'What are you doing here? It's been so long!'

Samar was a softer boy than his older brother, in both physique and soul. Quiet, even compared to Jai, and perhaps a little slow. But what Samar lacked in fierceness, he made up for with an innocent, forgiving nature that made him hard to resist.

Jai loved and admired both his brothers. He wondered: were it not for Leonid's reclusiveness, would he have grown to be their equal?

'Are we hunting today?' Jai asked, with as much bravado as he could muster.

Arjun saw right through him, stepping forward and wrapping Jai in a bear hug. Jai's head just cleared his brother's shoulder.

'So, the old man finally let you out of your cave,' he chuckled, pounding Jai on the back. 'You ride with us today. I'll see to it.'

Jai grinned uncertainly, eyeing the saddled horses hitched along branches of the trees that surrounded them. His fear of the large beasts embarrassed him and he cursed his own weakness. How could he daydream of riding a gryphon into battle if he could not even find the courage to mount a horse?

He shook the shame from his mind, instead taking in the wonder of his surroundings. The empire was more concerned with taming the wilderness of their lands than preserving it. This hunting ground, protected by Leonid since long before even Constantine was born, was the exception.

It was a strange place – a savannah of sorts, with yellow grasses and copses of trees scattered across it. Herds of beasts could be seen dotting the horizon and Jai wondered at the menagerie of animals released and hunted here. Most of the creatures out there he had only read about until now.

The contrast to the endless, uniform fields of wheat and corn was enormous. This was what the western empire had once been before the Sabines turned it into the world's breadbasket. With the Huddites gone, the Sabines now held the grain reserves that fed the ravenous Phoenix Empire in the far east. And, of course, they now had enough fettered Huddites to work them, and bolster the numbers of aging fettered left over from the War of the Steppe, all those years ago. That had been the real reason for the war, or so the rumour went. The invented excuse for the invasion had been so tenuous most couldn't even remember it.

Jai watched with bated breath as the man who had orchestrated the day, Constantine, emerged from his carriage, pushing his father's chair. For the briefest of moments, Jai caught Leonid's bleary eye, and the ex-emperor nodded imperceptibly. Jai was off the hook for today. If only to spy on the Dansk during the hunt.

'All so exciting isn't it,' Samar muttered. 'Did you see . . .'

He trailed off, open mouthed, then nudged Jai as a fur-clad Dansk girl stepped down from a nearby carriage, shading her eyes. It was Erica's handmaiden, if Jai was not mistaken, for she hurried to the princess's side as soon as she touched the ground.

Once more, Jai could not help but stare at the princess as her handmaiden helped her into her saddle. She was out of place, clad in ermine and lace, among the leather and gaiters of the milling hunting party. Still, like a white rock in a muddy stream.

Jai could parse little of her beyond her bearing, for the veil still covered her face. She sat straight backed, and ruffled the ears of her horse, seemingly at ease despite it all.

With so little to glean from the royal, Jai found his gaze drifting to her handmaiden. Jai could see why his brother was so taken with her – she was one of the younger women that had accompanied the hunting party and had long, pale hair that was as rare a sight in Latium as a free Steppeman. More than that though.

She was Dansk to her very bones. Dansk even in the way she walked, a swaggering gait that seemed almost theatrical. Her homeland was in everything about her, from the ice in her eyes to the sun-dusted freckles across her pallid, pink-touched cheeks.

This was not the soft, floral refinement of the painted-faced nobility of the court, nor the hearty charm of those few maids that worked in the palace. It was a harsh and sharp beauty that held Jai's gaze longer than he cared to admit. Samar required a swift prod to drop his own.

'Are these the hunting grounds?' Jai asked, shaking the girl's face from his mind. 'You've spoken of them so often it feels like I've been here before.'

Arjun grinned and clucked his tongue gently as a horse was brought to him by a servant. A black mare, one whose wild eyes made Jai take a step back. Arjun swung into the saddle and extended a hand.

'Ride with me,' he said, nodding over his shoulder at the back of his saddle. 'Titus has us here twice a week since . . . since I can remember. It'll be nice to see it for the first time again through your eyes.'

'Damn your heathen eyes,' a voice called out. 'Not today, arsewipe.'

Jai spun to find an unwelcome face glaring at him from among the morass of rushing servants and stomping horses. It was Corinth, pushing through the throng of servants and horses.

This was the man Jai had replaced over a decade ago. Indeed, it had been Corinth who taught Jai his first letters, though Leonid had taught him far more once Jai had the basics.

Rewarded for his long service by promotion to one of Constantine's cosseted personal servants, he was still asked to care for Leonid on the occasions Jai was unwell. This rare reminder of his former station was always blamed firmly on Jai.

'You go gallivanting off, I know exactly who's gonna be left to look after old Leonid,' Corinth growled, his bulldog face reddening. 'I've done my time. You—'

'Now now, Corinth,' a soft voice interrupted. 'Are your sponge baths with my grandfather not remembered fondly?'

Fear seized Jai, though it was nothing compared to the expression on Corinth's face. The man swivelled as if possessed, stammering nonsensical apologies until a single tut from Titus drew him to silence.

The prince turned slowly and gave Jai an appraising look, then nodded his head in the black mare's direction. Jai's fear of the prince far outweighed that of the horse, and he was soon scrambling awkwardly up the steed's side. He gripped Arjun's belly; suddenly aware he had turned his back on the prince in the process.

He swivelled in his seat, until he felt his spine creak.

'You do me great favour, in allowing Jai to ride with us,' Arjun said, turning the horse with a twitch of his reins and bowing his head in thanks.

'None at all, Arjun,' Titus announced, waving away the thanks. 'Why . . . your brother here was officially invited, was he not?'

And then, to Jai's utter shock, the prince winked at him before trotting away with a toss of his reins.

Never mind that Titus had forgotten Jai's name within moments of hearing it. In his entire life, Jai had perhaps exchanged a half-dozen words with the future emperor, and always on the periphery of his brothers. He felt a glow at the recognition. This . . . this was good.

Perhaps, with the arrival of the Dansk, his family's position in the court was to rise. Could it be that peace and forgiveness was the order of the day?

Or had Arjun called in a favour for Jai to get him out of Leonid's chambers, as he so often did.

Arjun and Samar had served as Titus's hunting companions almost as long as Jai had been alive, serving as his manservants whenever he left the palace grounds.

Arjun, in truth, was Titus's most favoured servant, somehow managing to soothe the young man's frequent rages through a mix of humility and flattery. He'd only been able to convince Titus to allow one brother to join him as a hunting guide. Jai did not begrudge him that, not least because of his fear of riding. Samar was too delicate to endure what Jai had to.

It was in many ways Arjun's place as a hostage that had made him so close to the prince. Titus was known for his fits of jealous anger, but it seemed he found it hard to feel envious of someone

so firmly entrenched as his inferior. Arjun's humble charm did
the rest.

Jai had always thought Arjun's looks would earn the prince's
ire, for though the blond, blue-eyed prince cultivated a reputation
as a dashing lover, he lacked much of a chin. Fortunately, the
prince considered the Steppefolk inherently ugly.

The horse shifted beneath Jai's haunches and Samar beamed
a wide smile at him as he mounted his own, smaller pony beside
them.

'Here,' Arjun said, passing back a cloth bundle. 'We've been
up since dawn preparing for this hunt. Best to get some food
inside of us.'

Jai shifted back in the saddle and unwrapped it, finding a
knife, as well as a hunk of bread and cheese. He cut some, and
the three boys sat among the rushing servants, chewing on the
humble fare.

In that moment Jai didn't think he'd ever felt so content.

'Won't you stay overnight, Jai?' Samar asked. 'We miss you.'

But Jai had no time to answer, as a servant blew on a hunting
horn. The black mare surged forward at a kick of Arjun's heels
and suddenly the world was a blur of wind and open savannah.
The hunt was about to begin.

Chapter 7

They did not travel far. To Jai's surprise, they were hardly out of sight of the rest of the party before Arjun had slowed his horse.

'Jai,' Arjun said, his voice low and coloured with something close to urgency. 'Has Leonid seemed different towards you lately?'

Jai frowned. It was not like Arjun to speak this way. Even when they had something serious to discuss, his brother would make light. It was as serious as he'd ever heard him be.

'No,' Jai whispered back. 'Why?'

Arjun shrugged, then paused and stared out over the plains.

'Titus has been spending less time hunting. And . . . he's become colder towards us somehow.'

'Leonid's treating me fine. More than fine,' Jai said. 'It could be nerves about the wedding.'

Samar's pony was not far behind and Jai saw the flash of worry as Arjun turned at the sound of hooves. Clearly, he did not want Samar to hear this. This was strange indeed.

'He's been spending a lot of time with Magnus,' Arjun said quietly, shrugging again. 'There's few that hate our kind more than that bastard. That's probably all it is.'

'One more year,' Jai said, forcing a smile onto his face as Samar caught up to them. 'And you'll never have to deal with him again.'

Arjun nodded, his typical care-free expression returning like a mask.

'Maybe they'll let you have a go this time,' he said loudly, as Samar pulled up. The other horsemen were not far behind.

The hunting party was smaller than Jai had first imagined, no more than a half dozen Dansk including the princess and her handmaiden, and Titus's entourage of three nobles, as well as Samar, Jai and Arjun to help them load their crossbows.

Constantine and Ivar had apparently preferred to feast on cold cuts in the open air, though Jai wondered if the fearsome Dansk king would have liked to join them.

'Today is a *special* day,' Titus announced. 'We hunt a new beast, never before seen in the hunting grounds. One caught by the Gryphon Guard and flown from the east some days ago, just for us.'

The nobles murmured in approval, but Jai hardly heard him. He was watching the Dansk, as ordered.

It was strange. Undoubtedly, Titus must have been properly introduced to his future bride on their journey from the coast to the palace, yet he did not greet her when she rode up, nor pay her any particular attention. In fact, he seemed more focused on his friends than anyone else.

'We've brought along these hunting crossbows, and our *loyal* guides,' Titus went on. 'Bolts as thick as a thumb – they can pierce even a dragon's hide.'

He winked at the Dansk and spun his horse to gaze out across the savannah. A veiled hint, Jai imagined, at the new guards at the palace who wielded the same weapons.

The veil that shrouded Erica's face made it impossible to tell

if she felt awkward. Her companions were oblivious, seemingly
unable to understand Titus's language; High Imperial. They
seemed more interested in the Sabines' horses than any specially
imported creature. Their own horses were small in contrast;
hairy, hardy things, better suited for travel in the bowels of a
long ship.

Instead, Jai gauged Erica's handmaiden's expression. Disdain.
She made little attempt to hide it, even flaring the nostrils of
her sharp, upturned nose. Jai imagined the grass-chewing beasts
of a carefully gardened savannah seemed quite pathetic when
compared with the great dragons, bears and wolves that roamed
the wilds of the Northern Tundra. The latter two were regularly
hunted for their fur, and to keep them from eating Dansk cattle,
if Leonid's diaries were to be believed. The former . . . well
better to lose a few oxen than a few limbs.

All three beasts, however, were favourites among the soulbound of the Dansk. Jai had even heard tell of bear-riders
battering through frontier town gates to allow the Dansk raiders
in to slaughter.

'What are we waiting for?' Jai whispered, suddenly eager to
see what beast Titus had brought to impress their guests.

Samar shushed him, rather uncharacteristically. Clearly this
was not typical of their hunts. Titus was looking back towards
Latium. And Jai could see a blotch on the horizon. No . . .
above it.

Soon enough, Jai could see a silhouette, swooping in a shallow,
lazy spiral to meet them. Was it Erica's dragon?

His breath quickened as it grew closer and closer, and even
Arjun choked back a gasp as the great beast skidded close enough
to lean out and touch.

A gryphon.

An enormous specimen, snapping jealously at Arjun's horse

as it folded its great wings. Only a shout and yanked reins from its rider quelled its aggression.

Yellow eyes flicked above a hooked beak, its gaze scaring a whinnying Dansk horse back a few steps, much to the nobles' amusement.

It was an older beast, one that had fought in the wars if Jai was not mistaken, for it was missing a toe on its front foot, and a crescent scar curved across its rump. Its feathering was golden and its fur tan, though Jai had seen dark-feathered gryphons, piebald ones and everything in between over the years.

This was the animal carved all over Latium, celebrated across the capital from statues to the engravings on the armour of every legionary in the empire. Only Leonid's red lion motif held a candle to the gryphon's importance, but that had been supplanted by the now de facto symbol of the empire since Constantine had taken power.

Jai eyed it as it raked a raised talon through the dry earth. It stood taller even than Arjun's mare, and could have rested its beak between the large horse's ears without lowering its head. A head crested by swivelling, tufted ears that Jai knew could hear better than even the enhanced ears of the gryphon's soul-bound rider.

He wanted to reach out and touch that space where fur and feather intermingled beneath the saddle, separating the gigantic eagle head and shoulders from a leonine posterior. Jai was not surprised that Leonid had been so drawn to the beast when he had first allied with the then little-known sect that had learned how to bond with gryphons all those decades ago. That small group of soulbound, training together and sharing knowledge, would go on to become the Gryphon Guard.

Jai's heart soared at the sight of the rare beast, willing its eyes to settle on him. How he wished he could soar just as these

Gryphon Guard did, much though they hated him. Sometimes it felt almost every night that he dreamed of the cool of the clouds and the sight of the world spread out at his feet, all within reach.

What idiocy, for someone who feared to ride a horse to dream of *flying*. He didn't need the Gryphon Guard sneering at him to feel inadequate and ashamed. He felt that way whenever he saw the great beasts in the flesh.

'Right on time,' Titus laughed, the clapping of his hands jarring Jai from his admiration. 'Magnus never disappoints.'

Jai's stomach turned a little as the great brute of a man who was Lord Commander of the Gryphon Guard dropped from his mount. The gryphon must be his totem, as beasts that had been soulbound were known.

The commander was a red-haired titan, with steely blue eyes, jutting jaw and a burn that marked him from cheekbone to jaw.

Magnus was well-known in the city and beyond for his cruelty, and the terrible violence he had inflicted upon the empire's enemies – not least the Steppefolk. It was a point of pride for Magnus that he had 'out-savaged' the savages.

To Jai's surprise, Magnus was not alone on his mount. A boy, younger than Jai by a few years, was waiting behind the bulk of the larger man. A thin, sallow-faced boy, yet one who held himself with the confidence of someone whose station exceeded his bearing.

A noble, by all appearances – but then, this was not surprising. The Gryphon Guard drew most of their acolytes from the noble families of the empire. Only second or thirdborn sons, of course, those with nothing better to do than dedicate their lives to the sect – few noble houses would give up their heirs to such risks.

Those who endured the training would be granted an attempt to bond with a chamrosh at the age of thirteen. Jai knew only a little of the Guard's secret methods of soulbonding, of the potions and pills taken to take the acolyte to the brink of death. He also knew that most who failed died in the attempt, and the survivors would forever remain in the Guard's service, lest they reveal what they knew.

The new soulbound would serve as squires until they earned an opportunity to bond with an infant gryphon. Again, many would die in the process, for Jai had heard the severing of an existing bond was dangerous and painful enough, let alone forming a new one all at once. But the survivors . . . they would become knights. Full-fledged Gryphon Guards.

'You see, I have spared no expense for us, Princess Erica,' Titus announced. 'Our Gryphon Guard have sent a tracker to speed things along – his totem seeks our quarry as we speak. Why, I am told Silas here is so gifted, he'll be spending a year with the Guild . . .'

Titus's words droned on, but Jai was once again distracted. For Silas was brushing a mop of black hair from his eyes and kneeling in the soil. Jai leaned closer as the boy narrowed his eyes and took a deep, snorting breath.

Silas's fingers contorted and a line sliced through the sand as if someone had taken a blade and scored the earth. His irises . . . *glowed*.

Jai stared, fascinated. No matter how many times he saw it, even small feats performed by the soulbound seemed a wondrous miracle.

Magicking.

That power was held by every soulbound, though only those trained knew how to use it. Rarer still were those who advanced far enough to do more than move a few grains of rice or spark a fire.

'. . . you may loose the final bolt, once we've taken the beast down.' Titus spoke on, and Jai watched Silas close his eyes, his face drifting blank. He was *feeling* his own soulbound chamrosh. Seeing with its eyes.

Suddenly Jai wished with every fibre of his being to be soulbound. For the ability to see beyond the walls of Leonid's chamber, or indeed the walls that housed Latium. For that feeling of being connected to something else.

Hell, he'd bond with a damned pigeon if that were possible – but only a few beasts were able to soulbond. But for every sect, and every beast, there was a different way to bond – and it was *always* dangerous.

Another dream. Another impossibility.

Better to focus on the task at hand. Watching the damned Dansk.

Chapter 8

With the attention of the group drawn to the golden gryphon, Titus finished his address a little lamely.

'Silas,' Titus said, his face darkening. 'Has your totem picked up our prey's scent?'

'Yes, Your Excellency,' Silas said, sweeping a finger along the line in the sand. 'We follow this line – my chamrosh circles above, but she is too far to see from here.'

Titus trotted closer, inspecting the direction of Silas's drawing.

'We ride!' Titus whooped. 'Come, Dansk, if your mules can keep up!'

He spurred his horse, and Jai had hardly a second to grip his brother before they were thundering along the ground. He dared not look back.

Jai saw, suddenly, the puerile incompetence of Titus. Offending his guests and future wife served no purpose. The boy was cruel, controlling and, though intelligent, it was of an educated kind rather than from natural cunning. And here, in the contemptuous way he treated his guests, Jai saw nothing but the bravado of a bully, intimidating and self-aggrandising in a childish attempt to impress in the only way he knew how. The prince was . . .

a product of his upbringing. And clearly one hiding a fear of the first woman he'd ever met equal to his station. He seemed unable to address her directly.

Focusing on the dynamics of the couple could only help keep Jai distracted from the lurching and juddering of the horse's movements for so long. He gazed at the horizon, hoping to see Silas's circling chamrosh above. No such luck.

It was going to be a long, painful day.

BY THE TIME THE horses slowed to a walk, deep in the savannah, Jai had long left the paltry contents of his stomach for the birds behind them. Finally, the circling chamrosh was high in the sky, and the whispered order to stop was given.

Now, the beast landed beside its master, who had loped alongside them on his feet, seemingly without breaking a sweat. Jai's awe at the boy's apparent strength and stamina was only rivalled by the sight of the chamrosh.

In all his years, Jai had never seen one up close. The Gryphon Guard's squires were rarely permitted to enter the palace, nor were given the free time to wander the streets of Latium. Instead, they were trained night and day on the Eyrie, or if they failed to rise to the rank of a Gryphon Knight when they came of age, kept on Latium's northern and coastal garrisons to patrol for Dansk raiders.

Though the chamrosh-bonded could not ride them due to their smaller stature, a well-trained squire was capable of seeing the world from the sky, watching through their totem's eyes. A chamrosh's sense of smell was also nearly as good as that of their canine cousins, which made them more useful still.

Jai took a moment to take in the gorgeous creature, wondering what it was like to have your very soul bonded to the wild-eyed animal. Silas certainly seemed none the worse for it.

The chamrosh was, just like its tablus piece, a gorgeous mix of hawk and canine, in much the same way a gryphon appeared a hybrid of lion and eagle. Or indeed a platypus with the duck and beaver – though he had only Leonid's diaries to help picture one of those; the old emperor had eaten one on his travels.

Chamroshes were sleek, tawny creatures, hardly larger than a hunting dog. Nor did they bear the front talons of their bird halves, as a gryphon did, instead having four canine paws. Jai could not help but be amazed at the tail wagging behind the beast, even as its hook-beaked head remained perfectly still, before swivelling to watch their approach.

Arjun rode alongside the prince and leaned close to whisper in Titus's ear. The prince raised a fist, stopping the column.

'Hush now,' Titus said, raising a finger to his lips for the benefit of the Dansk. 'Dismount that way. We approach on foot.'

They were in a low gully, deep in the heart of the savannah. The area was scattered with scraggly bushes and dry as parchment. It was at once barren and full of noise, for the air was stirred by the chirr of cicadas hidden in the knee-high grass.

'Why here?' Jai asked. The ground was soft and pungent here, with thorny bushes growing up the banks, tangling them.

'We're upwind,' Samar whispered. 'It won't smell us, but we can smell it.'

He took a deep sniff, then wrinkled his nose and winked.

'And sound won't travel well in a hollow, through all that,' Arjun added, gesturing at the vegetation.

But Jai was hardly listening, instead furrowing his brow and staring into the distance. Their target lay beyond. A dark mound of shag, half-obscured by silver-leafed shrubs – far enough that Jai could hide it from view with a thumb.

As they dismounted, Jai saw the Dansk men shrugging off their leathers and furs, stretching their muscles bare-chested. As for Erica and her handmaiden, they remained on their horses on a tussock nearby, watching while shading their eyes from the fast-sinking sun. Apparently they had no desire to take an active part in this hunt.

A whispered order from Arjun sent Jai scrambling toward the nearest Sabine noble, who, despite being bigger than Jai, could not wind the crossbow himself. Instead he sat, rubbing at his apparently injured palms and muttering curses.

Jai was swift to wind the crossbow for him, as the young noble growled 'hurry' at him. Already, Arjun and Samar were easing through the grass ahead, showing their charges the quietest, easiest path . . . and acting as a shield for their liege, should a snake strike.

For years, Jai had wondered at what it was his brothers did when they accompanied the prince in the savannah. Now he knew.

It took a huge effort to haul upon the crossbow's lever, the twine creaking back until it slotted into place. The noble did not even wait for Jai to knock a bolt, instead snatching at the crossbow and attempting it himself. The trigger went off as he did so, the string snapping forward with a crack so loud Jai was shocked their prey didn't bolt then and there. In the silence that followed the pair earned a death stare from Titus.

'Steppe-cunt,' the man-child spat, and Jai spun away as spittle misted his face.

The noble moved off on his own and Jai sat, frozen in shock.

Ahead, Jai heard a high-pitched squeal, and a whoop of triumph from Titus. He could hardly see, for his view was obscured by the shrubs ahead.

'Guide,' a voice hissed.

Jai turned and saw the handmaiden had leaped down and sidled close to him.

'I want to see,' she said, her accent no stronger than that of the royals she served. Jai was a little surprised to hear the Sabine language spoken so comfortably, but far from shocked.

High Imperial had long been used to some degree in many courts, even before Leonid conquered half the known world. Some said that the so-called Phoenix King in the far east was fluent in it. It had become the language of the Kashmere Road after all, and thus that of every merchant or envoy worth the name.

'The men too,' the handmaid said, nodding over her shoulder.

Jai stared, her strange beauty taking him aback for a moment. She was so close it almost made him nervous. She stared back at him, until Jai realised it was a pointed look.

'My mistress tells me there are . . . vipers in the grass,' she hinted.

'Right,' Jai whispered. 'Sorry. I'll go ahead.'

Somehow, it didn't seem right to tell her he had little idea of what he was doing. She'd lumped him in with his brothers. Then again, he'd done just the same to her with her companions, assuming she could not speak his language. Or the language he spoke anyway.

'Follow me,' Jai said, attempting to mimic the crouched, sidling gait he'd seen his brothers make through the grasses.

The laugh from behind him made him stop, and he felt the heat as the back of his neck reddened.

'We'll go quickly,' Jai said, with as much bravado as he dared. 'Hurry.'

Chapter 9

Jai came across Samar almost by accident, a stone's throw from where Titus hunted ahead. Jai almost tripped over him, for his brother was low in the long grass.

Samar sat on his haunches, staring dully back at them, and on toward the setting sun. There were tears on his face.

'Samar,' Jai called, uncaring of the noise. 'What's wrong? Why aren't you with . . .'

He trailed off as his brother sobbed, once. Samar shook his head, saying nothing. Older than Jai . . . yet so childlike, even now.

Ahead, Jai could hear a deep, grunting bellow, and louder cries of triumph.

'Arjun!' Jai yelled. 'Are you hurt?'

He turned back to his sibling, who stared on, vacantly. Seeing no injury, Jai began to run, leaving the Dansk behind. Now, he could hear the deep moans of an injured beast, and the whooping of the hunters ahead.

Jai lunged through the bushes that obscured his view, careless of the thorns that ripped at him.

Relief flooded through him, for there was Arjun, crouched

on his haunches. Unharmed. With his back strangely to the prince
and the melee, his face inscrutable.

'Arjun,' Jai said.

His brother met his gaze. Then lowered it.

And Jai saw.

Saw the beast, snorting lung-blood into pink mist, shuddering
as another bolt disappeared into its fur with a wet thud. Its
majestic head swinging back and forth, moaning as it collapsed
onto its shaggy belly.

A great, furred rhinoceros, taller by half than a stallion and
twice as wide, dark and huge against the horizon. Enormous,
and *real*. Its twin horns toppling like the mast of a sinking ship,
until it lay still. Jai might have thought it already dead, but for
the bubbling blood at the corners of its hoary lips, and those
soft, wet pants that misted the grass red.

It was a khiro. The prized beast of the Steppefolk. The source
of their milk, their meat, their transport. But more than that, it
was Jai's father's sigil. Their family's sigil. And Titus was slaughtering it before their eyes. Making them watch. Making them
help.

Titus's invitation to Jai had not heralded acceptance of him
and his brothers. Quite the opposite. It was a reminder of their
place. That even with the so-called barbarians of the north
welcomed into the court, the Steppefolk remained defeated
enemies. Their captive warriors were to remain fettered forever
more, and nothing about this marriage would change that.

'Arjun,' Titus snapped, holding out the crossbow. 'Load
another.'

Jai saw his brother shake his head.

'Damn your eyes, Arjun. Embarrass me in front of my bride
and your brothers will see the consequences.'

Jai did not know what moved his feet. Perhaps it was that

look on Arjun's face. His brother, who never let their enemy see his weakness. Broken in his shame.

The khiro groaned when Jai reached it. It trembled at his touch but did not move when he lowered himself to meet its gaze. He could see the pain in its deep, dark eyes. See the confusion.

Jai drew the cheese knife from his pocket, pressing it to the base of the beast's skull. It was the best way for a cavalryman to put down a broken-legged horse – he imagined a khiro would be no different.

'Permission to put the beast out of its misery, Lord Prince,' Jai called.

He dared not look at the prince. Had he overstepped? Or would the hunters loose a second bolt, careless of hitting Jai.

By now, the Dansk had caught up to them, observing the scene with curious eyes. If they understood the significance of the beast, they did not show it. And then, the handmaid spoke.

'My mistress asks that you do not sully your hands with the slaughter, Lord Prince,' she called. 'That you might lift her from her horse. But what an honour to see you bring it down. A noble quarry, well taken.'

Even Titus was surprised by the girl's fluid command of his language. The prince paused, contemplating her words.

'Perhaps it is fitting,' Titus said, suddenly taken with the idea. 'Yes . . . why not?'

He spat in Jai's direction and stalked closer. Hunkered down, to watch. He motioned with his hand, watching as if it were some spectacle.

'Go on,' he urged, smiling at Jai. 'Do it.'

'I'm sorry,' Jai whispered.

He drove the knife deep with a blow from his fist, and felt bitter tears sting his eyes as the beast stiffened, then fell limp.

As its last breath rattled from its chest, he could hear the buzz of flies, turning the congealing puddle of blood into a seething black morass. This wasn't hunting. This wasn't even sport.

'Samar! Get your fat arse over here,' Titus bellowed. 'You, the arsewiper, go to your fool brother.'

Jai reached Arjun as his tear-streaked other sibling stumbled out from the bushes, and the three stood, watching the prince. Titus strolled closer to the khiro and gave the beast a kick.

He jumped back in mock fear, then chortled to himself. He turned his back on them, and Jai heard the buttons of his jodhpurs pop open.

Titus took a wide stance, and then the splash of urine was apparent.

'You boys are going to cut this beast up,' Titus announced. 'And bring it back for the dogs tomorrow. And keep the head intact – I want it mounted.'

He bounced a little on his heels, before buttoning up his kecks.

When he turned, Jai felt the prince's gaze upon him. Yet while his brothers hung their heads, Jai met his eyes with his own.

'I've always wondered what the food of my people tasted of, lord prince,' Jai said. 'I thank you for the opportunity to taste it.'

Titus looked at Jai as if he'd been struck. Yet it seemed he could find no offence, nor impudence in Jai's response. And with the handmaiden watching, he could only lift his chin and retort:

'You mistake me.'

The prince leaped into his saddle and Jai stared on, past him, as the hunting party moved back to the gully, leaving the three brothers alone in the clearing.

They took a long while to speak or to move, not even when

the thunder of the hunting party's hooves faded into the distance. The rays of the dusk sun had lengthened and the khiro's body cast a long shadow. Jai sat back on his haunches, letting out a breath he had not realised he'd been holding.

'The . . . the *bastard*,' Samar sobbed.

Arjun threw an arm around his brothers' shoulders, pulling them in close.

'That jumped-up little prick thinks he's left us to be miserable. Instead, he's given us all evening and night to spend together. Let's make the most of it.'

Chapter 10

It was not in misery that they rode through the gates of Latium, but in joy. They were tired and bloodied to the elbows. Yet triumphant despite it all, glorying in the morning sun.

They had spent a night together beneath the stars. Feasting on the roasted delicacy of their people, usually eaten, so Arjun told Jai, only when the khiro could no longer produce milk or sire young. And then killed only in ritual, in respect and dignity. A cause for celebration, for a life well lived. Telling stories and laughing.

They'd agreed that the mother goddess of the steppe would want them to eat, despite everything. She, who they'd heard of almost as a fairy tale, from the mouth of Balbir.

It was Balbir they went to find now.

The fettered Steppewoman sent to care for him and his brothers, all those years ago. They had spent but a paltry two years together, living in the servants' quarters, before Jai had been charged with Leonid's care and his brothers sent to learn the ways of the hunt.

She, who had taught them what little they knew of their

people. Only Arjun, the eldest, had more than the vaguest of memories of their homeland. Now, Balbir worked in the house of a lesser noble, moved on from the palace as her age had caught up to her.

Balbir deserved to taste the khiro. They lived lives that were not their own – but all three felt guilty for not seeking her out more often as the years passed by.

The three boys made a strange sight, with their bloodied bodies and horses. Not to mention the makeshift sled of pelt and branches they pulled behind them, bearing a pile of butchered meat. At any other time, the guards would long have stopped them before they reached Balbir's mistress's home. But with the engagement feast being rushed, there were dozens of such sights as the fare from across the empire was summoned to the kitchens.

Latium was a strange city, a lone settlement a day's hard ride from the Silver Seas, on the western coast of the sprawling Empire. It was situated amid fields, woodlands and savannah, as if it were a small island in a sea of wilderness and scattered farmland, connected only by the long, winding bridge of the Kashmere Road.

In fact, it was more town than city, only keeping the latter title to make it seem grander. The entire place was dedicated to caring for the Sabine Court.

Clothiers, tailors, cobblers, milliners and jewellers, even armourers and blacksmiths were scattered in their dozens, fashioning goods to adorn the nobility, officials and military officers that lived near the palace. Court fashions changed seemingly with the wind, and the shops were always heaving with activity.

These the three brothers avoided, for patrolling guards kept suspected beggars and the unwashed away with a healthy introduction to their truncheons.

They avoided the crowded markets too. Food, of course, was

another sought-after commodity, and the stalls of exotic fruits, meats and spices were a constant in Latium. On the rare occasions where Jai could scrounge up enough coins, he would sample the cheap, castoff fruit that was bruised or misshapen. One of the few joys he had managed to find in this place.

Even down the side streets they could not escape being reminded that the Royals owned it all. The white, imported stone that paved the streets remained, and the buildings were embellished at every opportunity with cornicing, carvings and other such ornate displays. Everywhere, the iconography of gryphons, chamroshes and lions were emblazoned in mosaics, gargoyles, even the graffiti on the walls. Every inch was dedicated to honouring the Sabines and their charges. The only exception, tucked away in a back alley, was a monument to the fallen of the Crimson Death, honouring the dead from the plague that had taken so many, more than a decade ago.

Wherever they turned, the streets were heaving. For with the wedding approaching, and the nobility of two grand civilisations converging on the city, there was money to be made.

It was a relief when they reached the servants' entrance of the noble's home. By now, the morning was in full swing. They would be expected at their posts before long, and Jai was beginning to feel on edge.

Arjun knocked on the door, until it cracked open, and a suspicious eye peered out. At the sight of them, a matronly woman stepped out, her arms floured to the wrists.

'A fine time tae call, when the mistress expects her repast,' the woman complained, her voice thick with the Samarion brogue of the northern reaches of the empire. 'If'n it's Balbir you're wantin', she's workin'.'

Arjun rolled his eyes.

'Don't lie to us. Even the fettered don't start this early.'

The matron pursed her lips.

'You callin' me a liar?'

She lifted a hand and yanked at her blouse, revealing a tattoo there.

'Know what that means, eejit? I can tell no lies. That's how the mistress likes it.'

Jai grimaced at his brother's clumsiness. Samarions were both a people and a religion, with their homeland in the north of the empire. According to Samarion belief, to lie was a sin grave enough to sentence them to eternal hellfire. Few still practised truth-telling religiously, but those who did bore the tattoo of their order.

'Now be off with you,' the matron spat. 'You can go'n play happy savages another time.'

Jai saw Arjun bristle at her words. He scrambled down the horse's side and hurried over before his brother answered in anger. Ever since last night, Arjun had been like a raw nerve.

'My dear lady,' Jai said, bowing low. 'We apologise profusely for our expeditious visitation. We had only wished to grace your home with a gift of fine meat, as thanks for taking such care of our dear Balbir.'

The matron's mouth flapped open, shocked at Jai's florid, high-born speech. He was the palest of the three, being only half Steppeman. She couldn't quite tell what he was. He continued before her brain caught up with her mouth.

'A gift for your house. Meat of the khiro. All we ask, is you allow *all* the servants to sample it, fettered included. And tell them who gave it to them. There's more where this came from.'

He hurried to the sled, and chose the finest cut, a yellow-marbled hunk of rump.

The matron eyed it hungrily. Red meat was a treat even for a well-heeled citizen, let alone a servant such as she.

'Khiro, you say?' she muttered. 'Isn't that one of your filthy animals?'

'No filthier than a pig,' Jai said brightly.

He tugged the cloth that had held the bread and cheese and bundled up the meat, before placing it into the matron's arms.

'Please,' Jai said, bowing again. 'We Steppefolk owe gratitude to our hosts, whether fettered or freeman.'

The matron let out a grunt.

'Good tae know at least one of you knows your place.'

The door slammed shut. It was just as well, or she might have heard the curse Arjun hurled after her.

Jai took a deep breath, ready for a telling off. Instead, Arjun grinned at him.

'You always had a calmer head on your shoulders, Jai,' Arjun said, shaking his head ruefully. 'I was ready to tear her a new one. And where would that get us? A whipping for Balbir, and the meat in that shrew's stewpot.'

Jai shrugged.

'There's about a hundred of her running the kitchens at the palace.'

Samar jumped down, and Jai found himself wrapped in a hug.

'I'm sorry you have to deal with that,' he said.

'You're lucky I was scared of horses,' he joked, pulling his brother tight. 'Might've been you!'

For a moment too long, they clung on. Neither knew when they would next see each other. They, who lived in the prince's wing of the palace, and spent half their days out in the savannah. And he, for whom a trip to the palace gardens was a rare excursion.

'Go on, Samar,' Arjun said. 'Better cover up that meat before the flies get to it. We'll take it to the kitchens, let Jai head back on foot from here.'

As their brother dutifully obeyed, Arjun stood beside Jai. For a moment, the pair watched Samar in silence. There had always been some . . . distance between the eldest and youngest of the brothers, and in this pause after their night of bonding, Jai suddenly felt it more than ever. They were so different it was hard to imagine they would be friends in another life.

'It wasn't the horses that sent you to Leonid,' Arjun said, all in a rush, as if he'd been holding the words back. 'Hell, only took one day and you're riding like a natural. You're a Steppeman, whether you believe it or not.'

Jai looked up at him, surprised.

'Why then?'

Arjun sighed and gave Jai a smile.

'To serve Leonid they had to give you an education. To read. To write. To learn the ways of their court. Why do you think we are only allowed to serve the prince when he hunts, or feasts. Why never when he attends his father's council, or meets with the governors of the colonies?'

Jai stared at him. He'd always wondered at his selection. Thought it had been oversight. That *he* was an oversight.

'Why do they ply us with liquor and fine foods,' Arjun went on, 'and force us to spend our days away from the court? Leonid asked for you, specifically, because you are third in line, Jai – and might even have less claim than our uncle if it came to it. They could not allow one who might someday rule the Kidara tribe to know what you do. They'd rather us soft, and spoiled, and stupid.'

He leaned close, such that Jai could no longer hold his brother's wide-eyed gaze.

'They keep us apart intentionally. Hell, but for that stunt with the khiro, you'd have been kept from the hunt this day too. But they underestimate our love. Our loyalty.'

Jai forced back tears. It was the first time Arjun had said he loved him in a long time.

'In a year's time, when I turn of age, I return to our people and take our father's place. You think yourself an arsewipe. No. You are my secret weapon. In three years, you will be twenty too, Jai, when the peace treaty says we can return home. Wait but a little longer. Then I'll have you and Samar by my side. Just think what we can do then . . . together.'

He seized Jai in an awkward hug. Jai hugged him back and felt the tears flow freely.

'I love you too, brother,' he whispered. 'Three years, and we'll show them all.'

Chapter 11

Jai returned to the palace with a heavy heart. It was strange, to feel so sad after the good times. But glimpsing what life might be . . . it left him feeling so empty afterward.

It was some relief, then, that when he crept into his rooms Leonid was tucked up in bed, snoring loud enough to wake the dead. The result of a night of drinking upon Titus's triumphant return no doubt.

He wondered if the old man knew he'd been forced to hunt their father's symbol. If he would feel it cruel . . . or necessary.

Whatever you called the man, Leonid was ever the pragmatist. Hell, Leonid had been totally against fettering his captives, until he'd had the defeated armies of a dozen enemy states to contend with. And at his son's urging, Leonid had built the prisoner camps, to work their fields, forests and mines. It was only when Constantine took power that the practice was codified into law, legalising the fettered state. One of the many reasons Leonid's son was known as 'the Cruel'.

'You've returned.'

Jai nearly jumped out of his skin, only to realise the snoring had stopped. Leonid had spoken with his eyes closed.

'I have,' Jai replied. 'Sire,' he added.

Leonid nodded slowly, as if Jai's answer had told him more than that. Perhaps it had.

'My grandson. He's . . . young.'

Ah. So the old man did know.

'No younger than I, sire,' Jai said.

He kept his tone neutral, and his words factual.

Leonid sighed. Grimaced.

'My family owes you an apology, but I feel it is not what you seek. Speak, Jai. What can I do?'

He opened his eyes, and Jai saw the pity there. It was a rare emotion for the old man, and the proffered favour even rarer. He forced back emotion, parsing through his wants, one by one.

'Balbir,' Jai said, lifting his chin.

He'd ask for nothing for himself. His forgiveness was not to be bought by petty favours. Leonid said nothing. Of course, he did not remember her.

'She's fettered. Sent to care for us when we were children.'

'Oh?' Leonid asked. 'And what became of her?'

Jai could not hold back a derisive snort.

'Her contract was sold on,' he said. 'To some noble widow on the edge of the city. I ask that you buy her contract and give her over to my care.'

Leonid considered Jai's words. Cocked his head.

'And where would she be housed? Here with us?'

Jai shrugged.

'She can work in the kitchens with the scullery maids. Live with them too. But when my brother leaves, she goes with him.'

Leonid grumbled beneath his breath.

'She can return with your brother. But I'll not take a good fettered from an old widow. Balbir stays there until then.'

Jai felt rage then. It was but the work of a few orders to a senior servant at the palace, yet the old man could not go to the trouble. Still, he knew not to push his luck. In the end, her freedom was the far greater prize.

'Fine,' Jai said.

'Good,' Leonid said, clapping his hands and raising himself up in his pillows. 'Now, another game of tablus?'

EVENING SEEMED TO ARRIVE before Jai had time to catch a breath. In truth, he was elated that he had arranged Balbir's eventual freedom, had surprised himself at his own daring, and spent much of the afternoon trying to figure how to get a message to his brothers about it.

But Sabine feasts always began in daylight, and before long Jai was dressing the old man in his finest regalia and brushing what little hair the old emperor had left.

With Leonid almost ready, the perfumers came to have their way with the old man. It bought Jai a little time to get his own appearance in order, even if a small towel, Leonid's old soap and the bucket of water he kept in his room were all that was available to him.

'Come on!' Leonid called. 'I've been ready for an age.'

Jai groaned, still attempting to paw his damp hair into some semblance of tidiness.

The overpowering floral perfume favoured by the Sabine royals almost burned his nostrils as he took his place behind the old man, resisting the urge to gag.

'Shall I fetch the chamberpot?' Jai muttered, realising he was staring at the books again. 'Else we'll be back here as soon as you've emptied your first goblet.'

'Never mind that,' Leonid said, suddenly impatient. 'Move your lazy bones.'

Jai leaned forward and the chair trundled over the thick rugs and through the double doors that led to the palace proper.

'Tonight I will hear the conversation well enough,' Leonid instructed. 'But watch Ivar's eyes. See what interests him. That, I cannot do.'

'I will, Great One,' Jai said, already slipping into the formal form of address that would be required of him that night.

'And don't think I didn't see you making eyes at that princess yesterday. You'll focus on the task at hand, or you'll feel the back of mine.'

It was an empty threat – Leonid was hardly capable of lifting his pecker for a piss. But Jai knew that greater men had been executed for far less than ogling royalty. It seems the brief peace-making of the morning had passed. And his status as his father's son only stood for so much.

The feasting hall was not far from Leonid's chamber, a product of the time when the ex-emperor could still stomach rich food. Its double doors were open, and beyond Jai could see that they had more than just the Dansk royalty as guests.

Dansk men and women filled half the room, sat at the long tables with tankards in their hands. Even this early in the evening many were already drunk, quaffing beer and laughing uproariously. They were dressed in fine furs despite the heat from the great hall's crackling hearth, just as the Dansk hunting party had been.

'Their nobles,' Leonid muttered. 'And their generals.'

Jai wheeled the old man into the room, down the wide path that divided the room in two. Across from the Dansk, the Sabine nobility were also present, resplendent in all the finery the Sabine Empire had to offer. Every culture that had been subsumed by the Sabines was apparent in their clothing.

Fine silks from the south-eastern colonies and precious stones from the desert provinces were on full display. Blades of blue steel from the forges of Damantine were at the hip of every Sabine general. Even the food, sumptuous and spiced, came from the far reaches of the empire's territories, filling the room with the scent of cardamom and paprika.

It was a grand display of power, and Jai was already looking forward to the leftovers he would eat later, cold though they would be.

'Leonid!' bellowed a voice.

Jai stared in bewilderment as Ivar stood up from the raised table at the end of the room, some fifty feet from them, where he sat with his daughter. He waved the ex-emperor closer, and Jai found his feet obliging the foreign king.

'You sit next to me,' Ivar said, patting a space between himself and his daughter on the bench. Jai trundled Leonid up a small ramp, bringing him behind the seat.

Leonid grunted his approval, and slapped Jai's helping hands away as he stood haltingly and took his seat.

'Your son and grandson are tardy,' Ivar said, pouring Leonid red wine. 'But I don't mind. It's you I wish to dine with.'

He leaned closer, and Leonid lifted his chin to meet the king's gaze.

'How many times have we battled?' Ivar asked.

Leonid motioned for Jai to lift his goblet to his mouth, and the ex-emperor took a long sip and smacked his lips before responding.

'Only once,' he said. 'Long ago. You were but a pup back then. And you lost, as I recall.'

Ivar narrowed his eyes, but there was a sparkle there that told Jai he was finding the exchange amusing. Even so, Jai watched as Erica's arm slipped to the side, and lay a calming hand upon her father's own. Here was a man who was not averse to flights of rage.

Ivar relaxed, and chuckled.

'A tactical retreat. Of course, back then you were but an upstart ruler of a poor strip of farmland. Now look at this place.'

He gestured at the heavy silver of the cutlery.

'We've not fought since for good reason. You Sabines are too rich for my blood. A bit like this wine. Who do I need to thrash for a flagon of mead around here?'

He shouted this last question, and a servant scurried away to find him some. Now it was Leonid's turn to smile.

'Mead. Now there's a drink that kept me warm on campaign.'

Ivar inclined his head.

'I'll have a barrel of my best sent to you. Not that you'll need it – there's not much campaigning left! Except for the Great Steppe of course.'

And then, to Jai's surprise, the king's intense eyes turned to him.

'You, boy. You've the look of a Steppeman. Who's runt are you?'

'I am Jai, Rohan's son, Lord King,' Jai said, bowing his head low.

Ivar's face fell. He paused, in what Jai guessed was a rare moment of consideration for his next words.

'Your father and I battled many times along our border. A great warrior, and a good man. I was sad to hear of his death.'

He nodded to himself sagely, lost in thought.

'He was another of the great ones,' he finally said. 'We're a dying breed, Leonid. The age of war is over. And with this marriage, the age of peace begins.'

Leonid sighed and took another sip of wine.

'I do not regret its coming, Ivar. It is what I fought for. Do you remember how it once was? The petty squabbles, the endless warring states, from all sides. A peasant could not hold onto the fruits of their labour for more than a season before it was stolen by their own rulers for their soldiers, or invaders on a raid.'

Ivar grunted in half-agreement.

'I expanded my kingdom, and you founded an empire. We've done our jobs. We made the peace, today more than ever. Let the next generation keep it.'

He glanced up at Jai, who remained at his position above Leonid's shoulder.

'Sit boy, you're making me uncomfortable.'

Jai hesitated, and Ivar's face suddenly darkened.

'I'll not have you hovering over my shoulder. Sit and keep my daughter company. You'll not be standing much longer, one way or another.'

Jai still waited despite the threat, hoping Leonid would instruct him first. Erica shifted to make room, and he felt her hand pulling him down to the seat.

'Sit,' she whispered. 'Before he angers.'

Chapter 12

Jai felt like all eyes were on him as he took a seat, but he knew he had no choice in the matter. He snatched a napkin from the table, holding it like a shield, hoping anyone who noticed him would think he was seated to wipe Leonid's mouth. At the first sign of Constantine or Titus, he would stand. He doubted Ivar would beat him to pulp at the moment of the Sabine royals' arrival.

He was careful to keep his head down, even as he leaned forward and gave Ivar the side eye. But there was no information to glean there, for the great king's focus was entirely on Leonid, the two leaning their heads close and engaging in a whispered discussion.

'Is it always so . . . much?'

Jai turned, his heart in his mouth. Erica was facing straight ahead, her face inscrutable beneath the veil. He waited, wondering if she was addressing Leonid.

'Jai, is it?'

She *was* talking to him.

'Yes, princess,' Jai whispered.

He glanced to his left, and saw she had not yet turned to him. But her voice emerged from behind her veil once more.

'You are a prince?' she asked. 'If you are Rohan's son. Why do you wear the clothing of the servants? I saw you on the hunt too. Did Titus do that to shame you?'

Jai gulped at the question and parroted the response he'd given to many such questions in his years in Leonid's charge.

'As a hostage, I am in service of the Sabines. My elder brothers are true princes, so they are servants in name alone – they carouse with Titus, hunt with him, yet serve him, as all his subjects do. But my mother was a concubine, and I am the last in Rohan's line. I hardly count as a prince. So, I serve Leonid.'

Erica was silent for a moment.

'This is Sabine cowardice,' she finally said, contempt dripping from her words. 'When I am empress, we will secure our borders by the strength of our armies, not by holding blades to the throats of children.'

Jai struggled to keep a smile from his face, though being called a child sent blood rushing to his face. Erica could hardly be much older than himself.

'What can I tell you of the Sabine court?' Jai asked, hoping to change the subject. 'Soon, you shall be at the centre of it.'

Erica sniffed.

'The women here look like dolls. Their faces are painted, and they wear such clothes as I would suffocate in. Where are the shield maidens? Why do none carry blades?'

Jai lowered his head.

'That I cannot answer. It is the way it has always been. I am told the plainswomen fight alongside the men, as the women of the Dansk do. But I have never seen such things here. Nor can a woman lead her house.'

Erica brought her hands up to the table. These were not the hands of a lady of the court. No finely manicured nails, but chipped stubs that had been bitten to the quick. Even her fingers, now tightening into fists, were as callused his own.

'I'll not preen about the palace like a peacock in a Sabine pleasure garden, nor—'

Her words were cut short as the great doors to the hallway swung open. Jai almost leaped to his feet but was frozen in place by the sight that greeted him.

A dragon had entered the room, padding at the head of a contingent of Dansk nobles. A young one.

The beast was hardly larger than a pony, and a small pony at that. But it was as beautiful a creature as he'd ever seen, its scales a burnished bronze that glimmered in the torchlight, and large, dark eyes that were almost puppy-like.

'Ah,' Ivar called out, vaulting over the table in a single bound. 'My daughter's dowry has arrived.'

He stalked down the centre of the room, and to Jai's surprise, reached out to scratch the beast on the underside of its snout. The dragon let out a deep rumble of appreciation, pausing and lifting its head to give Ivar better access.

'This little one was born from my late wife's dragon and my own. The first newborn in a generation. If Titus cannot soulbond with it, it shall belong to my grandchild.'

His words elicited a tut from Erica, though Jai could not tell if it was annoyance or disgust. The dragon followed Ivar back onto the raised platform of the high table, leaping with a languid grace and settling beneath his seat like an adoring puppy.

The king took a hunk of jerky from his pocket, and the beast snapped it up, gulping it down and emitting a low purr of pleasure. Jai wondered if the legend of draconian fire breathing was a true one. He drew back his legs, just in case.

'Gold,' Titus's sly voice came from behind. 'An apt colour for the first dragon of the Sabine dynasty. Perhaps we shall change our crest from gryphon to dragon. What do you say, Father?'

Jai looked back and was horrified to see that the emperor and his heir had just emerged from the side door behind him. Jai leaped to his feet.

'In time, perhaps.' Constantine replied, his brows furrowing as he caught sight of Jai.

Jai rushed to extricate himself from the table and nearly fell over the bench in his haste. He swiftly resumed his position hovering behind Leonid's shoulder, as Titus went to take his place.

Titus was dressed in the full regalia of his station, resplendent in a purple robe, edged with gold filigree. His hair, as usual, was oiled back in the fashion of the nobility of the court, turning the gold of his hair a darker yellow.

Even his eyes had been made up with dark kohl, making the blue stand out against his pale skin. But he could do nothing to hide his weak chin, nor the piggish upturn of his nose.

Before the prince sat, he made a show of wiping fastidiously with a napkin at the hardwood seat, before dropping it at Jai's feet. An icy glare completed the performance, and then Jai could breathe easy as Ivar shifted a seat down from Leonid, and Constantine took the king's place at his father's side.

Heart racing, Jai waited for Titus's first words to Erica. But none came. Instead, the prince leaned forward, addressing his father.

'Shall we go for another hunt tomorrow?'

At this, Constantine raised a perfectly shaped brow, then turned away, murmuring softly to Ivar.

'Greet your bride, boy,' Leonid growled low. 'You were not raised a savage.'

At this, Titus reddened, a flash of rage crossing his face. Only now did the future emperor deign to speak to Erica, whose face remained inscrutable.

'Where is your dragon?' he asked.

It was a blunt question, not a greeting, but Erica inclined her head in polite fashion.

'She hunts, Lord Prince,' Erica replied. 'You have that in common with her. Right now, she feasts on a plump deer, caught in the forest east of here.'

Titus froze at her words, his brow forming a deep furrow. Then he leaned closer, and Erica flinched away. Love at first sight, this was not.

'You sense that? Through the soulbond?'

Erica nodded, but she had hardly drawn breath to reply before Titus interrupted her, his sharp eyes snapping to meet Jai's.

'Fetch Magnus, arsewipe,' Titus snapped. 'I've need of him.'

Jai stared dumbly for a second. Magnus? What need did Titus have of the commander of the Gryphon Guard? The pause earned further ire.

'Now! Before I have you beaten within an inch of your life.'

Jai scuttled back a few steps, if only to get out of Titus's vicinity.

'I myself have not attempted a soulbond,' Titus went on. 'It is dangerous with dragons too, is it not? Many die in the attempt, as with other beasts?'

Jai did not wait to hear Erica's response, knowing he had delayed Titus's request long enough. Further down the table, Magnus had just taken his seat, along with the other important generals and extended family of the Sabine dynasty.

The thought of even approaching the man terrified Jai. Even so he hurried over and hesitantly broke the man's brooding silence.

'Lord Commander,' Jai whispered. 'The prince . . . uh . . . requests your presence.'

Magnus grunted in response, and Jai could only stare at the ruddy back of the man's thick neck as he slowly turned toward him.

'Out of my way, whelp,' he growled, smoothing back his long, ginger hair.

Jai made room as the enormous man extricated himself from the bench and kept a few steps behind as Magnus approached Titus.

The commander leaned down, his size forcing him to bend almost double to bring his head level with the prince's.

A whispered conversation followed; one Jai could not quite make out. Magnus sighed, then bowed and stepped away.

'As you wish, my prince.'

He turned to Jai and stabbed a sausage-like finger in his direction.

'Follow me,' Magnus growled, walking towards the doors of the kitchen.

Jai imagined he was due to fetch something and followed in silence, catching only a brief glimpse of Erica turning toward them, and getting to her feet. He had only made it a few steps before he was yanked through the doorway, stumbling into the sudden heat of the stoves.

A hand lifted him by his collar, holding him high against the stone wall as if he were no more than a pup.

'You dare to sit in the prince's seat?' Magnus growled, his face filling Jai's vision. 'You think to embarrass him in front of his bride?'

'I . . .' Jai managed, before a vicelike grip clamped around his throat.

'It's been a while since I've killed a Steppeman,' Magnus hissed, bringing his face as close as a lover, such that Jai could smell his perfume. 'I'm going to savour you.'

Chapter 13

A slap from Magnus's meaty palm set Jai's ears ringing and near burst an eardrum in the process. Pain accompanied the darkening of his vision, Jai's mind trying to shut down at the suddenness of it all. His legs did not support him as he was released from the wall, and a hand took hold of his collar.

He was dragged in a daze through the heat of the kitchen, and then he was outside in the cold, his feet scrabbling for purchase on the cobblestones as he was dragged across the courtyard.

His collar choked him, twisted in Magnus's great fist, and he pawed at his throat, rasping for air, half-conscious though he was.

'Please,' he choked. 'I can't—'

'Save your begging for later, boy,' Magnus laughed, shaking him like a half-wrung chicken. 'You'll need it more then.'

The sky was overcast, with black thunderclouds gathering above. These were a rare sight, that somehow cut through the fog of pain and confusion that had overtaken Jai's vision.

Then the great spire of the Eyrie came into view, an hourglass column that towered above all else, even the lofty heights of the imperial palace. It was a grand construct, already raised above the surrounding lowlands by the cliff that bore Latium. Such was its height that the very top could only be seen on the clearest days, for it was often shrouded by the clouds.

Even now, as Jai was dragged ever closer, he could not see its peak. Only the great hollow that cut through its core, with a single platform borne by chains.

Jai had dreamed of a visit to the sacred training grounds at the tower's top. Of doing some grand favour for Constantine and being granted the right to attempt to soulbond with a gryphon chick.

But at this moment he dreaded the very sight of it. For he remembered the executions of the so-called traitor knights, though he had been little more than a toddler then. Ten unnamed riders accused of plotting to take power for themselves, or so the story went. There had been a swift trial, held behind closed doors. Then their summary hurling from the top of the tower that same day.

Of course, nobody but the Gryphon Guard knew who they were, or saw them being hogtied to their slaughtered beasts. Only their comrades saw the moment they were pushed from the edge. But Jai had heard their screams as they tumbled down. And he saw the red mist when they hit the ground. Jai had looked away after the first.

Such sights were a grotesque juxtaposition to the beauty of the palace, with its gardens, fountains and strutting peacocks. But an emperor did not stay emperor for long if his subjects were not reminded of their place now and again, and the deadly consequences of straying from it.

Jai now knew he would be another example. One more body

to be scraped from the surrounding plaza, a reminder to the Steppefolk of who truly ruled them. He lurched into the shadow of the tower, his bulging eyes catching glimpses of onlookers, their faces full of pity. He hardly noticed when the wooden platform began to rise. By now, his vision was little more than a tear-filled blur, and only the rattle and clank of the enormous black chains told him they were moving up.

'Your brother once told me you dream of flying, boy,' Magnus breathed into his ear. 'I've seen you lurking at our tables. Don't worry, you'll fly soon enough, sure as a goat's foot.'

Even as a child, Jai had wondered at the sacred sanctum of the Gryphon Guard, one so secretive that even Titus could not set foot there until he was emperor. Jai had volunteered in his scant free time to serve in the dining hall, ears straining for half-heard details. Clearly, he had not gone unnoticed.

The pressure eased on his neck. Now, with nowhere to run but over the edge of the ever-rising platform, Magnus relaxed his fingers, allowing Jai to take his first unimpeded breath in what felt like hours.

'Let me go,' Jai choked, wiping at his eyes. '*Please*. I only did as I was ordered.'

Magnus chuckled, and the soft, jovial sound was stark contrast to the cruelty Jai had seen in the man's eyes.

'Oh, I'll let you go,' he whispered, his breath hot in Jai's ear. 'When I'm dangling you from the edge by your craw.'

Jai had no retort, and even as his heart raced and nausea boiled his belly, his mind boggled at the sight of Latium, eyes widening at the great sloping expanse all laid out before him. By now, the platform had gone well above even the tallest of the grand spires and domes of the city.

He was higher than he had ever been, the cool wind above the city raising gooseflesh. His dreams had been filled with such fantasies, of just once seeing the world far below him. Even in that moment of his greatest despair, he devoured the sight with his eyes. With his death inevitable, the very air tasted sweeter, the colours of the world somehow more vivid.

He sucked in one more unimpeded breath, then another and another. Any moment, he expected the platform to stop, for Magnus's arm to crush his neck once more. But they rose ever higher, the nearby spires of the palace seeming as saplings struggling in the shadow of a great oak, and he perched at its top.

Then a sudden chill, and the view turned to white. They had passed into the cloudscape, and the mist soothed him like a salve, coating his body and turning horror into wonder.

This too began to fade, the world turning bright and blue, his view of Latium hidden by the immense bank of clouds. It was like the Gryphon Guard lived on another world, closer to the Sabine goddesses of sun and moon.

By now, he could hear the clanking of the platform mechanism above, though Magnus made no move towards him. He supposed up here there was nowhere to run.

For a moment he was tempted to make a move for the edge. To take the satisfaction away from Magnus. He shook the thought from his head no sooner had it arrived. He would fight until the last breath.

The clanking stopped, and Magnus's meaty arm swivelled Jai to face the other way. And there, in front of him . . . was the sanctum of the Gryphon Guard. The Eyrie.

Chapter 14

The Eyrie was shaped like an enormous bird bath, the bulk of it being made up of the thick stem that housed the rising platform, made from great pillars of granite that held up the dish-shaped terrace at its top.

It was upon this terrace which Jai now stumbled, the iron bar of an arm gone, replaced with Magnus's hand gripping a fistful of his hair.

Jai's eyes watered with pain, his entire scalp near-torn at the roots, but even that could not prevent him from taking in the view before him.

The terrace looked for all the world like the palace's hot spring baths, the ones that Leonid had once frequented, before he decided the heat made his bones ache.

Deep-veined marble tiles white, yellow and black stretched from edge to edge of the grand, circular platform, and greenery spilled from arrays of pots and hanging baskets. The air was cold, yet as Magnus shoved him to the floor, the stone was warm on his skin, touched by the unimpeded sun.

A pool of water at the centre of the terrace's sloping basin was the focus of the place, an impossible lake hundreds of feet across. At its centre, appearing for all the world like a floating temple, was a building. A place that must be a closely guarded secret if Jai had not known of its existence until that moment.

A hard prod with Magnus's foot shoved him towards the long marble bridge that led across the waters towards the building. He wondered at the structure's many pillars, cornicing and intricate carvings of swooping gryphons and armoured men.

But even this temple was not the most unusual thing in view.

For around the lake – in it – was the Gryphon Guard. Men walked unabashedly naked, or wearing but a loincloth to protect their modesty. They bathed in the shallows of a marbled beach, washing themselves in the water.

Jai saw mostly old men, and young acolytes, early in their training. The knights and squires would be on patrol at this time, especially with a foreign army at their very gates. As for the gryphons and chamroshes themselves, they would be in their roosts, built into the stem of the tower itself. He had hoped to see a chick, for they were an unusual sight, but it seemed it was not to be. The only sign of any flying beasts were distant silhouettes circling above the horizon.

It was but a moment of wonder before the fear seized his heart like a clenched fist. He tried to calm his breathing, and blinked tears from his eyes.

The secrecy of what he was seeing was both a blessing and a curse. Now Jai knew he would not leave this place alive. He had to negotiate.

'Magnus, please. I can be useful here, I can—'

A foot slammed between his legs, and a wave of nauseous pain curled through Jai's belly. It was all he could do not to vomit, though he earned himself a few seconds of reprieve as he curled up upon the marble.

'No fettered up here, boy,' Magnus rumbled, nodding to a passing elder. 'Nor mangy servants like you.'

Even as he spoke, Jai saw some of the youngest acolytes, some boys no older than seven, carrying buckets to the plants, watering them. Others scrubbed the backs of the older men, the water tinged grey by their sloughing skin. These boys were the workers of the Eyrie, their fates there yet to be determined.

Magnus seized Jai by his scalp once more, dragging him to his feet. He shoved him on, and Jai's feet trod the marble of the bridge.

Only then did Jai see the fish that swam in the clouded water. At first they were but orange and yellow shapes. Then he saw their long whiskers and gaping mouths, shifting through the detritus at the bottom of the great pool.

The shadow of the temple entrance passed over him and Magnus's palm clapped over his eyes. This was but a shortcut across the waters, and the cruel man clearly had no intention of letting Jai see more than he would be allowed.

Yet Jai could see through a chink in the man's fingers. Just a glimpse, before that too closed his view. Teenagers, older this time, sitting cross-legged in grand empty rooms. All had chamroshes curled about their crossed legs, beaked heads resting in the laps of their masters.

The youths, likely squires, were doing what all soulbound men and women could do with their totems. Soulbreathing.

What they did was invisible to the naked eye, yet Jai knew the invisible forces that swirled around them. They were absorbing the mana of the world, cultivating it to store within them and use for their own devices. The source of the power behind majicking.

The word alone was one he should never have heard, for the Gryphon Guard kept their methods a close secret. Only a misspent youth of eavesdropping had allowed him some small understanding of it.

Of course, there were other soulbound folks in the world. But few went through the kind of training that the Gryphon Guard did. And none had access to a generation of knowledge, scrolls and books accumulated by the sect since it was founded all those years ago.

Jai wondered if Erica, or indeed her father, were privy to such knowledge.

It was strange, to know of his impending death, yet to think of such things instead. His heart still rattled, his palms dripped with sweat, but it was hard to truly believe the world was about to be snatched away from him.

Some mad kernel of hope at the back of his head had sent him on a fantasy that he would be inducted into the sect here and now, rather than be thrown from its top at Titus's behest.

Clinging to that self-told lie was his only comfort as he stumbled through what he imagined was a long central corridor, inhaling the scent of burning incense, and hearing the echo of deep, humming breaths timed in unison.

Now, he felt the sun upon his face once more, yet the hand remained. They walked on in silence, a cool wind buffeting Jai until they stopped.

Light, bright and unfiltered, burst across his vision. For a moment, Jai was blinded as Magnus held him in place, so tightly that he could not move another step.

Then, he saw. Saw his foot hovering over nothingness, and Latium yawning in front of him. This was the fated place where the ten traitor riders had been hurled from the tower. A spit from the perfect circle of the tower's top, a launching place for riders on their first flights, or so Jai had surmised as he'd stared up and daydreamed.

'Was there not a meal waiting for me, I'd have some fun with you first,' Magnus whispered in his ear. 'Hell, I'd have killed you then and there if the prince hadn't wanted to make an example of you to his new guests. They'll hear of the shitstain you leave down there. Their nobles will walk this way, on their return to their army camp.'

Jai twisted in Magnus's grip, ripping his own hair, but it was no use. He might as well have been chained to the man's hand.

'Know this, boy. Your death is but a chore. Your life is no more worth remembering than a fart to me. Nor to anyone else.'

But Jai was more than that, at least to one man.

'I have served Leonid all my life,' Jai choked, sudden terror garbling his words. 'I know his every need, his every whim. Without me, he is lost. Let me live, Lord Commander. Punish me some other way, I beg you.'

Magnus chuckled. 'So the old man has to train a new arse-wiper. No skin off my nose.'

'It'll be the skin off your back,' Jai replied, putting as much confidence into his voice as he could muster. 'And more besides.'

At this, Magnus paused. A shadow passed above, but Jai's eyes were firmly fixed on the ground far, far below. People milled about, small as insects on a pavestone, oblivious to the drama unfolding above them. And soon he would be as an insect beneath a boot himself, the mess of his insides smeared to the ground.

'The man built the very tower we stand upon,' Jai went on, his breath rasping from the damage to his throat. 'Hell, he built this empire. Anger him at . . . your . . .'

'His anger will matter very little soon enough,' Magnus said, chuckling as he tightened his grip. 'It's a shame that you will not live to see it.'

Jai tried to speak, but he had no breath left to give. Time stretched.

He hung above the world, feet kicking. Still, he hung there. Second after second. Almost a minute of pure, unadulterated terror. It seemed Magnus wanted his fun after all.

And then, it came.

A roar and a blast of wind, such that both he and Magnus staggered back. Two great wings blotted out the sun, and Jai could smell the stink of blood as the beast's open maw continued its bellowing.

Jai could only writhe in his captor's grip as Magnus bellowed in return. The man's hand outstretched, fingers dancing. A glow formed there, and the very air seemed to thrum around them. Then . . . the hand lowered.

'Take him,' Magnus grunted.

Jai fell back onto the marble ledge, the iron bar of the commander's forearm falling away. He flinched as the dragon's claws clicked closer, its head lowering to stare into his eyes. Its pupils were black ovals in pools of honey, and they expanded as the head drew closer. Somehow, it was as if the beast recognised him.

'Boy!' Magnus barked.

Jai turned.

He didn't see the fist coming.

Chapter 15

A song echoed through the receding darkness of Jai's mind. It was one he knew, yet he knew not how. A melody of melancholy, and words that spoke of loss, of longing for home. Words of his people. A language he had half-forgotten, yet still understood.

Then, a memory. Of wizened hands stroking his brow. Lulling him to sleep. Only now, they lulled him awake. The lullaby, for that was what it was, stopped.

Fingers touched his nose, his eyelids. Water dripped through his lips, and he brought out his tongue to lap at it. He was thirsty. So thirsty.

'He wakes,' said the voice. 'I knew you would live. Rohan's bloodline does not die easy.'

She spoke with an accent. The same one he had once sported, all those years ago. And he knew that voice.

Jai opened his eyes. And recognised the face that swam into view. Balbir.

But strangest of all was not her presence, but the room in which he lay. He was in a bed rather than a straw-lined cot. The room was not sumptuous, but there were rugs upon the floors, and curtains on the windows. That there were windows at all would have been surprise enough.

'Where are we?' he croaked, after Balbir poured more water into his mouth. It hurt to speak, for his jaw felt as if it was made of broken glass.

Balbir smiled. She had been old even when he had first known her, yet she did not look like she had changed a day. That same, shrivelled walnut face. Those same warm dark eyes, deep-set and inscrutable.

'You can thank your new friend for the room. She paid for it herself. Say what you want about that princess, she has a conscience.'

Only now did he remember. The dragon . . . and Magnus's fist. Instinctively, he touched a hand to his jaw, feeling the swelling there.

'Her dragon brought you down itself. Carried you in its own claws, left you on the palace steps.'

'I owe her my life then,' Jai whispered.

'And more besides,' she said. 'Her handmaiden has visited every night to nurse you. I imagine the little royal has had to learn how to brush her own hair.'

She cackled at that, though soon her laugh turned into a hacking cough.

'Every night?' Jai asked. 'How long have I been here?'

'A week,' Balbir said, once her fit had subsided. 'A blow from one as powerful as Magnus would kill most, though I suspect that was not his intention. A soulbound warrior, and one who has ascended, no less, can knock a flagstone from a wall without grazing a knuckle. You were lucky to survive.'

Jai did not know what she meant by ascended, but it was not that which had caught his attention. If he had survived a week, it meant he was safe from Magnus's wrath. Or indeed, that of Titus. At least for now.

'Don't worry, that Dansk king and Constantine have far more important things to argue about than the life of a lowly Steppeman,' Balbir said, as if she could read his mind. 'I'm told the young heirs have forgiven each other and plans for the wedding continue. Why, it is but a few days away now, if the rumours are true.'

Jai lay silent, surprised by how much the sound of her voice lulled him.

'You're right. Rest is all you should focus on. Drink, eat. Heal. When your patron sent for me, I was told you must return to work as soon as you awaken. And go you will, for I dare not lie.'

Jai grimaced.

'I thought that princess had a conscience.'

Balbir chuckled at that, and shuffled towards the door.

'It was not your princess that sent me,' she chuckled. 'It was Leonid. You've friends in high places, my boy. Keep them sweet – I suspect they're all that are keeping Magnus's hands from your throat.'

She sniffed, and Jai took her in as his eyes adjusted to the paltry light filtering through the curtains. He saw the hunched shoulders, and those callused hands. She wore a fettered servant's robes, along with the symbolic shackle, locked upon her wrist. Though her garments were well cared for, they were so ragged as to likely be the only clothes she owned.

Yet after all this time she still wore her braids, as unmarried women of their folk did. She had not been broken by this place.

Of course Leonid had sent her. Who else? It was just a shame he'd had to pay for it with his face.

'I waited too long to ask for your freedom, Balbir,' Jai whispered, horrified at the state of her.

'Pah,' she said, waving his words away. 'Your uncle sold me

to these Sabines when his nephews needed a nursemaid. Sold you and your brothers too, though you wouldn't know it. Not that it matters now.'

Jai took her hand, feeling the leather of a decade of hard work there.

'You don't belong in this place another second,' he whispered.

She smiled then, and it was in that smile that her years fell away. Her hands grasped his own.

'I smell the air of my land each day. I feel the dirt beneath my feet, and see the sun rise each morning. Do not worry about me, my boy. My body is here, but my mind . . . my mind is not.'

Jai felt tears start in his eyes and turned his head to hide it.

'Anyway, I'll be out of this city soon,' she said. 'My mistress sold my contract on.'

'What?' Jai demanded, wincing as he sat up too fast. 'Leonid said you'd be going back with Arjun, when he comes of age!'

Balbir chuckled darkly.

'Oh, that he did. In fact, his messenger said as much, when he sent for me. Only, he never mentioned payment. Why do you think my mistress sold me on so quickly?'

Jai tried to quell the rage building inside him. Of course. He had only made things worse.

'I'll be glad to see the back of these Dansk anyway,' Balbir muttered, unaware of Jai's melancholy. 'We've had two staying with us, and I've been scrubbing my hands raw cleaning after them. They throw their bones on the ground when finished, as if there are dogs waiting to gnaw them. And whether man or woman, they spill more beer than they manage down their gullets. Yet the Sabines call we Sythians heathens. Now they marry one.'

Jai grinned, for it had been a while since he'd heard that

word. The Sythia was the name the Steppefolk used for themselves, though they identified by their tribe first and foremost.

Balbir got up, wincing as her knees cracked at the movement.

Jai stuttered, almost speechless with anger.

'I'll talk . . . Leonid won't . . .'

She held up a finger.

'You use all the favours you have to keep yourself safe, child. Clean up now, before the innkeeper throws us out for the smell. There's a bucket by the door. I've better things to do than watch you wash your balls.'

She stomped out of the room, closing the door behind her before Jai could regain control of his tongue. Beside him, a bowl of vegetable broth sat cold, a film glazed across its top. He leaned over and took it.

Heal he would. And suck up to Leonid he would, too. He needed to curry all the favour available if he was going to convince the old emperor to buy Balbir's freedom. After what Jai had been through, the old emperor would have to listen.

As he spooned the first mouthful and gulped it down, he could not help but think how close he'd come to death. It had been so strange, how long Magnus had held Jai out over the edge. And his words . . . they tugged at the recesses of Jai's mind. That Leonid's anger would soon not matter . . . and that Jai would not live to see it.

Chapter 16

J ai's legs were strong enough to hold him upright, though he could only manage a short trot to the bucket by the door before he was out of breath and unsteady on his feet. A week of healing had taken its toll, with little more than the paltry food and water Balbir might have spooned into his half-conscious mouth.

As he pressed his face against the cool wood, he heard footsteps approaching. Footsteps too sure and fast to be that of Balbir.

In that moment, Jai remembered he was not safe. Jai knew in his state, he could not overcome an assassin, nor even a child armed with a wooden spoon. He was far too weak for a fight.

No, better to feign unconsciousness and try to take them by surprise. Wincing, he staggered to his bed, lying down once again in the shrouded gloom and shutting his eyes even as he heard the door open and shut. Had he heard the rattle of the door locking, or had he imagined it?

There was a sigh. The creak of the wicker chair close by his bedside. Then, he felt it. The soft touch of a finger beneath his chin, pressing painfully into the soft flesh there. Was that to test if he was awake? Or . . . something else?

The finger withdrew somewhat, lightly grazing his skin. And . . . a glow. He could see it through his eyelids, the red-tinged darkness turning orange, then yellow.

He felt the finger running across his skin, at once hot and cold as it traced a pattern.

Jai had a flash of memory. Of Magnus's outstretched finger, and the glow there as he prepared to attack the dragon. The assassin was going to take his head clean off. With magick.

He bellowed and lashed out, his hand tangling in his attacker's hair. Yet no sooner did he rise than a palm slapped him down onto the bed once more, with such strength that the wind blew out of him.

For a moment he wheezed, eyes streaming, expecting the kiss of a blade beneath his chin. Instead, he heard muttered curses in a language he could not understand. But he recognised the accent, and as he rubbed his eyes clear, he saw who his supposed attacker was.

She was dressed in simple garb. No fancy furs, as he had seen her in before, but even so her sharp, elfin face was unmistakeable. The princess's handmaiden.

'What were you doing?' Jai wheezed.

'Helping,' the girl snapped, brushing at her hair where his hand had caught in it. Despite her lowborn status, she clearly cared for it, and it shone even in the gloom. But it was another glow he was drawn to. The fading light of her fingers . . . and in the irises of her eyes.

'You're soulbound,' he said, his brow furrowing. 'You were magicking.'

The girl froze at that, then spoke in a casual voice.

'You are mistaken.'

Jai shook his head, then winced at the movement. This explained her strength, though in truth, slamming him back onto the bed in his weakened state was no great feat.

'I recognise the glow,' he said, lifting a hand and waving his fingers.

The girl sighed and chewed her lip, assessing him with a wary gaze.

'Fine,' she said. 'But you'll take that to your grave, you hear? I risk much, coming here. But my mistress insisted.'

Jai nodded slowly.

'Please,' he said. 'Continue.'

The girl lifted a hand, then brought it to his chin once more. Now he could see the glow properly. A soft, white light. It was different to the golden blaze that Magnus had made.

He looked at the ceiling, feeling awkward as she closed her eyes in concentration.

The feeling of hot and cold returned, but this time he allowed her to continue her ministrations. Slowly, the feeling spread through his jaw. It was like cool water, washing away pain. Yet, despite the finger placement, it only affected the side where he had been injured, as if the light sought out the wounds within.

Then, just like that, the girl yanked her hand away. Her face was drawn and pale, eyes slightly vacant. She sat back on the chair, and took a deep, shuddering breath.

'Thank you,' Jai whispered, touching his chin. The pain remained, but far less than before.

The girl shrugged and stood to leave.

'Wait,' Jai pleaded. 'What is your name?'

She almost ignored him, then turned back.

Her sharp, oval face, softened by an upturned nose and the wide, blue eyes that were so common among her people. Wary, deep eyes, that seized his gaze and would not relinquish it.

She was beautiful, though it was a harsh, wild beauty, unlike the cultivated glamour of the women at court. He'd never known a girl like her before.

'Frida,' she said.

'You are the princess's handmaid?' he asked.

Frida held his eyes and nodded, though everything about her face told him she wanted to leave. Even her feet were pointed at the door. He had no right to keep her longer. But he needed one more thing from her.

'Please pass my thanks to your mistress,' he asked. 'And tell her one more thing.'

He stopped, realising he had hardly thought his next words through.

'Out with it then,' she said. 'But think carefully. She's a fickle friend to those that take advantage.'

Jai took a deep breath to buy time. Then he spoke haltingly: 'I think Magnus wanted her dragon to save me. It was like . . . it was like he was waiting for it to show up.'

Frida chewed her lip.

'What possible reason could he have for that?'

Jai had no answer for her. He had no idea what Titus had said to Magnus.

'I don't know. But he said something strange. That Leonid's rage will matter little soon enough, and it was a shame I wouldn't be alive to see it.'

Frida laughed.

'Well, now I think you're paranoid. The man is ancient. Surely that is what he meant – that he will surely die soon anyway.'

Now it was Jai's turn to bristle.

'You were not there,' he said. 'It was the way he said it. And who are you, to determine if the future empress should know or not. I *owe* her. This is my way of repaying that debt.'

Frida glared at him for a moment, then relented.

'Fine. I'll tell her for you.'

With those parting words, she strode out of the room, leaving the door slightly ajar behind her.

For a moment Jai considered remaining in bed. Waiting until evening to make his way back to the palace. But he couldn't risk waiting. Who knew where Balbir would end up tomorrow if he didn't get Leonid to intervene.

Jai sighed. Washing could wait. He had to talk to Leonid.

Chapter 17

Frida's healing had made a huge difference, and he wondered whether she had returned many times in the hopes of catching him alone to do it.

Soulbonding was rare across the world, in part because of the risk of death. Yet it came with advantages. Enhanced strength and senses for one. What was it they said about the knights of the Gryphon Guard? That they could hear a maiden's fart at a hundred paces, and smell it before she'd aired her skirts.

Jai wondered what beast the handmaiden might be bonded to. Healing was known to be one of the harder forms of majicking, so Jai suspected a cave bear. It was the rarer, larger, more predatory beasts that yielded the greatest soulbound warriors, with the ability to perform great feats of majick.

Dragons and gryphons were said to be the best to bond with, then manticores, chimera and other rare predators of the wilds. For the Dansk, their great bears and direwolves were most popular. As for the creatures of the steppe – khiroi and mammoths were leaf eaters both . . . Jai had an inkling they were less desirable.

Either way, the healing had helped. It was that, or the soup had worked miracles. He made it to the door in half the time, and only took a few panting breaths before he stumbled into the corridor.

Jai was able to deduce from a glance out of the window where he was. He was in an inn known as the Red Lion, so named after Leonid and his sigil. According to legend, Leonid had killed a cave lion with nothing but a hunting knife, returning home covered in blood, a crimson pelt thrown over his shoulder.

Jai knew from the old man's stories that he had killed it with a bow, and the blood had come from his amateurish attempt at skinning it with said knife. Yet the old man was not one to pass up a good story, and had allowed the assumptions of his friends to turn to fable.

The sorry remains of the poor lion still lay at the foot of the old emperor's bed. Jai had slept on them enough times when Leonid was ill and needed close watch.

In any case, the inn was not far from the palace. He snuck past the owner without notice, for the portly man was snoring behind a desk near the entrance. Then he only needed to scurry down a few side streets before he reached his destination; the back entrance to the palace – the kitchens.

As always, they were a hive of activity. The entry yawned open, its heavy doors unbarred, and he could almost feel the heat from within, as if it were an open mouth. If he could guess, the Dansk nobility were still taking advantage of the Sabines' hospitality.

At a time like this, the Sabines were on high alert. There were many guards supervising the unloading of various meats, fruits and vegetables that had likely travelled halfway across the empire to grace the royals' plates. Jai was just glad that he still wore the uniform of a palace servant – sweat-stained though it was. It was better that nobody knew he had woken just yet.

He approached the nearest cart, where a potbellied man was swearing at the various scullery boys who were lifting enormous melons from its back. Jai's belly grumbled at the sight, but he was quick to take hold of one of the yellow fruits.

Before he could even move towards the kitchens, the man's hand had seized Jai by the scruff of his neck, forcing him to turn back.

'I've not seen you afore,' the man growled. 'You'd better deliver that to the kitchens, sharpish. If I see you stray, I'll have your hide for a rug.'

Jai tried to do just as he said, but the hand remained in place.

'I'm volunteering today,' Jai explained, already struggling with the weight of the enormous fruit. 'I'm usually a manservant, but I've been sent to help.'

The man's eyebrow lifted with some incredulity, taking in Jai's scruffy appearance, and what Jai imagined was a bad bruise along his jaw.

'I had to borrow this uniform. Look, I'll take it in right now, you can watch me.'

The man slowly released Jai but did not dismiss him.

'You'll not find melons like this in all of the empire,' he growled. 'Not even straining a bodice in Leonid's fabled whore-house. I've carried these through storm and snow, on bandit-infested roads, and across the Nambian Desert. So if I find out that a single one is missing when the quartermaster opens up his coffers, it'll be your head. Get it?'

'Got it,' Jai muttered.

'Your name?' the man asked.

'Rohan,' he said, after a half-second too long of hesitation.

The man narrowed his eyes at Jai, then nodded.

'Not many who'd own up to a name like that,' he said. 'Be off with you.'

Finally, Jai was free, though he'd earned himself some curious looks from the guards for his trouble. Still, he could do nothing but walk through the doors, struggling pathetically with the melon after the week of not eating.

As luck would have it, his uniform did the trick, and the guards simply chuckled in amusement as he twice had to rest the melon upon the floor, and twice subsequently snatched it up after a cry of outrage from the fruit seller. Some assassin he would be.

No sooner had he crossed the threshold to the kitchens proper did an impatient quartermaster direct Jai to place his melon with the others, as he checked items off a list upon his parchment.

Within minutes, Jai was through the kitchens and scampering down the dining hall. It was strange to walk past the place where Magnus had kidnapped him. Despite the hubbub of the kitchens there was a normalcy to his surroundings that felt at odds with the danger he now faced.

He moved as quickly as he dared. There was always a chance that Magnus, or one of his gryphon guardsmen, would be eating a late lunch.

Jai was happy enough when he reached Leonid's rooms, nodding to the guards as he made his way through. He only hoped they would not tell anyone they had seen him.

Only when he entered Leonid's room, the old man was not there. This was worrying. Leonid would never leave his chambers without a good reason.

Clearly the room had been packed up. The old man's clothing was missing, as was one of the large trunks that usually sat at the foot of his bed. Which meant he had not just left for the afternoon. No, he would likely be gone for a while.

Jai hurried to his room to gather his belongings, knowing he could not remain here unsupervised. But upon entering his little room, he realised he had almost nothing to take. No clothes that were any better or more useful than those he wore now. No keepsakes worth taking for the few days he hoped he might be away. No food, no trinkets. Within a minute, he had gone through all he owned.

He sat on the bed and laid out his haul.

Outside of a few loose coins, all he'd really found was Leonid's old razor, one he had saved for his own grooming. Rusted though it was, it might give him half a chance against a potential threat. And if he was honest with himself, he might use it to shave the fledgling whiskers from his face before Frida returned, in the washbasin he had seen in his room at the inn.

He felt just a little guilty for giving the Dansk handmaiden so much thought when he should be focused on Balbir. He was suddenly uncharacteristically aware of his appearance.

But then, it was rare for him to speak to such a beauty. Or indeed, girls in general.

Most of the servants in the palace were male, for many were retired legionaries from Constantine's wars. And there were plenty of them, though their battles had been nowhere near as bloody as those of Leonid. These recent wars were mostly tidying up rebellions and finishing off the few migratory tribes that had found safety nestling in the mountainous region between the Northern Tundra and the Great Steppe.

And even if there were not so many veterans seeking employment, with Titus's mother dead in childbirth, there were no women in the royal household in need of handmaidens and female company. As for the few scullery girls that did occasionally frequent the palace, most seemed to view Jai as more of a curiosity; as a strange prince from a savage people; servant to a dying old man who never left his room.

Jai sighed as he peered into Leonid's quarters through his

open door. He looked at the books, the trophies and writing materials. He had felt a prisoner here his whole life. Like a weevil in an aging songbird's gilded cage, living among the muck. With Leonid not here to keep a wary eye . . . would anyone even notice if he disappeared?

He could beg a favour from Frida. Balbir could say he had died in the night. He doubted Leonid would ask for proof, and if he did, she could say his body had been taken to the plague pits; that rotting, stinking mass grave at Latium's cliff-base where only grave robbers dared tread.

Hell, he could even steal whatever trinkets he could from here and use them to buy Balbir's freedom. Or Frida's silence. Certainly over a decade of labour more than made up for what he'd take – he would feel no shame for theft.

But as his mind turned to the many relics of Leonid's victories, he heard the front door swing open, and the sound of hushed voices. Immediately, he was dizzied by the sudden pounding of his heart.

He reached out and swung the door near-shut, glad for the thin partition of wood between him and whoever had walked in. For a moment he wondered if Leonid had returned, but the voices were too loud to be the old man, and one too deep.

So he steadied his breathing, letting the world's spinning come to a halt. Then, slowly, he crawled over to the door, and put his eye up to the crack of its hinge. Immediately his heart began pounding once more.

For there was Magnus. And Titus.

Chapter 18

Jai clamped a hand over his mouth, watching as the two peered about the room before splaying themselves along the two reclining chairs opposite the hearth. The two were here for privacy, of that there was no doubt, for their conversation ceased until Leonid's great oak doors had closed behind them.

'Are you sure it is safe to speak here?' Titus said, his voice so low Jai had to focus to make the words out at all. 'Why not our usual place?'

Titus was peering around the room with a curious eye. It had been some years since the young man had visited.

'The Dansk are here now,' Magnus said, 'and there's plenty of soulbound among them. They might be listening.'

Titus snorted derisively.

'You give them too much credit. Those barbarians wipe themselves with snow.'

'Regardless,' Magnus said, allowing a low chuckle, 'the old man has had this place charmed by my own men, if you recall, to prevent any uninvited totems from crossing its threshold. Not even a Huddite mouse-spy's rodent could squeeze into here. Paranoia and the decrepit go arm in arm.'

'Fine,' Titus said. 'Tell me.'

Magnus spoke quietly in response, his words unintelligible, until an impatient groan from Titus raised the big man's voice once more.

'. . . trees. No fires, as agreed. But any longer and they *will* be discovered.'

Titus snarled.

'Had that bitch not sent her dragon to hunt there, I might not have had to create that distraction with the plainsboy. Do you have any idea how much of her dowry I had to return to win her family's forgiveness? She thinks me a monster now.'

Jai's stomach twisted at the young prince's words. Titus might resent his forced marriage, but calling his future wife a bitch was . . . something else. And he knew exactly who the 'plainsboy' was. His near-execution had been staged, it seemed.

'Does it matter?' Magnus chuckled. 'The dragon pup is the real prize, and it's not like they'll be taking any of that gold back with them. You're just lucky the princess cared enough to intervene.'

Titus examined his fingernails.

'I suppose you are right. Though from what I hear, that boy is so unimportant that his uncle Teji has not even sent a formal complaint. Not that it matters, I could take a piss on Rohan's grave and he'd do little more than grandstand. There's no appe-tite for war in that one.'

Magnus grunted in response.

'I should have killed the little shit there and then. To think that he's set foot within our inner sanctum, yet still draws breath.'

'Patience, friend – just a few hours longer. The time soon comes where we'll do as we please. Is that not, after all, what this is all about?'

Magnus grunted again, but Jai could see his great fists balling up with concealed rage.

'My men will bring him to me by nightfall. My spies have found him and some old plainsbitch holed up at the Red Lion. Oh, and the princess's handmaiden has been visiting him too.'

'Good,' Titus replied. 'Let the Dansk bitch focus on the little runt. He's proved most useful, as it turns out. Keep him alive until it's done.'

'Sire please. I can't wait that long. One night early won't hurt,' Magnus urged. 'Like you said, the boy is a nobody. I'll make it look like he died from his injuries.'

Titus sighed, but did not contradict him.

The prince's silence sent Jai's head spinning once more. Not for his own safety, but Balbir's. They knew where she was. He had to warn her.

In fact, he had more warnings to give now. But they spoke too cryptically for him to understand what he needed to warn the Dansk of. It made no sense.

'So, is everything prepared?' Titus asked, the long pause finally ended. 'Their early arrival has thrown off our plans. We'll need every loyal knight and squire you have; I don't trust the palace guards to react with the speed we need them to, even if they are now equipped correctly.'

'They know what to do,' Magnus replied. 'The question is, will it happen on time?'

Titus sniffed.

'I am assured it will. My man in the kitchens has been feeding his larks for weeks upon nothing but the seeds of hemlock. They are immune, but their flesh is so impregnated with the poison, just a few of their tongues will do it. I'll personally serve him an entire bowl of them. The trial at the feast proved its efficacy.'

It was all Jai could do to steady his breathing. He knew the more powerful soulbound had far greater senses than those of a normal man, and one hoarse breath would be all Magnus needed to discover him. Jai was lucky the man had let his guard down.

'Then, if you have no further need of me, I will take my leave,' Magnus said. Jai heard the big man getting to his feet. 'You want my advice? Go through with the marriage, have a try of that royal bitch's quim. We can afford to wait until then.'

Titus chuckled drily.

'I've had enough Dansk whores this week to sate a war-weary legion. She'll be no different. And there's nothing to stop me from having her afterwards. You can keep her when I tire of her.'

Magnus laughed, already heading for the exit.

'You do that, and I'll fight a hundred wars for you.'

He rapped his knuckles on the door, just out of sight, and the guards heaved them open. Soon Jai was alone, with only Titus in the room.

Now the emperor-to-be sat alone. The young man was hardly older than Jai, yet in the gloom, he looked almost haggard. Away from his audience, he sagged and the skin beneath his eyes was dark.

Jai watched Titus stand and run his hands along the artefacts scattered throughout the bookshelves, a fallen king's shield here, a bloodied flag there. Jai realised he and his brothers were just the same to the young heir – a reminder of past victories; pawns to trade. Little more than the trophies upon Leonid's walls. Now, Titus wanted trophies of his own. Not the hand-me-downs of a bygone era.

Clearly, he was done playing second fiddle to an old man. No, third fiddle. After his father. He wanted to make a name of his own.

There was no staying here. Not after what Jai had heard. There was to be a bloody coup, and he wanted no part in it. He had no choice but to escape this place for good.

'You'll see,' Titus murmured. 'You'll all see.'

Jai saw. And he'd seen enough.

Chapter 19

J ai walked swiftly to the great doors, wincing as the object
he had stuffed down his threadbare trousers chafed against
his skin. Of all the valuables in Leonid's room, most were
too large or too noticeable to be seen carrying out of the
palace.

He'd been quick in his search, fearful of Titus's return and
knowing the room like the back of his hand. But there was no
coinage to be had, for what need had a royal for such a thing.

There was, however, one item he had managed to take. One
that had belonged to his father, such that it was still rusted with
his blood from the execution. In that theft, he felt no guilt.

It was a gorget, made from fine, blue damantine steel. If he
dared to wear it, it would sit upon his upper chest, with a rim
protecting the bottom of his neck. Would that it had protected
his father's better when Leonid had swung the axe.

At its front, sitting just above the heart, was the sigil of his
father's house and tribe – the Kidara. A male khiro, the great
horned beast he had been forced to kill.

It was fitting that his ancestors had chosen that symbol. The
khiroi were the lifeblood of the Great Steppe. Those huge beasts

of burden that carried the tribes' very towns upon their backs as the herds migrated with the seasons.

Both wild and tame, it was they that cropped short the long grass of the endless steppe – and they that fed the great predators that made his homeland a dangerous place at the best of times.

Jai rearranged himself a final time, then stalked through the doors with all the confidence of the prince himself.

'Where is Leonid?'

The guards at the doors stared straight ahead, ignoring him.

'I have his medicine,' Jai said, holding up the small pouch that contained his razor and coins. 'I'm the one who looks after him – you've seen me.' He shifted his weight onto one hip as the two guards stared straight ahead. 'Of course, if he gets sick and dies, they'll blame me first. But when they start pulling out my fingernails, I'll have two more names to give them. Yours.'

The older of the two scoffed at Jai's words, but the other blanched slightly. It was this one that Jai turned his attention to.

'What was it that they did to that Huddite spy, all those years ago? Was he the one they fed alive to the gryphons? Or was that the court jester who took the piss out of Constantine's beard?'

'That bear-shit-eating Dansk king is ill,' the boy muttered, earning himself an eye roll from his partner. 'The royals and their guests have taken themselves to the royal rooms at the baths to help him sweat it out.'

'Ill?' Jai asked, his ears pricking up. 'Ill with what?'

But his questions had earned him the ire of the older guard, who launched a kick that sent him sprawling across the plush red carpet of the grand corridor.

'You fuck off now,' the man said simply.

Jai fucked off.

His mind raced as he hurried back through the palace corridors, the rusted razor now clutched in his pocket. Little use it
would be against a soulbound assassin, but it gave him some
comfort.

Magnus knew where he slept. And soon enough, Balbir would
go back to the room. Whether Jai was there or not, any killer
would have few qualms about slitting the old woman's throat
while they waited for Jai to return.

But surely he owed Erica a warning also. Now he knew what
the so called 'trial' had been. Testing the poison upon Ivar. The
soulbound king had survived their first attempt, it seemed. But
now Titus claimed he had an entire bowl of poisoned larks'
tongues. Enough to kill him dead.

Either way, Jai knew he would never get close to any of the
royals. His best chance would be to return to his room, get
another message to Frida that way. If Balbir arrived first, then
the Dansk were on their own.

LEAVING THE PALACE WAS easier than entering, and with each
step, his resolve grew. His plan to escape with Balbir had gone
from a fantasy to a reality in the thousand steps it had taken
to reach the inn once more.

Once there, he crept past the still-sleeping innkeeper and
returned to the room. He prayed that Balbir would return soon.
Before an assassin came for both of them. Within, he bathed
himself as best he could, using a pail of water and the razor to
try to make himself presentable.

There was even a bar of soap, unscented but serviceable. After
washing, he left his clothes to air by the window and put on
the gorget, tracing his fingers along the insignia at the front. It

was perhaps the closest he had ever felt to his father. Quite literally, in many ways, for the sigil's engraving was made all the more visible by the black blood dried within its cracks.

The armour sat heavy upon his shoulders, its crescent bottom beginning just above his sternum, and ending in a loose collar at the base of his neck.

'You wear it well,' Balbir said.

Jai spun, to find the old woman sitting upon the bed, her beetle brows furrowed at the site of him. How had she moved so quickly?

Jai hurried to cover himself, earning a cackle from Balbir.

'Nowt I've not seen afore, Jai,' Balbir chuckled. 'I've seen your twig and berries since afore you knew you had them.'

Jai reddened, unsure of what to say. 'We have to leave,' he whispered, plucking his kecks from the windowsill and pulling them on. 'I returned to the palace to ask Leonid to buy your contract. Only, he was not there. Magnus was . . . and . . .'

He sought the words to explain what he had heard, but they jumbled in his head. He did not know what he knew exactly.

'Something is going to happen, very soon. If we can get a message to Frida, we should, but for now I need you to pack your things. We're—'

A bony hand clapped over Jai's face, shoving him back against the wall. It took a moment for Jai to realise it was Balbir. She had moved with such speed he'd been taken unawares.

She glared up at him with her dark eyes, and a single finger pointed to the ceiling. Jai's own eyes turned there, seeing a trickle of dust falling through the beam of light from the curtains.

He looked to the door, but Balbir shook her head. Leaned in, close as a lover.

'We run; they'll hunt us down before we reach the front gates. We kill him now; we've bought ourselves some time.'

Jai's eyes widened and he shook his head. But Balbir was already moving, stooping low and scuttling to the shadows beside the window. She pointed Jai to the darkest corner of the room.

It was a mad plan. An old lady and a damp, half-naked boy, taking on a soulbound assassin. She had not even a weapon in her hands, and he just a rusted razor.

The razor was slippery in his palm, sweat already forming despite his lack of clothing. It was a simple weapon; a floor-sharpened metal shard embedded in a handle of corkwood. He hid it behind his back. The element of surprise was all they had going for them.

Now he saw the shadow at the window. That long shaft of light that divided the room in two flickering, then darkening. There was a sudden glow . . . not from outside . . . from inside the room.

An explosion of glass. A man, moving impossibly fast, blade extended. Stopped short, even as Jai screamed, slashing wildly at the air.

Only the man never reached him.

Jai stood frozen, razor trembling. But the man was as still as he, but for a twitching face, and eyes that darted from Jai, then to the razor. For a moment, Jai wondered if this was some sort of challenge, waiting for him to make the first move.

Then, Balbir faded into view, as if Jai's eyes had adjusted to the gloom. He saw her fingers clutching the man's nape, pinched like an eagle's claw. Her face was scrunched as if in agony, and the glow from her fingers and eyes was a dark, deep red. A red that was fading.

'Now,' Balbir croaked. 'Before I lose him.'

Chapter 20

J ai had never killed a man. Never even been in a fight, unless being roundly beaten by guardsmen or other servants counted. He glanced at the old woman to his side. There was no choice here. Nor time. He did not look the man in the eye when he cut across his throat. Only felt the soft tug of flesh as he drew the blade through, and felt the hot blood spill, almost caustic, over his hands and feet. Jai felt numb.

Still, Balbir held the man until his gurgling abated. Her fingers never moved, and afterward his body hung like a marionette. Dead, yet frozen in place.

Then, with a great sigh, Balbir let him fall. Collapsed, kneeling in blood. Her breath rasped in her lungs, eyes rolling back into their sockets.

Jai gently took her in his arms, careless of the blood that now soaked them both. He lay her on his bed. She was so light, lighter even than Leonid.

His mind reeled at the discovery of her abilities. Again, he had been aided by one of the soulbound. Frida had surprised him. But Balbir shocked him.

'Water,' Balbir hissed.

Jai was swift to find the gourd of water and put it to her lips. She drank greedily. Her face was more drawn somehow, as if the crosshatching of lines had been etched deeper into her face.

Beads of sweat broke out on her forehead, and for a while she twitched, the corners of her mouth bubbling white. But after a few, long breaths, she calmed.

Jai had hardly spoken to a single soulbound person in his life. Now, they seemed to be everywhere. He stroked her head, and then felt his gorge rise as blood smeared across her brow. He turned, threw up upon the floor. Then again, and again, until tears and snot ran from his nose.

'I killed him,' he gagged through the words. 'Like I w-*ugh* . . . slaughtering a pig.'

Balbir's hand took his wrist then. Her hands were surprisingly strong.

'It is good to mourn your enemy's death, especially when you did not know them,' she whispered. 'But only after the battle. We are still in the midst of it.'

Jai gulped and wiped his face with the bedspread. Cleared his throat and took a seat beside her. Balbir smiled and lifted a hand to brush his face.

'Of all Rohan's sons, you bear his likeness most,' she whispered.

Jai smiled and shook his head.

'I am only half Steppeman. How can that be?'

Balbir tutted and gave him a light slap.

'Contradict me at your peril. If I say it is so, it is.'

'And yet you lied to me,' Jai grumbled, wincing and rubbing his cheek.

Balbir groaned, waving at him dismissively as she sat up a little.

'Bring me that soup,' she said, avoiding the veiled question. 'I must recover my strength.'

Jai spotted a fresh bowl of soup, still steaming upon the counter. She must have brought it with her upon her return earlier. His belly grumbled, its scent surpassing even the metallic tinge of blood in the air, but he diligently brought it to her and fed her a few spoonfuls.

'I am a spy, my boy,' Balbir said, sighing after a large gulp. 'Or at least, I was one. Your grandfather convinced your uncle to send me to care for you boys. Old and hunched as I am, he did not think I would be suspected – just another captive from the war. I would have my totem carve messages in the earth for him to read. Of course, I could do little but let him know how his grandsons fared . . . and after a few years, not even that. With your grandfather's death, I was forgotten. And I preferred it that way.'

She sighed and closed her eyes.

'My Sagara still lives, though her eyes are more cataracted than mine. I see her world through a haze. But I still feel my old land through her. I am there now. I feel the earth beneath the pads of her feet. I can smell the fresh-cropped grass, hear the songs of our people as they bring the herd in for the night.'

'Sagara is a khiro?' Jai asked.

The old lady nodded, and Jai saw a sadness in her eyes. She took the bowl then, guzzling the rest of the soup. He marvelled at the old woman's courage. The deaths of spies captured by the Sabines were legendary in their savagery and were always public.

There had been some Huddite spies caught just before Jai had been sent to Latium, but he knew the story well. It had been one of Constantine's first acts as emperor. It was said by some that they were not spies but rather scapegoats so the new emperor could make his mark.

The five men and women had been barrelled and left in the market square, their heads exposed for any to hurt. Noses, ears, eyes – those were the first to go, for the urchins of the streets were as cruel as they were desperate.

But this was not what made their deaths so terrible. It was what was packed into the barrels with them. Faeces, milk and offal were poured in before their sealing, and the liquid putrefied inside. Maggots writhed and burrowed into the spies' flesh, bodies rotting from the outside in, their wails rending the air.

By the end, their throats were slit in the night by someone who took pity. Or, more likely, a nearby vendor who knew the stench and noise was bad for business.

'I thank you, Jai, for not hesitating,' Balbir said, her voice quieter now. 'My mana was almost spent. A few seconds more and he would have slaughtered the both of us.'

Only then could Jai look at the man. He had thought it would make him sick again, but instead, he felt strangely empty.

The man wore no armour, nor insignia. His face was as plain as any he'd seen, neither handsome nor ugly. Even his sword was a simple thing, made of pig iron. Jai wondered at the care Magnus had taken to hide the assassin's origins.

'What happened to his beast?' Jai whispered. 'Will it not warn his brethren of his death?'

Balbir shook her head.

'Some say a piece of the man's soul now resides in his beast. But it is but a beast, and loses the acuity that so many totems gain when the bond forms. Without him to guide it, it will be unable to pass on any message. If we are lucky, it has flown off in distress, without anyone noticing it has gone. I could smell it on the roof before . . . I cannot smell it now.'

Jai breathed deeply. 'What now?' he asked.

Balbir shrugged and lay back.

'If we run this very moment, we have a chance. But a slim one. Better that they do not look for us at all. Beyond that, I know not. Until a few minutes ago, you were to go back to Leonid, and I to go back to scrubbing floors for a new master. If you've a plan, I'll listen.'

Jai brought his knees up to his chest.

'My plan didn't involve a dead assassin in our room.'

Balbir's hand lashed out, slapping him.

'It does now.'

Chapter 21

R eady?' Jai asked.

He felt sick. Their plan was precarious and relied on chance more than anything else. But it was the *only* plan.

Balbir nodded, then heaved as they rolled the man's body onto the blanket and wrapped him up to his neck. He lay there, eyes half-open, mouth agape. Balbir shut them both with gentle fingers.

Now the assassin wore Jai's clothing, and Jai his. He was conspicuous, as his outfit was bloodied . . . but that was a problem for later.

'You are sure?' Jai asked.

'He is but an empty vessel now,' Balbir whispered. 'And I will need to defile him to save us, before the night is done. But first, I must soulbreathe.'

Jai cocked his head, fascinated. Balbir settled back, cross-legged, as he had seen the acolytes of the Eyrie do.

'I can do this alone,' she said. 'This will take hours, for I am not the cultivator I once was, and my totem is far. If they come while you are here, we both die.'

Jai grunted.

'The assassin was waiting for your return, I am sure of it. So whoever sent him might assume he is still waiting.'

'Even so,' Balbir muttered.

'You think I want to make that journey without you? I've hardly set foot beyond the walls of Latium. If another assassin comes, I'll wake you up and we'll deal with him together.'

'On your head be it.'

She breathed in, then out, slowly.

'The lungs, the bellows,' Balbir whispered. 'The heart, the hearth. The stomach, the cauldron. The blood, the filter. The core, the cast.'

Her voice was hardly audible, yet her chest seemed to double in size as she took great gulps of air. Jai wished he could see what he knew was happening. The mana of their surroundings, trickling into her body like fine dust. What happened beyond that, he knew little of.

For a while, he watched her. Then scrubbed at the front of his shirt and his moccasins until the washwater was pink and the stains faded so as to look like he'd not had more than a violent nosebleed.

The killer's clothing was far softer and cleaner than the scratchy servant's uniform. Unexpectedly comfortable, Jai dozed on and off as Balbir sat, her only movement the deep in and out of her chest.

It was only when he woke, perhaps hours later if the angle of the sunlight was any indication, that he noticed it. Something was in his pocket, something small and soft, but he could feel it there.

He pulled it out. It was a note.

Whether it's done or not, take a shift at the palace before the eighth bell. All trusted hands are needed.

There was no signature or seal. Likely a message passed from Magnus, to a captain, to the assassin. The man looked young, hardly more than a boy. Likely this had been a test of his loyalty, or some such nonsense.

What this did tell him was how much time they had before the assassin would be missed. And he had just heard the seventh bell ring a few minutes earlier. He had to speak up.

'Balbir,' he said.

'I know, boy,' Balbir muttered, getting to her feet. 'The hour grows late, but my power is still only a little. Let us hope it is enough.'

Already the old woman was stooping over the assassin's body, a hand outstretched over his face.

'Forgive me,' she whispered, as her eyes started to glow.

Her hand began to blaze orange, even as her fingers danced in front of the man's closed eyes. Then, the flames poured forth, materialising as if from nowhere. Jai turned away as the stench of burning hair and flesh made him gag once more. At least this time, his stomach was practically empty.

The orange light began to fade, but the stench remained. Balbir sighed and finally Jai turned. He averted his eyes, but not until after a glance at the ruin that the flames had left behind.

'You are lucky he is black of hair and tanned from the sun,' Balbir muttered. 'Or I'd have to do his hands and feet.'

Jai felt his gorge rise once more, but resisted. Another glance told him that the face was unrecognisable. He could have been Titus himself, and Jai would not have known.

'Now, you need to leave – through the way he came,' Balbir said, jerking her head at the window.

'Repeat the plan to me,' Jai whispered.

'I'll wake the innkeeper as if I have just arrived, then return in a panic and have him call the town guard and tell them of your death. I'll wait until they've taken the body to the plague pits and meet you by the front gates.'

Jai nodded.

'Good,' he said. 'They will think the assassin got sick of waiting for you and killed me – and I suspect you're not important enough for them to mount too great a search . . . no offence meant. He's supposed to return for the eighth bell. Let us hope there is enough chaos in whatever happens tonight that they think he died in the fighting . . . if there is any.'

He stood to go to the window, but Balbir tugged at his sleeve.

'There is every chance the town guards will be in Magnus's pay,' Balbir whispered. 'They might kill me all the same.'

Jai felt his heart twist at her words, knowing that this was *his* plan.

'I cannot do it for you,' Jai said, squeezing her hand. 'Would that I could.'

'No, I care little of that. It is that I have knowledge. A gesture passed from my ancestors that may be forgotten in my death. I am the last in my line – I have watched all my grandchildren buried, one after another, through Sagara's eyes. I would have you pass it to the soulbound of the Steppefolk.'

Jai hesitated, and Balbir gripped his collar, forcing him to meet her gaze. She looked so frail, in the dusk light. Her eyes were filled with some emotion he could not understand. Regret? Longing?

'Indulge an old woman, in what may be her final moments. It is but one gesture. The others I must hope will already be known.'

Jai nodded and sat down once more.

'Quickly now,' he said. 'The eighth bell approaches, and who knows if they will shut the gates when . . . whatever it is happens.'

She lifted her hands, and contorted one of them into a strange shape, tucking her thumb beneath the second knuckle of her middle finger, and bending the other fingers at crooked angles. It did not look dissimilar to what Magnus had done.

'It is a charm; majick that is cast upon an object or person to change them. This will make you hard to see. The shade spell. You can cast it on yourself, though it only works in low light. My family have used it for years while hunting in the long grass, but as you saw earlier, it has other uses. It is one of the reasons I was chosen as a spy. The Huddite mouse-spies know this skill too.'

Jai tried to memorise it, imitating her crooked fingers as she tutted and shifted them to her exacting specifications.

'Pah. It will have to do,' she grimaced, then pushed him towards the window. 'Go, boy. If I am not there by the eighth bell, begin your journey. I will catch up with you on the Kashmere Road.'

Jai wished to hug her. To thank her. Something. His throat felt raw as he watched her. She was as close to a friend as any he had. As close to a mother as any he had.

But she had already turned away, heading for the door. Instead, Jai girded himself, and mounted the windowsill. There was no way of getting word to Frida — it was time to leave this place. The outside world awaited.

Chapter 22

J ai cursed as he limped along the cobbles, wishing he had taken more care when dropping to the ground. He did not know how soon the eighth bell would come. But the squares with the sundials were too crowded, and he dared not be seen.

Steppefolk were uncommon in Latium, mostly due to the animosity felt by the veterans that made up the palace and town guard. On top of that, he looked odd enough with his bruised face. Not to mention that his bloodied tunic was much more obvious in the light of the setting sun.

He stuck to the shadows, taking the side alleys, using the Eyrie as a reference point to head for the main gates.

Luckily, there were areas where the underclass lived – the servants and even the few fettered that were kept behind doors. Here, he blended well enough, though he had to take a circuitous route around the city centre.

The journey took longer than he had wanted, and he wondered if Balbir had arrived ahead of him as he hurried with head bowed. But there was no sign of her when he finally arrived at the enormous black gates that had stood for nearly half a century, built into a high wall bisecting the base of the jutting cliff.

It was no surprise that the gates were still open, for despite the frenetic energy outside the kitchens that morning, still more food was being brought through, alongside carriages with wealthy guests from across the great empire.

Guards watched from towers in the walls, while more still patrolled the grounds. But they only cared about what was coming in. It would be so easy to slip outside and begin the long journey on foot. But there was no sign of Balbir.

And as he loitered, the guards began to eye him. Pickpockets were rife in Latium, despite the punishment of losing a hand. Jai knew that the guards were not particularly overzealous when it came to due process, and would as soon enact justice in a back alley as on a clean medical slab at a prison.

It was then that he saw her. That flash of pale hair, and the heads turning to look at her as she walked past. A Dansk maiden was a rare enough sight in Latium, let alone one of such beauty. Frida. It had to be.

The girl was moving swiftly, almost running as she ducked and dodged through the crowds. But then, she was soulbound. If she wanted to, she could probably barge a furrow through the crowd without so much as a falter in her step.

His shock at seeing her here almost made him forget she was the very person he wanted to see. He could kill two birds with one stone. Or at least, prevent Titus from doing the same to the Dansk dragons.

'Frida!' he bellowed.

If she heard him, she did not show it. If anything, she seemed to pick up speed. In seconds, he would lose her. A bell tolled – its source Constantine's grand cathedral, still under construction.

The brassy clang reverberated across the city, echoing through the streets. Some people even stopped to listen. It was the great Bell of the Huddites, stolen in an early campaign from their holiest of temples. The instrument was famed for the purity of its sound, but all the sound did was set Jai's heart beating fast. The eighth bell. It was allowed to quieten before the next knell, and the note hung in the air for nearly a full minute.

A second toll rang out.

He didn't think. He had to warn her of what was to come. Wasn't sure if it was revenge that drove him, or a sense of gratitude. The gates were right there. Balbir had told him to leave now.

Three tolls.

Jai's feet took him after Frida. At first, to see where she was headed. Then, to see which street she had turned down. Soon he was running too, grunting through pain as his jaw bounced at the movement.

A fourth toll.

'Frida!' he yelled.

Passers-by leaped out of his way now, seeing the frantic, bloodied boy haring through the streets. He knew this was foolish. That he could be arrested for far less than the commotion he was making.

But in a single breath, he could hurt Magnus and Titus to their cores. Change the course of history. No man in the empire could say that.

Frida moved even more swiftly now. She was running, there was no doubt about it. But of course, she had heard him yell. She was soulbound.

'I have to warn you!' he bellowed. 'Stop!'

Five tolls.

By now, she was out of sight. But he knew where she was going. Latium's baths. Frequented by the wealthy of the city, the natural hot springs there were one of the many reasons Leonid had made this strange spit of land his capital.

Exhausted, Jai allowed himself to turn his sprint into a trot. He stopped at the baths' pillared entrance. It was a strange structure, a man-made cave mouth that led deep underground – the product of a younger Leonid's fancies. There was no sign of Frida – but surely she would be inside?

A sixth toll sounded . . . and he saw them.

Now he knew he had miscalculated. The place was surrounded by a dozen Gryphon Guard, resplendent in their full dress. Bronze moulded over steel armour, they almost glowed gold in the light of the setting sun. Scarlet cloaks marked them out from the surrounding crowds, who waited for just a glimpse of the visiting bride.

A seventh toll set their murmuring silent, even as shadows flitted through the sky. Jai looked up and saw the silhouettes of gryphons, wheeling and watching for signs of danger.

What would a bloodied Steppeman look like, sprinting his way through a crowd toward the place where the royal family were sequestered? Many a madman had tried to kill the Sabine royals before, and each had been slaughtered before the royals had even taken notice.

He could easily be one of them. Already he began to turn, to fight his way back to the gates. The crowd behind him shifted, and a woman cried out as she was barged aside.

Jai took but a single step, before a heavy hand slammed down upon his shoulder. The eighth bell sounded, so loud he could feel it in his chest.

A death knell.

Chapter 23

Y ou're late.'
Jai was spun around and found himself looking into the angry eyes of Corinth. The man was no gryphon rider, but rather Leonid's old servant, who filled in for Jai when he was sick.

'Where are you running off to?' he demanded. 'You've had enough time off. If I have to wipe Leonid's arse one more time . . .'

The relief Jai felt was swiftly receding.

'I need Leonid's medicine,' Jai said, thinking quickly. 'I forgot it back at the palace.'

Corinth gripped his shoulder and pulled him toward the baths.

'I was sent to pick up all his medicines last week,' Corinth said. 'And a book every day since. He's been staying with the emperor since Ivar fell ill.'

He held up a dusty tome, and Jai realised the man had spotted him on his way back from the palace. Poor luck, but far better than a Gryphon Guard.

'He's in good health, but someone has to wash the piss-stains out of his kashmere, and it's not going to be me.'

Jai tried again.

'Seriously, it's a medicine he doesn't—'

A backhanded slap silenced him, setting his ears ringing.

'You lazy little shit,' Corinth growled. 'I heard you've been awake since this morning. Even been back to Leonid's chamber. What took you so long to come back?'

Jai was dazed, his jaw aching from the blow. It had been a mistake, asking the door guards where Leonid was – what good had that information done him? They must have sent word to Corinth. Clearly he had complained about his new role to them.

'I . . .'

Luckily, Corinth wasn't interested in the answer.

By now, Jai was in plain view of the Gryphon Guard, and any struggle would just draw more attention. And even if they didn't take note of him; out of breath as he was, he'd be lucky to take ten steps before Corinth caught him.

None of his choices were good ones. If he was lucky, he might be able to give Corinth the slip once they were inside. One thing was for certain. His only chance to meet Balbir now would be on the road.

Worst of all, their plan to fake his death was now almost in tatters. His only hope was if his supposed time of death could be confused. Who knew how closely Magnus would investigate?

Either way, Jai kept his head down as he was frogmarched between the Gryphon Guards. It was fortunate that these fully fledged warriors had been keeping an eye on the Dansk army when Magnus had brought him to the tower. The worst could happen if one of them recognised him.

It was a relief when he stepped into the shadow of the baths' entrance, passing between two grand pillars and into the torchlit stairway that led deep into the bowels of the earth.

Jai had been here many times before, with Leonid. He imagined the old man was not happy to have been sequestered in this place. Hot water made the old emperor's bones ache, he said - as almost everything seemed to these days. His presence here suggested that the rumours of Ivar's sickness might be worse than he'd been told. The royals were on lockdown. This looked like assassination-watch, in a place with only one way in and one way out.

As they descended deeper, more guards could be seen lining the stairs. To Jai's surprise, there were almost as many Dansk as palace guards. Clearly the royals had been staying here a while, though, as Corinth moved unimpeded.

It was a sumptuous, echoing place, and when they finally reached the end of the steps, they were thoroughly searched by two guards to allow them past. Jai's razor was confiscated, and he was glad he had cleaned the blood from it before leaving his rooms.

Usually, he was overjoyed at the chance to soak in the hot baths – when Leonid visited, he was allowed to use the facilities while the old man was pampered by beautiful masseuses. That part, the old man *did* like, though Jai suspected he no longer came because his . . . *little general* (as Jai had once heard Leonid call it) . . . no longer rose to the occasion.

Finally allowed through, Jai walked on across the mosaic floors, every inch painstakingly depicting some Sabine victory in battle. It turned his stomach to see dead Steppefolk piled high upon a battlefield, apparent window dressing behind resplendent Gryphon Guards and cheering legionaries.

The air was hot, warming his head as the heat rose. Torches flickered upon the granite walls, the smoke mingling with the heady steam that filled the corridors, filtering up through clever draught holes in the ceiling. Corinth pulled him inexorably onwards, passing by the parts usually open to the affluent public, then the nobility, and finally the private area of the royals.

The royal entrance was a grand, stone-carved archway, and Jai had to be pulled bodily over its threshold before being patted down again by another palace guard. Escape seemed impossible now. The only silver lining was he suspected Titus and Magnus would not be here. But Leonid would be. And though the old man was half-deaf and half-blind, his mind was as sharp as ever. If anyone would see through his tenuous body swap plan, or even be motivated enough to investigate, it was him.

Better not to be seen by the old man at all.

'This is Leonid's manservant,' Corinth said to the men standing guard, handing the book over to Jai. 'He's taking over for me.'

The guards seemed disinterested, but nodded in acknowledgement.

'All right, arsewipe,' Corinth growled, shoving Jai forward with a foot in his lower back. 'This is where I leave you. Next time you get sick, work through it. Or I'll make you wish you'd died from the fever. If Leonid needs me, I'll be back on watch at the entrance. Don't make me come back here.'

Jai did not reply, instead staring after the man's retreating back. So, his attempted execution was not common knowledge. That would be Leonid's doing.

'Strip,' the guard who had patted him down said.

'I . . . what?' Jai said.

'Emperor's orders,' the guard said.

'Why?' Jai asked. Was the poisoning common knowledge?

'Do you want me to beat you first?' the guard growled. 'Nobody enters here with a single thread. Leave the book too – we'll check it and have a fettered girl bring it.'

Jai hesitated, slowly unbuttoning the top of his tunic to buy time. He could turn back. It's not like they would stop him – they didn't know what he was here for.

He could wait until Corinth was up the stairs, then make a

run for it; hope that the bodyguard didn't spot him as he hurried down the steps. But if he did, the Sabines would start hunting for him before he even left the city, dead body or no.

Even if they didn't catch him he'd have broken the terms of the peace between the Steppefolk and the Sabines. He'd be lucky if his uncle didn't hunt him down himself.

And . . . he was here now. The damage had been done. Why not keep on?

It was the sight beyond the guards that made up his mind. There were two passages ahead – one for the men, and another for the women. With only royals and their personal servants allowed past this point, he knew Erica and Frida would likely be alone in the women's section.

He could warn her. Ask for her help.

'Well?' the guard demanded.

Jai pulled his shirt over his head for what seemed the hundredth time that day.

'All right,' he said. 'I'll strip.'

Chapter 24

It was easy enough to slip into the women's section, for the scented mist was so heavy here that the guards were visible only as hazy silhouettes from where the corridor diverged into two.

The floors had been cleaned since last he came here. The women's section had been abandoned ever since Titus's mother died, and left to moulder. Now the tiles shone again, though he could still see where the grime had been pushed to the edges of the walls by a swift mop.

He padded deeper down the corridor, wishing he had explored this section before. All he knew was that this area was far smaller than its male counterpart, thanks to its late single occupant of yesteryear.

As he walked, he could not help but feel a draught about his nethers, and the swing of his family jewels. He had nothing to cover himself, so he walked with both hands cupped below.

Embarrassment at the thought of being seen naked was but a passing feeling. Terror soon overcame it, for only now did he realise that the faux pas of sitting in Titus's seat paled in comparison to violating the privacy of a royal lady. If Titus didn't kill him for doing so to his betrothed, Erica might well kill him herself, warning or not.

When the passage finally opened into a single room, he was relieved to hear the soft murmur of women's voices. She was here. It had to be her.

He took a tentative step deeper into the room, making out the steaming pool of water at its centre. Before he could take another, he felt a sharp stab in his throat . . . and the press of soft skin against his back.

'Take another step, and it'll be your last.'

The voice was so close he could feel her hot breath against his ear, steam on steam. Dansk. Female. It was all he could think, his mind a blank.

The pain sharpened, and Jai knew a weapon was pressed against his jugular.

'Please,' Jai whispered. 'I am Jai, son of Rohan. I have come to warn the princess. Let me do so and I will take my leave. I need not go further.'

The pressure upon his neck receded a touch, though his captor pressed closer. He tried not to think of the soft mounds pressed against his upper back . . . or the thatch of her pudenda brushing against his buttocks.

'I told you I would tell her,' the voice hissed. 'Why do you think we are here, you fool?'

Frida. Of course it was her.

Jai closed his eyes, his mind still working at half-speed. Honesty was his only option, but his memory of what he had overheard in the long hours since seemed to meld and shift.

'I returned to Leonid's chambers and overheard Titus talking with the commander of the Gryphon Guard. They plan to betray you tonight. They spoke of . . . unspeakable things they would do to Princess Erica. And do not eat the larks' tongues. Did her father eat any last night?'

His words tumbled out in a garbled mess, a stream of consciousness that at least sounded true to his ears. But still, Frida did not stir. He only hoped his loins would follow her example.

'I saw you,' Jai whispered, careful not to move. 'Outside, near the gates. I followed you here, as you ignored me. I could have left, but I chose to come here and warn you. *Please*. Don't let it be in vain.'

Finally, the weapon left his neck, and Jai saw a long, sharp hairpin before it was slipped out of sight.

'Close your eyes,' Frida whispered, shoving him aside. 'And then get into the pool. I'll allow you an audience.'

Jai did as he was bidden, pressing his eyes so tightly closed that purple shadows danced in his vision. But not before he caught an unintended glimpse of her slender frame disappearing across the room, her long, golden hair brushing the gentle curve of her lower buttocks.

The image seared into his mind like a brand on a steer, and he was glad he could leap into the water of the pool at Frida's eventual summons – though cold water would have been far more helpful.

Still, as he waded forward, the danger of his situation soon outweighed his moment of lust. He would be lucky to leave this place alive, let alone survive the next few hours. Something big was coming.

'Elaborate,' an imperious voice called. 'I heard every word you spoke with Frida. Hell, I heard you talking with the guards. You are lucky my father is ill, or he may well have heard you too.'

Gone was the friendly tone of his last conversation at the

feast. Her voice was harsher somehow. If she had been trusting before, she was certainly not now. Jai gulped and moved closer.

It was true. Anyone could be listening.

'Ill with what?' Jai asked. 'They spoke of poison. Of . . . testing it.'

He heard a sharp intake of breath.

'Hemlock poisoning,' Erica said. 'We know the signs – why, it is not so many years ago that my mother died from a cup intended for my father.'

Jai's head jerked up at that. Would Constantine have dared . . .

'Was it . . . ?'

'A cousin, seeking the throne for himself.' She spoke so matter-of-factly. This was a woman used to loss. 'He was dealt with.'

Jai remained silent.

'In the normal quantities it only cripples the power of a soulbound – it takes a lot of it to kill one of us. A few days hence and my father will be well again. You are telling me this assassination attempt was not some disgruntled Sabine noble from the border provinces . . . but Titus?'

'Aye,' Jai said. 'It came in the larks' tongues.'

There was a pause, and Jai thought he could make out one of them whispering into the other's ear.

'Frida tells me my father was not offered any last night,' Erica finally said. 'More likely it was in his mead. But no matter. We won't be eating food from your kitchens again, regardless of whether you came here today. Tell me this, my apparent ally. Why test it? Why risk this forewarning, rather than kill him outright?'

Jai had no answer.

'I can only say what I heard,' Jai said, panic rising in his chest. 'But there's more. Did Titus tell you where Magnus was taking me?'

Another pause.

'He did,' Erica said. 'And I told him to stop it. He said by the time a messenger arrived, you'd be long dead. So . . . I sent my dragon for you.'

'There is something in the woods he does not want you to see. By sending me somewhere only your dragon could intercede, it drew it away from the forest.'

'*Her* away,' Erica said.

'My apologies,' Jai whispered.

He stood in the hot water, sweat trickling down his brow. Erica was right – this plan made so little sense. Poisoning Ivar just enough to put his guard up . . . what sense could it make? What was it that Constantine had said, when the Huddite spies were put to death?

If you aim an arrow at an emperor, you should pray you don't miss.

'It's true,' Erica finally said. 'He gave me permission to bring you back. Even offered to return some of the gold from my dowry if I'd forgive him for his cruelty. Not before I spoke my disgust, mind you.'

'And I thank you for it,' Jai said. 'But does this not seem strange? The Sabines can be cruel, but to execute a peace-time hostage for such a low transgression as sitting in their dinner seat, at the behest of their father-in-law-to-be, no less, speaks of utter hubris and foolishness. Titus is no stranger to both, but even this seems beyond his petty insecurities.'

Another long silence, and Jai felt every second. Judgement, it seemed, was about to be passed. It would be so easy for Erica to order Frida to kill him, if not do it herself. He could be just another rapist, killed by a soulbound woman defending her honour.

'My kingdom,' Erica said, her voice softer now. 'Has been in a state of war for nigh on a century. Men are taken from their farms and fishing boats to defend our borders. Our coffers are emptied to make ships of war, weapons and armour, rather than roads, bridges and grain. Dead boys are sent home in haversacks, killed on cattle raids to feed our starving populace. How else has a kingdom as small as mine withstood the power of an entire empire for so long?'

Jai remained silent.

'I give myself gladly to this petty brute of a prince,' Erica went on. 'So that I may raise my child to be a kind ruler. So that every captive Dansk warrior taken as fettered might find their freedom. So that my armies can return home, and care for their families as they once did.'

Erica let out a long sigh, and Jai could just about see her silhouette in the mist. She seemed so small without her dragon.

'You're a stranger to me. You may owe me your life, but your story is confused. First it is Leonid who is in danger, then it is my family. You speak of things hidden in the forest, yet my dragon has hunted there since and seen nothing but the beasts of the earth. Perhaps whatever was there has been withdrawn and returned tonight. Perhaps not.'

Jai now realised he hadn't thought any of this through. He'd seen Frida and run. Never once thought just how insane his story sounded.

'What would you have me do, Steppeman?' Erica asked. 'Reject the wedding, after all the expense lavished upon us? March our men back to their ships, and continue this endless state of war?'

'Use your father's poisoning as an excuse,' Jai blurted.

Erica let out a bitter laugh.

'Who would believe us? In fact, who would we even tell? Don't you see, if I back out of this wedding, your empire has the perfect excuse to kill us all before we've walked a mile. It would be an unforgivable insult. Wars have been started for far less. Genocides too.'

Jai felt sick.

'This was all a trap,' he said, so quietly he did not even hear himself.

'Or you are wrong,' Erica said.

Jai shook his head, half impressed, half in disappointment. 'You speak of the dangers of attempting to escape the trap,' he said, raising his voice. 'But speak nothing of the consequence of walking into it blindly.'

'Not blindly,' Erica said, her voice quiet this time. 'Thanks to you. But I have no other choice.'

Jai couldn't believe his ears. He understood she had few options, but to do *nothing* . . . it was unthinkable.

'You have to get away,' Jai said. 'Leave here.'

'You're asking me to throw away my kingdom's one chance at peace on the muddled accusations of a stranger.'

Jai, for the first time, felt rage. Thick and caustic, filling him with righteous energy. He wanted to roar, and beat his fists upon the water. Instead, he bowed his head.

'I almost lost my last chance at freedom to come here. I still might. So I don't care what you do. I'm leaving.'

He turned, almost expecting for her to call him back. Instead, there was only the hiss of steam, and the drip of condensation from the walls.

There was nothing left to do . . . but run.

Chapter 25

The guards were ambivalent as Jai pulled on his clothing, and he was surprised to find that his coins remained in his purse. Even his gorget was returned to him, though with a raised brow from the guard that handed it to him.

And then . . . some soft-spoken words, behind him.

'My father has suffered in your absence.'

Jai's entire body seized at the words. That voice was unmistakeable. He had heard it many times, yet it was the first it had *ever* addressed him directly.

Constantine.

Jai turned slowly, to see the emperor in all his naked glory. The man stood unashamed, a look of annoyance on his face.

This was a man capable of terrible cruelty. A man whose empire was built on the backs of fettered. Yet as he stood before Jai, the acorn nub of his penis almost lost in a nest of pubic hair, arms crossed over his sunken chest, that knowledge was hard to parse.

'Forgive me, Your Imperial Majesty,' Jai said, bowing as deeply as he could. 'I was unconscious until today. I came straight here.'

The emperor sniffed, his perfectly trimmed goatee trembling. 'Illness is the excuse of the indolent. See that it does not happen again. Typical savage sloth . . .'

The emperor muttered further and snapped his fingers at a guard who brought his clothing on bended knee. Jai swiftly began to pull his tunic off over his head and was glad the guards had the sense to not mention he had just put it on. Constantine's anger was legendary, and he had even been known to have messengers whipped when bringing news of poor harvests.

It was not too late. He could still escape – clearly Constantine was leaving. If he just hid for a few minutes until the emperor had departed . . .

'Hold it, boy.'

Leonid's tremulous voice emanated from the mist. Only now did Jai see him, his chair being pushed along by a naked fettered girl, her body painted in ochres to accentuate her figure, wearing naught but the manacle of the fettered upon her wrist. Jai averted his eyes, so that he would not see the misery in hers. A recent Huddite war-captive. Of that there was no doubt.

'I am glad Balbir has brought you back to me. Dress me and return me to my chambers,' he said. 'We must prepare for tonight.'

THEY TRAVELLED BY PALANQUIN, as was customary for the royals when using the city streets. They even brought each vehicle down the stairs, so that Leonid's chair did not need to climb them.

Jai was thankful, for the royal procession was flanked by the Gryphon Guard, scarlet cloaks billowing, gryphons circling above. Constantine travelled with his son and a haggard-looking Ivar, and behind, Erica and Frida used Titus's palanquin.

Leonid seemed completely at ease, his eyes closed, customarily silent. His fingers tapped a marching tattoo on his belly, as if he were hearing it in his head.

To Jai, it was a relief. And at the same time, a disaster. He still had a chance; a quick trip to the kitchens for Leonid's dinner, and he could slip out.

Who knew how chaotic the night would be – he could be just another dead man in a night of butchery. Certainly that would be the excuse that Magnus wished to use. The trick for Jai would be making sure he wasn't *actually* one of them. His one advantage was that as far as Magnus knew, Jai was already dead – assuming the city watch reported it to him.

'You will dress me, when we return, in full regalia,' Leonid muttered, eyes still closed. 'But no need for the perfumers.'

Jai startled, his escape planning interrupted.

'Why not?' Jai asked, cursing the catch in his voice.

'With Ivar's suspected poisoning, I have the perfect excuse not to attend.' Leonid said, waving his hand as if it were hardly worth repeating. 'I shall watch the ceremony from my balcony. No need for perfume if nobody can smell it.'

Jai's ears perked up at that. It would be the perfect time to leave, when all eyes were on the ceremony.

'Of course, Great One,' Jai said.

'None of that formality, boy,' Leonid said, waving him silent. 'I've had enough grovelling from that fool Corinth to last a lifetime.'

He harrumphed and settled deeper into his couch. Then he lifted a skeletal finger, as if remembering something.

'I spoke with Titus,' he said, eyes still closed.

Jai's heart began to thunder. Leonid paused, as if waiting for Jai to speak.

'Yes . . . Great One?' Jai said lamely, unable, in his fear, to slip into informality. Leonid grimaced and spoke on.

'You'll live,' he said simply, scratching an itch upon his beard with a liver-spotted hand.

Jai did not know what to say. After a few more moments of silence, he spoke up.

'I thank you. I hope . . .'

He trailed off, unable to find the right words.

'Magnus,' he said, blurting it out as the silent stretched over-long. 'My life is forfeit to him. I have seen their sacred temple.'

'Pah!' Leonid spat, dismissing Jai's words with a shaken head. 'I built the damn thing for those ingrates. Half emptied my coffers to do it too. The cost of their continued allegiance.'

Jai's ears pricked up at that. This *was* new information. Leonid had always been open with Jai in his stories in that they had helped him achieve his victories – he was not *that* full of hubris. Yet he had always been cagey on the details.

Jai knew that one of Corinth's main tasks in transcribing Leonid's old journals had been replacing the names of the Gryphon Guards with only their rank and title. Jai imagined it was the old man's way of taking all the credit, such that his achievements would be remembered as his alone, long after he was gone.

'Are they worth so much to you?' Jai asked, suddenly embold-ened by Leonid's apparent disdain for them.

Leonid sighed.

'Eyes in the sky, my boy. Worth every coin, and more besides. Why, when Rufinus . . .'

The old man often disappeared into reveries and Jai did not interrupt, instead peering through the curtains to see where they were. Already the poor men carrying the palanquin on their shoulders were mounting the palace steps, those at the back forced to lift them above their heads so as to keep their carriage level.

Whether or not Leonid was taking the threat of poisoning seriously, no chances were being taken by their bodyguard. Soon enough they would be delivered to the door of Leonid's chamber.

For a moment Jai wondered if the old man could protect him from Magnus. Certainly the safest place in the entire palace was Leonid's room – deep within the complex; so far back that its rear windows looked out over the escarpment's highest point, and the Black Forest beyond.

In a few years, Jai would be free to return home anyway. If he could survive Magnus that long.

'If you are so scared of Magnus, you must remain by my side until I can speak with him,' Leonid snapped, jarring Jai from his internal debate.

Jai cursed under his breath. So much for escaping during the ceremony. Unless he could find an excuse. There was no time to think on it further, for there was the soft thud as their palanquin was lowered to the ground. They were back at Leonid's chamber once more.

Chapter 26

Leonid was quiet as Jai dressed him, his mind seemingly on other matters. It was as if, by some instinct, the old lion knew that something was afoot.

Jai's mind was scattered. He didn't know what to do. Whatever plot Titus and Magnus had cooked up was plainly focused on the Dansk. Jai'd likely survive the night if he stayed put, holed up in a room protected by some of the strongest charms in the empire.

Then they'd be focused on the inevitable war. Jai might well last three years, if he never left Leonid's side.

Jai glanced at his master's face as he buttoned the robe for him. Perhaps he should tell Leonid about the plot. But then, what could the forgotten old man do to prevent it?

And would Leonid even want to prevent it? Jai believed he would.

Perhaps he would take it to his son, the emperor himself. Constantine did not seem aware of Jai's near-murder, or his injuries. What else might the man not be privy to? Titus wanted war, while his father had tired of it. Was the young prince forcing the emperor's hand? Or was it all driven by his revulsion at the idea of marrying a 'Dansk whore'?

But it was all far too great a risk. One word of this to Leonid and he'd have no chance of escaping.

He'd warned the Dansk – that was enough. He owed nothing to anyone. Except perhaps, Balbir. With any luck, she'd be far from here by now. He only hoped he'd be able to find her when he made his escape.

Jai focused on finding an excuse to leave the chamber. Dressing Leonid took no time at all, the man's usual fastidiousness diminished since he was only to be seen from the balcony.

'Would you like your crown tonight, Great One?' Jai asked.

Leonid grunted a refusal.

'Save it for the real ceremony,' he said. 'It hurts my neck if worn too long.'

Jai furrowed his brow.

'For the . . . what are we dressing for?' he asked.

Leonid turned his pale eyes to him and snorted in mild amusement.

'They were not embellishing when they said you were unconscious,' he mused. 'The wedding is tomorrow. Tonight is only the wedding rehearsal.'

Jai was even more confused.

'Rehearsal. Why?'

Leonid tutted in annoyance but did answer. It seemed Jai was in his good books that day. Perhaps the old sod had missed him.

'We have a thousand dignitaries coming from all over the empire, even from kingdoms across the Silver Seas. All watching the union of our great houses. It is customary to rehearse the ceremony to avoid accidental embarrassment – and it's an excuse for another feast. Even before the empire, it was the done thing.'

In a way, Jai was relieved. All the key players would be busy, and if he made an excuse to leave during something as seemingly mundane as a rehearsal, Leonid might be more inclined to allow it.

'Will we attend the ceremony?' Jai asked.

Leonid looked at the balcony that overlooked the courtyard. He didn't need to say anything – it was not the first time they had watched and even taken part in ceremonies below.

There were few responsibilities left to the old man; those that Constantine and Titus had no interest in. The bestowment of knighthoods, lordships, even the graduation of the Gryphon Guard acolytes to squires were chief among them.

Leonid would make a short speech and grant their rise up the Sabine ladder of aristocracy with a wave. Of course, Jai's presence at Leonid's side on those occasions was inappropriate, so he had taken to sitting at Leonid's feet behind the balcony, rising to steady the old man or whispering to remind the old man of a forgotten line or phrase. He was still able to watch the ceremonies, tedious though they were, through one of the ornate gaps in the balcony balustrade.

This occasion would be no different. Within minutes, Jai was in position at Leonid's feet, peering through to see the pomp and splendour of the event from perhaps the best vantage there was. He'd made sure to keep his head down as he wheeled Leonid into place, so that none would see he was still alive if they happened to look up.

The rectangular courtyard was as large as a small amphitheatre, and was indeed designed for viewing in much the same way – for it was surrounded by long, pillar-studded corridors of multiple storeys, with balconies of their own. Indeed, Constantine was not averse to throwing grand events of theatre and opera for the nobility of the kingdom, and as many as a thousand people could watch the spectacle below.

Today there were none of the crowded onlookers, craning their necks to see over those in front – for this was the rehearsal, with a far more intimate guest list. Instead, the many guards that he had seen in full regalia seemed to have doubled in their numbers. Moreover, the deadly crossbows that he'd noticed, unusual for legionaries, were loaded and in their hands.

The apparent threat to Ivar's life must have been the perfect pretence to double the guard. And as he peered more closely, he saw nothing to suggest that the princess had gotten cold feet. The servants still walked their rounds, sweeping up a fallen petal here, polishing a mirror there.

In all his years, Jai had never seen such expense. Rose garlands spiralled around every pillar and balcony, while candle-lit crystal lamps sparkled like jewels on plinths. Every torch in the building seemed to have been lit, even as the last rays of sun still warmed the horizon.

Servants still scurried in and out of the kitchens, placing fluted glasses charged with exotic liquors and platters of fruit at intervals alongside the arrayed seating.

Even from here Jai could smell the aromatics as each of the kitchen doors swung, their spiced scent drifting tantalisingly with the breeze, mingling with the rosewater poured into the four foaming fountains at the courtyard's corners.

The soft, brassy notes of the bronze cornu sounded from a small military orchestra, punctuated by exotic drums, and the melodic notes of a lyre player in a flowing dress.

The ninth bell rang, the peals quieter this far from the cathedral. The very sound set Jai's teeth on edge. Could this be the signal for the slaughter to begin?

At the tolls, the servants retreated into the palace once more, encouraged by the cries of their handlers. Soon, the place held only the guards, musicians, and the servers.

Then, the music changed tone, to something triumphant and jaunty. Notes rose and fell as the great doors opposite the balcony opened and Jai watched in surprise as the guests, both Dansk and Sabine, filed into the courtyard in all their finery.

Tension eased from his shoulders, and he let his breath leave his lungs. How could Titus stage a betrayal amid all this? Or were the soldiers and the Gryphon Guard a contingency – if in Ivar's death, the Dansk became violent? Perhaps the king's death was the cost of this union. Perhaps Erica had accepted she must pay it.

Leonid muttered something under his breath.

'May I help you, Great One?' Jai asked.

'Something is wrong,' Leonid whispered. 'Very, very wrong.'

Chapter 27

J ai stared up at the old man, then down at the courtyard once more. What had the near-blind man seen that he had missed?

'What is it?' Jai asked.

Leonid shuffled to the edge of the balcony, peering out as the guests took their seats, the tempo of the music rising ever higher.

'Look at the colours of the guests. What do you notice?'

His voice was low and urgent, and Jai was swift to answer.

'Many wear orange, with gold edgings. Still others wear pale blues with white lace. I cannot make out their sigils.'

He felt the shadows of understanding begin to form.

'The colours . . . they must be the liveries of two families. Why so many?'

'You see no other colours, boy? No reds or greens?'

Jai was silent.

Leonid cursed beneath his breath. 'The Corvins and the Blacktrees. Noble families whose landholdings and wealth once rivalled ours, from the far reaches of our empire. Their territories are almost kingdoms of their own – but they bend the knee to us. Our military is too powerful for them to challenge, though not so strong as to prevent them from underpaying our taxes each year.'

Jai cocked his head.

'So?' he asked.

'To invite so many of their families to the rehearsal honours them, allowing them to feast and celebrate with us twice, when they are the least deserving of such. It is a poor decision. Titus chose his guests – so he must have some other reason to bring them, and to snub those who might have been invited in their stead.'

Jai closed his eyes tightly, trying to figure out the convolutions of Titus's plan. Did he intend to slaughter these nobles too? He could only marvel at Leonid's intuition. Even when he could only see blurred colours, the man saw more than he did.

He looked closer now, eyes flicking from face to face. There were others among the visiting families, some Jai recognised as lesser nobles from across the empire – having observed their audiences with Leonid when the old man still performed the onerous task of receiving visiting dignitaries. Most of those he could see had their lands upon the borders of the empire, just as the Corvins and Blacktrees did.

'The idiot milksop thinks this rehearsal invitation will force them to give lavish wedding gifts,' Leonid muttered. 'Does he not realise that it will cost the goodwill of every one of our closest allies?' He continued to curse, as Jai now looked to the servants.

During the wars, many Steppefolk soldiers had been captured by the empire, fettered to be worked to death in camps across the empire. As part of the peace agreement, those that survived the duration of the war would be released to serve as fettered servants across the empire or work the fields in Leonid's newly conquered lands.

This was the deal the Huddites had rejected following the first defeat of their army. Of course, had they surrendered upon the declaration of war, as kingdoms such as those ruled by the Corvins and Blacktrees had done, they might have only had to pay heavy taxes. Continued defiance . . . well, death or fettering were the only choices left to those that took up arms.

So, it was not uncommon to see Steppemen working as fettered across the empire. Usually they worked the fields, unable to adjust to life indoors. But today, it seemed every servant present was a fettered Steppeman. But why? None of this made sense.

Finally, he took in the guards. Not their fine uniforms and armour, nor the ugly crossbows clutched in their hands. But their faces.

They were young. Not the usual veterans of the palace, but young men. Most looked as young as he was, some younger. He didn't recognise any of them either, and he'd been in the palace long enough to know the usual guards. He'd been beaten by them enough times.

These were Gryphon Guard – each one likely an acolyte, or a squire awaiting their knighthood. Boys, indoctrinated in the Gryphon Guard ways for years. As for the older members, they were nowhere to be seen. Nor were there gryphons circling above. What could be so important that they were elsewhere? Jai could only imagine they were keeping watch on the Dansk army.

This was happening. Something was happening tonight.

'Great one,' Jai whispered. 'I must eat something, or I might faint. Let me fetch you something from the kitchens.'

'Stay there,' Leonid snapped. 'I've need of your eyes. Tell me which other nobles my fool grandson has invited.'

Jai knew he had to leave soon. Within minutes the entire place would be locked down. Who cared if Leonid knew he was disobeying him. So long as he didn't think Jai was escaping, he'd assume he'd died in the inevitable slaughter below.

'I will return,' Jai said. 'I will fetch your dinner and—'

'My doors are sealed,' Leonid said mildly. 'Magnus charmed them just this afternoon. Only one of my blood may open them at this point. A precaution, after the threat to Ivar.'

'You can open them too, can you not?' Jai asked.

Leonid looked down at him sharply.

'Yes. But if you think I'll risk my safety even a trifle to sate your greedy belly, you are mistaken, boy.'

Jai cursed under his breath. His next best option was to throw himself off the balcony. Though somehow he doubted he would get more than a few feet before the guards descended on him.

So he had to wait. Wait until this was all over, and then find another way out of here. Stick by Leonid's side until Magnus and Titus were miles away, and he was but a forgotten footnote in the day of their greatest triumph.

The music was picking up tempo. The guests were all in their seats – Dansk seated in rows to Jai's left, and Sabines on the right. A rich, red carpet went down the centre, and at its end a decrepit high priest stood, hands shaking.

The Sabines had long forced their own religion upon the imperial populace, even adopting their dead ancestors into the pantheon of gods. Jai was surprised there was no member of the clergy from the Dansk religion, a *gothi*, to perform the ceremony too. Perhaps there was one for the supposed real wedding, on the morrow.

They came, then. The great doors swung open, and there walked Titus, accompanied by his father. The pair walked slowly, allowing applause to wash over them. To Jai's surprise, Titus looked the picture of good humour – it was the emperor's face that looked waxen. As if he knew what was coming.

Behind, Titus's entourage followed, a dozen men and boys stepping in tandem with the orchestral drums. These were the usual pack of cronies – the heirs of the various kingdoms that formed the empire, as well as the hostages of those that did not.

Among them were Jai's brothers and several of his cousins. He saw Arjun's tall frame clearly.

'Speak, boy. Tell me more.'

Again, Leonid grunted in annoyance, as Jai explained that his brothers were in the wedding party.

'The fool has no appreciation for politics,' Leonid grumbled. 'A wedding rehearsal is an opportunity to reward those . . .'

Jai tuned him out, for now his eyes were directed heavenward. Moonlight was all that remained to light the skies, but even in the darkness, he could not miss the gleam of scales as two enormous beasts spiralled to the ground.

Dragons. One black, one green, descending with such speed as to elicit gasps, even a single, garbled scream from a more sensitive guest. But they alighted with such grace that the scream remained unaccompanied. They shifted uncomfortably, trapped between chairs and the courtyard wall, before folding their wings and resting upon their bellies.

Only then did the great doors open a final time, and the sight of the veiled princess drew murmurs of awe from the onlookers.

The mock-ceremony was about to begin.

Chapter 28

They came, step by faltering step. Even Jai could see Ivar was unwell, the bullish man pale-faced, sweat dripping from his brow. He wore the same clothing he had worn when Jai had first seen him – the same bear skin, bare chest and leather gaiters. Hell, it hardly looked like he had been to the bath house at all.

Erica, however, was resplendent, though her face was veiled as before. Her gown was made of the purest ermine fur, draped about her slim body with frills of white lace and silver filigree. She held her head high and her back ramrod straight, despite the weight of her father upon her shoulder.

Ivar looked worse than Jai had thought, but the man still managed a smile and a wink at Titus when he left his daughter next to him and the music fell away to silence.

The high priest began to speak, his throat bobbing with nerves.

'Let us pray,' he uttered, his voice high and querulous. 'Such that this couple may be blessed by our great pantheon.'

Heads bowed, even those in the Dansk side of the audience.

'Heliana, our great goddess of the sun, bless this couple with your light. Let it be so.'

Voices murmured under breath.

'Let it be so.'

It was typical, at least as far as Jai knew, to request the blessings of the gods collectively. A strange choice to name each one, for it would extend the ceremony by at least a half hour. But then this was an auspicious occasion.

'Silene, our great goddess of the moon . . . ' the priest droned on, and Jai could not help but tune out. His religion, such as it was, had little in common with the vast range of gods that the priest was about to name.

Instead, he looked for Frida. Found her, standing with head bowed, close to the dragons. There was no sign of any plan to save her princess or king. They had walked into the lion's mouth. Now, it would feed.

Yet, in the very moment that every guest's head was bowed, eyes closed in worship or respect, the soldiers upon the balconies did not move. If ever there was a time to strike, it was now.

But there was nothing. Only a young man dressed in yellow near the back, vomiting into his hat – too much liquor and not enough sense, Jai supposed.

For a few seconds, Jai allowed himself to believe all would be well. That Titus had backed out of his plan – that it was just a childish fantasy that Magnus had indulged.

Then . . . it happened.

Constantine stepped forward. Fell to his knees.

For a moment, Jai thought the emperor had been overcome with religious fervour, despite the dry delivery from the priest.

It was only when he toppled forwards, sprawling upon the marble, that Jai knew something was terribly wrong.

'—goddess of . . . emperor!' the high priest garbled, but his words could hardly be heard over the gasps of the guests.

'What is the meaning of this?' Titus bellowed, kneeling beside his father. 'Fetch a doctor!'

A Dansk noble leaped to his feet, as if to get help. But he had seen what Jai had – the great double doors blocked by an inpouring of guards, Magnus at their head. Guards who were advancing, with blades drawn.

The emperor was not the only one who was taken ill. Now, more people slumped in their chairs – more still vomited. Just like the boy had . . .

Jai looked to Ivar, then Frida, seeking a hint that this was their doing. Their horror-filled faces said all Jai needed to know.

More guests collapsed – not all of them, but enough. And none of them Dansk.

This was becoming more and more obvious, and Titus pointed a trembling finger at Ivar.

'You did this!' he screamed.

A masterful performance.

'Inside,' Leonid hissed. 'Get me inside.'

Jai hardly heard him.

Erica snatched at Titus's sleeves, even as Ivar was surrounded by the prince's entourage, Arjun among them. Titus held a blade to his betrothed's throat. And upon the balconies . . . the crossbowmen stepped forward.

'Crossbows!' Jai screamed, leaping to his feet.

Jai didn't know if Ivar heard him. Certainly there was enough screaming in the hall to drown him out.

Yet the dragons flared their wings, even as the cruel crossbows began to spit. Ivar's black dragon wrapped his great wings and body about its smaller counterpart, protecting its flesh with its own. For a few seconds it endured, shuddering as each bolt punched into its scaled hide.

Then the green dragon burst out, hurtling into the sky. Jai saw a figure clutching its back, saw the dragon's sides shuddering as it was struck. Then it was gone, into the night.

Ivar roared, fists knocking Jai's brothers back, despite his weakness. Then a blade burst through his throat, silencing him for good. Magnus's.

No sooner had the brute dealt with Ivar than he strode towards the dying black dragon, raising his blade high. It glowed white, the air surrounding it shimmering with heat. He dragged the blade along the beast's exposed white belly, spilling its guts in a single stroke.

Bloodied to the elbow, he grinned with savage abandon, moving to join the other guards. Guards who ignored the twitching, foam-mouthed figures on the ground. Ignored even the emperor, who lay dead.

No, it was the Dansk that they surrounded. Men, women and children. Old or young, it did not matter. They were all encircled by interlocked shields, blades held at the ready above. A crossbow bolt spat out into the middle of the crowd. A blonde child let out a keening cry, a feathered stump planted in her belly.

Jai could not look away when the screams began. Not until he saw the blades rise and fall, heard the drum of desperate fists upon shields. Not until he smelled the blood.

Tears blurred his vision, and he averted his gaze. Leonid said nothing. He sat. Stared. His face was inscrutable.

It did not take long for the slaughter to end. One side was armed, the other was not. And most of the Dansk were not soulbound. Only a single guest, a woman, gave them any trouble. She broke free with gouts of flame and fury. Even reached halfway to the doors before a bolt took her through the spine. Her baby, swaddled to her chest, wailed and cried, until a hobnailed boot silenced it for good.

And then, it was over. The Dansk were dead. Their princess, captured. Their king, murdered. And down there, among the blood, amid the cries of the dying and the mourning . . . Titus smiled.

Chapter 29

Jai went to move Leonid's chair. It was no good to stay here any longer. One glance toward their balcony, and he would be next.

'Nay, boy,' Leonid growled, clutching the wheels with white-knuckled hands. 'I must see the whole of this.'

There was rage there. But directed at whom, Jai did not know.

So Jai crouched once more, watching as Titus grasped Erica by the shoulder and shoved her to her knees. His father lay forgotten, motionless. The prince had not even checked to see if the emperor was alive.

There was silence in the square, even among the few imperial guests that had survived the poison. Only the occasional sob or choked breath disturbed the courtyard turned charnel house.

'Finish the ceremony,' Titus snapped, jabbing a finger at the priest. 'As if it were the morrow.'

The high priest mouthed wordlessly at the air, unable to speak. He had been sprayed with Ivar's blood, and he wiped at his face as words began to tumble free.

'Rhea, great goddess of fertility, bless this couple with the same fertility you bestow upon our land—'

Titus raised his blade this time.

'I said *finish* the ceremony. Marry us. Now.'

The high priest choked a second longer, then spoke the words in a jumbled rush.

'I declare you husband and wife, in this life and the everlasting.'

Titus laughed aloud, pulling bloodstained fingers through his pale hair.

'Let's see then,' he said. He yanked the veil from Erica's face.

Jai saw the girl, as did every onlooker. She was nothing like he'd imagined – her face round, eyes wide with fear. He was almost ashamed to look. He only knew one thing: if she dared to use her powers, Magnus was hovering just behind her, a glowing blade pointed in her direction.

'Pretty enough,' Titus announced, yanking back her hair and displaying her bare face for all to see. 'But who is to say what a murderess looks like.'

Magnus stepped forward and whispered something in the prince's ear.

'Ah yes,' he called out, sweeping his knife at the remaining guests. 'Our uninvited guest. Bring her!'

He shouted those final words, and the doors swung open again.

They dragged the woman in, for she could not stand on her own. She left a bloody trail behind her, where her nails had been ripped from her bare feet.

At first, Jai did not recognise her, for he was high on the far side of the courtyard. But then he saw the smock and heard the words Titus spoke.

'A plainsbitch, sent to assassinate my father. We knew she had delivered something, we just did not know what it was. She provided the poison. She, who has been plotting for years. Working with Dansk filth.'

It was Balbir. If she was alive, there was no sign of it. Clearly she had been tortured, and beaten so badly her face was almost unrecognisable. Samar and Arjun's faces were filled with horror at the sight.

'Did you all not see Ivar's illness?' Titus yelled, turning in a slow circle as he addressed the courtyard. 'He did it to himself, attempting to administer the poison to my father on their very first meal together. Do any of you deny this plot between those steppe heathens and this fat fuck?'

He punctuated the question with a kick to Balbir's body. At this, Jai saw Arjun bristle. The young man stepped a little apart from the rest, as if to remind Titus of their friendship. But he did not speak.

'She confessed,' Magnus rumbled. 'Eventually . . .'

'Bring her closer,' Titus ordered, ignoring the display.

Magnus strode forward, gripped her by her hair and lifted her, her bloodied feet dangling above the ground.

Jai felt numb. Willed himself to move, even if to ball his fists, yet his limbs would not respond.

It was just as well. Nothing he could do would change this. Even if he threw his life away in the attempt, it would be little more than a distraction.

'Is she alive?'

Magnus shook her like a ragdoll, and Jai heard a faint, gurgled moan.

'Speak, bitch!' Titus yelled, slapping her across the face.

'She's got no teeth,' Magnus rumbled. 'Not anymore.'

Jai felt his gorge rise as Titus let out a chortle, but forced it down. He saw the sudden terror in Arjun's face, his tan face paling unnaturally. They'd recognised Balbir.

Balbir's hand rose. Just enough to be noticed. She crooked a finger and let out a croak.

'Oh, you've something to say?' Titus laughed, lifting her chin and peering into her face. Again, she crooked her finger, and he leaned in. Her hand rose higher and Jai held his breath.

There was a flash of light and Titus flew back, skidding across the marble. He lay there groaning.

For a few heartbeats, there was silence, Balbir falling limp from the effort. Magnus lifted her high, then slammed her head into the paving, his great hand crushing her skull to a pulp. He snorted and wiped his hand on her smock.

Now, Jai vomited. She'd wasted the last of her power trying to help him escape. Had she not done so . . . Titus would be the one dead now. Had she not gone to the guard for Jai, she would never have been captured.

He looked up through stinging eyes as Titus struggled to his feet, limping back to Balbir's corpse. The prince spat on it, then looked up, his eyes blazing with rage.

'Take them,' he roared. 'Take them now!'

It was done so quickly, it took Jai a moment to realise what had happened. Blades were raised to his brothers' throats, and still more servants found themselves surrounded by raised swords. All Steppefolk. The soldiers moved methodically, as though expecting the order.

Any pretence of this all being spontaneous seemed to have been forgotten. But then, who else was left in the courtyard but those loyal to Titus? Only those few surviving imperial guests, and the palace guard. Jai doubted either would survive the night.

Steppefolk were lined up and forced to their knees in front of Titus, their protests falling on deaf ears. Behind each stood a guard, their blades just above the collar bone.

Arjun and Samar remained motionless, but for the tears streaming down Samar's cheeks. Only Arjun looked defiant, his back straight, his eyes burning with fury, never leaving the prince's face. Jai clasped a hand to his mouth, as if it might stop him from crying out, though every fibre of his being wanted to.

Titus waited for his men to slap the shrieking servants into silence.

'Take me in,' Leonid croaked.

Jai ignored him.

It was when Titus raised his hand, ready to signal their execution, that Arjun spoke. His voice was clear and calm, his chin high.

'You would forget our years of service and friendship?' he asked.

'It is you who has forgotten it, traitor,' Titus said simply. 'You're lucky I give you a swift death. That is your reward. Rohan's line dies with you.'

Despite the bravado, Jai heard a catch in his voice.

Arjun looked up towards the balcony. Nodded, at Leonid. No . . . not Leonid.

Jai.

Their eyes locked. Arjun's lips trembled, averting his gaze back, but he still mouthed a word. One Jai could not hear, though he understood its meaning. And felt the love and support behind it.

'Go.'

Pride suddenly spread across Jai's heart. Pride at his brother's courage. Pride at being a Steppeman, and Rohan's son. But it did little to assuage the horror that had wrung all sense from him and left him frozen, his mind somehow racing and yet empty. Horror at the knowledge of what was coming.

'Are you really this stupid?' Arjun said, raising his voice so all could hear. 'This will mean war. A second war. Your people almost lost last time.'

He nodded to Ivar's corpse, though his eyes were fixed on

Erica. As if inviting her to speak. Or act. But she remained silent, her eyes upon the paving. In shock, or something close to it. She hardly seemed to notice the many crossbows levelled at her.

'I welcome war,' Titus said, laughing. 'I was born for it.'

His mirth sounded fake – his chuckle a little too long, the pitch a little high. It seemed Arjun had picked up upon it, for he spoke with slow care.

'Perhaps you are right,' Arjun said. 'Perhaps this spy did help kill your father. But who is to say that our leaders sanctioned her treachery?'

There was a catch in his voice. He too had been raised by Balbir. He too mourned her loss.

'It is not too late, old friend,' he said, his voice suddenly full of warmth. 'I can return home and take my place as king of my tribe. We will ally with you and invade the Northern Tundra from the east. Together we can revenge this great injustice.'

Titus stilled. Considered.

Then he stepped forward and slit Arjun's throat.

Chapter 30

Jai forced himself to watch. Told himself he was numb and could not look away.

It was Samar's cry that he knew he would always remember. And how that cry turned to a gurgle from the kiss of an imperial blade.

Only when the last of the Steppefolk fell did he turn away. Almost left Leonid there on the balcony, so lost was he. Thoughts could take no hold in his mind. They were flighty, elusive things, and his limbs worked almost of their own accord as he pushed the old man back to his room.

Jai sat at the end of Leonid's bed. Even from here, he could still smell the blood. The very air was thick and coppery with it, claggy in his throat and on his tongue.

His gorge rose, and he heaved once more. Spat bile into the carpet, not caring about the mess. They'd be washing his blood from it soon enough.

He sat. Stared.

There was no escaping this. Even if by some miracle, Leonid chose to let him go, there was no way he would be able to leave the palace unnoticed. From the screams outside, the guards were not done with their work.

This was to be a night of butchery. There'd not be a single Dansk or Steppeman left alive in Latium by morn. Himself included.

He wondered, dully, if the remaining imperial guests – the witnesses – would be allowed to leave. Those few who had not eaten the larks' tongues, as Constantine must have. He doubted it.

'Jai?'

Jai looked up. Leonid had swivelled his chair and lowered his head to meet Jai's gaze.

'I'll live, will I?' Jai muttered, for once not hiding the bitterness in his voice. 'Wasn't that what you said?'

Leonid pursed his lips and let out a deep sigh.

'My son is dead,' Leonid rasped. 'My empire is at war. Why should I care if you live?'

He spoke half to himself, or so it seemed to Jai. Almost as if . . . he was unsure in his own words.

For a moment, Jai wanted to seize the old man. To beat him until the tyrant opened the door. Jai's life was forfeit anyway. Why not give himself that thin chance of escape? Why not take some revenge?

But somehow, still, Jai did not hate the old man. Not as tears traced the wrinkles in Leonid's face and fell onto liver-spotted hands. Hands that shook.

Jai was no monster. Until this day, he'd never once lifted a hand in anger to hurt another. Leonid was guilty of countless sins. But Jai was not his judge, nor his executioner. Only the gods, if they existed, could do that.

'I'll not survive this night,' Leonid said.

Jai looked up at that.

'Oh?' he asked.

Leonid shook his head, as if his words were beyond Jai's comprehension, then scratched at his chin. He looked at his knuckles, surprised, then smiled ruefully.

'Stubble. First time in what . . . a decade?'

Jai sniffed. Clearly Corinth was not much of a barber.

'You've cared for me, boy. In your own way,' Leonid murmured. 'A man is shaped by the deeds of his youth. Remembered for the deeds in his maturity. But what of his eldership? Then, he is not seen as man at all. Only a shell, waiting to become memory of the man he once was.'

His voice was quiet. Almost regretful. It was a new colour on the fractious old man.

'I have done terrible things. I sit here, in a prison of my own making, paid for with the blood of a thousand thousand innocents. And for what?'

Jai could almost laugh. Here was the man who had once ruled half the known world. A man who wanted for nothing. And he was wallowing in self-pity.

'You have—'

'Quiet,' Jai hissed.

He'd heard something. A rattling at the room's double door. And a glow, at their four edges.

'Away with you,' Leonid hissed. 'Into your sleeping place.'

Jai did as he was bidden, if only because he no longer had a razor to hold to the old man's throat.

Once again, he found himself hiding in the small cupboard he had called home for almost a decade. He felt detached, the world around him dreamlike. Once again, he was eavesdropping on Titus.

'Grandfather,' Titus cried out, as soon as the doors opened.

He hurried into the room, hands spread wide. His face was

scrunched up, bawling like a babe. But there were no tears there as he threw himself at the old man's feet, hugging the skinny legs to his chest.

Leonid extended a hand, resting it on the boy's head. His face was dark and troubled.

'I could not save him,' Titus wailed. 'But I revenged us. Our Gryphon Guard fly, even now, to instruct the governors of our cities that we are in a state of war, and they must begin conscription before sun sets on the morrow.'

He looked up at Leonid, the mask of his apparent grief slipping for a moment as he considered Leonid's face.

The old man motioned for the boy to stand. Titus did so, brushing at his own crumpled purple finery. He only succeeded in smearing his hands with blood. *Arjun's.*

For a moment, Jai was tempted to rush out. To choke Titus to death, end the Sabine dynasty once and for all. It was only the bloodied blade at Titus's hip that stopped him.

'I have a legion in the forest, ready to ambush the Dansk Army,' Titus said, filling an increasingly widening silence as Leonid considered him. 'By sunrise—'

'Where did this legion come from?' Leonid asked, his voice serious as a grave. 'The agreement was only one legion would accompany them.'

Titus stammered.

'They – I summoned them. When Ivar fell ill . . . I thought . . .'

He trailed off, and then hung his head. It was a lame act, the boy's bravado shrivelling under the stern eye of his patriarch. A poor cousin to the performance Jai had witnessed in the courtyard.

'I could not marry her, Grandfather,' Titus blurted – suddenly a child once more. 'Not a Dansk whore. Father didn't even ask me.'

Leonid said nothing. His limpid eyes were unblinking, and Titus continued, words spilling from his mouth in an uncontrolled flood.

'I planned to betray them. I had Magnus's men stationed with the palace guard. Invited our rivals as guests so as not to place our allies in danger.'

'And the Steppefolk?' Leonid asked.

Titus's shoulders sagged, but his mouth ran on.

'When Magnus's men brought me that plainsbitch, showed me the poison she'd prepared, I knew they'd been planning this for years. I had to show strength, Grandfather. You, of all people, must understand that.'

Leonid, again, said nothing.

'I did not know then that she was working with the Dansk. I had thought Ivar and Erica were her target. Without the Dansk to occupy our legions, the Steppefolk could never stand against us.'

It was a plausible enough story. Jai would almost forgive Leonid for believing it.

'But I was right to betray them, wasn't I?' Titus ploughed on. 'Ivar poisoned father. Poisoned our guests—'

'Poisoned himself?' Leonid asked. 'By accident, wasn't that what you said?'

Titus had no answer for that, and Leonid let out a soft snort of derision.

It was perhaps only in that moment that Jai fully understood the depths Titus had sunk to. Because now, Jai knew, it was not Ivar the larks' tongues had been for. Or at least, not primarily. They'd only poisoned Ivar to be sure of its potency . . . and to weaken the soulbound king for his murder. That, and for an excuse to double the guard and bring the Gryphon Guard's acolytes into the palace.

Still, Jai could not believe the boy had murdered his own father. The guests from the rival kingdoms, yes. There was some sick genius there, in framing one set of enemies for the murder of another and slaughter the former in turn. But to kill his own father? It was madness. Jai might have thought it an accident, had he not heard what he had in this very room, but a few hours earlier.

'Grandfather,' Titus whispered urgently. 'Let us finish what you started. Let us conquer this continent from the Silver Seas to the Oceans of the Sunrise on the Phoenix Empire's coast. Our men will seize the riches owed us by the weakened Corvins and the Blacktrees and use our replenished coffers to mount a campaign the likes of which have not been seen since your ascendancy.'

Leonid lifted his head, locking eyes with his grandson. There was so much, in that look. Both Sabines knew, Jai saw, what had happened that night. It was a thing unsaid.

Almost a full minute passed, before Leonid finally spoke.

'Summon the generals, boy,' he said. 'If it is war, then we must win.'

Jai saw the relief in Titus's expression as the boy nodded in agreement. Relief . . . and shame.

'It is already done,' Titus said, turning to leave. 'I have called upon the heads of all the great families as well, to support us in our hour of need. And of course, they will need to be here to witness my coronation.'

He was almost at the door, when Leonid called out.

'There will be no coronation,' Leonid said. 'Not for you, anyway.'

Titus stopped. He did not turn. Only spoke one word.

'Why?'

Jai could not see Titus's expression. Just the reddening of the boy's neck.

'I gave my throne to your father,' Leonid went on. 'Because it was mine to give. Now he is dead, the throne returns to me once more. And I choose to keep it.'

This time it was Titus who remained silent.

'You have never fought a battle, boy, let alone a war.' There was sadness in Leonid's voice as he spoke. 'I will guide us through this storm until you are ready. Mayhap it will be before it is all done. But now . . . I cannot allow it.'

Titus walked on, his back straight as a rod. His hand hovered over the door's handle. Then it slipped down, to the key in its lock.

He twisted until there was a loud click. The boy's shoulders shook and his hand moved again. Slid to the blade at his hip.

'So be it,' Titus said.

Chapter 31

Leonid held up a hand as Titus advanced, and to Jai's surprise, the boy paused. The old man keened with sudden effort, his knuckles whitening as he lifted himself from the chair. He stood on trembling legs, with lifted chin and curled lip.

'The Lion of the Sabines will not die with bended knees,' he growled. 'I cursed the day you were born; when you took your mother from us. Now, I curse it again on this day that you took your father. Would that your mother could see what I see. Would that the world could. A snivelling pup. A traitor.'

Titus's face blackened with rage and he took three short steps. The blade flashed as it buried itself deep, bursting through the old man's back. The force of it toppled Leonid back into his seat, and the man's moan of pain covered Jai's own gasp.

'You'll die a slow death,' Titus hissed, leaning down and pulling Leonid's face into his chest. 'With piss in your pants and your guts in your lap.'

He grunted with effort as the blade sawed to the side and Leonid gasped when his entrails spilled out of the wide slit. The old man's eyes were blank, his soundless mouth opening and closing like a beached fish.

'I had hoped you would be grateful,' Titus said, wiping his blade upon Leonid's doublet. 'I have made possible your grand vision of a united land, all under the Sabine banner. But you let cowardice betray you.'

He shook his head ruefully.

'And then my father, who was content to nibble at the crumbs of glory you left behind. Ignoring the riches to the east and marrying me to a barbarian. Was that his plan? To put a half-Dansk runt on our throne? It is he who is a traitor. And you . . . you are no better.'

He spat at the old man, but only succeeded in wetting his own chin. A second attempt speckled the old man's face. Jai, despite it all, felt his hackles rise at that.

'Magnus told me we would have to kill you, but I came alone to give you a chance. I should have known better.'

Leonid twitched, his eyes staring and vacant.

'When I come back with witnesses to "discover" your corpse, I'll blame that plainsboy you're so fond of. We've his body already. Why, I'll make a show of it, parade the corpse through the streets until its rotted. Think of it. The Dansk killed my father, the Steppefolk killed you. The perfect reason for my actions this day. So perfect, it's as if the gods themselves guide my fate. But then, my ancestors are among them, aren't they. You'll be with them too, soon enough.'

He laughed at that, even as Leonid began to shake in earnest.

'Your ancestors . . . piss on you,' the old man croaked.

'Not before I piss on you, you old fuck. Every morning, if you're buried close enough.'

The lock clicked, and Titus opened the door, just wide enough to squeeze through. The four corners glowed once more at its close.

Then Jai was alone . . . alone with a dying emperor.

* * *

JAI DID NOT KNOW what made him go to Leonid. There was little Jai could think of to ease his final moments.

But what else could he do? The door was impassable and the courtyard a charnel house. His best plan was to arm himself somehow – ambush Titus when he returned. He might even get a few blows in before Magnus turned him to ash.

Jai removed his shirt and pressed it to Leonid's belly. The old man grimaced, but nodded thanks. Already, blood was soaking through to Jai's hands. It would not be long now.

'Water,' Leonid croaked, adding his hands to Jai's.

Jai fetched some. It was stagnant, left over from a week ago, but Leonid gulped it down greedily. Finally, he leaned back. Sighed.

'You . . . are the only friend I've left in this world,' Leonid whispered. 'The son of my greatest enemy. The gods . . . have a sense of humour.'

Jai wiped the dribble from the old man's beard.

'Is there a prayer I can speak?' he asked. 'When you . . .'

Jai trailed off. He knew not what else to say. Leonid let out a bitter laugh.

'I'm not fated for the heavens in the Beyond, my boy,' Leonid said, his voice weak now. 'I know where I'm going. No last plea will change the gods' minds. If this ignominy is to be my end, then they've not forgiven me my sins.'

Jai lifted the pitcher to Leonid's lips, but the old man turned his head away. His eyes were already growing glassy, and the veins of his face were as blue spiderwebs, fading into sight with paling skin.

'I'll wait with you,' Jai murmured. 'Until it's time.'

Not that he had any other choice. But the words brought a smile to Leonid's face.

'Seek the winesop in the phoenix,' he said. 'Beg his favour . . . and his forgiveness of me.'

'Hush now,' Jai said, stroking the old man's brow. 'Now is the time for prayer.'

But Leonid was rambling, his gaze distant, unfocused.

'You've read almost everything in this room,' Leonid said. 'Perhaps, it is time to finish. That has always been the key to your freedom.'

He laughed and Jai hushed him once more. Leonid gripped his wrist and turned his eyes to Jai.

'After all, why not?' Leonid chuckled, a strange smile upon his face. 'When my family becomes my enemy . . . what does my enemy become?'

His last breath petered out, punctuated by a final exultation.

The Lion of the Sabines may not have died on his feet. But he did die laughing.

Chapter 32

Jai sat with the dead emperor a while longer. He closed the old man's eyes. Covered him with a blanket.

He knew he had loved Leonid. It was a love borne of long years of companionship. Of knowing the old man truly. If Balbir had been the closest thing he had to a mother, then Leonid was the closest to a father.

Not a good one, by any means. Nor a kind one. But a father nonetheless.

He had been Jai's gaoler and Jai's ward. His master and his charge. He'd been there for what felt like Jai's entire life. Jai mourned the monster. Or what the monster had become.

Leonid seemed to have been losing his mind in his final moments. Speaking of places and things that made no sense – and a task Jai couldn't possibly attempt even if they did. He'd be lucky to survive the next hour, let alone have a chance to search for . . . a drunkard inside a rare beast.

But the man's last words had also reminded Jai of the gulf that had existed between man and boy. Of that unspoken thing. Jai's father.

In over a decade of Jai's stewardship, Rohan's name had

hardly passed either's lips. Nor had Jai touched Leonid's journal of that time period. Some years into Jai's arrival, Leonid had placed the volume, perhaps out of respect, on the lowest shelf in the very corner of the boudoir.

The many other journals had been expanded upon, then carefully transcribed by the cathedral's monks. Certainly, Jai had spent enough time writing down Leonid's thoughts – why, he'd probably written half the contents of these shelves.

These books had gilt letters and were bound in rich vellum. Jai knew some of them almost by heart, particularly the ones where the Gryphon Guard went into battle. But the one that documented the War of the Steppe remained in its original form.

This one was made from yellowing, loose leafed pages, rough-joined with string. These were the writings of a man on campaign, scrawled upon the back of a war horse, or jotted in half-sleep through days of drawn-out conflict.

Jai had always wondered about that. Was it out of embarrassment that Leonid had not immortalised those years? Certainly it was a war that had almost brought the Sabine Empire to its knees. Had there not been a decisive battle, both peoples might have ground each other down to collapse.

Whatever the reason, Jai knew he should read it. If this was to be the end of Rohan's line he could at the very least learn a bit more about the man whose line ended with him.

Before he sat down to read and await his death he took the time to search the shelves for a weapon. Perhaps he might attempt to avenge his brothers when the time came, or at the very least earn himself a quick death in the attempt. If Titus returned without Magnus, or accompanying bodyguards, Jai might just manage to kill him.

But every blade on the shelves, whether ceremonial artefact

or bloodstained trophy, had been blunted. Jai suspected this had been done years ago in case a servant turned upon Leonid.

With little other choice, he armed himself with the heaviest, thickest blade he could find, a heavy falchion – planning to wield it as a metal club. Blunt or not, it'd bash Titus's head in. He ignored the armour, knowing it would weigh him down in his ambush and do nothing to protect him from Magnus's majicking.

Only then did he allow himself to shuffle to the room's darkest corner and sit cross-legged as he had done as a child at Leonid's feet, listening to his tales of glory and plunder.

He took the journal. A single, ragged volume, hardly thicker than two fingers. He brushed dust from the first page; one that doubled as a cover.

The writing was scrawled at an angle, as if dashed off in a hurry:

Heathens. People of the Plateau. Steppefolk.

They bear many names. Yet I cannot recall hearing any of them until my empire touched their borders. Once, they warred among themselves. A fragmented culture made up of a dozen major tribes. Something is different now.

Twice, my generals have sent a cohort beyond our borders, in pursuit of their raiders. Twice, no man has returned.

1200 men. Gone.

Too long have I languished in this palace and let the business of war be led by lesser men. It is time to scour the rust from my blade.

Jai tried not to let that first word get to him. *Heathens.* It was an insult used so interchangeably with Steppefolk as to be rendered common parlance across the empire.

He had spent his entire life being told he was a heathen. That his people were savages. Blood drinkers, head hunters. Transients. Vagrants.

Yet he knew so little of his own people that he could not deny it. Being raised Sabine, he too felt his stomach turn at their rumoured traditions.

He admitted it was strange to him that Steppefolk had no cities, towns or even villages. That each day they packed up their yurts and moved on to new pasturelands. That they mined no metal, nor grew any crops.

Even those things that Balbir had taught him were half-forgotten. And his own memories were now little more than dreams.

Did he really want his last thoughts on his ancestors to be shaped by the mind of the man who had reason to hate them most?

Jai knew he was lying to himself. Knew the real reason he didn't want to read on. But he allowed himself to put it back.

Only, as he went to do so . . . he saw something. It was a rusted lever, built into the shelf behind.

For all these years it must have sat there in plain sight. Leonid had known Jai would never go near the journal. It was no wonder.

Jai leaned forward. Pulled it, then pulled harder, straining as a rusted mechanism screeched in protest.

There was a rumble, then the *clack-clack-clack* of chains. Jai held his breath, turning to see what might happen. Knowing the excesses of Leonid's youth . . . anything could. The very ceiling could shift aside, if the younger emperor had wished to sleep beneath the stars.

Instead, there was a final, soft click . . . and the creak of wood behind him. Jai felt a draught and spun slowly once more.

'The key . . . to my salvation,' Jai whispered.

The shelf had swung back, leaving a dark gap at its edge just wide enough for him to squeeze through. There was no light . . . only that soft breeze that told him that somewhere beyond there was a way out.

It was then that the door rattled. For a brief, panicked moment, Jai hesitated. This was his one chance to kill an emperor. To avenge his family.

But did he not owe it to his family to live on? To continue Rohan's legacy?

It might well have been cowardice that made him step through the gap. Or perhaps it was loyalty to his father that made him snatch up the journal and leave the sword to hide the lever in its place.

None of that mattered as Jai shoved the shelf closed behind him with a final, loud clank. Because for the first time in what felt like his entire life . . . Jai was free.

Chapter 33

He stood there, alone in the darkness. Pressed his ear to the wood, listening for Titus's feigned wail of despair. But he heard nothing. *Saw* nothing.

There was no longer even a draught to guide him. It was as if he had suddenly found himself in a dank cave, deep within the recesses of the earth.

He might have believed it too, had he not known the truth of it. He was in fact hundreds of feet above the rolling valleys that surrounded the palace – somewhere inside the jutting escarpment upon which Latium was built.

Jai let out a long breath he had not realised he'd been holding. For the moment, he was safe. In fact . . . he was more than safe. Of all the people who had seen him since he had awoken, almost all were dead.

Constantine. Leonid. Even Arjun.

And Balbir. Poor Balbir, who had kept his secret till the end. For had Titus not said that they had Jai's body? Her silence meant even Magnus must think him dead.

But that didn't mean things would be easy. Every Steppeman and woman and Dansk in the city would be hunted now. Even if he found a way out of the palace, the danger was not over yet.

To compound it all, he had to travel the length and breadth of the largest empire in history. Few inns would take him. Fewer carts would let him hitch a ride.

He, who had hardly set foot beyond Latium's walls, would have to live off the land. One problem at a time though.

For now, he just needed light.

It was lucky then that after rolling and stuffing the diary into his pocket and some fumbling against the rough-hewn walls, his hands touched a candle and tinderbox. Clearly Leonid had used this route before.

The tinder was dry and sparked easily enough. Soon, he could see his surroundings. A cave made of damp, uneven stone.

Within moments, he was walking down a steep passageway. It might as well have been a spiral staircase, but for the slope in the stead of steps. Somehow, Jai doubted this was by design for a wheelchair, and more from the speed such a secret place would need to be built. If the dust that coated the candleholder was any indication, Leonid's last visit had been long before he'd been confined to the chair.

In truth, Jai was surprised that this passage had not been affected by Magnus's charm. But then, he had been able to exit via the balcony too. It must have been the main door that had been charmed, and that alone.

As he descended, the air became cooler, prickling his skin with gooseflesh. Water dribbled from the ceiling and he could see from the first bumps of stalactites that this place had been constructed many, many years ago. Perhaps even in Leonid's youth, when the palace had been first built.

It seemed endless and silent but for the drip of water and the echo of his footsteps. Every few seconds, a cold droplet would thud into his hair or shoulders, sapping the warmth from his bones.

What was this? A secret escape in case of a coup or an assassination attempt? Certainly it was working that way.

And then finally there was a break in that deep, spiralling snake of a passage.

An entryway, yawning in the side wall. No door, nor rug. The space beyond might have been a natural cave, could he not see the pick marks around its edges.

Jai wondered whether he should continue on his way – his first priority was to get away from Latium. Yet he knew soldiers would be hunting for Steppefolk in the city streets. Perhaps waiting would be better. Surely they would be tired of slaughter by the early hours of the morning.

So he stepped through into the darkness. And now he saw signs of what this place had once been.

Moth-eaten curtains divided up a huge chamber along with various furs and rugs. A huge bed, so large it could fit ten men, sat at its centre. There was even a small hearth set deep in the wall.

In an instant, Jai knew what this place was. It was a place joked about in taverns, or sworn upon in ribald exhortations.

Leonid's fabled whorehouse. Or rather, whore-room, by the look of things.

No emperor wished to be known to sleep with prostitutes. It was unseemly, not to mention the potential for easily identifiable bastard progeny who might later claim the throne. Certainly not while married – and certainly not in his own bedchamber.

This place must have been Leonid's solution. Jai only dreaded to think where the entrance might be. A fat lot of good this secret passage would be to him if it emerged into a room in an actual whorehouse.

More likely, though, it would be somewhere discreet. Where the courtesans would have been able to enter without drawing suspicion. So Jai sat upon the bed, ignoring the dust that billowed as he flopped back.

Just an hour or two of sleep would help, but he had no way of telling the time here. No, he'd have to stay awake — the sooner he was on his way, the better.

If only there was a way to while away the time.

Unfortunately, there was nothing of value in this place – whoever arranged Leonid's visitors must have taken everything. There must have once been furniture here, as well as drink, if the broken shards of wine bottles, and dust outlines on the threadbare rugs were any indication.

All gone now. Still, as Jai took in the walls of the room, he saw colour there, among the ragged remains. A flower, painted upon the wall. And three stick figures.

They were childish. In fact, he now saw the toys scattered in that corner of the room. A carved horse, its leg missing. A doll, one so ragged that it looked like rats had nested within, with gaping empty eyes. He shuddered at the sight.

He examined the stick figures more closely. A man, woman and child, holding hands. And the man wore . . . purple. An emperor's clothing.

Chapter 34

The room had undoubtedly once been a brothel – the signs were all around him. There was even the goddess of courtesans, Ishtore, depicted in stone above the doors. But it was also something else. Or had become something else.

It could be that Leonid's favourite lover had a child; a daughter if Jai was to guess. That she would play in the corner while they . . . did business.

It wasn't quite the wild orgies that the tales spoke of, though undoubtedly this place had started that way. There were even murals upon the walls, long overtaken by mould and rot, that seemed to have once depicted such things.

But he imagined something different. He pictured Leonid fathering a child. One who would visit here, so he could pass the time with both mother and daughter. Perhaps, in time, they had drifted apart.

He explored the room further, tracing his hand along the rough, damp walls. To see the brothel-turned-playroom. See the markings of the child's height upon the wall – she'd grown almost up to his belly before the marks stopped.

There were no dates written anywhere to hint at when this

had happened. Jai knew this place had remained untouched since he arrived in Latium. Certainly, Leonid had not been sneaking off in the night when Jai had moved into his chambers.

Whoever had once been here, they were long gone.

By the time Jai had explored every inch of the place, he felt like the hour was growing late – though in truth he had lost track of time. He had only lingered to allow the city's guardsmen to grow bored of their search for Dansk and Steppefolk.

He wished there was something of value there – something he could barter for coin or safe passage. No such luck. There was nothing that had not been taken by the place's rot and damp.

So he continued on his way, down the spiralling passage. The deeper he went, the damper it became, such that he could hear the trickle and drip of water all around him. At the same time, the air became less stale and heavy.

He thought he could feel the beginnings of a breeze upon his face. But . . . there was a stench in the air. At first, he thought he was imagining it. Or perhaps the smell of his own terror-sweat had reached his nostrils.

Soon, though, it was too strong to ignore. It was a smell that Jai was all too familiar with. He'd smelled it before as a child when the Crimson Death had reached Latium. When the royals had holed up in their deserted palace, eating cold cuts and fruit, sleeping in dirty sheets, while plague ravaged the streets outside.

For weeks, the bodies had been left to moulder where they had fallen, skin stained with the disease's tell-tale red rash. It was only when the Gryphon Guard, immune from the sickness as soulbound, cleared away the bodies that the stench had left the palace.

This was that same smell. Death. Rot.

It was only when Jai reached the end of the passage, where

the fetid air was almost unbearable, that he realised where he must be. This was where he'd dreaded he might end up tonight. Or at least, his body might.

The plague pits. So called for their first use, when the Gryphon Guard had carried the hundreds of plague-stricken bodies to the edge of the palace's cliff. Tipped them down, to rot in the natural hollow at the base of the rock face.

Few ventured there now. For it was where all bodies of the unwanted and forgotten went. The dead fettered and servants, the vagrants and orphans. Cheaper to pay a watchman to dump their bodies there. The stench, by heaven's grace, was too far below to reach the palace.

But it was close to these festering pits that Jai emerged, once he had forced his way out through an overgrown crack, one choked with vines and brambles. It was no surprise, then, that none had found the secret entrance to Leonid's brothel, for the area had become a diseased burial ground.

Outside, the stench almost made his eyes water.

In the new moonlight, he blew out the candle. Pocketed it. Best not to draw attention to himself. He allowed his eyes to adjust to the darkness, praying he was alone, and shivering at the cold of the winter night.

Jai had pictured this place. Had nightmares, even, that it was where he might end up. He'd always imagined a great hole in the ground, where thousands of bodies floated amid a slurry of maggots and liquid putrefaction.

Instead, it was more a shallow, long-grassed valley, with wild-flowers and young saplings. Here and there, Jai could see the old bones of the dead. They did not seem out of place, more like driftwood, or fallen branches.

Nature had reclaimed these hills.

Then there were the bodies. He tried not to look at those

strewn about, in their various forms of decomposition. Some were shrouded, but most were not. Their eyes seemed to stare at him, accusing. They had the assassin's eyes.

Whump.

Jai heard a wet thud nearby. At first, Jai thought it a loose rock. But then he saw the next one, plummeting from above.

A naked body, falling in deathly silence. Then another, and another. Jai rushed back to the passage entrance, huddling in its shelter. He covered his eyes, then his ears. It was the noise at the end of each fall. The wet impact, punctuated by a crackle of bones.

The Gryphon Guard were throwing bodies off the cliffs. Stripping them of their fine clothing first, of course, and of their jewels and trinkets. His brothers would be among them. Jai didn't want to see it. Didn't want to have to bury them with his bare hands.

Jai heard a crash. One so loud he almost felt the ground tremble, and his eyes flew open of their own volition.

Ivar's dragon had fallen too. Hardly a stone's throw from where Jai crouched, its huge black form splayed like a beached whale.

And then, the gruesome hail stopped. Clearly the dragon had been the last to be hauled from the courtyard to the cliff's edge.

Only now did Jai begin to plan his escape, the reminder of the danger he was in almost falling into his lap. He could not walk to the city gates and begin on the Kashmere Road. That was as beaten a track as had ever existed, and was patrolled by hundreds of imperial legionaries.

No, he would have to head for the Black Forest, no more than a half mile's walk from here. Once through, he could hide in the cornfields and walk the dirt trails used by those who could not afford the tolls on the great highway. He'd be at greater risk of ambush from bandits, but he had to make a calculated choice. He only hoped whatever Titus was hiding there had left the forest by now.

East. That was all he knew. Oh, he'd seen maps of the continent. Knew he'd be skirting the long, winding line of the Kashmere Road through the many territories of the empire, and then on through the spine of the Petrus Mountains that ran down its edge.

If he was lucky, he'd meet another group of refugees, hitch a ride on a carriage or cart. Perhaps some of Latium's Steppefolk on the run, or Dansk merchants laying low.

For now, his feet took him closer to the dead dragon, if only to glance at it as he headed for the treeline, not far in the distance. But something made him pause.

The dragon had held up pretty well in its fall, though the impact had spilled its great guts into a pile beside it, steaming in the icy air. Already, a feast of flies were buzzing.

It was not this, however, that caught Jai's attention. It was the beast's chest. Above the great rent where Magnus had slit its belly, a second, jagged hole had been punched into its sternum. Someone, or something, had torn out the beast's heart.

Not only that, but its protruding, swollen tongue and open mouth revealed someone had yanked free all its teeth. The men above were vultures of the worst kind.

'It'll be close,' came a voice. 'Look, there's the dragon o'er yonder.'

Jai's stomach lurched. Behind the bolt-studded hump of the dragon's belly and chest, someone was coming. And they were close. Too close for him to retreat back to the passageway.

Footsteps . . . and the snap of brambles, drawing closer. There was only one place left to hide.

Chapter 35

Why'd you not take it afore you chucked 'er off the clifftop?' a second, whinier voice asked.

It was muffled, but Jai knew they were just outside. Outside the still-warm belly of the dragon. He buried himself deeper into the entrails with slow deliberate movements. If he could still see moonlight, one glance inside would likely reveal his presence.

'You heard the princeling,' said the first. 'Hollerin' 'bout cleanin' that mess up. You wanna stop to cut a ring off a Dansk whore's twat-twiddler with that mad bastard watchin'?'

'That's Emperor bastard to you, sirrah,' the second giggled, in a mockery of the accent of the upper class. 'He'll be crowned soon, mark me.'

'All I knows is, that noble was one of the first we tossed over,' the first said, ignoring his companion. 'Afore the emperor ran off and they could search those other deaduns' proper-like. We'd best hurry – we won't be the first to think of this.'

'A good day for us,' the second said.

'Nowt good'll come from all this,' the first muttered. 'War's acomin', no two ways about it.'

'War's coming?'

It wasn't difficult for Jai to see who the brains of the opera-
tion was, but he found it hard to focus, for he was swallowing
over and over to prevent his gorge from rising. Within the warm
belly of the beast it stank of blood and shit, and he could feel
the burn of spilled stomach acids along his side. Each breath he
filtered slowly between his teeth, as if that would somehow help
with the fetid air.

'Slaughterin' half the Dansk nobility'll do that. Wake up and
smell the entrails, you daft prick.'

'Then find the sodding ring afore we catch the Crimson Death.'

There was a muttered curse, and a moan of disgust.

'She's one of these,' the first said. 'Look, must be this one.
She had a ripe pair on her, that I remember.'

Jai heard the scrape of a blade being drawn. Then the sound
of sawing back and forth, and of gagging.

'Keep a lookout, or you'll not get your share,' the first growled.

'These guts smell something rotten,' the second moaned, his
voice queasy. 'You see Magnus carve the thing open?'

There was only a cry of triumph in response.

'Got the fucker,' the first crowed. 'That fuckin' bone was a
bastard to get through.'

'We ought' cut off the dragon's claws,' the second said, and
Jai felt the dragon shake as it was kicked. 'Make a necklace.
Worth something, no?'

'We've been 'ere long enough, and this blade'll do nowt 'gainst
dragon bone,' the first growled. 'There'll be more bastards comin''
soon, and not just the usual graverobbers neither. Those Gryphon
Guard are a greedy lot. If they weren't busy slaughterin' and
rapin' heathens in the city they'd 'ave been 'ere by . . .'

Their voices began to fade, but Jai forced himself to remain,
sheer terror overcoming his discomfort. Just hearing the way the

men spoke told him those sick bastards would murder him just for the fun of it.

Only when he truly could no longer bear it did he begin to crawl out, scrabbling his nails along the slimy folds to pull himself forward.

In the darkness, he could hardly see. He could just feel the weight of the dragon's insides, as he gasped breath after stinking breath.

There was something hard, blocking his path. He shoved at it, desperate to escape the dank embrace of the fleshy prison surrounding him. It shifted, and he latched a hand upon the broken spar of a rib for purchase, heaving until the blockage plopped free, and he could take a single breath in the air beyond.

The air was full of the same stench, and of the rotting corpses beyond, but in the icy moonlight it felt fresh as a mountain stream in his lungs. He gasped again, careful to breathe through his mouth, and emerged from the beast's slitted belly like a newborn, slipping and sliding until he was birthed onto the grass.

He lay there for a moment, shivering in his blood-wet clothes, and letting the horror subside.

Only when the moonlight was hidden by a cloud did Jai rise to his feet, clutching his arms to his chest. The temperature was dropping fast, and the soaking clothes made it all the worse. He could see the heat steaming off him.

He had to move, for there would be more scavengers on their way. He'd heard there were plenty of vagrants who made a living stripping the dead, even doing the grisly work of taking teeth for dentures. Word of the slaughter at the palace would reach them soon enough.

What was another dead body, and a Steppeman's at that? They'd rob and murder him for the shoes upon his feet, let alone the handful of coin in his pocket and the Damantine steel hidden beneath his tunic.

Already, he could see ragged figures picking their way closer, still some distance away. They seemed hesitant, and Jai could not blame them. The sight of what might be a resting dragon with a bellyful of human corpses . . . tended to do that.

He went to take a step, and stumbled on something heavy ahead of him. He frowned. He hadn't seen a boulder here before. Had the guardsmen left something behind?

Hoping it might be something useful, he knelt down and ran his fingers along it. It was . . . scaly. And ridged, like the crocodile skin of Leonid's scabbard.

But strangest of all . . . it was warm. Warm from the dragon's steaming insides. It had been in there with him.

He was holding a dragon's egg.

Chapter 36

He ran.

Ran like a madman, fuelled by excitement and fear in equal measure. He tripped and slid through the long grass, the egg held close to his chest. If a dragon's teeth were worth so much, he knew this would be worth a fortune. After all, was the golden dragon pup not supposed to be a large part of Erica's dowry?

Certainly, it would be enough to buy him passage to the Great Steppe. If he played his cards right. Or rather card . . . The egg was all he had.

He looked back and was relieved to see none of the scavengers had followed him. For once, his luck seemed to have changed.

His thin clothing was torn and muddied by the time he'd fought his way through the thickets to the forest edge, but that was hardly the worst of it. There was not an inch of him that didn't seem covered in a thick layer of bloody viscera, dragon-bile and half-digested excrement. He was shivering in earnest now, the wetness of his clothes drawing the heat from his skin.

The only warmth came from the dragon egg, still steaming from the heat of its mother's insides. He clutched that round ball to his skin, its form like that of a grapefruit. A heavy one at that.

Worse still, the assassin's shoes were soft and thin, such that the wearer could feel the contours of the ground. They would hardly last a few days of rough terrain, if his feet didn't rub themselves to stumps first. They were already beginning to blister.

His chest heaved, unused to the effort. When had he last run?

He couldn't approach anyone wealthy enough to offer a fair price for the egg. Or anyone at all really, covered in filth as he was. He'd be lucky not to freeze to death that very night.

For a moment, he looked back. Wondered if he might steal shoes from one of the few dead that had not been stripped of their finery already. But already the grave-robbers were beginning to swarm, going about their grisly work. Like the flies, this was a veritable feast for them.

The forest was ominous. It was ancient, made mostly of ironwood, a tree whose lumber was too dense to shape for furniture and too heavy for ship-building. This was largely the reason the forest had been left intact.

Jai had never set foot in a forest. Hell, even the sight of these wild trees was novel, for they were stark contrast to the manicured orchards in the palace's pleasure gardens.

He'd seen the forest often enough at a distance – that enormous dark swathe amid the flaxen patchwork quilt of fields. Never had he imagined it so terrifying a prospect. Then again, he'd never pictured this place at night either.

Out in the open there had been moonlight. Enough to see a fair way when the clouds parted. But just one step into the forest and he was swallowed up by gloom. A few more and he could hardly see a hand in front of his face.

This was his only choice. There was nowhere else to go. All he wanted to do was curl up into a ball and sleep. Forget the chill that was making him shake so hard his teeth rattled. He resisted that temptation with every fibre of his being. Even a homebody like him knew that would mean death – he'd read enough stories of soldiers, frozen in their sleep on the ground. He had to keep moving, or he would die where he lay.

So he lit the candle, his hands shaking as he clashed the flint and steel from Leonid's secret passage. The small flame was his only source of warmth and light.

It was a paltry illumination in the murk, no more than enough to keep his feet from tripping, and to stagger between the great trunks.

In deepest shadow, he walked on. Walked until his blistering feet went blessedly numb.

He walked not to reach somewhere. He might as well be walking in circles for all he cared in his stupor.

Jai walked for warmth. To buy time, until the morning sunned the forest. For something to do as his shivering breaths came in short gasps and the world began to tilt. As the darkness seemed to yawn, beckoning him ever onwards.

When he fell, it took him a few moments to realise it, so numb was his body, so lethargic his mind. The candle sputtered in front of his face, then flared as a dry leaf caught flame.

Fire. How could he not have thought of it? Jai brushed more leaves together, glad his hands were not entirely numb yet thanks to the warmth of the egg. He was just able to pick up twigs with trembling fingers.

The leaves smouldered and crackled, and Jai was careful to stoke it slowly. He had built fires before, in the grand fireplace of Leonid's chambers, but that was with pre-prepared tinder and bone-dry logs.

These twigs were damp. He added more leaves, but Jai's fledgling fire was already going out. He could feel the heat seeping from him as he sat upon the cold, wet ground. He did not have time to attempt another fire if this one failed.

The edges of his vision were darkening, the world warping around him.

Now, he sacrificed all the tinder in the box that had come with the candle. This flared bright, and he could see the great, creaking branches of the trees above.

Only then did the first twigs catch flame. The heat was a godsend. He piled on still more twigs, and any dead wood he could find in the vicinity.

It was when all the wood he could find had been piled onto the fire that Jai removed his stinking, blood-soaked clothes, hanging them to dry on a low branch.

He trembled, naked as a newborn, curling on the damp mulch of the forest floor around the fire, so close that the hair upon his wrists singed. The egg had fallen close by, and this he clutched close to his sternum.

It was leathery and rough, heavy as a stone. Strangely, the surface was still as warm as when he'd first picked it up. Warmer than it had any right to be.

But the fire . . . the fire was dying. And so was he.

Chapter 37

It did not take long for Jai to be left in utter darkness, curled naked beside a pile of smoking, musty wood. There was no tinder to light another flame. Only the flint and steel, that might smatter sparks upon more damp leaves if Jai only had the energy to get them.

But Jai could hardly feel his body, let alone move it. The brief reprieve from the cold had bought him but a few more minutes, and now the winter night would take him for good.

He felt shame. Shame that he had failed, so utterly, even with the good fortune the gods had chosen to bestow. To get so far, only to die shuddering in the dark. To rot, forgotten, alone in the murk of the woods.

He wished he had waited longer in that chamber. Wished that he had tried to avenge his family. Avenge his people. Avenge humanity for that matter. The war that was coming would set the whole continent aflame.

Jai could not go back. He could not carry on. He could only clutch the egg close to his chest. Feel the heat beneath its leathery exterior. Feel . . . movement.

It was hardly perceptible. A faint reverberation within, as if a tiny fist had tapped upon his chest. Somewhere inside there was a living creature. Another being he had failed.

Would the egg survive, clutched in the arms of his wet, frozen corpse, so deep in the forest? He imagined the small beast emerging someday. No mother to care for it. No food but Jai's rotted remains.

He pitied the unborn creature. It had done nothing to deserve this.

Jai could feel the last weak pulses of his heart and pressed the egg closer. As if the warmth of it might spur his heart on and keep him alive just a few minutes longer.

And somewhere within that egg, he could feel another heartbeat. Almost hear it. Fast and strong. Jai yearned for his own to echo it.

Instead, it slowed further. The darkness deepened.

In his mind's eye, Jai saw his body fade. Flesh, skin, bone and sinew; all melted away. So did the forest and everything else until only two pulsing lights remained.

One was his own heart. A weak, sputtering thing, like the fire just minutes ago. The other flashed so fast and bright it might have blinded him, were he not dreaming.

Jai willed his light closer. Yearned to be near that other. To not die, here, alone.

And then he saw his light move, through sheer strength of will. Jai put his all into it, even as he felt himself convulse and twitch upon the soil. It didn't matter. Nothing else mattered. He had to touch that glorious, pure light.

But his movement was slow. Like the turning of a rudderless ship in a shallow harbour. So slow as to be imperceptible.

Jai's light was fading, until it was hardly there at all. And then, as his light dulled to near nothingness . . . the other twitched towards his.

The two lights met.

A jolt ripped through Jai's body. Pain, like nothing he'd ever felt. Agony in its purest form. As if his very soul was being torn from him . . . answering the call of another.

He felt that other. Liquid fire, burning a hole into his chest. But Jai welcomed the pain. It meant he was alive.

He pulled towards it. Opened himself up to it. He could feel it pooling inside, scorching a path through the darkness. Then coalescing. Forming something, deep within him. A mote of solid, concentrated light.

A kernel. A seed.

It was within his heart. Powering it. Warming it.

Chilled blood moved sluggishly through his veins once more. He faded back into existence. The wreck of his body, still twitching and spasming, began clawing its way back from the edge of death.

Jai opened his eyes.

The world was brighter now, even in the night, and growing more so with each passing second. He could see with crystal clarity, the murky canopy above suddenly riddled with moon-beams – silver-tinged spars that Jai could almost touch.

He was no longer cold . . . but feverish. Feverish and ener-gised. His very body steamed, flushed red as he'd never seen himself. And the egg. The egg burned hot too.

It twitched.

He let it fall and scrambled back. There was something stir-ring within.

He heard a thud. Then another, and another. The leathery ball's surface distended with each blow until suddenly there was a crack and the shell ruptured.

A pale, glossy thing slid out from the egg and onto the earth, landing there in a pool of liquid.

Jai . . . felt it.

Felt an emotion not of his own – a sudden elation. Joy at the feeling of cold. The feeling came from somewhere close by . . . but within him all at once.

The cat-sized creature lifted a long, slender neck. Peeked at him over the crumpled remains of its egg. Eyes of lapis stared out, boring into him. And a porcelain-scaled snout, snuffling at the air between them.

He felt . . . *love*. There was no other word for it.

A deep caring, warm in his chest, edged with worry. And without knowing how, Jai perceived this dragon had sensed his fading light. His soul, burning out.

It had saved him. Saved him by lending him its own bright light. Deemed him worthy and shared its soul with him. He was . . . bonded with this thing. Numb with wonder and cold, the realisation hit him like a hot slap. He was soulbound.

This all felt like it was happening to someone else. *Soulbound*. All he could feel was relief that he was alive.

A snout nudged closer, snuffling towards him along the soil. It stopped between his legs, gazing up at him with large, round eyes. They were turquoise blue, so rich in colour that they almost seemed to glow. A stark contrast to the opaque, milky scales that layered the creature's exterior.

It cocked its head and purred, low and deep. Crawled closer; nuzzled against his thigh. With trembling hand, Jai stroked its flank.

There was a flash of pleasure. He felt it in his chest. Again, that feeling of otherness. He could feel what this creature felt. Its emotions . . . even the touch of another.

This was what they called the meld. That connection that drove some soulbound insane. That invasion of one's mind, and the occupation of another's.

There was a reason some beasts were never bonded with. No man can live with the alien thoughts of an insect within his head. Even the famed mouse-spies of the Huddites hardly lasted a few years before they became gibbering wrecks.

Jai closed his eyes, feeling the beast leap languidly into his lap. It was so light. So small. No larger than a housecat.

The beast trusted him absolutely. And he it.

Chapter 38

Jai awoke.

He did not remember falling asleep. Exhaustion must have overcome him. That, or the dozing consciousness he shared had pulled him to slumber with it.

He felt hunger. Or the dragon did. It was hard to tell where one feeling began and the other ended.

Jai rose, scanning his surroundings. But the beast was nowhere to be seen. Jai didn't worry though. He could sense it. It was somewhere to his right, deeper in the forest.

It was on the move. Hunting.

There was the scent of something else. Something small and squeaking. He pictured the wriggling thing between his jaws, crushing down to—

Jai shook his head, slapping his cheeks lightly. Beyond, there was a snap . . . and *pleasure*. The taste of blood, rich and heavy.

The dragon was in no immediate danger. Best to focus on himself. There were things to do. Too many, really. But the first thing was first.

Fire.

It did not take Jai long to light a new one in the cold light of day, though in truth, he had no need of it. He felt the chill, yet it had no impact on his damp, naked body. No shivering, no gooseflesh. No numbness of any kind.

Rather, he used the fire to dry his still-damp clothing.

The world was so very different, now. The edges of things seemed more in focus. More vivid, more colourful. He could pick out crushed berries upon the ground a hundred feet away. Smell it too. Hear the chirr of the insects in the trees, the crackle of branches from the soughing breeze above.

So this was what it was to be soulbound. The world the same, but more of it. Jai's mind reeled at the intensity of it all. He attempted to parse the conflicting sounds, smells, sights . . . yet it took all his focus not to clamp his hands over his ears and squeeze his eyes shut.

He realised he had walked barefoot over the thorns and fallen branches without discomfort, and snapped dry branches for the fire with little effort.

Through his years of eavesdropping on the Gryphon Guard, Jai knew a little of soulbonding. Knew the various potions and pills their acolytes imbibed to aid in the attempt, and the twitching, choking death that followed if they failed.

How had he managed to do it without their guidance . . . without the lessons of a hundred generations? And with a dragon no less.

Many had attempted to bond with these fabled, mountain-dwelling beasts. But only the Dansk had succeeded.

It was a secret they had guarded jealously for centuries. It gave Jai some small pleasure that Titus did not have it. Though he worried for Erica and what might happen to her if she did not give the secret up. He suspected it was the only reason she was alive.

Soulbound.

Him? Impossible.

He shifted closer to the fire, wrinkling his nose as his frozen clothes began to drip. The scent was not a pleasant one. Nor was the sight for that matter.

He wondered what would make a more palatable sight to those he might come across on his travels. A filthy, naked wild man of the forest? Or a far filthier clothed man, covered in blood and shit.

Neither seemed a good prospect. But at least the latter made him feel human.

He was only glad that Leonid's journal had survived the experience . . . well, mostly – it was a good thing he had already read the front page. It remained tucked in a tight roll inside his pocket.

Jai took a moment to breathe. To *think*. He closed his eyes.

Concentrating, he sucked in a deep gulp of air, held it, then let it out slowly. Almost as if he were puffing a pipe. This was what he had seen Balbir do when she had soulbreathed at the Red Lion. It felt right, somehow. And at the very least, calming.

Of course, Jai had no idea how to begin the act of soulbreathing. For now, he just wanted to understand his new body. What it had become.

He felt strange. Not only because of the changes in his flesh and wellbeing, but the feeling of something . . . *new* within. He sought it out, exploring the recesses of his mind like a tongue tracing teeth.

It was almost by instinct that his mind shifted into that dream-state of the night before. It felt like a door had opened in his mind. Or rather, been blown off its hinges. There was no closing it again.

He could see a shell there – a hollow, crystalline structure. Floating in the dark centre of his very being. And inside was something . . . liquid. Pure, bright, and cleansing. Like molten light.

Moreover, there was a thread. An umbilical cord, almost, towards a second bright light. Stretching out into darkness, towards a distant star. The thread pulsed with light. With *thoughts*.

This was beyond his comprehension, and the thin knowledge he'd garnered from half-heard conversations of the Gryphon Guard acolytes did little to help. He only knew that strange shell's name.

A *core*.

It was hard to pull himself away from that ethereal state. He could have stared at those golden lights for hours, floating, out-of-body, in that dark, weightless ocean.

There would be plenty of time for that, in the long nights ahead.

Jai stood up. He needed to find his dragon.

He could feel it. Out there, in the trees. Chewing on gristle, revelling in the salt-copper tang. And as he focused upon that feeling . . . it only grew stronger.

Jai felt its eyes upon him before he heard it. Even felt the jolt of recognition, and regret for having forgotten him while it hunted.

This mind . . . it was intelligent. Sharp and bright, and ruled by emotion. Different to his own in a thousand ways, but similar in far more.

It was part of him. That was the strangest thing. It knew him like he knew it. Not his memories, or the details of his life. But everything else worth knowing.

It knew his petty jealousies. His shame. His darkest fears. Knew how he saw himself, and how he was. And it judged him for neither. Almost . . . loved him for it.

He knew this in the same way he knew his dragon was kind. That it wanted to be loved. That the mewl it let out was because it missed the mother it had never known.

The little one knew that she had died. Felt her body grow colder.

'Come here, then,' Jai whispered.

He needn't have spoken. The dragon sensed his welcome. It came racing up to him in a scattering of earth and leaves and dropped something in his lap.

'Shit!'

Jai leaped away, and the dragon chirred in consternation. A decapitated squirrel lay forlornly at the beast's feet, and the dragon nudged the bloody morsel closer to him with its snout.

Round, turquoise eyes looked up at him, as if to ask if it had done wrong. The beast's gaze was . . . beautiful. Like staring into twin lagoons in a sea of snow.

'Sorry little one,' Jai whispered.

He sat back down, reaching out to touch the dragon's head. Stroked along its nostrils and blunt snout, marvelling that he could be so close to a *dragon*. Felt the heat of its breath misting his face.

It chirred reproachfully and nestled into his lap once more.

'What are we gonna do, little . . .'

He leaned to the side and checked the hatchling's nethers.

'. . . lady.'

Jai rubbed the cool, opalescent scales and crooked a finger, running it the length of her back. Her languorous, spur-tipped tail lifted like a cat's in return, and he scratched the skin around each protruding nub of bone along her vertebrae. They were nothing like the long spines of her older counterparts.

He lifted each of her four legs, tipped with sharp claws that extended when he pressed his finger into the pad of her foot.

She wriggled as it tickled her, and nudged his hand away with her short snout, then snuffled at the air once more, eager to sample the cornucopia of scents that made up the forest.

He traced her webbed wings with some care . . . for they were folded tight against her back, such that they were almost invisible. Even gentle pressure from his finger could not lift them, though the little beast did seem to appreciate when he gave them a good scratch.

Perhaps they would unfold in time. But he suspected that, much like a bird, a newly hatched dragon was incapable of flight.

It was almost self-indulgent, the feeling of petting the little beast. He knew where to scratch, where to rub. His own body was covered in gooseflesh at the pleasure of it.

Only when the dragon began to doze did Jai stop. He sat still so as not to disturb her, and used a stick to prod the squirrel into the embers of the fire. Refusing the dragon's gift would have been rude, especially since he sensed the little thing had room for more. Moreover, his plan to avoid others on his journey meant he would need to live off the land. In a few days, a squirrel would probably feel like a luxury.

He was no cook, but the initial stench of burning fur was soon replaced by the char and crackle of cooking fat. Soon enough, Jai was able to gnaw at the limbs, but the mouthful of flesh he eventually peeled from the tiny bones was not nearly enough to fill his belly.

Jai had heard legends that some of the more powerful soul-bound did not need to eat at all, preferring to live from the mana they cultivated alone. He had thought that a sad existence, but after the squirrel . . . he kind of understood.

Chapter 39

Jai's eyes fluttered open. He'd been dozing, letting the warmth of the rising sun lull him in and out of slumber. He hunched close to the warmth of the fire. A fire that now only smouldered.

Sighing, he carefully lifted the dragon from his lap and tweaked the edge of his hanging clothes. They were crusty, but dry enough.

He groaned in disgust, but pulled the clothes on, wincing at the parts that were still a little slimy. The stench was far worse than before. But he supposed with his new senses that was to be expected.

The dragon twitched. Then she jolted awake, her racing heart setting Jai's own apace with it.

He knew instantly why. Recognition had seized her mind. A familiar scent, though not one Jai could divine amid the jumble of thoughts flooding their connection.

And then the dragon was in the thickets, racing away from him.

'Come back!' Jai groaned, staggering to his feet.

She heard him. Ignored him.

'Is this how it's going to be?' Jai called out.

Nothing. Not even an emotional response to what Jai knew the dragon would recognise as Jai's annoyance.

He groaned and placed the diary, flint and striker in his pocket. He looked around for the rest of his things, then realised there was nothing else to take. So he pulled on his soft shoes once more and launched himself into a jog.

'Damn, little one,' Jai huffed. 'We'll have to get you a leash or something.'

It was strange, to feel the distance between them. He could tell the dragon was far faster than him. With each moment, it felt as if it drew further away.

The creature was desperate. Almost frantic. Jai could not parse the reason, but the grief it felt was so palpable as to make him sob.

Jai forced himself to ignore their connection, focusing on his own emotion. That was far more preferable; he was near-bursting with elation.

Because he could *run*.

It was almost like flying. Twice he launched himself too far off the ground, stumbling and rolling in a burst of soil and fallen leaves. His feet no longer hurt beyond the blisters from the night past, and his breath only came fast after the first minute of running at full tilt. Now he understood that joy when the royal hounds were allowed to run wild on a hunt. He was free.

Free.

Jai would have run faster, were he not so unused to the strength of his legs. And though he thought he'd survive running full-tilt into an ironwood tree . . . he wasn't entirely sure his teeth would.

And then . . . his dragon stopped.

She had sensed something new. Something unexpected.

Fear pulsed through her like a drug, such that Jai struggled to separate her terror from his own. Already, a cold sweat had broken out on his forehead as he slowed, catching up with the little beast.

She had stopped in the approach to a ravine formed by an outcrop of rock to her left and a fallen tree to her right. A hollow in the forest floor, muddied and marked by the imprints of hoof, paw and claw. Vegetation grew thick on either side.

Now, Jai could smell what the hatchling had. A thick, animal stench, and that of blood and entrails. Not unlike the smell of the dead khiro as he and his brothers had butchered it. But this was more than that. Stronger, and tinged with the smell of carrion.

The dragon's sinuous form wound up a loose boulder to look into the shadowed canyon. Jai crouched beside her, staring into the darkness.

He put one hand upon her back, stoking her smooth, cool scales, and the comfort it gave her echoed in his mind.

Then her back arched and she let out a low growl.

There was something there, waiting in the shadows. Snorting. Snuffling.

Hunting.

Jai scrabbled in the dirt, his hands coming upon a dead branch rotted off the fallen tree. A flimsy thing, replete with twigs and half-dead leaves.

And then he saw them. Red eyes, shrouded in gloom, deep in the ravine.

'Come, little one,' Jai whispered, his heart hammering in his chest. 'We'll find another way.'

A branch snapped as a shaggy form stepped out of the murk. A spotted, furry, leonine thing, square-headed and pug-nosed. Spotted from snout to tail, with a short mane.

But it was the fangs Jai could not tear his eyes from, those long, yellow sabres on either side of its mouth that gave the beast its name.

A sabretooth. Its face was red as its eyes, caked with dried blood from whatever it had been eating. Jai saw the furred hump on the ground; rotted prey mauled beyond recognition.

This was no lion; lazy cosseted beasts that lived fat off the cultivated quarry of the hunting grounds. It was a tiger. A lone ambush predator, feared across the empire and beyond.

A low rumble resonated from the hollow and seemed to shake Jai's very chest.

Jai's brothers had told him of their sightings in the savannah. Even Titus, with his posse and dozen crossbows, would give these beasts a wide berth.

'Little one,' Jai whispered, wishing he had given his totem a name as he backed away.

He knew not where the dragon's emotions began and his ended. Fear, anger and a fierce protectiveness confused Jai's mind enough that he could do little more than stumble back as a fanged blur lunged out of the ravine, scattering leaves and dirt.

A pink maw flashed, and all Jai could do was brandish his branch, hurled back as a great weight slammed into his chest.

He felt the beast's jaws clamp about his neck, and the metal of his gorget screeched. The sabretooth echoed the sound, its tooth snapping clean away before it reared back in pain.

Jai let out a garbled scream, ramming the flimsy club even as jaws snapped and heaved around it. Hot breath, fetid and coppery, spittled Jai's face. The branch was all that kept the yellow fangs from closing about his throat. The sabretooth snarled and thrashed, insatiable.

Splinters rained down on his face as Jai shoved and kicked, scrabbling back. The beast followed, the fangs inches from his eyes, filling his vision and slashing his brow. He felt the scrape of tooth on bone.

Blood spurted and Jai panicked, screaming mindlessly as he thrust with all his might, earning himself a few inches of respite.

Terror. Pure, unadulterated terror. And . . . a flash of courage. Of *love*.

A blur of white flared above, and the pressure lifted. The beast reared, lifting its paws from either side of Jai long enough for him to see the dragon clinging to its mane, her tail stabbing and darting like a scorpion's sting.

Jai kicked out as it reared again, jack-knifing into a crouch, using the leverage to twist the branch aside, and the slavering tiger with it.

It was enough to allow him to leap back just as the branch snapped, leaving him with a jagged spar.

The tiger rolled and the hatchling scrabbled away, scampering to Jai's side. Together, the pair faced the beast, Jai clutching his broken branch like a short spear.

A gasped breath. Then another, and another. Each a surprise as the sabretooth roared, spinning and snapping at the air.

Jai saw then. Saw its sightless, jellied eyes, where the hatchling had stabbed it blind. The pair waited, frozen, and Jai could practically hear his heartbeat, his pulse twitching his hands.

This battle was not won yet. The tiger prowled, snorting and pawing at its face, blood dripping in the dirt. It snorted at the ground, and only now did Jai see the enormous muscles of its thick neck and forelimbs. Were he not soulbound, he could never have won the battle of strength between them.

Jai took a pace back and a twig snapped. Instantly, the tiger spun toward them and it lowered its head to the ground. Snuffling.

And Jai remembered. Remembered how Leonid told him he

had finished off the lion all those years ago. But that had been a hunting spear. And he . . . he only had a broken branch.

Jai crouched, careless of the noise. Planted the branch's base into the ground, grinding it as deep as he could . . . and screamed. Screamed out his fear, his exhaustion, his self-doubt.

The tiger leaped, so fast Jai hardly believed it. One bound. Two.

Jai hurled himself aside, bundling the hatchling into his chest. Heard the snap of the branch and rolled, rolled, rolled until he came to a stop against the fallen tree's side.

For a moment he dared not open his eyes. Then he heard the whimpering from beyond.

The sabretooth took a step toward him. Then another, and another. It stopped, its entrails tangled in its own legs. For the beast had ripped itself on the jagged spar from belly to tail, disembowelling itself. The branch dangled, buried, half-broken, beneath its tail.

The tiger let out a low moan before collapsing to the ground. It stared sightlessly at Jai, keening and shuddering.

Jai did not wait to watch it die. Only gathered the hatchling into his arms . . . and ran.

Chapter 40

J ai did not know how long he ran. Only when the hatchling wriggled in his grasp did he slow, panting with the horror of what they had encountered.

He leaned against a tree, his chest heaving. He knew the danger was gone, but his body did not. Only a pulse of concern from the dragon slowed his breathing and he closed his eyes, sliding down the trunk, oblivious of the damp of the ground seeping into the seat of his pants.

The hatchling lapped at his brow and Jai lifted a hand. Winced, for the sabretooth had sliced him to the bone.

'Thank you,' Jai whispered. 'My heart.'

He felt something hard and cold tangled beneath his shirt. He tugged it free to find the long, yellow canine of the beast, snapped at the base. Jai let out a relieved gasp, pocketing the trophy.

The dragon mewled and he gathered the hatchling into his arms once more. For a minute they sat, both revelling in their survival.

Jai had never felt more alive.

He had thought he had known terror back in the palace. But

no, that had been dread. A heavy cloud of fear and anticipation, punctuated with moments of misery and horror. This . . . it had been a mindless, unthinking thing. And it had set his soul aflame.

More than anything he felt love, pulsing from the little beast like a heartbeat.

Love.

His whole life, he had never felt loved. Not truly.

His brothers had loved him, true. But it was a love borne of duty. A love unspoken, and little felt.

Yet as the little beast nuzzled into his chest, mewling with concern, he knew it then. It was like a cloak, warming him. Settling his racing heart.

'Would that you could speak,' Jai whispered, lifting the hatchling like a babe, staring into its sapphire eyes. 'For I would tell you how dear you are to me.'

She lapped at his face, letting out a purr of joy.

She knew. Of course she knew. Just as he did.

He scratched beneath her smooth chin and felt the pleasure echo through his soul.

At this moment, he knew not where he began and she ended. *This* was the meld. Spoken of as a burden, an animal intrusion into the mind by so many of the Gryphon Guard. What fools they were.

It was only when he had calmed that the hatchling pulled from his iron grasp. She nipped at his hand and Jai released her, a little surprised.

'What's the rush, little one?' Jai whispered.

And he realised he did not need to hear her response to know the answer.

He closed his eyes.

There was something out there. Something . . . familiar. Calling to her. A primal, unknowable thing that even she did not recognise.

He sensed, rather than felt her scamper away. He stared, and saw her pause, looking back at him.

She let out a yelp. Then she was haring into the forest.

Jai groaned, hauling himself to his feet. And allowed himself a smile.

His totem was a courageous, stubborn little thing.

IT WAS SOME RELIEF when the dragon seemed to slow and Jai felt himself draw nearer. In truth, he too was beginning to slow. He was stronger, true. But not tireless.

And he could sense something strange happening in his mind. A slow draining . . . as if his strength was being stolen somehow.

He stumbled to a stop in a rush of soil and pebbles. The little dragon was moving slowly now. He could feel her ahead of him, stalking something beyond. And Jai could smell something. Something all too familiar.

The scent of blood. Fainter in his own nostrils, but far greater in those of his little companion. It was confused. It had been running towards . . . a friend? A sibling?

The thoughts were so foreign in his mind, it was hard to tell. It mattered little. Jai didn't want to be near anything remotely bloody or dead again for as long as he lived. Whatever the dragon had found . . . they'd best steer clear of it.

'Come on . . .' he hissed beneath his breath. 'We don't have time for this.'

The little hatchling was crawling slowly upon her belly. Approaching something in a clearing ahead. It was ignoring his mental calls for its return completely.

'Cheeky little . . .'

He felt the blade against his skin first. Then the tug of fingers in his hair, yanking his head back to expose his throat.

'Tell me how you found me, or I kill you where you stand.'

Jai recognised the voice. The accent.

The blade pressed close to his throat.

'Frida,' he managed. 'It's . . . me.'

There was a sharp intake of breath and the blade withdrew. 'Jai?'

He was shoved forwards and allowed himself to collapse to his knees. Best not to show his new-found strength.

'Frida,' he whispered, half to himself. 'You made it out.'

He did not turn, instead raising his hands in supplication. After last night . . . who knew what she thought of him.

'You're . . . are you hurt?' she asked. 'You look . . .'

Only now did Jai realise what a horror he must look.

'Oh,' Jai said. 'I'm fine. It's not my blood.'

He was yanked back to his feet by his hair and shoved forward once more. Her sympathy was apparently short-lived.

'Don't turn around,' she hissed. 'I don't trust you.'

Jai sighed and did as he was told. Somewhere ahead, the dragon had heard their words. It was circling back. Jai tried to impress upon it that he was safe, closing his eyes and visualising that distant light . . . but a shove from Frida jarred him from his thoughts.

'Stop there,' Frida said. 'Turn.'

Jai stopped. Turned.

The girl looked dead on her feet. Her face was even paler than her usual complexion, and her eyes were unfocused. She'd clearly been crying, though he'd hardly believe it from the fury behind her eyes.

It was strange to see someone dressed in a fine green dress with hair pinned and braided standing in the underbrush, bloodstained and dirtied. Though he imagined he looked far more bizarre than she.

'Whose blood is it?' she demanded. Jai realised he must look like a living demon, so covered in blood and dirt was he.

He didn't want to lie to her, but he didn't want to tell her about his dragon unless he had to. And he needed her on his side.

'Not mine,' Jai whispered, wincing at the half-truth. 'Leonid's, and others. I hid among the bodies.'

'Is he dead?' Frida demanded.

Jai nodded, unable to look her in the eye.

'Two Sabine emperors for one Dansk king,' she hissed, bitter tears in her eyes. 'Titus paid more than he won.'

Jai shook his head.

'Erica was captured too.'

He didn't mention the many other deaths – of his brothers . . . and their nobility. Frida was no longer listening.

'My . . . she lives?' she asked.

Jai nodded, and she cursed bitterly beneath her breath.

'They'll demand a ransom,' she growled. 'And she'll break under torture, of that I've no doubt. She knows the secret to soulbonding with dragons. Titus will be soulbound to that hatchling soon enough, if he has the strength to survive it.'

Jai closed his eyes and sensed his own hatchling approaching. It was in the bushes, just a few feet from them.

'Come on,' Frida growled, prodding him forward. 'You're going to tell me how you managed to murder a Sabine royal and then escape. This could be another of their tricks.'

Jai felt anger then. It was all he could do to push the emotion away, for the dragon almost leaped in reaction to it.

But for now, she held in place. Out of fear, more than anything. She had seen something ahead that had left her terrified of Frida.

'My brothers are dead,' Jai said through gritted teeth. 'And I've been through hell. So forgive me if I don't stick around to beg your trust. You can follow me if you want. But I'll not stand here to be insulted like this.'

He held his breath and jogged beyond the reach of her blade. Then he stopped.

Because there, in front of him . . . was a second dragon.

Chapter 41

J ai was frozen. He couldn't move. Not in the face of the
pitiful sight that greeted him.

The princess's dragon had been struck with more than a
dozen crossbow bolts, their feathered ends studding its emerald
torso. The wounds were still open and the blood on the ground
had frozen, churned to red slurry with the beast's writhing.

This close, he could not believe its size, for its body stretched
out of sight, into the gloom of the woods. Even the khiro from
the hunt would have been dwarfed by the enormous beast, for
it was as long and wide as two carriages, nose to tail.

How it had reached this far into the woods, Jai didn't know.
What he did know was that it was dying.

Its emerald chest rose and fell so imperceptibly that at first
Jai thought the beast had already passed. Only the movement
of its yellow eyes told him it still lived, and the blood that
bubbled from the nostrils at the end of its long snout. Now he
knew who had escaped upon the dragon's back.

'Jormun flew as far as he could,' Frida whispered behind him.
'But he could take me no further. They will come for him soon.'

She let out a sob and fell to her knees beside the beast.

'Can you heal him?' Jai asked.

Frida traced her fingers along the beast's side and it let out a low, mournful growl.

'I tried, but he's past what I can fix. I've hardly the mana left to ease his pain.'

Jai felt a twinge of guilt, wondering if she had wasted her mana on him too, as Balbir had. But there were too many wounds. No one could heal all of them.

Frida's brow was soaked in sweat. Her body shook, and her hands trembled. It was strange. Why was she suffering like this?

She had not a single injury, or at least not that Jai could see. She was soulbound, so surely the cold was not affecting her. Had she been poisoned, like Ivar?

'No,' Frida whispered, falling to her knees and lifting the beast's horned head into her lap. 'No, please, be strong, my love.'

Jai knelt beside her. He had no words to say. He knew not the bond between this handmaiden and her mistress's dragon.

But she didn't need to go through this alone.

The beast let out a long sigh. Its huge side heaved once and then . . . nothing. It was so still, there in the depths of the forest. Even the wind seemed to have stopped its soughing.

Frida cried out, in a scream of anguish that seemed to never end.

But it was more than that. For as Jai went to offer comfort, such as a hand upon the shoulder could give, Frida collapsed back.

Her eyes stared, unseeing, and her mouth began to foam. Her body contorted and twisted, heels drumming a tattoo upon the ground. Jai could do little more than hold her head away from the soil.

'Frida!' he yelled, lifting her from the ground. Her skin was ice cold.

This was no poisoning. This was something else. Her pupils had expanded to twin dark circles, such that he could hardly see the blue of her irises.

Worst of all was her face. It was a rictus of fear, contorted unnaturally to a silent scream. As if she had seen something horrifying and could not look away.

Then, as swiftly as it had begun, she went limp. Her face returned to some semblance of peace, though it was drawn and haggard.

'Frida,' Jai whispered. He slapped her on the cheek and her head lolled in his lap. 'Frida!'

Nothing. It was only through holding up the empty tinderbox to her nostrils to see the faint steaming of its surface that he knew she was still alive.

Jai tried to understand what had happened. This was too sudden, too close to Jormun's death to be coincidence. There was a chance she had poisoned herself, but Jai knew better now.

Frida was soulbound to Jormun. Not Erica.

Could this mean that the princess was not soulbound? It made a sick sense. Bonding with a beast was dangerous enough at the best of times. Perhaps Ivar had chosen not to risk the life of his only heir for the sake of tradition. Perhaps he had arranged for her handmaid to be bound to the dragon instead.

Whatever the case, the dragon's death had devastated the young woman, both physically and mentally. He had no idea what would happen to her now.

He dared not move her. Not when she was hardly breathing. Instead, he set about building another fire. One that would warm her clammy flesh.

She looked so much smaller than she had before. Fragile even.

Frida's sweat-darkened hair was plastered across her face, and he brushed it clear. Her skin had gone as pallid as his dragon's scales and the shadows of the forest hollowed and harshened the sharp features of her face.

There was a pulse from the thread in his mind. A feeling of . . . concern. He could sense the hatchling's eyes on the back of his neck.

'Come out,' Jai called.

He didn't know why he said it – the dragon could surely not understand speech. But she understood the sentiment behind it, at least to some extent.

Jai heard the patter of feet and a sudden weight upon his shoulders. The hatchling's scales were hot to the touch, like the warm porcelain of a teacup. He leaned his head against her side.

She rumbled happily at his attention and the reverberations relaxed Jai's body, if not his mind. So much had happened, he'd hardly had time to think. What did Frida mean for his plan?

Jai's heart raced. If he was smart, he'd leave this girl here. It would only be a matter of time before the gryphon riders came for her, or indeed for her dragon. He suspected she had only survived this long because most of their beasts were flying to the corners of the empire, notifying rulers, governors and generals of the coming war. That, and the men were raping and murdering their way through half the servants and fettered in Latium – killing any witnesses to the atrocity there.

Legions would be conscripted, borders fortified. And the great monster that was the Sabine Empire on a total war footing was about to wake from its slumber.

Had Frida's dragon not been mortally wounded, and had she been anything other than a handmaid . . . there would be dozens of Gryphon Guard chasing her. Even so, his hatchling had found Jormun and Frida by scent alone. A single acolyte on the hunt for them might find them just as easily.

He should take his hatchling and go. Right now, while nobody was looking for him. He could disappear into the great unwashed of the empire. Keep to the backroads, live off the land.

He could make his way back home.

Instead, he gathered the dragon into his arms and began to look for firewood. Frida had answers he needed. She could teach him what it was to be soulbound, even how to care for his dragon.

In his heart of hearts though, he knew why he did not leave her. He did not have it in him to leave her to die. For had he not almost suffered the same fate, before the little dragon saved him?

He stared at the pale, stricken girl. And hoped she would last the night.

Chapter 42

'Ash,' Jai said.

He paused, then scratched the stubble upon his chin. 'Nah, that's more a boy's name.'

The fire crackled, belying the eerie silence that had settled upon the forest. Dusk was approaching and Jai was distracting himself as best he could.

Twice, he'd almost lost his nerve and left. It shamed him to know that. But it was shame, too, that kept him there. The shame he would feel at leaving Frida alone and helpless, lying motionless by the fire.

Curiosity, too, stayed his feet. He wanted to know more about his hatchling. Right now, every moment was a discovery for the little beast. And every discovery, a joy.

Her tail whipped back and forth as she scampered about and he almost hushed her as she chirred with excitement.

He could feel it with her, as if he were experiencing the world for the first time. The dragon was like a puppy, haring about the clearing, chasing after one scent or another. He chuckled as she leaped and snapped at a passing bug, and failing to catch it, scrabbled at the earth to scarf down a worm.

It was the strangest feeling, to be hungry and full at the same time. To both retch and salivate at the taste of the worm wriggling down his hatchling's gullet.

By now, he had begun to understand their connection better. He could feel it by closing his eyes and returning to that increasingly familiar dream-state.

In his mind's eye, he and the hatchling were two crystalline vessels, floating in an abyss. Twin, distant orbs connected by a powerful thread, one that pulsed back and forth with such frequency that it was at a near-constant hum.

When he allowed his mind to wander, the emotional noise of their connection was near deafening. He could hardly register what was in front of his own eyes when that happened. It took a great deal of focus to filter it out to the bare minimum.

In truth, it was a wonder he'd managed any sleep last night at all, though he supposed when the hatchling had fallen asleep the hum must have died down to a soft murmur. Not to mention that what he'd experienced was more akin to unconsciousness than slumber.

Naming the little thing was his main distraction for that early evening. He'd tried a dozen names, but few seemed to stick.

The dragon was a happy, awkward little thing, true. But when she sat upon her haunches and stared at him with her big blue eyes, there was majesty there. This was a noble beast, and not one that would someday be spoken of as the great dragon 'Snowball'.

There was one name, however, that Jai kept being drawn to. For the dragon was born into it. Melded to him by it. *Winter*. There was a cold, steely beauty in that name.

Winter. That was it.

A soft sob drew Jai from his contemplations.

Frida stirred. Her lids opened, and she looked at Jai with glazed eyes. As if sensing his trepidation, Winter disappeared behind the hump of Jormun's body, peeking between the great spines of its back as the girl sat up.

For the moment, she simply stared into the fire, ignoring Jai completely. Despite her great strength, she looked so fragile in that moment. No . . . broken.

'You're soulbound to Jormun,' Jai said. 'Aren't you?'

The words came unbidden, and he winced at their awkwardness. But if Frida felt the same, she did not show it.

'I felt his death,' she breathed. 'It is . . . unspeakable. I almost thought I would follow him.'

'You were bound to this dragon,' Jai said, pressing a little further. ' . . . Did Titus know he was not marrying a soulbound princess? That Erica's handmaiden was the one who controlled the dragon?'

Frida blinked slowly, then shook her head and staggered to her feet.

'Does it matter, now?' she asked dully. 'Jormun is dead. And so will we be, soon.'

She pulled her dress tighter around her shoulders.

'They'll be racing to find us,' she said. 'If they well-knew the scent of a dragon, we'd be long dead. I should harvest the soulgem now. Destroy it, before they get hold of it.'

Jai frowned.

'Soulgem?' he asked.

Frida nodded towards Jormun's chest.

'When a totem dies, their core dies with them and becomes a soulgem. If one harvests it, it can be used in many ways. An ingredient in pills and potions . . . or consumed directly.'

Her voice was monotone, as if she were a child repeating the words of a tutor from memory. And her words were cryptic too, but Jai absorbed every morsel of information as greedily as Winter had devoured the forest's bugs.

Jai tugged the dagger she had threatened him with earlier free from his belt-loop. It was a pretty thing, made from a strange, pale metal. Little more than a paper-opener, but sharp enough. Having searched her near-empty saddlebags, he knew it was the only blade they had.

'I can do it for you,' Jai offered.

She sniffed and shook her head.

'No. Faster to forge-cut with an iridium blade.'

Frida held out a hand. Jai hesitated, then handed it to her.

He might be soulbound, but Frida was too, and she was trained in the majicking arts. Her beast had died, but he knew that most of her power remained. If she wanted to hurt him, she could, whether he gave her the blade or not.

Her fingers tightened upon the narrow handle of the blade. Soon, there was a hum in the air. And the blade was glowing orange . . . then white.

'I hope I have time,' she whispered, swiftly slicing into the beast's side with a fizzle and hiss. The blade's colour was already fading back to orange, but the girl worked swiftly, sawing a circular hole in its flesh.

Her hand plunged into Jormun's side and withdrew a clenched, red-clotted fist. Before Jai could see what was within, she stuffed it down her bodice, blood and all. She let out a long breath and collapsed back onto her haunches.

'That used most of my mana,' she whispered. 'But at least it's done.'

Now Jai understood the jagged rent in Winter's mother's chest. Magnus must have harvested that soulgem himself.

With this new knowledge, however, came urgency. Magnus would want to get his hands on Jormun's soulgem, not to mention the rest of the Gryphon Guard. The chaos of an unexpected war had given them some breathing room, but the stench of the rotting dragon corpse would bring as many riders as flies.

'Are you strong enough to travel?' Jai asked, getting to his feet.

A soft chirr of excitement came from behind the beast.

Frida leaped up, wild-eyed. She stared down at Winter, who chose that moment to let out a nervous burp.

'By the All-Mother,' Frida gasped.

Chapter 43

Frida turned upon him, her blade raised.

'Who sent you?' she hissed.

Jai backed away, hands raised in supplication.

'I can explain. I—'

'The princess must be dead after all,' she hissed, cutting his words short with an accusatory jab of her dagger. 'You are Titus's creature, sent to learn how to bond with his hatchling. Or . . .'

She stared at Winter, eyes starting in confusion.

'No . . . you must serve those treacherous Nordlanders. How have . . .'

Again, she stopped, staring with panicked breath. Her confusion was palpable.

Behind her, Jai saw Winter bristling, her eyes fixed upon the dagger. Within moments, she would leap.

'No,' Jai whispered to her.

Winter ignored the sentiment and gave a low growl. She was a protective little beast.

Slowly, Jai reached out and pushed Frida's blade down. The knife was blazing hot to the touch, and he winced at it . . . but it was only uncomfortable.

Frida must have noticed, for her eyes widened at the sight.

'You are soulbound,' she whispered. 'You . . . you are a Gryphon Guard?'

Jai shook his head, unable to find the words to explain. Winter, however, was of a different mind. She leaped up, her little claws digging into his tunic, then slid languidly onto his shoulder. She chirruped happily, and Jai knew that it was from gladness that the blade had been lowered.

Frida's mouth gaped, and a choked breath escaped her.

'What is this?' she croaked.

'I'm – uh. *We* are soulbound,' Jai stuttered.

Frida stared, wild-eyed, and Jai could only stumble lamely through his explanation, the carefully rehearsed lines he'd practised earlier immediately forgotten.

'The black dragon . . . it had an egg. And I was freezing to death, and it was warm. So I held it close, you know? I didn't mean to. It just sort of . . . happened.'

The Dansk handmaiden swayed on her feet. Then she burst out laughing. Hysterical gales of laughter.

'You?' she laughed.

It was a mad laughter, one verging on the edge of tears. She slapped at her own face.

'Wake up,' she moaned.

Jai could only stare at his feet. He felt guilty somehow, as if he were a thief.

'I'm sorry,' Jai said. 'It wasn't my choice. Winter . . . she saved me.'

Frida waved away his apology.

'*You've* saved *her* from those Sabine cunts. For now anyway.'

She sniffed. Reached out a hand, ignoring the dragon's growl of protest.

She tutted, and scratched the little beast under her chin. Jai blushed red as he felt waves of pleasure overcome him. Frida caught herself as Jai let out an involuntary grunt, and withdrew her hand.

'Well, you're not lying,' she said. 'You're well melded. And Winter is a good name. Not in the tradition of the Dansk, mind you. Better to have named her for her mother. But it is a good name.'

Winter let out a low rumble at the withdrawal of Frida's hand and attempted to tempt her back with a preening stretch of her neck. No such luck.

'She's a white one,' Frida said, leaning closer. 'Small too. Hatched too early.'

Her misery, at least for now, had been overtaken by curiosity.

'Is white rare?' Jai asked.

Frida chewed her lip and half closed her eyes, as if trying to remember something.

'It is,' was all she managed. 'Most die in their eggs, stillborn.'

Jai nodded, as if this were the most normal thing to be discussing in the world.

'Do their colours matter?' he asked.

Frida shrugged.

'So the tales say. Though I have not seen any differences, and one colour can birth another as easily as not. Jormun . . .'

Her breath caught in her throat.

'Jormun was young, so I cannot be sure. But he never showed any difference from Winter's mother, Lind. And Lind was a black dragon – the most common of them all.'

She sighed.

'The truth is, I don't know. The Dansk royals do not . . . did not keep records like the Gryphon Guard do. There are just stories, and some old letters Ivar gave me. Most, I learned from him, and he was quite content to leave the past where it was.'

Jai cursed under his breath, wishing there was more she could tell him.

'We should move. If they catch wind of a living dragon, they'll hunt us to the farthest reaches of the continent. Titus was practically salivating over his golden hatchling. He'll be glad to add another for his children . . . if any woman would bear that monster's spawn.'

Jai couldn't agree more about leaving. It felt like he'd been trying to do just that for days now. Already, the light was fading, the blue of winter sky beginning to blush darker.

'I'm ready,' he said.

'Let me gather my things,' Frida said, wrinkling her nose.

It took her but a moment to go through her saddlebags, stuffing their contents into a simple sack. Clearly most of the pockets had been emptied for the ceremony.

Jai was almost offended at how little they seemed to have prepared for the betrayal. Had he not warned them? But then, who would have thought Titus would do something so . . . insane? Only he, it seemed.

'You have money?' Jai asked.

They would need it on the road ahead. Especially if Jai wished to purchase any new clothes.

Frida sighed. She was exhausted. 'I didn't think Dansk coin would be worth much in the empire. I've little of value, but this blade. And I'll not part with it. My mother gave it to me.'

Jai frowned.

'She was soulbound too?'

Before Frida could answer, the wind shifted. It was a sudden gust, but one that carried a stench with it. Blood. And the sound of screams, blending with the breeze.

Frida did not wait for him. Did not even stop to put out the fire. Instead, she ran.

She was faster than Jai thought possible. So fast that by the time he had kicked dirt over the fire and turned in pursuit, she was almost out of sight. But worst of all . . . she was running towards it.

Jai made his decision unthinkingly.

He followed, feeling that great joy of running once again.

In running, Jai felt a freedom like no other. He had dreamed of flying. And now, after so many years . . . did he dare hope he might live to do so?

It felt like flying. To feel the wind rushing through his hair, the trees blurring by. Even beneath the great canopy of the forest, Jai could see the winter sky filtering through. He could feel the space of the wide world and revelled in it.

Yet, he could not let himself be distracted by his elation, for already Frida was outpacing him. He could hear the distant crackling of branches where she ran, but it was hard to pinpoint its direction. The world was so *loud*. It was like trying to focus on someone shouting at him from across a crowded room, except the rest of the crowd was clamouring for his attention at the same time.

He slowed after a few minutes, listening.

It was only when Winter leaped from her ride upon his shoulders and led the way that he was able to pick up the pace once more. Apparently, the little hatchling was much more adept at tuning out the onslaught of noise than he was.

And all the while . . . the sounds of battle, and screams, grew louder.

Jai ran, he knew not how long. Only the lengthening rays of the sun gave him any clue, turning from sunset to dark. Yet Winter kept on, unneringly, even as Frida fell out of earshot and the little hatchling was forced to rely on scent alone.

So it was a shock when he near-sprinted into Frida's back.

Again, he could smell that far-too-familiar scent. The copper smell of blood, thick on the wind. But there was more to it now. This was the stench of battle. Of piss- and shit-filled keks, both from the living and the dead. Of fresh-churned mud and blood, body-odour and sweat.

They were near the edge of the forest, though still shrouded in shadow. There had been men here. Many of them. So many that the forest floor had been trampled into near-quagmire.

This was what Titus had hidden in the Black Forest. An entire army.

For that was what it was, out in the fields beyond. A legion, in the midst of battle.

No . . . not a battle. A massacre.

Frida was silent in the face of it all. There was not a sob, nor even a whimper. Only tears, streaming down her drawn face, as she gazed at the great slaughter of her people.

From even the shallow incline and distant view that the treeline afforded them, Jai could well see what fate had befallen the Dansk. His soulbound eyes saw further now, and every colour was as vivid as the murals of Latium's great cathedral. Though in that moment, he wished they were not.

Two legions had trapped the Dansk army. Twin crescents of scarlet-cloaked soldiers, encircling a struggling knot of men at its centre. This was the dreaded manoeuvre that had won Leonid his first battle. The Pincers of Carcinus, as he had called it.

Jai could tell what had happened. Or at least, he could guess. The Sabines had waited until sundown, when the Dansk oft worshipped their All-Mother goddess. They had approached using the cover of the forest and the wheat fields upon either side. Then, as the last light began to fade, the Sabines had fallen upon the praying warriors.

Only one Dansk legion was ever supposed to be near the

palace. This had been a condition of the marriage, or so Leonid had said. For among them was Ivar's personal bodyguard, and with them, the cream of the entire Kingdom's warriors. A show of strength, but one vulnerable to betrayal.

They had been right about that, of course.

On a good day, the best of the Dansk might well have beaten a single Sabine legion. But two? Jai was surprised they had lasted so long. It was testament to Dansk resolve.

'We do not have to stay,' Jai whispered. 'Some things are better known than seen.'

Frida's lips hardly moved, but he heard her nonetheless.

'I watch so that I do not forget.'

He did not begrudge Frida her resolve to watch to the bitter end. Had he not done the same as his own family were slaughtered?

The wind gusted, bringing with it the cries of the murderous and the dying. An unnerving chorus, raised to crescendo. But amid that horrible strain, a soft chirr drew Jai's eyes to Winter.

The dragon was pawing at Frida's dress, and even Jai felt his stomach wrench at a sudden feeling of pity. So strange, to feel the consciousness of another.

For a moment, Frida looked down, numb to the creature's charms. But when Winter leaped into the girl's arms, the hatchling had her.

Frida gathered Winter close to her bosom and pressed her cheek against the dragon's porcelain snout. Then she sobbed gently as the darkness drew in, and the wails began their long, slow journey into silence.

Chapter 44

It was Frida who first spoke when the killing was done. 'We should not linger.'

Her voice was taut and Jai had no desire to argue the point – he'd been feeling that way the moment the sun had sunk behind the horizon.

'Where to?' Jai asked.

Frida said nothing at that. In fact, she seemed to almost shrink at the question, the determination in her fading as fast as it had been summoned. Just like Jai, she'd clearly not thought that far ahead.

Jai got to his feet, trying to square the strange feeling of contentment and warmth with the deep chill. But of course, this was only Winter. She did not know what terrible world she had been born into. She was, in all ways, an innocent.

A desire to protect her came over him, and with it a hint of embarrassment at such a feeling being on display. For it was as if the very centre of his being had been turned inside out, and Winter could not only see it, but feel it, taste it.

This was an intimacy Jai had never shared with another. In fact, the closest relationship he'd had was with Leonid, tragic though that was. And certainly the old man had never known Jai's inner thoughts. Now, they were laid bare.

Winter seemed to be taking the whole thing in stride. But he supposed this was all the little beast had ever known. To have another consciousness in her mind was *normal* to her.

He might have thought that this was the secret to bonding with dragons. To do it while they were still in the egg. But the golden dragon that Titus was supposed to bond with was almost an adolescent, if a comparison to Winter was any indication.

'I don't know,' Frida finally said, breaking her long silence. 'Where were you going before Winter found me?'

Winter stirred at the mention of her name. She was an intelligent little thing, and had already learned that word's meaning. He wondered if she would learn other words. Who knew what the true intelligence of a dragon was? Only Frida, of the two of them.

It was a reminder of why he had hitched his wagon to hers. Now to convince her to do the same.

'I was going to cut across the land,' Jai said. 'Travel through the wilderness. Rejoin my people. I'm sure if you come with me, they will help you return to the Northern Tundra.'

Frida sniffed at that.

'We've raided the Steppefolk almost as much as the Sabines these past years – your people have no love for us. Any tribe that finds us would sooner abandon me to the wilderness than escort me home. Or worse. Bad men live among all peoples.'

Jai thought on this . . . and a realisation hit him so hard, all other thoughts were dashed from his mind. Winter let out a concerned chirp, jarred by the sudden emotion.

'With my brothers dead, I am the last of Rohan's line,' Jai said, his breath coming thick and fast. 'My uncle has held the

throne for Arjun for over a decade. With my brothers gone . . .
I am surely next in line. I can protect you.'

Only now had he truly understood this. For the first time in
his life . . . he was a prince in more than name alone.

Frida crossed her arms, the edge of her lip curling with disdain.
There was a harshness beneath that cold beauty.

'You are the heir to one of a dozen tribes, many of which
have warred for centuries. Who is to say we will come across
your own tribe first? You're more likely to be ransomed to your
uncle, or even the Sabines . . . and I held for ransom.'

Jai's sudden excitement faded at those words. Of course. He'd
not thought things through.

In fact, he knew very little of his people and their politics. It
was a topic Leonid had fastidiously avoided. Frida, it seemed,
knew more of his own people than he did. That was a strange
feeling.

Still. He needed her to come with him. Without her . . . he
realised he knew almost nothing of the world.

'I might say the same of the Dansk for myself,' Jai said. 'A
handmaiden will have little influence at the Dansk court, soulbound or no.'

Frida bit her lip, looking at Jai with a searching gaze. Then
she nodded slowly.

'There is a place, some way north of the Kashmere Road.
Where the far eastern border of the Northern Tundra meets the
western edge of the Great Steppe. The Petrus Mountains protect
that border of the Sabine Empire, and with more direct routes
into both our lands it is unlikely that the war will be fought
there. Not unless Titus thinks himself clever. We can part ways
at the border crossing, and travel to our respective peoples.'

Jai perked up at that.

'That's perfect!' he said.

Frida shook her head and spoke in a low murmur, almost to herself.

'It is a much longer journey, but that is not our greatest problem. There are few passages through the mountains, and most are protected by Sabine fort and garrison. I know traders are allowed through in peacetime, but by now they'll be sealed tighter than a nun's . . .'

She paused at Jai's raised brow.

'. . . palms at prayer. There may be a way through, though, paths that a few can travel where many cannot.'

'How do you know all this?' Jai asked.

'Erica and Ivar have been raiding the empire's borders for years. I picked up a few things, serving them so closely.'

Jai nodded slowly. He was not sure if he'd have made the same choice. Beyond being soulbound, he was of little use to her. But any suspicions of her intentions were blown aside by his fear of being alone. That, and a desire to learn everything he could about his hatchling.

'For now, I can guide us, but I must see the stars to do so. So, we travel by night, rest by day. Less chance of being seen.'

'Agreed,' Jai said. Though, in truth, he was ready to curl up and sleep. Not to spend the night tramping through the forest.

'I have one condition,' Frida said. 'If you disagree, we part ways now.'

Jai set his jaw.

Surely she didn't want . . .

'If you want Winter, you can't have her,' he snapped.

Frida raised her hands.

'I would never ask such a thing, even if it were possible. No, it is a question of time. I cannot waste months travelling by foot across the length and breadth of the empire. My people need me.'

Jai was confused.

'What other choice do we have?' he asked.

Frida let out a bitter laugh.

'The same as everyone else who wants to travel east,' she said. 'We take the Kashmere Road.'

Chapter 45

The ink dripped in the moonlit snow, black spreading like a bruise. Jai poured more into Frida's hair and then averted his eyes, trying not to glance at the soft slope of her bared shoulders.

She'd pulled her dress halfway down so as not to stain it . . . though by this point it was so ripped and ragged, he wasn't sure anyone would notice.

'That's enough,' Frida said. 'Save some for next time.'

Jai shuffled back and let her get on with rubbing it into her tresses. Her pale blonde hair was a dead giveaway for her Dansk origins – rare enough in the empire to catch attention.

She was lucky to have had an inkpot within the pockets of her saddlebags.

Jai had been wary of stopping in a clearing where a passing Gryphon Guard might spot them from above. Especially as they would be even more visible now winter's first real snow had fallen.

But Frida had said she needed to see the stars once more to orient herself before they continued on their journey – one Frida estimated might take them two months.

With the constellations obscured by clouds, she took the opportunity to enact her disguise while there was still melting snow on the ground. Diluting the ink was the only way to make it last.

As he waited, Jai took the opportunity to place Leonid's journal in her sack, as well as the purse, tinderbox, striker and flint. They'd be safer there. Leonid's journal had become even more ragged and bloodstained than before, if that were possible.

Frida had emptied her bag's contents upon a rotting stump, and Jai began to put those away too. A quill, a lead stylus, a water gourd they'd refilled with snow. And a book.

Jai absently flicked through it, wondering what Dansk letters looked like. To his surprise, there was no writing within. Only drawings. Sketches, really.

But they were beautiful. Fragments of what she saw on the wing. An arched window on one page, a bird in flight on another. He saw the palace skyline and the rolling hills beyond.

He looked up, feeling guilty. Glancing at illegible Dansk runes was one thing, but this felt like he'd broken her trust. Luckily Frida was still busy, holding handfuls of hair up to the moonlight to see if her plan was working.

It was a reproachful stare from Winter, perched opposite, that reminded him to close the book. That was a strange thing. He could sense the dragon had no understanding of what he was doing, or *why* it was wrong for him to look. But the guilt was enough for her to make a judgement.

'Who needs a conscience when they've got you, eh, Winter?' he muttered, flipping to the end.

Jai was about to put it away when something caught his eye. A face, taking up one of the last pages that'd been used. He might have ignored it, had he not recognised it.

It was him. Eyes closed, a hunched shoulder blocking most of the view of his swollen jaw.

It was the first time he had seen himself beyond a simple reflection, and she had captured his likeness well.

His long lashes, and the thick brows above them. The fledgling stubble dusting his hollow cheeks, and those full lips that marked him out from the thin-lipped Sabines.

Yet he hardly recognised himself. For he looked . . . peaceful. She must have drawn him when he was sleeping.

Quietly, heart beating fast, Jai replaced the book. It was just as well, because Frida was looking back at him when he looked up once more.

Her plan had worked, somewhat. That pale, lustrous hair was now a dirty grey-black, though in places he could see where the ink had stained her skin. That, and the roots near the scalp were far lighter. It would do at a distance. A shawl might have been a better idea. And her blue eyes were so common among the Dansk, as to give her away to any that might look too closely.

'I'll wait until these clouds clear,' she said, half-wincing at Jai's doubtful expression at the sight of her. 'Then we can keep moving.'

She turned her back on him once more.

Jai only wished it was not snowing. He might be better able to handle the cold, it was true, but the slushy snow had soaked through his fragile shoes until they were hardly worth wearing. There was one advantage in it though, and he took it now.

'I'll be right back,' Jai said.

He hurried into the gloom of the forest, until he was sure Frida could no longer see him. Winter followed. She was curious. And just a touch protective.

Satisfied, Jai stripped off, until he stood barefoot in the snow, holding the stinking bundle of rags that were his clothes.

Jai did the best with what he had, soaking the clothing in the wet slurry of snow, wringing them so tight they almost ripped.

But he was not done yet. It felt like a lifetime since he had been clean, and while the clothes had borne the brunt of the mess, he was still covered in blood and offal from head to toe.

He took a handful of snow and began to rub it on his face. Blood ran down him in rivulets, enough to colour the snow at his feet red from what had been in his hair alone.

Soon he was snatching handfuls of leaves, scrubbing at his body, his hair. Anything to be rid of that foul stench and encrusted blood.

Before long he'd turned that small patch of forest into what looked like the site of a massacre, with a bloodied slurry surrounding him.

Finally, he was able to run his fingers through his hair without tangling them in a clotted clump. To touch his bare skin, rather than a filthy crust.

He felt almost reborn. For a minute, he jumped up and down in the snow, attempting to warm himself. In truth, he did not feel much colder than when he had been clothed. Were it not for Frida, he might well have continued on naked.

He pulled on the trousers alone, leaving the shirt hanging on a branch. The shoes, he hurled into the bushes.

When he returned, Frida allowed him a rare smile.

'You're looking like yourself again,' she said. 'But I think those clothes need to go soon as we can find some fresh ones.'

Jai grinned, glad the tension was finally receding.

'Well, if you ever lose me in these woods, you can smell me out,' he replied.

Frida shook her head, hardly hearing him. Her mind was elsewhere already.

'Come on,' she said. 'We've a few hours of night left.'

Chapter 46

L ucky you,' Frida said. 'Go on. I don't need a soulbound's nose to tell me you need a wash.'

Jai eyed the sluggish green water of the creek they had found and crouched beside it. They had stopped before sunset, taking shelter beneath the ample cover of an ancient weeping willow.

So thick were the trailing branches, it was almost as if they were inside a leaf-walled hut. One with its own private bath in the corner.

'I don't know . . .' he said, dipping in a finger through the crust of ice at its edge. 'Could be danger—'

Water sprayed his face as Winter took a running dive. Jai spluttered, wiping his face as Frida let out a rare laugh.

'Don't be so prissy,' she said, the edge of her lip twitching. 'In with you. I'll boil some water and see what I can scrounge up for us to eat.'

Jai watched as Winter carved a languid circle, swimming in the algae at the water's edge, the pale porcelain of her scales and turquoise of her eyes stark and beautiful against the vivid green.

She gazed at him and let out a trill of displeasure at his hesitation.

'Scared of ruining your fine garments?' Frida asked, bemused. 'Don't worry, I'm sure it'll come out in the wash.'

One companion teasing him was bad enough. Two was just humiliating.

Jai leaped in, knees clutched to his chest. He let himself sink to the bottom as he adjusted to the winter-chilled water, revelling in the cool against his skin. He grasped the weeds on the creek bed and opened his eyes to a green-tinged world.

Before, the shock of cold would have been almost painful. Now, it was just a fact. His newly soulbound body could handle it.

In the cool dark world of the creek bed, Jai stared up at the surface. It was so peaceful down here. Another world. Silent and safe.

He was cocooned in the fronds of an underwater garden, where silver fish darted in shoals like starlings flocking above the palace skies.

Seconds ticked by and Jai watched in wonder as Winter glided through the water, her tail undulating, small wings pulsing. She circled around and around him, her joy so palpable Jai almost wanted to cry at the thrill of it.

She was flying. Almost.

A minute must have passed by already, yet Jai felt no need to rise to the surface. Nor did he wish to, for the glacial water was sloughing the filth from him like a second skin. He twisted nimbly in the water. He felt . . . reborn. Restored by the wild waters at the edge of civilisation.

As another minute passed, and then another, Jai was only just beginning to feel any strain in his lungs. So that was something else new. Soulbonding. What other tricks was it hiding? Elation sparked in him.

And then . . . it happened. A cramp, deep in his chest. Like a fist had seized his heart.

Winter released a stream of bubbles in alarm as Jai felt his body convulse, toppling him face first into the silt bed. For a moment, he thought he had been poisoned. He choked out a gout of bubbles that streamed to the surface.

Then black liquid erupted from his mouth, clouding the water dark. His skin burned, as more spewed from his pores, caustic and hot.

Jai's inner world opened unbidden. And . . . he could *see*.

See the pathways of his body, pulsating. Dark grime that clung to every part of him, pushed out by seeping, golden light.

And then, just like that, it was over. Jai kicked up to the surface. This . . . this was something new.

Jai erupted from the water, letting out a whoop after a long, gasped breath. At the creek's edge, Winter spun in a tight circle, chirping happily at his return. He breathed hard, sweeping algae from his arms and shaking his head.

'She's a natural,' Frida said, hardly looking up from the fire she'd set. Only moments had passed, and she had noticed nothing above the surface. 'Look what she brought for us.'

Jai stared as she dangled a half-eaten fish up for him to see.

'She left us the head,' she said. 'I'm going to roast it.'

The normalcy of it all was too much. Jai made a face, and she snorted.

'Take it as a high compliment from a hatchling. A dragon gives you liver, kidneys, head or heart, you've done something right. Or any hunter for that matter. You Sabines eat the muscle of your animals, throw away the best parts. To us, that is madness.'

Jai felt the joy and surprises of his swim receding, and the dark dread of his reality begin to seep back.

'Call me a Sabine again, it's the last you'll see of me,' Jai muttered.

He looked away from her and gathered Winter up into his arms. She mewled, sensing the sudden change in mood. A wet, fishy tongue lapped at his face, and he groaned, dropping her like a bag of hot sick.

It was then that he saw, as he half-turned back toward the fire. Saw Frida's haggard face, and the bitter anger in her eyes.

She was not his enemy. The Sabines were. He could forgive her a slip of the tongue.

'I am sorry,' she whispered, so quiet only his soulbound ears could hear it.

Jai urged Winter to Frida, and allowed himself a smile as the girl fussed over the little beast. It was hard to separate out the little dragon's adoration of her from his own confused feelings.

He cleared his throat and approached Frida's small fire. She had even dragged over a pair of old logs while he had been underwater, and he sat down heavily, staring into the flames.

For a moment all was silent, but for the crackle of flame and trickle of water. Then a yawn from Winter broke the silence.

'You must know a lot about dragons,' Jai said.

Frida sniffed, her head turned away from him.

'Did . . . how did you bond with your dragon?'

'Jormun,' Frida muttered.

'Sorry. Jormun,' Jai said.

Frida stared into the flames, and only now did Jai see the furrows past tears had made in the dirt on her face – she must have been crying earlier. She made a forlorn figure in that ragged, emerald dress.

'My mother . . . she was the one who knew dragons. Better than anyone. When she passed – unexpectedly – most of her knowledge left with her. I had so much more to learn.'

She paused to sniff, but Jai did not speak. She was thinking. Weighing him.

'In my culture, any of noble blood may petition the king to attempt a bond with a dragon. I will not tell you of my parentage, or my family line, lest we be captured – they can ill afford a ransom, especially now we are at war.'

Jai nodded along, trying not to let his eagerness show.

'Few make the attempt, for it is dangerous, more so, even, than for a Gryphon Guard's squire to bond with a chick. And we must do it alone, according to tradition, usually before a boy's voice breaks; before a girl has shown her first blood. Which means if we fail . . . we die.'

Even Winter, it seemed, was listening intently, though Jai knew she was only mirroring him. She too was still struggling to parse their shared emotions.

'King Ivar would not let the princess take such a risk, for he has but one daughter. *Had*.'

She set her teeth and shook her head like a dog as if to rattle away the grief.

'When Queen Astrid passed, Ivar swore he would never take another wife. So if Erica died in the act of soulbonding . . . his line would end. Many times, she tried to sneak out and attempt it herself. Once, she even made it to the nesting grounds, high in the mountains. But I followed her.'

Frida finally smiled, as if remembering a fond memory. He had seen that same look on Leonid's face, many times.

'Erica could not live with the shame of it. So I was assigned to her. That way she could ride, as her ancestors had. She could be loved by her people.'

She fell silent. Whatever had precipitated the sudden rush of confessions, it had been replaced by grief once more.

'How?' Jai asked.

Frida looked up at him.

'How did I soulbond?'

Frida gave him a level gaze. Then put her head in her hands.

'The Dansk have hidden the secret to bonding with dragons for centuries. You think I would tell you, deep in the territory of our greatest enemy? Where we might be captured at any minute? A trained soulbound can withstand torture. But you . . . you'd give it away in a second.'

Jai bristled a little at that, though she was probably right.

'Can I guess then?' he said. 'I near-froze to death, back there. And your folk, they come from a land of near-perpetual winter. The two are connected.'

Frida glanced at him, then let her head fall.

In the soft glow of the firelight, she looked lovely. Jai found it hard not to stare as she pursed her pink lips, and her eyes almost seemed to glow blue as they flicked up to seize his gaze.

'You know it, and now the Sabines do too. The princess will tell them, when their torturers get to work. The secret is out.'

She prodded at the flames with a stick, her face dark at the mention of her imprisoned mistress.

'Will you bond with another beast?' Jai asked. 'Perhaps it is wise, with—'

Frida's gaze snapped to him and he saw anger in her eyes.

'How could you ask me such a thing?' she said, her voice bitter.

Jai held up his hands.

'I am sorry,' he said. 'This is all new to me.'

'Happy now?' Frida asked. 'That you know our secret?'

Jai shrugged.

'It won't do me any good, I'm not going to bond with another dragon. Are there even many more left to bond with?'

Frida's face grew even darker.

'There are but a few dozen dragons left, and fewer still of an age to be bonded with. With the death of Jormun and Lind, none of the Dansk's dragon totems remain fertile – there are but two others. Dragons are a dying race, much as we try to help them.'

Jai felt great sadness at that.

'How is that possible?' Jai asked. 'How can these dragon totems be so old as to be infertile, if they must be bonded with as hatchlings.'

Frida raised an eyebrow at that. Almost as if she were impressed.

'There is an exception,' she said. 'If a dragon has bonded with a person before, they may bond more easily with the next. And dragons live for over a hundred years. Lind herself once belonged to Ivar's mother, and her father before her. Hatchlings . . . are rare – a dragon might hold a clutch of eggs in their belly for a decade before laying them, but few of those hatch. The age of dragons is passing.'

Jai sucked in the knowledge, wishing he had paper to write this all down in. Nothing in Leonid's journals had ever hinted at this. In fact, they hardly ever mentioned dragons – a product of never invading the Dansk Kingdom.

'Your gift to Titus. It truly was worth a kingdom's dowry.'

'And a golden dragon at that. We haven't seen one of those in even my mother's time. My god, if I hadn't loved Jormun so, I might have begged for him to be mine. When full-grown, he could take on five gryphons in the skies and win. Jormun, he could just about handle three.'

'Is it his colour that makes him so special?' Jai asked.

'It is said the golden dragons are almost twice as large as the rest, and he is a prime specimen, thick of bone and scale, proportioned perfectly. While Winter, lovely as she is . . . well, a white dragon's rarer than a golden one, but she's a runt, there's no sugar-coating it.'

She wiggled her fingers at Winter, who yapped excitedly at her.

'Who's a little runt,' she cooed. 'You are. You are!'

Jai let Winter scamper over to her, and ignored the smug look on the dragon's face as Frida clutched the little dragon to her chest.

He'd let the two have each other, this night.

Chapter 47

With daylight came a welcome warmth, but they pushed on despite their exhaustion. Both he and Frida were desperately hungry, and sleeping on an empty belly seemed impossible.

It was a relief when they reached the border of the forest and emerged into an expansive field of harvested corn.

'What is this?' Frida asked.

She pulled down the stalk of a corn plant with its fruit – one of the few cobs the farmer must have missed, since harvest was weeks since – eyeing the hairy, yellow kernels with suspicion. It was old and had almost gone to seed, but right now it looked like the most delicious thing he had ever seen.

'Hello?'

Jai caught the furrowing of her perfect brows and remembered that hardly anything grew on the Northern Tundra.

'It's corn,' Jai explained. 'The number of these I had to peel in the kitchens when Leonid wanted to punish me . . . you pull the leaves off like this, till you're left with just the yellow.'

Jai demonstrated, fascinated at the look of wonder on her face. She snatched it from him and bit into it, tearing off a hard chunk. She chewed . . . once. Then sputtered, pawing at her tongue. Jai had to resist the urge to laugh at her crestfallen face.

'Yes, I should have said, we usually boil it and eat it with butter, but . . . we'll probably have to roast this one.'

Frida sniffed.

'Rabbit food.'

Jai ignored her, instead reaching into their bag and pulling out his fire making kit. He'd gathered some tinder earlier, stuffing a fluffy-headed flower known as 'old man's beard' into his pocket. Balbir had taught him that one.

Frida looked almost impressed as he crouched on the ground, striking his flint upon the steel to dash sparks into the clumped tinder.

No . . . not impressed. Bemused.

Because after Jai had spent a good minute swearing at the small pile, attempting to light it, a jet of flame spurted over his shoulder.

Frida gave him a smile and wiggled her fingers.

'Forgot, did you?'

'OK, you *have* to teach me how to do that.'

Frida shook her head and gave Jai an only *slightly* condescending pat upon his shoulder.

'You can't do that yet. It takes practice. You might manage a spark – hardly an advantage should we be caught.'

Jai grumbled under his breath and added some twigs to his fledgling fire.

'Couldn't you have helped me out?' he asked Winter.

The little dragon had spent the last part of the journey napping around his shoulders, her smooth, porcelain head tucked beneath Jai's chin. Now, she plopped to the ground and stretched.

'Too early for that too,' Frida said. 'If she can at all. Some dragons never manage to breathe fire. And it'll be a while yet until she flies, too.'

Jai groaned at those words.

This soulbound thing isn't all it's cracked up to be.

'See, I need to know this stuff,' Jai said. 'Is there *any* majicking you can teach me?'

This was what Jai had been hoping they would have discussed already – but they had hardly spoken that day. The Dansk handmaiden was not the most conversational of people. But then, she had just lost so much, she would hardly be in the mood for small talk. And he supposed Frida spent a lot of time observing the princess's activities silently, watching over her mistress.

At his words, Frida appraised him with a reluctant gaze, before nodding slowly.

'There might be something,' she said. 'But only after we've eaten.'

JAI HAD ENJOYED LEARNING the limits of his new body, finding that he could maintain a fast jog for most of the morning with only a few breaks. Frida, on the other hand, had to slow down for him. She was faster and stronger than him, that was for sure. Perhaps it was something to do with being 'ascended'.

He'd heard the term once or twice, when serving drinks to squires, but knew little else about it.

Their meal, if six ears of poorly cooked corn could be described as such, was over.

Now, in a flattened patch of their own making in the midst of a cornfield, Frida had him sat cross-legged on the ground before her.

'Gather Winter into your arms,' she said. 'You must touch. Without her, soulbreathing is far harder, and slower. Few can advance on the path without it.'

Soulbreathing. Jai's heart beat a little faster at the word.

'The path?' Jai asked.

'Do you truly know so little of the soulbound?' she asked. 'What of your Gryphon Guard? Do they hide their practices so closely?'

Jai nodded.

'I've read every book on Leonid's shelves, but few go into the details of the Gryphon Guard. He even had his journals rewritten to remove their names.'

He sighed ruefully, then hurried on as Frida chewed an impatient lip.

'Leonid claimed to have used them primarily as scouts and messengers. It's almost like he didn't want them to take the credit for his success. But their great tower tells a different story.'

Frida nodded politely, but he could see that was not what she meant. She spoke slowly as if to a child. 'What we call the path is the progression of a soulbound through their stages of power. Right now, you are probably a first level soulbound, also known as the *body-cleansing stage.*'

Jai glanced down at his soiled clothing.

'Yeah, might not be the best time to do that.'

Frida snapped her fingers to get his attention again.

'No, not the outside of your body. The inside.'

Now Jai was really confused.

'Surely by now your body has begun to eject the impurities within?'

Jai was struck by realisation. Of course. This was what must have happened underwater. The black liquid.

'What . . . is it?' Jai asked.

'Corruption,' Frida's voice said. 'We are all born with it, and it grows as we age. It is in the air we breathe, the food we eat. Only the mana of a soulbound is able to remove it.'

Jai could think of nothing to say. This was news to him.

'It is said that the soulbound are more beautiful. This is why,' Frida said. 'Your eyesight will improve, your skin become unblemished, and you will become stronger. Some of it would have been cleansed when you bonded with Winter – perhaps you did not notice, filthy as you were. By now, you'll have expelled much of the rest.'

Jai let out a breath, glad that the worst of it was over. It had not been . . . pleasant.

'I think I am done with that now,' Jai said.

'Then you are a second level soulbound, or close enough.'

'Level . . .' Jai said, leaving the unasked question hanging in the air. He had an idea of what it meant, for he had heard the term used when he had served the Gryphon Guard. But no more than that.

Frida raised a brow.

'I suppose you'd have no reason to know. I will teach you. For Winter's sake.'

Jai felt his blood flush to his cheeks. Was he not worthy of a lesson otherwise, after all he had done for her? Only his curiosity, and pity, held his tongue.

'Levels are shorthand for how powerful a soulbound you are, and how far you've progressed along the path. A third level soulbound is more powerful than a second level soulbound. Simple enough?'

'Right,' Jai said.

'You've passed the first level – body cleansing. That means your body is in peak condition. You'll be stronger, faster and have better senses than before. You will heal more quickly, and never need a seeing-glass in your lifetime. But you'll not have the true strength and speed of a soulbound without using mana constantly. Only when you ascend will your strength and speed be permanent – using mana only to enhance it further.'

Jai cocked his head, listening intently.

'At the second level, you'll be using mana automatically. Your core will send mana where it thinks it is needed, and it will enhance your strength and senses. Fun while it lasts, but not much use when you run out.'

Jai remembered the initial hours of when he had first bonded to Winter. How fast he'd run, how powerful his senses had been.

'You have to learn to stop your body from using it all up. It is not something easily taught. When you learn how to seal your core and use mana only when you wish to . . . that's when you reach the third level.'

'How do I reach the fourth?' Jai asked.

Frida pursed her lips, thinking.

'That is when you ascend. Right now, your core is but a small kernel. You must expand it so that it can store more than just a thimbleful of mana. By filling it to its limit and then pushing beyond it, you will stretch your core. It is painful, but necessary.'

She frowned as if remembering her own experiences doing the same.

'Once it doubles in size, the walls will thicken until they are opaque. Only then will your body ascend. The first true mark of a soulbound, though still very early on the path.'

Jai nodded slowly. He knew that the acolytes of the Gryphon Guard only became squires when they had ascended.

It was strange, for the goal of ascending seemed so distant. And yet, it was but the first real step to becoming a soulbound warrior.

'I can't wait,' Jai whispered.

Frida let out a small chuckle.

'Sorry,' she said, and Jai saw her smile for perhaps the third time since they had met. 'I just . . . I thought you would know more. If Ivar knew what had become of his prized dragon's egg, he'd laugh so har—'

She stopped, catching herself. Her smile faded and she cast her eyes downwards.

It was easy to forget it was not just her dragon she mourned, but her king, and the flower of the Dansk nobility.

Jai could see that, even in her grief, Frida was enjoying the lesson. He supposed having to pretend her dragon belonged to Erica meant she didn't get to discuss it often.

And Jai had more questions.

'So how long until I can ascend?' Jai asked.

Frida had the decency to hold back a laugh, though not quite enough to hide the fact she had from Jai.

'Eager one, aren't you? You should bide your time. It's a dangerous thing. You must never try to ascend alone, lest you swallow your tongue, or bite so hard you shatter your teeth. It is a brutal, painful thing. Not everyone survives the process.'

'Well, then at least I should learn to soulbreathe. Surely we will move faster if I can replenish my mana.'

Frida looked beyond the cornfield, apparently eager to move on. Then she nodded.

'You're right. You'll run out of mana soon if you don't.'

Jai called out to Winter and she came scampering over to him, chirring with the excitement she sensed from him. He gathered her into his arms, pressing her to his chest, feeling the cool scales like a balm there.

'Close your eyes,' Frida said, with only a hint of impatience. 'You'll find it easier that way.'

He did so, and instinctively he knew to seek out that strange, introspective state.

'Breathe slowly,' Frida said. 'Listen only to the sound of my voice. Look within and seek out the light.'

He took several deep breaths, letting any fleeting thoughts and worries fade away. In his mind's eye, he could see the light, cutting through the recesses of his mind like a miniature sun.

'I see my core,' Jai said.

Frida's voice sounded distant as she spoke once more. And slow too . . . her words dragging ever so slightly, echoing faintly through his mind.

'That's good. Faster than most. Some take many days to unlock their mind and see their inner existence.'

Jai felt a little smug at that, but then instantly lost sight of it. He grunted and furrowed his brow. Seized the perspective once more.

So much for that.

'When the soulbond happens, both your soul and your beast's become hollow. Their interior unravelled to form the thread that connects you, making room for the mana to pool within. Your core is part of your soul. Protect it, for it is a fragile thing.'

Jai focused closer, seeing the vessel's crystalline structure and that glowing, pure liquid within. He could not be sure, but it seemed that the amount had dropped quite substantially since he had last seen it.

Mana.

Of course! That was what the liquid was.

'Now, look closer. See the darkness, not the light.'

Jai did as she said. Stared out into the black abyss that surrounded his core.

Only, it was not an abyss. As he looked closer, he could see that the core was deep within an amorphous black chamber. And there was a flow there. A rhythmic ebb and pulse, like the beating of a heart.

No . . . it *was* his heart. He could see the great arteries, black tunnels against dark walls. He was seeing his organs. His core was at the very centre of his heart.

Of course.

He let his mind expand, as if looking from a great height. Now, he could see the warren of conduits beyond the organs.

'I see . . . passages,' he said. 'Hundreds of them.'

'Those are your channels. Ghostly passages, ones that follow the same path as your blood. It is through these channels that the mana must pass, and be filtered, until it reaches your core.'

'How?' Jai asked.

'You have looked within. Now, look without.'

It took Jai a few minutes to expand his consciousness. To see beyond the dark confines of his body to the bright world beyond.

This world was not one of cornfields, silver skies and winter sunlight. No, it was an ocean. An ocean of tiny stars.

'See the mana flowing. It is in the air, in the earth. It is everywhere. It comes from all life. Even you and me.'

He saw it. Currents, eddies and great drifts of mana, floating like a fine, glittering dust. He could almost sense it flowing around Winter and Frida, their outlines silhouetted amid the tumult.

And Winter, dear Winter, was surrounded by the stuff, a golden aura that swirled about her. Mana, drawn slowly into her. A totem indeed.

'You must soulbreathe, Jai,' Frida whispered. 'As only the soulbound can. Breathe. Let your lungs fill like a longship's sails.'

Jai gulped in a great breath of air, and now he *felt* that golden dust enter him. Percolating inside him, settling upon the inner walls of his being.

'Let the vacuum of your core pull the mana through.'

Jai had no idea what that meant.

'Draw it in,' Frida said urgently. 'Force it if you have to. Push it into your core . . . gently.'

Jai returned to his heart's chamber. There was his core, floating, a thin thread stretching from its side to another, distant light. One that could be seen passing through the walls of his being.

'Your core,' Frida reminded him, her voice gentle. 'Look to your core.'

Jai *looked*.

His core was part of *him*. More him than the rest of his body. He could feel it, much as he might feel the nose on his face.

Now . . . he breathed in . . . with his core.

It was agony. There was pressure pulling on his heart, as if his entire inner mind had squeezed like a fist.

And in his lungs . . . the mana passed through. Sluggishly, into the thin network of capillaries, turning from gas to liquid. The golden, fluid light washed through the channels, dissolving the last remnants of the gunk that had once resided there.

It was like cool, crystal-clear water down a parched throat. Smoothing, cleansing, dissolving. It was . . . clean. Almost a relief, as if he had cleared a blocked nose.

Jai watched as the first motes of mana reached his core, seeing one alight on its surface. And down that golden cord that connected him to his totem, more still pulsed through, trickling into his core like a spring.

He could feel Winter's mind so clearly. It was beautiful. Innocent. He wished he could reach out and touch her. Even as he felt the agony of soulbreathing, he sent her all the love in his heart. And felt it returned twice over.

And then, Winter shifted, nuzzling closer to his chest. It was enough to break the trance, snapping Jai back to the dark behind his eyelids.

Jai opened his eyes and let out a long breath.

'Feel good?' Frida said.

Jai sighed. He did, but there was something bothering him. He felt . . . sticky.

'What is . . .' he began.

Only to see black upon his skin. Little spots of it, seeping from his pores. He sniffed at it and was glad he could detect no odour.

'For you, that was probably the last of it.'

Jai grunted.

'It's a wonder the soulbound are not known for their stink.'

'Why do you think the Gryphon Guard have that pool up there? Their acolytes bathe themselves after they cleanse their channels. It takes a few weeks with a chamrosh, as they're weaker than dragons and gryphons.'

'Why do I have any mana at all?' Jai asked. 'I never soul-breathed before.'

'When you and Winter bonded, she gave some of her mana to you. Every time you use strength or speed beyond what your cleansed muscles can achieve, it saps a little of what you have. When it is gone, you will be stronger than you were before because of your cleansed body, but not by nearly as much.'

Jai gritted his teeth, annoyed at himself. How had he used so much?

'You can't have much left. You should be careful, using it so liberally.'

'What?' Jai spluttered.

Frida gestured at him.

'You've been running non-stop, with almost no food or sleep for . . . two days now? You think that doesn't come with a cost to your mana? You'll be lucky if Winter has much left to give you either. A beast's mana comes in a slow, constant trickle, without cultivating directly. They rarely have enough to spare.'

Jai grimaced, then gathered Winter into his arms and hugged the beast to his chest. She was a wonder, sure enough.

'How am I going to soulbreathe when we hardly ever stop for a break?'

Frida shrugged.

'We'll figure it out. For now, we need to get to the Kashmere Road.'

Chapter 48

The great causeway that cut through the heart of the empire and on into the mysterious Phoenix Empire was easy enough to find. Almost every path lead to it, one way or another.

By now, they had traversed far enough from the palace to relax a little – the Gryphon Guard would likely be searching the woods and fields, not the road. Even so, Jai was still wary of being seen by anyone.

They might no longer be hunted as an escaped prince and handmaiden. But as Dansk and Steppeman . . . they would still be under suspicion, given the state of war between their peoples and the Sabine Empire.

Now, as the sun neared the end of its journey toward the horizon, they peered over a ridge to where a gentle, grassy slope led to the cobbled double-wide carriageway. Donkey-drawn carts, hand-pulled rickshaws and a smattering of walkers peppered the way, and there was no chance of travelling far without encountering someone, as Jai had hoped.

On either side of the road were cornfields, brambles, and rocky, uneven slopes. Jai knew they could not simply skirt its edges on foot, for they would be slowed significantly . . . and they were likely to garner even more suspicion if they were spotted doing so. Somehow fighting their way through thorny bushes in the dark of night did not seem faster either.

'What now,' Jai said. 'Soon as I'm on that road, they'll spot me. No doubt we'll make a suspicious pair.'

Frida regarded him thoughtfully – looking up then down.

'You're not a full Steppeman. You've a different look about you. A hint of the steppe, it's true. But to those who don't know better, you might look like a man of mixed parentage from another region. Perhaps the Nambian desert?'

Jai bit his lip. It was true that he was not always assumed a Steppeman – it was only the rarity of he and his brothers as 'free' Steppefolk in Latium that made him stand out. Beyond the occasional servant and fettered, most of the city's inhabitants were Sabines. Only the visiting merchants were an exception, and these stayed in the plaza markets – they never set foot on palace grounds.

As he eyed the passers-by upon the road, few were typical ruddy Sabines. Some even had the black-toned skin of the Shambalai region, from the far southern reaches of the empire.

'You may be right,' Jai said. 'I don't have their accent, nor do I grow my hair out and plait it, as Steppefolk do.'

'If they ask, we'll tell them you're half-Nambian,' Frida said. 'You'll be fine.'

'And what of you?' Jai asked.

Frida pointed at her hair, giving Jai a face that said 'Isn't it obvious?' Jai rolled his eyes in response.

'You'd better make a shawl,' he said. 'Your hair looks like someone poured lamp oil on your head.'

Frida bristled, but Jai ploughed on regardless.

'Have you *looked* in a mirror?'

The bristling eased back a notch.

'And maybe keep your eyes lowered,' he said. 'I could spot that blue a mile away.'

Frida's lips twitched at that, though Jai struggled to read her expression. But she did as he asked, ripping a wide swathe from the bottom of her dress as if it was so much rice paper, and wrapping it about her head.

'Anything else?' she asked.

Jai shrugged.

'Oh, you know. Just the *dragon* we've got with us.'

Frida's eyes widened – as if she'd forgotten how unusual a sight Winter would be.

'She'll have to follow us by the wayside until we can buy something to hide her in. She's fast enough to keep up.'

Jai thought for a moment, then nodded. They had no other choice.

He turned to the little beast and picked her up in his hands. She chirred and attempted to sniff his face.

'Now you listen, girl. We need you to follow us . . . but you can't be seen. Like you're hunting a squirrel, right?'

As he spoke, he tried to relay the meaning of his words to Winter. He needn't have worried though. The little beast was swift to wriggle free, scampering down the cliffside, sniffing for prey. She was hungry too, for she'd turned her nose up at the corn, though Frida had confirmed dragons did eat food other than meat . . . in a pinch.

Jai was sure she'd understood. Pretty sure anyway.

Now was the moment Jai had been dreading. There was no time to hesitate, for Frida was already trundling down the slope to the windswept road.

None of the other folk even gave them a second glance. They kept their eyes on the road, trudging ever onwards. A haycart trundled past, the donkey at its head turning its head as it passed them. Its driver did the same. A matronly woman, who pinched the tip of her nose.

Hitching a ride was going to be harder than he'd thought. Or at least, until he didn't look like a dirty, barefoot vagrant.

'So, Jai,' Frida said, apparently having the same idea. 'We've a long journey ahead, Kashmere Road or no. I don't think ragged trousers and bare feet will cut it, do you?'

Jai grimaced.

'I doubt a trader will stop for us,' he said.

Frida nodded slowly, her eyes darting left and right. Her nonchalant air had dissolved in the face of so many passers-by.

He noticed something strange, then. A man had overtaken them. This wasn't *that* unusual – they weren't travelling fast and had kept their pace only to a brisk walk.

But he was a hunched, decrepit man. And there was nothing significant in sight ahead. What was he heading towards?

Jai craned his neck, wondering if perhaps he was attempting to beg a lift from the cart. Yet, the man kept turning his head, looking behind him.

Now another party overtook them, this time an entire family, clutching each other's hands. Jai turned. Stared.

'We'd better hurry,' Jai whispered. 'Don't want to be caught up by that lot.'

Frida turned. Her eyes widened at the dustcloud upon the horizon, and the shining, scarlet cloaked men at its head. The legions were on the march.

Chapter 49

The Kashmere Road was peppered with more villages than could be named on a single map.

Frida and Jai had reached their first: a little village known as Elvetham, and now stood at its gates, glad to have reached it before sundown. While they planned to travel at night, the hunger in their bellies was taking its toll and they'd agreed to spend one night in a rented room, with food. Jai hoped he had coin enough for it.

The legions travelling behind them had already stopped to make camp, so they were safe for now. They just had to set off again at the break of dawn.

'State yer business,' a voice said.

Jai turned to see a grizzled gate guard, one far past his prime. He was so old that he leaned upon the spear he carried, and the armour was so rusted that Jai wouldn't have been surprised to learn he was a veteran of Leonid's wars.

'Room and board for the night, and new clothing,' Jai said, realising it was their strange appearance that had drawn his attention. 'We were waylaid on our travels by bandits.'

The guard scratched his stubbled chin, looking at them with

mild curiosity. Jai could have been any vagrant walking the way, begging for alms. But Frida, in her ripped green dress, looked an easy mark.

'Ain't many bandits on this part o' the road,' he said. 'Not when there's a legion so close by.'

Frida flashed the old man a smile and touched him softly upon his mailed elbow.

'We stopped for a picnic and left the trail. Why, if only you'd been there to protect us.'

The old man perked up at that and returned her smile with a snaggletoothed grin.

'Sorry t'tell yer, the Manticore's full tonight,' he said. 'There's more'n enough folk on the road these days. Trouble's a' brewin' yonder. Few want to be caught in it.'

Jai cursed under his breath. The dream of a hot bath and actual food in his belly was fading fast.

'They'll not let you in like that, anyways,' the man said, before hawking and spitting off to the side. 'Now . . . 'ave you money?'

Jai considered this.

'Some,' he ventured.

'I'll give ye a shirt,' the man said. 'One *denarius*.'

Jai hesitated, and the man spat again and began to wander off.

'You've a deal,' Jai said.

The old man turned, a grin upon his face.

''Av it then,' he said.

He yanked the mail over his head, then his own shirt. It was a rough, homespun thing, made of sackcloth. But Jai took it gratefully, if only to curb the pitying glances of every person that walked by. He'd rather none look at them at all.

The guardsman replaced his mail and began to wander away the moment Jai fished into his purse and allowed him to snatch the silver coin.

'Sir,' Jai called out. 'If the Manticore is full, is there another tavern or inn that might have room?'

The man turned reluctantly, as if eager to be away. Jai was beginning to suspect he'd overpaid for it, and the man was worried Jai was going to realise that fact.

'There's another place a half-day's walk down the road, but it'll be morn afore you reach it. But if you leave the road, there's a couple places. Same owner o' this one.'

'Can you . . .'

But the old man had hurried off. The pair stood there for a moment and then Jai pulled the shirt over his head. Despite his bare feet, he was beginning to feel human again.

'You reckon I paid too much for this?' Jai asked.

Frida shrugged.

'You're asking me? I've never even touched a Sabine coin. Do you think you did?'

Jai winced and admitted something that until that very moment, he hadn't realised was strange.

'That was the first purchase I've ever made,' he said.

Frida stared at him, horrified.

'What?'

'The palace treasurer deals with it all. If Leonid needed something, he just called for it and it would come. If I needed something . . . well, he'd do the same. But he didn't think I needed much.'

Frida prodded his purse, still clutched tightly in his fist.

'So where did this come from?'

Jai sighed.

'They're coins I found over the years. Mostly when I scrubbed the floors of the mess hall, or went on an errand. I don't even know how much I've got.'

He pawed through the bag's contents, counting them. Frida

looked on, curious. Somehow, this was supposed to last them all the way to the edge of the empire. And he'd just traded away his most valuable coin for a shirt on his back.

'I've got ten *semis,* three copper *as* and one *sesterius,*' Jai said. 'That was my only *denarius.*'

Frida looked at him blankly.

'A *semi* is the smallest coin. Then two *semis* to an *as,* four *as* to a *sesterius.* A silver denarius is worth four *sesterii,* or sixteen *as.*'

She chewed her lip.

'You got ripped off,' she said. 'But there's an advantage to being an outlaw. You can steal, too.'

She grinned and flashed him the silver coin in her palm, before dropping it back into his purse surreptitiously.

Jai felt a flash of fear that they'd be caught and found out.

'We'd better move on before he notices,' Frida said, a bit more casually than Jai would like. Jai took a step toward the road, but a soft hand upon his shoulder stopped him.

She nodded at a nearby market stall, where the owner was transferring its contents of fruit, vegetables and dried meats to a handcart.

'But let's buy some food first.'

She plucked the purse from his hand.

'Let me do the negotiating this time.'

Chapter 50

There's nowt around 'ere,' the barmaid said, raising her voice to be heard above the inn's racket.

They were in the Manticore, checking to see if the guard had been telling them the truth. Even stepping inside, the answer had been obvious. The place was heaving, filled wall to wall with travellers of all kinds. Many would likely be sleeping on the streets tonight.

'The guard said there were other taverns,' Jai said. 'Same owner?'

The barmaid rolled her eyes and looked pointedly at the other punters waiting for a drink. She began to move down the bar when Frida flashed her a coin. The maid turned back with a sly grin.

'Like I said, nowt,' she said, holding her hand out for the coin. 'But buy me a drink an' I'll think on it. A pint'll cost more'n that though.'

Frida darted out her hand and pulled the maid close.

'Listen, wench. I can offer a hot slap or this cold coin. What's it to be?'

The barmaid seemed unabashed, for she was twice Frida's

size, with hands large as bootsoles, and rougher too. But when she'd plucked ineffectuality at the white knuckled fingers clutching her pinafore, she sighed and pointed in a southerly direction, beyond the doors.

'There's two inns down there, my love,' she said. 'Down the goat trail. Closest's the Chimera on the left fork, t'other's the Jackalope on the right.'

Frida released her and handed her the same coin she'd flashed. The barmaid looked surprised, perhaps at the fact Frida had honoured their bargain. As they began to make their way out, the maid called after them.

'If'n those'r full, you ought to try the Phoenix. 'Tis a ways further down the Kashmere Road, then turn north, just afore the turnpike.'

Jai turned to thank her, but Frida shoved him on. They were out the doors, walking into the cold night once more.

He could sense Winter, munching on something that tasted far more delicious to her than Jai reckoned it should. He could almost feel the crunch of cartilage and bone in his own mouth.

'Winter's close,' Jai said. 'She'll follow us off the path. She's better at sensing where I am than I her, I can tell.'

Frida nodded.

'That's always the way, for any beast. They understand our intent better than we theirs. Perhaps because they have no words of their own. But you'll get better, I promise. Just takes time and practice.'

Jai gestured vaguely at their surroundings.

'Plenty of opportunity for that while you're on the run, eh?'

Frida grimaced, but nodded.

'We'd better find somewhere to rest soon. I've so little mana, I can hardly summon a spark to light a fire. I need to soulbreathe.'

Jai couldn't have agreed more, keen to cultivate mana of his own.

'Well, seeing the packed-out tavern there, I wonder if the detour is worth it,' he said. 'If we're slow, the legion will overtake us. And I don't think we want to attempt to walk by them, dyed hair or no.'

Frida frowned.

'Surely they're no more likely to recognise us for what we are than any other traveller?' she asked.

'Most imperial citizens just want to live their lives, stay out of trouble,' Jai mused aloud, his mind turning back to the many beatings he'd endured from the guards at the palace. 'But the legionaries . . . they've a long-held hatred for the Dansk and Steppefolk, not to mention anyone else outside the empire. And not just the veterans. The young lads'll have been trained up on a diet of war stories and loathing, at least if they're from the cities. It just takes one to have a suspicion.'

Frida chewed on her lip, swaying slightly. Exhaustion was beginning to take hold. And with both their mana reserves nearing their end, they'd have a hard night ahead.

He looked beyond the still-open gates, where the sun's last meagre light allowed sight of the rugged goat path across the road's cobbles.

'Come on,' Jai said. 'We'd better get going. Sundown's early in winter here, but we'll need to wake well before sunup if we're to beat the legion. A Sabine legion can march more than five leagues in a day. They'll be up at the crack of dawn too.'

Frida sniffed at that.

'With a bit of mana, I could do that before luncheon,' she said.

'Well I can't,' Jai snapped. 'Unless you're volunteering to carry me. So let's move for the Chimera. Every second we waste here is another not sleeping or soulbreathing.'

Frida looked affronted at his tone for a moment, but

relented, it seemed, when Jai sagged against the tavern wall with exhaustion.

'All right,' she said. 'We'll risk it. Let us hope there are still rooms. Look, there's others headed that way.'

She was right too. A smattering of travellers had turned onto the trail, some not even glancing in the small village's direction. A few might be headed home, but most had the look of experienced travellers about them, clutching walking staffs and broad-brimmed hats.

'What do you think?' she said. 'That's a dozen rooms taken in that group alone. Maybe this Phoenix place she mentioned is more likely to have space for us.'

The word jarred something in Jai's memory. He'd hardly heard the barmaid before, but now he remembered Leonid's dying words. What he had thought was gibberish. Leonid had mentioned a phoenix. Or was it *the* Phoenix?

'The . . . winesop,' Jai murmured, scrunching his eyes as he tried to recollect the exact phrasing.

Frida frowned at him.

'We head for the Phoenix,' Jai said. 'I've a good feeling about it.'

The Dansk handmaiden gave him a hard look.

'No carousing,' she said. 'You may have been locked in a dusty room most of your life but it's sleep or soulbreathing, you hear?'

Jai nodded absently, still trying to remember what the old man had said.

Either way, they were going. Leonid had saved him once. Perhaps he would again.

Chapter 51

I t was getting late, and there was still no sign of any turnpike. The only thing that gave them some hope was that there were few travellers about now. While the Kashmere Road was patrolled by *contubernia*, squads of ten legionaries that kept the peace and sought out bandits, even they stopped to camp at sundown.

Bandits preyed on the tardy and the foolish in the dark of night. Whoever was staying at the Phoenix that night would have arrived there by now. Since Jai and Frida's plan was to travel by night anyway, that die was already cast.

'If that barmaid lied to us, I'll run back there and give her the beat down of her life,' Frida growled.

Jai didn't reply. He was of good mind to do the same. At this point, Winter was rustling along the ridge. Her full belly was finally not the complete antithesis of Jai's own, as he munched on the paltry supplies they'd been able to afford with their small collection of coins.

Half had been saved for their board that night, but the rest had been used to purchase a sackful of vegetables. He crunched on a carrot now, still wishing he could have something warm in his belly.

'Is that the turnpike?' Jai asked.

He could see the flickering lights of what might have been a row of flaming torches. They walked further, peering into the darkness ahead.

Finally, it came into view. A large gatehouse had been built across the road, with imperial guards stationed at its top. Walkers would simply skirt around its edges, but anything larger than a handcart would struggle to manage the rough terrain on either side and would be forced to pay the toll to pass through its gates.

Luckily, they didn't need to do so, for the path north was also just visible in the moonlight – a narrow trail flanked by brambles. Jai might not have even considered it, were it not for a splintered sign nailed to a sapling with the faded word 'Phoenix' scratched onto its surface.

It was an ill-lit path, with branches and dead wood encroaching at every step. Little of the moonlight filtered through the thick vegetation, though the eyes of his newly cleansed body saw better than they once had.

Jai didn't think this was going to be a high-class establishment. That suited him well, though. He needed a bed and a bath, not fine furnishings. And they certainly couldn't afford them.

'Winter,' Jai called out.

He was feeling uneasy, stepping off the path. Best to keep her close.

The little dragon whipped through the underbrush swiftly at his summons, chirring excitedly as she leaped into his arms.

He held her close, feeling the warmth of her porcelain scales against his skin. Somehow, he'd already begun to miss her in the short time they'd been apart. Even if he could sense her the whole time.

'Did she eat?' Frida asked, as they turned onto the trail.

'Yes,' Jai said, scratching the little beast beneath her chin. 'And then some.'

Frida sniffed.

'Good,' she said, 'Winter's small. Smaller than any other dragon I've seen. Born too early, I'm sure.'

Jai felt a guilty twinge at that. But it wasn't his fault. And runt or no, she was still the best thing that had ever happened to him. He cared not a jot if she was smaller than other dragons.

'Let's hurry,' Frida said.

Jai was grateful now for his enhanced senses, though they were waning with the collapse of his mana reserves. By now, he had barely a few droplets pooling at the bottom of his fledgeling core.

He was even more grateful due to the treacherous path, strewn as it was with sharp rocks and divots that would break a pack animal's leg easily enough, if not his own. Jai wondered at that – this ruled out the Phoenix being in a frequented village, or even a venue set up for the majority of the Kashmere Road's travellers. So what *was* this place?

In fact, it was unusual that the guard had not mentioned it either. Only the sign and the path's existence gave him faith they were headed for anything at all.

Half an hour passed by before Frida said she saw the lights of torches and heard the raucous sound of revelry that told them they were heading in the right direction. Jai had to concentrate hard to even get a hint of it. His mana was well and truly gone now.

Jai felt Winter's anxiety tick up a notch. Enough to give him pause. But he could not read the little beast's senses as he wished. He only knew something that troubled the dragon was ahead.

'There's—'

'I smell them too,' Frida said. 'More than one, I reckon. They're not moving, and there's no fire. Suspicious.'

Jai sniffed at the air and listened intently. But his mana was so depleted even the cold was getting to him. He might as well have been his old self. This didn't bode well for a fight.

'I hear them. They know we're coming.'

But then, neither did the fact that they had only one weapon between them. That, and an infant dragon.

'Winter, follow at a distance,' he hissed. 'Don't come unless I call you, you hear?'

The little dragon wasted no time, scampering into the darkness so quickly that even Jai swiftly lost her. He didn't like the twinge of emotion he'd felt from her at his words. But beside the hurt, there was . . . a stubborn quality to it.

'What's the plan?' Jai asked.

Frida was walking faster now, the dagger clasped behind her back. Her confidence did little to assuage Jai's anxiety. They were heading into an ambush.

'Follow my lead,' Frida said. 'If we run, they'll give chase, and we cannot afford to fight this. We must make them think we are not worth it.'

Jai saw them before he smelled them. They were not trying to hide, it seemed, instead standing in plain sight across the path's centre. Four of them. Three men and a woman, and all holding a weapon of some kind.

Luckily, only the woman held a sword – the others brandished staves made from rough-hewn branches. And they stank, each and every one of them. They were dressed more like vagrants than organised bandits. Even in the gloom, he could see there was hunger in their eyes. A sick, desperate hunger that surpassed all else.

'So kind of the Phoenix to send a greeting party,' Frida called out.

She approached them with a nonchalant air, even waving at the men as they slapped their staves into their palms.

'Oh yes,' the woman called out, raising the sword and jabbing it in their direction. 'We're here to escort you through the dark. Never know what unsavoury characters you might run into in the dead of night.'

She was better spoken than Jai had expected from the state of her companions. In fact, she even wore a leather chest-plate, compared to the ragged sack-cloth of the others. Their leader, then.

Frida smiled at the bandit's words, and Jai was amazed at how at ease she seemed. His own palms were sweating profusely, and he was already looking around his feet for anything he might use as a weapon.

'Best wait for the next lot then,' Frida said. 'We've no need of protection.'

The woman chuckled drily.

'Oh, we insist. My sister sent you for the Phoenix, or do I tell a lie? She only sends folk that . . . need our services.'

Jai's heart fell, realising what had happened. Apparently the barmaid hadn't meant to help them at all. Crossing her palm with brass rather than silver might have been a mistake.

'Is there even such a place?' Jai asked.

His voice sounded shrill, and he cleared his throat.

'Oh yes,' the woman said, looking over her shoulder. 'But you'll be headed back the way you came. The Phoenix isn't for the likes of you.'

Frida lifted a hand. Pointed it at them.

'They say the soulbound can kill a dozen men with a single gesture,' she said. 'But I've never managed more than three.'

'Ooooo,' the leader said, lifting a hand in mock fear. The other men sniggered.

And then, Frida's finger began to glow. A spark emerged, warping and twisting in the air. It cast her face in an ethereal golden light.

'Step aside,' she said. 'And we'll forget we ever saw you.'

The spark drifted away from her, slowly crossing the gap between them. Soon, Jai could see each and every one of the dishevelled troop of bandits. Men hardly better dressed than himself, bearded and dirty. Their eyes were sunken, their cheeks hollow. Few looked like they'd had a decent meal in weeks. He almost pitied them.

The spark seemed to have spooked the men, for they were exchanging glances, gauging the pair. Frida let her hand fall from behind her back, revealing the dagger.

Jai stepped forward, standing beside his friend. He lifted his hands, balling them into fists. His experience with punching had always been on the receiving end, but he knew at the very least how to square up. He'd witnessed too many scullery boys scuffle to not.

'Where's your beast?' the leader asked. 'It'd be here if you were smart. Or maybe you're bonded to a mouse.'

She pointed her blade at them, and her companions shifted their stances, as if preparing to charge.

Jai closed his eyes, taking his connection to the hatchling with a gentle grasp.

'Winter,' Jai whispered, half to himself. 'Make yourself known.'

In the darkness to Jai's left, there was a growl. It was a guttural, savage noise, such that Jai might never have thought it her, had he not asked her to make it.

Still, the men remained in place.

A shadow darted behind the crew and one of the men cried

out. He lowered a hand to his calf and held up a bloody palm. Jai sensed Winter's anger, and he tried to order the beast to remain where she was. He received back only a sense of furious disagreement.

'Last chance,' Frida snapped. 'My *mouse* has your taste now. I won't be able to hold him back much longer.'

The leader glanced to the side as the bushes crackled from Winter's movements. Another growl sounded, even louder than before.

'You've got ten seconds,' she said.

The leader lifted her sword.

'Take them!' she screamed.

Frida's hand whipped up, her entire body launching forward in a deep lunge. Jai heard a thrum in the air, and the woman staggered. For a moment, Jai did not understand what had happened.

Then, the bandit clutched her chest. Fell to her knees, and Jai saw the hilt of the dagger clamped in the woman's hands.

A yowl from the darkness set even Jai's teeth on edge, as Frida contorted her hand, her finger glowing once more.

'I'd rather not waste my mana,' she sniffed, looking at her glowing fingertip as if inspecting her nails. 'But by all means, join your friend.'

In the darkness, Winter howled.

The remaining bandits did not even say a word. They turned as one and ran into the darkness.

Jai realised he'd been holding his breath.

'Frida, I . . .'

The girl held up a hand, silencing Jai. It was only when the men were out of earshot that she strode forward, yanking her blade from the still-twitching bandit's chest. Blood spurted and the dying bandit grasped at the hem of her dress, muttering unintelligibly. Frida kicked her onto her back and began going through her pockets.

'Her boots are too small, but take her kecks,' she said, yanking the bandit's belt and scabbard free. 'Quick, before she bleeds on them.'

Chapter 52

J ai was still in awe of Frida as they trudged up to the tavern. He knew life among the Dansk was tough but . . . this was no pampered royal servant. The handmaiden knew how to handle herself.

The Phoenix was as grotty a building as Jai had ever seen. A lone structure at the end of the trail, constructed of what looked like it had once been a shepherd's hut, with ramshackle additions tacked on as an afterthought.

This was not a retreat for weary travellers, nor even local folk. Rather, this had the look of a hideout. A place for the undesirables of the Kashmere Road. Jai wouldn't have been surprised if the bandits had bedded down here after robbing them as they had planned.

The wind had picked up as the hour grew later, and Jai was glad of the new clothing. Already the branches of the surrounding trees were rattling and swirling leaves into the air. He crossed his arms and set his teeth, resisting the urge to shudder.

'Perhaps we should turn back,' he whispered. 'I'm trousered now, plus we have a sword and some coin. We should take the win, camp out by the turnpike. We can sleep with a roof over our heads tomorrow.'

'I can't take another night on the road,' Frida said. 'It's too cold, even for us. We need time to rest, to soulbreathe.'

'Fine, then we go in,' Jai said. 'You're soulbound. We both are. With your majicking, we could burn this place to the ground if anyone gave us trouble.'

Frida snorted.

'I had barely enough mana to make that glintlight. Didn't have enough for the second. I put most of what I had left into that throw. I'm tapped out.'

Jai blanched at that, and his heart began to beat baster. Until that moment, he hadn't realised how much of his fragile sense of safety was tied to Frida's protection. Without mana, she was just a strong warrior with a dagger.

He looked her over. Her green dress would look out of place, it was true. The material was too fancy, and too colourful.

'I probably wouldn't look amiss in there,' Jai said. 'But your dress . . .'

Frida sniffed at that. Looked down at her body and shrugged.

'You know the difference between a noblewoman and a courtesan?' she asked.

She lifted a hand to her shoulders and tore at her dress until her shoulders were exposed. Then she took the plunging laced neckline that dipped towards her cleavage, and ripped it even further so that the swell of her breasts was visible.

'Clothing,' she said triumphantly.

Jai averted his eyes, but he'd seen enough. Her hemline was already short from when she had made the shawl, but these changes were far more revealing. She looked like the ladies he'd seen loitering on Latium's street corners in the early hours. The muck and wear of their travels only compounded Frida's lowborn appearance. She really did look like a noblewoman no longer.

Jai was almost too exhausted to think. A chill gust cutting through his threadbare shirt made up his mind. Without mana, a night outdoors would be one of biting wind and cold, damp ground.

'All right,' Jai said, swaying on his feet. 'Let's go in. We'll take whatever room they have available and go straight there. Winter can keep watch outside in case the bandits return while we sleep. We'll carry her tomorrow in the vegetable sack, so she can sleep through the day.'

Frida didn't reply. Instead, she barged through the tavern doors, leaving Jai no choice but to follow.

Inside he was met with a wall of warm, stinking air.

'Close that door!' called a voice. Jai swiftly obeyed.

The inside of the tavern was surprisingly empty. Indeed, there was hardly anyone there at all beyond a handful of men throwing bones upon a table – the source of the uproarious noise Frida had heard earlier.

A man eyed them from behind the bar, rubbing a filthy dishcloth over an even filthier drinking horn. A sign above his head showed Jai their limited choices.

Wine: 1 semi

A ladle and a barrel of foamy liquid with scum floating on top sat beside the barman. Whatever 'wine' was on offer, it wasn't made with grapes. All he knew was it smelled like vinegar.

Frida prodded Jai forward and he realised that he had to act the part. He scrunched his eyes closed, trying to wake himself up, then swaggered forward, a hand grazing the hilt of the sheathed sword at his hip.

'Barkeep,' he said, trying to affect the air of a low-born man. 'I've need of a room to bed this wench. Quickly, if you can. She's charging me by the hour.'

The barman hardly looked up at him, instead jerking his head at the other end of the room. There Jai saw that the back section of the hut had ragged curtains hanging from the ceiling that partially obscured an area of straw-stuffed mattresses and cushions. A few men could be seen laying there. In one corner, two naked bodies writhed rhythmically, unperturbed by a few onlookers sprawled nearby with their hands stuffed firmly down their trousers.

No walls, doors or windows here. So much for their plan of having Winter keep watch.

'Bed's two *as*,' the man said, finally looking up. 'Take whatever's free. Well's out back. If'n you've got valuables, I'll keep 'em safe.'

He gave Jai a near-toothless grin and held out his hand. Jai was glad Frida had let him keep hold of the sword and bag – going back to his supposed escort for money might look just a *little* suspicious.

Having palmed two *as* into the man's hand, Jai turned back to Frida, who wiggled her fingers in his direction, then winked and blew him a kiss. He motioned for her to join him and he chose a bed in the far corner. It was further from the fireplace, where most of the other occupants had gathered, but at least they had two walls at their back.

Jai's cot in Leonid's wardrobe had been small but comfortable, for it was made up of Leonid's old duck-down pillows. Yet as Jai settled down onto what was little more than a straw filled sack, it felt like settling on a cloud.

Frida busied herself rearranging the curtains to afford them some modicum of privacy and lend weight to their supposed plan to sleep together. This elicited not a few groans of disappointment from the onlookers. This didn't last long though, as their attention turned back to the copulating couple in the opposite corner, whose moans were nearing a crescendo.

Above, Jai could hear the sound of the wind, then a soft pattering as it began to rain. Somehow, it made their little alcove feel safer.

'Frida,' Jai whispered, scraping the rusted sword's blade from its scabbard. 'I'll take first watch. Will you sleep or soulbreathe?'

A soft snore from behind him gave him his answer.

Chapter 53

Jai's eyes grew heavier in the dubious comfort of the Phoenix's interior, but he forced himself to stay awake for now. As much as he'd like to join Frida, he knew that her sleep was more important than his. *She* could soulbreathe properly while awake. He could not.

Luckily, quiet fell in the inn as the night drew on. The barkeep disappeared into a back room and the remaining patrons settled their debts and turned to sleep too.

It was some relief, to settle on the dusty pillows, and pull the sack-cloth blanket over his lap. Two nights of sleep on the damp ground had been bad enough, soulbound or not. In his mind's eye, Jai sensed Winter. She was nestled deep in a pile of dead leaves, somehow cosier even than he.

But she missed him.

He tried to think how to keep her with him, but his tired mind was struggling to collect his thoughts.

A twitch from Frida gave him pause. She lay like a scared child, knees clutched close to her chest. Her lips parted and she let out a low moan.

He wished he could wake her from her nightmare. But she

needed this sleep. And she needed to mourn, even if in slumber. He supposed he did too. But when he closed his eyes he could see Samar's eyes; saw when the blade had cut Arjun's throat. Felt Samar's heartbreak. Arjun's disbelief and sudden agony and the moment the light had faded from his eyes.

It was too painful to think about. The memory filled him with a rage he could hardly contain and left him feeling utterly powerless.

Revenge. It seemed impossible now.

He cursed himself, for not staying in that chamber. For not attempting to kill Titus when he'd had the chance.

Had he been a coward? In that moment, he'd told himself that his best revenge was to live.

He and Frida would be lucky to reach the border; he'd be luckier still to make it back to his tribe. But he would. He swore it. Swore on the memory of his brothers. Of his father. Not just to live. To rule. To claim his birthright.

None of that was possible if he was powerless. He *had* to grow more powerful.

Jai closed his eyes.

He prepared to explore himself once more, glad that the curtains prevented the other occupants from seeing he had his eyes closed.

By Jai's estimation, each and every one of the inn's customers was a bandit, cutthroat or rogue of some sort. He only hoped he had looked intimidating enough to keep them from seeing him as an easy mark. Somehow . . . he doubted it.

Knowing this might be his only settled time for a while, Jai decided to try to soulbreathe, even without Winter to aid him. He closed his eyes and took those deep breaths, allowing his mind to drift to that strange, dream-like state where the mana of the world came into view.

It was a painstaking process, but this time, Jai took Frida's words to heart. Jai allowed his mind to explore the network of passages between his breath and his core. He found a direct route. And *breathed*.

The pain of squeezing his core and drawing mana through his newly cleansed channels was helpful in keeping him awake. That, and the occasional bubble of emotion he sensed from Winter, who was dreaming of chasing squirrels.

Slowly, the motes of mana drifted through his channels; so slowly he could hardly see them move at all. Again and again, he squeezed at his core, and it felt like a fist had seized his heart.

He persevered. Watched as the motes coalesced, like oil on a hot pan. As if dust had turned to liquid, flowing, drip by drip, into the chamber that held his core.

Finally, the first trickle reached the crystalline core, melting into its walls and passing through. Filtered further by its shell, the mana turned from a dull gold to aureate light.

Yet the very moment it entered, the purified mana flowed out once more. Swiftly now, as if it had a mind of its own. Seeping into his flesh to warm his cold body and making the cuts and scrapes of the day tingle as it accelerated his healing.

Before long, it was all gone.

Jai set his teeth . . . and began again.

He pushed through the agony of soulbreathing for what felt like an age, but he imagined was likely no more than an hour. It was almost therapeutic, to see that thin trickle reaching his core. Yet there was hardly more than dregs left at the bottom of the tiny kernel that was his core when he stopped again.

It was no wonder Frida was out of mana, though he knew that with a larger core, and more practice, he'd improve in future.

Over and over he strained, even as the small reserve he had

built dissolved into his body like cold water down a parched throat.

By now, his core was *hurting*. After all, he had been squeezing a fragile shell. Jai looked to Frida's sleeping form. Saw the pain there, even in her troubled sleep.

Pain that now lived in the back of his mind too. The memory of his brothers was imprinted on his very soul. Their faces as Titus's blade did its work.

The bastard Sabines had taken them from him.

Jai closed his eyes and took a deep breath.

Rage.

It was a powerful motivator.

JAI FORCED HIMSELF TO soulbreathe until he could bear it no longer; when each breath felt like he was inhaling ground glass and forcing it through his veins. Only then did he finally examine his handiwork.

Jai was pleased when he did so. He'd built up a small reserve, though it was a fraction of what he had beheld when he had first bonded with Winter.

Still, a few more nights of this and he might just manage to partially fill his core, replacing what remained of the mana Winter had passed to him.

By the time he was done, the Phoenix was silent but for the wheezes and snores of sleeping vagabonds. He had no way of telling the time, but he was sure his watch was well overdue a reprieve.

For a moment, he was tempted to delve into Leonid's diary. But in truth, he still dreaded to read it. To know his father's final moments. How his people had been defeated. Subjugated.

Sleep was more important.

Frida was still sleeping, her darkened hair spilling onto the mattress and that flawless face finally settled in dreamless sleep. Jai almost didn't have the heart to wake her.

But he knew that she needed to soulbreathe herself, to do more than bluff with a . . . glintlight . . . if they were ambushed again. Given their plan to travel in darkness, and their very first night's experience on the Kashmere Road, Jai had no choice but to gently shake her awake.

To her credit, Frida did not complain. Instead, she gave Jai a nod and a whispered thanks, before settling into a cross-legged pose not dissimilar to his own. She began breathing rhythmically.

Jai was tempted to sleep right away. He even tried to for a few minutes, curling up on the cushions, using their vegetable sack as a pillow. But the day's long walk through the forest had left him sticky with sweat and grime, and his nails were bloodied where he had stripped the fallen bandit earlier. Not to mention the last of the grime that the body cleansing stage had left upon him.

He knew they would not have time to wash come morning, nor have a nearby water source at their disposal for quite some time.

He stood and stumbled toward the front door, so exhausted that he was dizzied by it. Just a quick shock of cold water from the well, a scrub with the mouldering sackcloth he'd brought with him, and he'd be able to sleep. Or at least, that was what he told himself.

As Jai unbarred the door he felt eyes upon him. Or perhaps he sensed the halting, uneven breath of a drunk, and the smacking of his lips as he gulped down more wine.

Jai turned toward him with as much confidence as he could

muster. He locked eyes with a man glowering at him from the corner. A balding, heavy set man with a silver-streaked red beard that rested upon his ample belly. He held a tankard in his hand, and threw it back without blinking, staining the silver in his ruddy beard brown with drink in the process.

Jai lifted his chin as he'd so often seen men do when faced with a possible foe. At this, the man only grinned, and raised his drink.

'Don't forget behind your ears,' he grunted. Then he burped and blew Jai a kiss.

Jai grimaced and pushed his way out into the cold night air, searching for the well the barkeep had told him about. It was easy enough to find, positioned beside a ramshackle outhouse that stank to high heaven.

Jai was glad the rain had stopped, but the wind was still bitterly cold.

Within minutes, Jai was dunking his head in a bucket of well-water so cold that he'd had to drop the bucket with force to break through the layer of ice that had formed upon it.

Somehow it was more a relief than a shock as he scrubbed himself with the sackcloth, wringing the grime of the last few days onto the soil by the well. He supposed he had warmed up while he'd soulbreathed, and his mana reserves were still just enough to keep him from shivering more than a little.

Then, he heard it. Or rather, Winter did, pulsing with alarm.

Soon enough, he heard it truly. Crashing amid the brambles. And voices. There were men, stumbling in the darkness.

Jai ducked behind the well, listening intently. He could just about hear them.

'. . . killed 'er dead, throwin' that knife.'

'You think I care Tullia's dead? I owed the fucker money.'

This second voice was female, and educated, even more so

than the bandit Frida had killed. She spoke on as feet stamped and shuffled on the frozen ground. These men were cold. Impatient.

'Now boys, have I looked after you tonight?'

There was a chorus of *ayes*. More than before. Jai peered over the well's edge and felt his stomach lurch with shock. There were almost a dozen men there.

Hungry, lean men. He could smell them. Smell the booze, fresh on their breath. Whoever this new arrival was, she'd likely given it to them as payment. Jai dreaded to guess for what service.

'I've no mind what you do with that Dansk bitch,' said the woman. 'Or her savage servant . . . but I suggest you turn her in for the reward. I'd say that's pretty generous of me, it being my tavern'n'all.'

More *ayes* followed. So . . . this was the owner of the other taverns too. A wealthy woman . . . what could she want with the likes of them?

Jai shifted his grip on his blade, trying to remember how much mana remained within him. Would those last dregs give him the strength to put up a fight?

'So lads, I've only one thing to ask in return. I've need of the white dagger that killed poor Tullia. You said, did you not, that she was soulbound, and Dansk by her accent?'

'Yes ma'am,' came the enthusiastic response of the first speaker.

'Then that's all I need. Her dagger. And the body of whatever little beast she's bonded to. If it was small, it must be but a pup.'

There was a clearing of someone's throat, and then Jai saw someone shoved forward to the front of the group.

'Camilla, please . . . she showed us her majicking. Lights in the dark. And she . . . like he said, she killed Tullia.'

Camilla sighed.

Jai peered at her from behind the well.

She was well-heeled, though she wore trousers rather than the traditional smock or petticoats of a Sabine woman. And she was older than she sounded, for her dark hair was dusted with grey. She looked out of place standing before the pack of vagrants.

Yet she spoke to them as if this was just another day for her. Jai had no doubt who employed the bandits in these parts. And they'd walked right into her tavern.

Camilla raised a finger and stabbed it the way they had come.

'You think a Dansk would give two shits about sparing the lives of a few bandits if she could kill them soon as look at them?'

Her question hung in the air and she sighed again at their silence.

'If she's a Dansk in fancy clothes, it means she's a noble on the run from that slaughter at the palace. And if she let you lot see her and live to tell the tale, that means she wasn't strong enough to kill the four of you and keep you quiet.'

Silence.

'Noble means money, lads. And you can keep all of it.'

That did it. The ten men began to murmur among themselves. Some slapped each other on their shoulders, while others muttered under their breath, psyching themselves up.

Jai had only one card left to play.

'Winter,' Jai breathed. 'I need you.'

Chapter 54

They stormed into the tavern in a thunder of feet, but without a single word spoken. Clearly, they wanted to catch their targets asleep.

Behind them, Jai darted forward in a half-crouch, gathering Winter onto his shoulder as he did so.

He stuck out a hand, catching the door before it slammed shut, and slipped in after them. He needn't have hurried.

Ten men, plus Camilla, stood uncertainly in the gloom of the tavern interior, an assortment of staves, clubs and knives held out in front of them.

'On,' Camilla hissed. 'Find her.'

Again, one bandit was shoved forward, a trembling lad no older than Jai. He was handsome, in a fragile sort of way, the effects of poor living yet to hollow his cheeks. His weapon, little more than a rusted spear, shook in his hands as he crept closer to the maze of curtains beyond.

'Go on, lad,' one of the bandits whispered. 'Slit her throat for us and you can have a double share.'

The boy hesitated, then drew a tight, quick breath and ducked beneath a hanging sheet. Seconds passed, with the other bandits peering into the still, curtain draped interior.

Jai held his breath, still crouched in the lee of the door. The men were now advancing, step by faltering step. And up in the rafters, a sinuous form leaped from beam to beam.

Jai sensed Winter reach Frida. Felt a flash of concern, then triumph. The handmaiden was awake . . . and she'd know that if Winter was there, something was amiss.

Camilla muttered beneath her breath.

'Cowards. You should rush the bitch.'

She was so close to Jai that he could have reached out and tied the woman's bootlaces. Instead, he rose, ever so slowly. Waited for it . . . and . . .

A boy's scream ripped through the air. Men stirred from their sleep, shouting in confusion.

Now.

Jai lunged, clapping a hand over Camilla's mouth, and slamming the flat of his blade so hard against the tavern owner's throat that she choked through his fingers.

'Right, then!' Jai yelled.

A handful of the bandits spun around, and Jai yanked Camilla's head back, just as Frida had done to him before. Winter pulsed with relief and Jai knew Frida was safe.

'You think you're facing one soulbound,' Jai growled, forcing Camilla to step deeper into the gloom. 'But you're facing two.'

More bandits turned now, and confused sleepers stumbled into the open, weapons drawn. Frida remained somewhere in the darkness behind them.

'Frida! Are you all right?' Jai bellowed.

There was silence. And then, the body of the boy erupted from the sleeping area, tangled in a mess of clothesline and ragged sheets. He slid to a stop at the arrayed bandits' feet.

'I'm not all right,' Frida called out, now visible as more curtains fell. 'I'm *angry*.'

Camilla twitched in his grasp and Jai pressed his lips close to her ear.

'Try me,' he hissed in a voice tinged with as much madness as he could muster. 'Warm my hands with your blood.'

The twitching stopped. Jai urged Winter into the rafters once more, closing his eyes to send her out of harm's way. She did as he requested, sensing his urgency.

'You've miscalculated,' Jai called out, searching for fear in his opponents' eyes and finding it. 'So, here's what's going to happen. You're all going to line up against the bar. My friend there is going to walk to me. Once we're safely away, our beasts will follow. Don't think about coming after us. We'd kill you all where you stand, but you'd not be worth the mana.'

He closed his eyes and sent a desire to Winter. Above, a guttural growl set bandits spinning, weapons pointed at the darkness above.

'Sound like a mouse or a pup to you?' Jai asked.

He drew an exaggerated, impatient breath, and shoved Camilla forward a step, letting the sword's edge slip around until it pressed against the base of his captive's skull.

'Move,' he said. 'Or your boss'll be breathing through her throat. Then who'll pay for your drink?'

A few of the bandits took notice of that, but still they glanced at each other, indecisive. Without Camilla, they lacked a leader. Well, Jai would give them a very motivated one.

He relaxed his blade a fraction.

'Speak,' he hissed.

Camilla was only too happy to oblige.

'Move,' was all she said. 'Swiftly!'

Bandits shuffled aside in angry silence, as did the rest of the tavern's patrons. Frida took a few wary steps forward, waiting for a clear path to the door.

A clap sounded from the fireplace. Then another, and another.

Jai flicked his eyes to the side and saw the bald, rotund man who had raised a tankard to him earlier.

'A fine performance,' the man laughed, his words slurring ever so slightly. 'Why, I've no' seen better in Latium's Colosseum.'

Jai ignored him and dug the blade's tip deeper into Camilla's neck.

'Do as the boy says,' Camilla snapped. 'Ignore this drunk cunt.'

'Now, now,' the bald man said in a broad Samarion accent. 'See, you were right the first time. That Dansk lass over there's had barely enough mana tae throw that poor dead lad across the room. Nobody soulbreathes at this time of night unless they're desperate for it.'

'Shut your mouth,' Jai spat. 'Or my beast'll give you a new one.'

A growl from above punctuated his words. The man lifted his eyes with an amused glance.

''Tis no mouse,' the man said. 'But it'll be nigh' the same size, I'll wager.'

'Rufus, there's a damned sword to my neck,' Camilla growled at the man, before turning back to her accomplices. Jai didn't like that the pair knew each other by name.

'Boys, I'll pay you all for the night's work,' Camilla pleaded. 'Just step aside. Let the bitch through.'

Rufus stood, swaying on his feet, even as the bandits did as they were bidden, sidling toward the bar with clear reluctance.

The man pointed at Jai with an unsteady finger.

'As for the boy, well, he's got ye' in a fair pickle, and he's no' lyin' that he's a soulbound either. But he's probably out of mana too, if his shiverin' earlier was anythin' to go by.'

Camilla perked up at that.

'Now, even if he had the guts tae put that rusted old thing through your throat. He'd be pretty quickly cut tae pieces. And milady over there, well she'll no' make it out alive either. Especially if yon' lads over there take your side.'

The newly woken patrons were listening intently. Jai did not like where this was going. He swallowed, hard.

'We've hardly any money,' Jai called, instilling as much confidence as he could into his voice. 'Show them, Frida.'

Frida was swift to yank the purse from her bag and pour some of its contents into her hand. She tossed these into the room, and the coins rolled across the floorboards.

'Coppers and brass,' she said.

'Now, you're after her iridium blade, or do I no' have ye pegged, Camilla?' the bald man went on.

Jai's heart fell at that. The blade . . . it had value. And Rufus had let the whole tavern know.

Camilla nodded ever so slightly, then let out a whimper as Jai jabbed the blade hard enough to draw blood.

'So you see, lads. The real prize ain't in her capture. It's no' her coin. It's yon dagger there. A whytblade. Made of iridium. So rare, there's only a handful of blades like it in all the empire. Why, a Gryphon Guard'd bugger his own mother just tae have a shard of it.'

The tavern's occupants hung on every word he said. And slowly, eyes turned to the blade in Frida's hand. A simple, short blade, made of pale metal. Even in the dim torchlight, it was almost as pearlescent as Winter's scales. It was unmistakeably unusual, though Jai didn't know if this Rufus spoke the truth. Frida's silence told him it might be. He was sure he wasn't the only one who thought so.

'Give me a scenario where I come out alive, Rufus,' Camilla hissed at the bald man.

'There isn't one,' Jai growled back. 'Not unless Frida walks out unharmed.'

He grasped the woman by her long hair, earning himself another whimper. Frida took a few steps into the open, her hand raised threateningly, as if she were about to cast some charm or spell.

Rufus ignored it, even strolling in front of her pointed fingers.

'Now, I tell you all this because I've somethin' tae offer any or all of yous. My services. You see . . . I'm for hire.'

Rufus spread his hands. He was a large man, broad shouldered and so tall he was but a few inches from the low rafters. Were it not for his enormous belly and red-tinged face, Jai might even have guessed him a soldier. But in his state? Jai was surprised the bandits were even hearing him out.

Rufus reached down to his side and slapped a short scabbard at his hip. It was unusually thin, almost a rapier, but just wide enough to have a cutting edge.

'Mersss . . . enary services,' he half slurred, half burped, then gripped his hilt with a flourish.

For a moment, there was silence.

Then laughter came. At first a few chuckles, then gales from both patron and bandit alike. Only Jai, Frida and Camilla remained tight-lipped, for it was their lives that were in danger.

The man remained silent, seemingly oblivious to the mirth of those around him. He stood apart from the rest, closer to the entrance, with the bandits still crowded at the bar, and the patrons peering out from the curtained sleeping area further in.

'Openin' bid?' Rufus asked, proffering a palm.

More laughter. The big man was deadpan, but Jai found none of this amusing. The old drunk had turned Jai's plan on its head. With a blade worth an apparent fortune in Frida's hand, there would be little chance they could leave with it still in tow. And from the look on Frida's face . . . she wasn't ready to part with it.

'Leave the blade, girl,' Camilla called out. 'And you've got a deal.'

'You'll let us go, will you?' Frida spat in response.

One of the bandits raised a hand, turning to his comrades.

'Listen here lads,' he said. 'Methinks Camilla there ain't the one who ought' be negotiating. Seems to me it's us boys are what's twixt her and the door.'

He stabbed a dirty finger at Camilla.

'No share for you, you ol' sinner.'

Camilla spat a curse at him, even as Jai blinked sweat from his eyes. Somehow, his hostage had suddenly become worthless.

'Only if'n we get a share,' one of the patrons called. More weapons were drawn, as a large party of those overnighting in the tavern began to rise to their feet.

'Oi,' bellowed Rufus. 'I *said*, who's gonna hire me.'

One of the bandits was within a few feet of Rufus, and now he stomped up to the old man.

'Shut your ugly mug,' he said, bringing his head close. 'We're doing *bisnis* here.'

Rufus smiled broadly, his feet scraping into a fighting stance. The big man leaned away and Jai saw the scabbard's top *glow*.

'Make me.'

Chapter 55

The bandit lashed out . . . but his fist never made impact. Rufus's blade thrummed, once, flaring bright.

There was no blood. Only the man's steaming stump, and the meaty thud of his arm falling to the floor. Rufus kicked out with his foot and sent the man skidding across the floor in a crackle of broken ribs.

'Now,' he said. 'Who's got an openin' bid.'

Rufus sheathed his sword and raised his palms non-threateningly, even as pandemonium broke out in the Phoenix. Men scrambled away from him, while bandits rushed to the side of their fallen comrade.

The maimed man looked dazed, staring at his stump as he wheezed out a mouthful of blood. Jai saw with a heady mix of horror and amazement that the wound had been perfectly cauterised with that single, white-hot stroke.

'See, I could take yon blade,' Rufus called out. 'But I'm no thief. I'm here tae save seein' my favourite tavern burn while yous fight it out. Unless . . . someone else wants tae get a taste?'

He spoke slow and loud, his voice carrying despite the sudden rush of voices and feet.

'You surprise me, Rufus,' Camilla choked aloud. 'What secrets have you been hiding?'

Jai could only stare, his mind incapable of processing what he had seen. Rufus was . . . soulbound? And had a whytblade of his own?

The heavyset man ignored Camilla, instead repeating his demand.

'Openin'. Bid.'

'Ten denarii,' called a tavern-goer. He was forced to raise his voice over the gurgling moans of the dying bandit.

'Fifty,' said a bandit, suddenly entirely disinterested in his gurgling comrade.

Rufus grinned broadly, splitting his silver-red beard with tobacco-stained teeth.

'Payment comes first,' he said, nodding to the bandit who had spoken last. 'So you eejits better have the coin on you. Same goes for you, Dansk girl.'

The bandit's grimace almost matched the one on Frida's face. Jai didn't think that slovenly crew had more than two coins to rub together. But he and Frida were hardly better off. And Rufus knew it.

'How do we know you'll keep your word,' one of the tavern-goers called out.

Rufus glared at the man, then tugged back his shirt, pointing to a tattoo there. The mark of a true, anointed Samarion. Truth-tellers, lest they be damned to hellfire. Rufus stabbed a finger in Camilla's direction.

'Tell 'em, Camilla. Why you allow me tae drink here, day after day. Have I ever skipped a debt or broken the rules of this place?'

Camilla hesitated, then inclined her head as much as Jai's blade would let her.

'No,' Camilla allowed. 'Your word is good here. For all that's worth, since it's clear I know you not at all.'

'So, fifty denarii,' Rufus said. "Tis less than I expected. But I'll take it, unless . . .'

He let his words trail off. He waited . . . then began to draw his blade.

'You drink for free,' Camilla snapped. 'For one year.'

Rufus's grin grew wider.

'Now we're talkin',' he said. 'Now we're getting tae the meat of it. That'll beat fifty.'

'The way you drink,' Camilla muttered, 'it'd beat a hundred.'

Jai jabbed her with the blade, if only to do *something*. He couldn't think straight. A soulbound? Here?

Rufus's presence was maddening. Right when Jai had been so close to escape, he was suddenly in an apparent bidding war for his own life – one they were ill-equipped for. Would Rufus chase them if they made a run for it? Certainly, the others would.

Jai felt like they had no other choice, he just didn't know whether to run Camilla through in the process. Would whatever slim advantage that gained them be worth another death on his conscience? It was perhaps only this debate that stopped him from bellowing for Frida to follow and sprinting out of the door.

These panicked thoughts were all that went through Jai's mind other than the feeling of Winter shifting to the rafters just above him. If they were going to run, she'd be ready.

But would Frida? The girl had hardly moved, instead staring at Rufus with furrowed brow.

Deep within the tavern, half-hidden by the ragged curtains, the largest group of the lodgers were in frantic, whispered discussions. The jingle of coins was apparent, and Frida shifted on her feet, her eyes still fixed on Rufus. The man was between her and the doorway. He waited patiently, humming a little tune.

'Five hundred sesterii,' the tavern-goer said triumphantly. He held up a heavy sack and jingled its contents.

Rufus closed his eyes, as if calculating in his head.

'All right,' he muttered. 'That's plenty more'n a year's worth.'

'Three years,' Camilla snapped. '*And* a hundred sesterii. Tomorrow.'

The tavern-goer threw up his hands. Rufus nodded his head slowly in response, pursing his lips as if giving the offer due consideration.

'Fine,' he said. 'I'll . . .'

Frida cursed, so loud and so long that even the drunk Rufus stopped speaking. Or at least, Jai assumed it was cursing. It was in Dansk.

'The whytblade,' she said through gritted teeth. 'I'll trade you for it.'

Rufus turned to her, a look of mock surprise upon his face.

'Oh yes?' he asked. 'Just like that?'

Frida nodded slowly.

'We've no other choice.'

Now Jai saw the cunning in Rufus's words. Of course. It had been his plan all along. This was a bloodless, easy victory for him. Frida was going to hand the blade right to him. And somehow the bastard had managed it without having to go to the trouble of stealing it.

'Think about this, Rufus,' Camilla snarled. 'You do this, you'll never drink here again.'

Rufus swayed on his feet.

'After tonight . . . I can ne'er drink here again anyway.'

Frida stomped forward, flipping the blade with a practised twist of her hand, before offering it, handle first, to Rufus.

'Wait!' Jai called.

Frida glanced up at him, but pulled the blade back before Rufus could take it.

'You said this blade is priceless, right?' Jai said.

Rufus grinned and nodded.

'Aye, lad.'

'How long would you work for us?' Jai asked.

Rufus furrowed his brow. He hadn't expected the question.

'One week,' Jai said, before the drunken man could answer. 'You protect us for one week, and you can have the blade.'

The man was silent, but behind his apparently inebriated gaze Jai saw a fierce intelligence. Calculation. Guile.

'Nah,' the man said. 'Seller's market. What other choice have you got?'

'It's no choice at all,' Jai said. 'Because we're as good as dead or captured whether we make it out of here or not. We walk out of this place with just one sword between us, these bastards will hunt us day and night. Hell, I think this one would pay just for the privilege of gutting me herself.'

'You better believe it, kid,' Camilla snarled.

Jai resisted letting his relief show on his face. Exactly what he'd hoped the woman would say.

'Now, if they know that you'll protect us for a week,' Jai said. 'They'll leave us be.'

Rufus snarled at that.

'You can fuck off.'

'Then kill me,' Frida hissed. She yanked at her dress, exposing her sternum. 'Carve out my heart. Because if the only service you're offering is to let us walk out that door, you might as well. They'll catch up with us long before I can cultivate enough mana to protect us.'

This time, Rufus said nothing, frowning at her with apparent annoyance.

It was as if the balding man had convinced himself he was doing a good deed, or at the very least thought he was not committing a bad one.

Jai stared at the man. And wondered.

'I've something else,' Jai said. 'A message for you from an old friend.'

Rufus laughed at that.

'You're a cheeky little savage, I'll grant you,' he said. 'But you've done enough bluffin' for tonight. I don't know you, nor you me. Even our kind host there knows nothin' more'n my name.'

Jai lifted his chin. What he was about to say was a guess, nothing more. But he'd come all this way. Even sought this place out. And if anyone in this room was to be the winesop, it was this mysterious soulbound man with a blade worth a fortune.

But he could not say it aloud. Any mention of the name Leonid was bound to stir the rumour mill, and they were conspicuous enough. Or at least, stir it more than all this already would. But there was something he *could* say. Something that only the folk from Latium would recognise.

'It's from the Red Lion,' Jai said, hoping the famous tavern would shroud his true meaning. 'I bring dying words.'

Rufus did not react, at first. Then his face began to darken, his very skin reddening. This was unexpected. This was . . . rage.

Rufus took a step towards him. Then another, his hand resting upon his blade's hilt.

Jai closed his eyes, waiting for the man to rip through him like rice paper. Instead, Rufus spoke in a slow, deliberate voice.

'Aye lad,' he said. 'You've got a deal.'

Chapter 56

J ai did not so much step through the doorway as he was hauled bodily through the door by Rufus. Camilla was tossed aside with an indignant squawk.

'You tell me what that bastard said,' Rufus said.

His voice was low, urgent. There was little of the bemused drunk Jai had seen before. This was a different beast entirely.

'I . . . he . . .' Jai was dazed at the sudden change of temperature and light, stumbling back over the sodden earth.

The man towered over him, his ursine figure blocking out the light of the open door. The sour ale-stink of his breath was overpowering, and Jai plucked ineffectually at the sausage fingers grasping his shirt.

Winter barrelled through the swinging door behind them, snarling with a savagery Jai had not yet seen. Rufus turned, raising a hobnailed boot, only to freeze as Jai cried out.

'Stop!'

The little beast veered away, spraying sodden soil, before skidding around and leaping onto Jai's shoulder in a flap of wing and claw. She snapped at the man's hand until Rufus withdrew it with a grunt of surprise.

Behind him, Frida stepped through the doors as well, and Jai caught a glimpse of men peering out at them. None had dared to pursue them. There was only Camilla, screaming obscenities, before Frida slammed the door in her face.

Jai began to stammer out an answer, but Rufus held up a thick, trembling finger. The bald man stared at Winter, at first in shock . . . then something else. There was . . . a pained look in his eye.

'Well then,' Rufus growled. 'Looks like someone wasn't fibbin'.'

He turned and stomped, seemingly into the wilderness. Certainly there was no path that Jai could see. But Frida followed without question, and Jai had no choice but to do the same. After all, this mountain of a man was all that stood between them and being hunted through the night by a few dozen ruffians.

For a few minutes, Jai could do nothing but stumble over the uneven ground, dodging branches as Rufus pushed through brambles and hedgerows, crashing through the woods like a great, red-bearded bear. By now, Jai could see the first hints of sunlight cresting the horizon. He couldn't imagine spending another day without sleep.

They had paid an old drunk to protect them. One who might be soulbound, and who held a whytblade, but still a drunk. Jai was beginning to think that they were wandering aimlessly.

'Can we at least use a glintlight?' Frida asked. 'My dress is being cut to ribbons and I've nothing else.'

'You'd best be rid of it soon,' Rufus said. ''Tis a poor disguise. And no. No light. We're being hunted now.'

Frida scoffed at that.

'If you think those buggers are gonna let you go, think again, lass,' Rufus said. 'You've bought yourself a day, nothin' more. That Camilla didn't become owner of three taverns without a fair dose o' wits.'

'What are you talking about?' Jai demanded.

'Afore long, yon lads'll realise that a dozen well-armed men can take a soulbound warrior on a good day. And they don't see me 'n' Lady Frillyskirts over here as warriors, or you, besides. We're just lucky all Camilla could scrounge up tonight was a bunch o' vagrants. But give her a couple days and some coin, and we'll have a right crew o' cutthroats on our tails. Maybe a couple o' soulbound mercenaries or two, if she's willin' tae pay for it.'

Jai felt his stomach twist at that. To be hunted . . . properly hunted. That wouldn't help their chances at all.

'Probably makin' an agreement with the rest o' the tavern now,' Rufus went on. 'Of course, I could take 'em. But they don't know that.'

'So go back,' Frida said. 'Kill them for us. You work for us now, right?'

Rufus chuckled darkly.

'Oh yes. Let's leave forty-odd men cut tae pieces with a whytblade in a tavern. That won't draw the Gryphon Guard's attention. Only thing keepin' you safe from 'em is the greed of those cunts in the Phoenix. That and they're no' exactly . . . friends o' the authorities.'

'Fine,' Frida snarled. 'Let them hunt us. That's what you're here for.'

'By the looks of your dragon there, lass, I've a feelin' you're not lookin' for any more attention,' Rufus rumbled. 'I've a feelin' I could sell you and that beast for more'n a whytblade. Lucky for you I've no desire to deal with the Sabines or their ilk.'

He spat contemptuously at the mention of the royals. It was enough to shut Frida up.

They walked on in silence, until Jai began to think they were being led into a trap. He only let himself relax a little when he saw their destination. At first, he thought it a haystack or a hillock. But as they neared he saw it was a ramshackle cabin.

It was . . . unusual. Even in the moonlight, it looked like it did not belong, built in the shadow of a gnarled tree on uneven ground. Vegetation surrounded it, and moss even grew up its walls and upon its roof. This was a lost, forgotten place. And apparently, it was Rufus's home.

'Come on,' Rufus growled, as Jai heard the rattle of keys. 'They don't know this place. We'll lay low here tonight. Get ready for wherever you're headed. East, I imagine?'

'The Kashmere Road,' was all Frida replied.

Rufus shrugged and kicked open the door. The interior smelled to Jai like a bear's den . . . if the bear had a penchant for stale booze and unwashed balls.

Still, it was warm, and Jai's eyes were so heavy, he had to lean against the doorway to stay standing.

Rufus ducked beside the hearth, tossing logs into the fireplace. Then, his hand gestured, and there was a spurt of orange light. Jai heard a crackle, and the room was bathed in the warm glow of fire.

Within, there was little of note. A cot, a hearth, a chair, desk and table. It all looked built by hand, rough-hewn from knotted trees and uneven stone. Even the furniture was hand carved, as if Rufus was a wild man of the forest.

Stranger still, there was no beast to be seen. Unusual for a soulbound.

Then Jai felt Rufus's eyes on him. Black beads beneath beetling brows, glowering with unspoken emotion. They stood in the centre of the single room, the space feeling much smaller as the enormous man ducked inside.

Frida took a seat on the lone chair, if only because they had little room for anyone else.

'So lad,' Rufus said. 'You tell me how a plainsboy and a Dansk noble ended up in the Phoenix, at a time like this. And with a message from a man not so long dead that he's still coolin' on the slab. You tell me, boy, and you *convince* me. Or I'll cut pieces off you till you do.'

Frida bristled at his words, but Jai held up a hand. Somehow, Winter felt less concerned, though Jai knew she could sense the aggression behind Rufus's words.

But . . . for some reason, in that short period between the Phoenix and the hut, the little dragon had lost her antipathy for the old rogue. Instead, she seemed to view him with curiosity.

Not that it mattered. Jai believed him well enough. The man owed them nothing, and it seemed only a warped sense of honour had kept Rufus to their bargain.

'How we came there I can tell you on the road,' Jai said. 'But I'll tell you who I am. I have been Leonid's personal manservant for most of my life. Never have I heard your name spoken, nor had knowledge of your—'

Rufus lunged towards him and Jai yelled out in shock. But before he could react Jai felt himself wrapped up in an embrace and a great ham-hock of a hand battering his back, knocking the wind out of him.

'You!' Rufus cried out. '*You* killed the old cunt. Rohan's bastard! Never did I think . . .' He trailed off, his words devolving into laughter once more, his rosy drinker's nose reddening even further. Jai choked and spluttered until Rufus released him.

'I didn't . . .' Jai stuttered. 'I . . . you've heard of me?'

Rufus chuckled.

'We've all heard of the plainsboy who murdered old Leonid. And the Dansk king who poisoned Constantine. Half the empire knows by now, that snake Titus made sure of that. And the other half know by now that the legions are on the march.'

Rufus ruffled Jai's hair, his hands sticky with ale.

'Had I known that, I might've gotten you out o' there for nothin'.'

He winked at Frida.

'Deal's a deal though.'

Jai cleared his throat before Frida could retort. She looked in as foul a mood as he had ever seen her.

'Like I was saying. I don't know why Leonid wanted me to find you. But you were in his final thoughts.'

He hesitated. Telling Rufus that Titus had murdered his own father and grandfather, all so he could take the throne before his time and start a war for his own personal glory, might not sound *convincing*. Nor was Jai sure if he even wanted it to be known. Certainly, Rufus seemed more amenable to them when he thought Jai had murdered the old emperor himself.

'So, then,' Rufus grunted taking a seat on the cot. 'What did the old bastard have to say?'

Jai closed his eyes, thinking back to those last words. He could not remember them exactly, but . . .

'He begged your forgiveness,' Jai said. 'And your favour, for me.'

Rufus said nothing. His face was suddenly expressionless.

Jai continued. 'He even helped me escape . . . so I could get to you, I guess. Before I . . . you know.'

Rufus chewed the edges of his moustache. Then he got up, slapping his knees.

'I'll make sure we weren't followed. You rest for a few hours – we'll be on the move all tomorrow.' He pushed through the door, out into the night.

Jai hadn't needed Rufus's warning. Nor did he even request the cot. Instead, he slid to the floor beside the fire, curling up upon a thin, deerskin rug. Winter slipped up his shirt into the hollow of his stomach, pressing her warm scales against his skin. That alone felt heavenly.

Rufus could come back and murder them in their sleep. Or the bandits might slip by Rufus and do the same. None of it seemed to matter. Jai would wager his life on the flip of the coin if he could get just one hour of sleep.

Chapter 57

J ai felt as if he'd hardly shut his eyes before Rufus was slapping him awake. It was like being lifted and shaken by a bear.

'We leave now.' Rufus muttered, dropping Jai on his feet as soon as his eyes fluttered open.

Winter was already awake, somewhere on the roof by Jai's estimation. And Frida was outside. He could see her through the open doorway, combing her hair in the morning sunlight. The ink had almost all run out in the drizzle of the night before, but the lustrous sheen that marked her as Dansk had still not returned.

Sunlight. That meant morning.

'We should have left hours ago,' Jai whispered.

'We tried tae,' Rufus grunted. 'Twas like waking the dead. And your little beastie weren't too happy with me manhandlin' you. But . . . I think even she got tired of waitin' and let me near this time. Fierce little one, ain't she?'

There was the scent of cooked bacon in the air, but all Jai saw was an empty skillet. That and a thick red tongue lapping at the moustaches surrounding it. So much for hospitality.

Rufus stood, brushing his knees. 'Did the old bastard let you sleep in all day?'

'He hardly left his bed,' Jai muttered, rubbing the sleep from his eyes.

Rufus's hand shoved him out into the warmth of the sun.

Frida was sitting on a rock in the clearing before the house. 'Took you long enough,' she muttered.

'Sorry. If I was conscious, I'd have . . . woken myself up,' Jai said lamely.

She shrugged, and her slender fingers began to make quick work of her hair, plaiting it into a loose braid.

'Gave me time to soulbreathe. Last time I'll let us get caught like that again. It was stupid. *We* were stupid.'

Jai scratched his chin and sensed a sudden drop before feeling Winter alight on his shoulders. Her wings had flapped once before folding into her shoulders.

He grinned. A good sign.

'So,' Rufus said, clapping his hands loud enough to make Jai wince. 'Where now, my erstwhile employers?'

Jai didn't know what to say. Somehow, he'd expected Rufus to know where to go next. Clearly, Frida had thought the same, for the swift retort Jai had expected was not forthcoming. Rufus stared at them each in turn, hand stroking his red beard.

'Shall we play happy families for the week? Or perhaps your highness might want tae go for a nice stroll back the way we came.'

Frida glared at him.

'Don't call me that.'

Rufus cackled.

'Not you, *milady*. Why, I was speakin' tae King Jai of the Kidara, first of his name. You should curtsy tae him. What an honour it must be.'

Frida snarled and lashed out. Her hand moved in a blur, so fast Jai flinched.

There was the slap of meat upon meat, and Jai almost felt the air shake at the impact. But he did see her knuckles buried in Rufus's meaty palm, and him snapping his fingers closed around them.

'All tae be expected,' Rufus said, almost gently, as Frida cried out in sudden pain. 'You're a soulbound. And no' a bad one, neither. You're no' too happy about the arrangement that *circumstances* have forced upon you. No' me, you understand. *Circumstances*. Say it with me, lass.'

'*Circumstances*,' Frida gritted out. Jai saw her hand dart for the whytblade at her side, but Rufus had already stepped away.

Immediately, she collapsed to the ground, nursing her hand.

'Nothing broken,' Rufus said cheerily. 'Just wanted tae get that out o' the way now, afore we set off.'

Jai knelt beside Frida and Winter leaped from his shoulder to hers, nuzzling her cheek. She lifted her good hand and scratched the little beast under her chin.

'I'm OK,' she said, more to Winter than Jai. Then, 'You're no ordinary soulbound, are you?'

'No, lass,' Rufus said. 'Not bloody likely. You're ascended, true, but you're barely a fifth-level soulbound at best, if you even know what that means. I remember when I was at your level. My balls hadn't dropped yet.'

Frida cursed bitterly under her breath. Rufus leaned in, listening with a hand cupped around a conch-like ear.

'Oh, I've never put anything up there before,' he chuckled. 'But I'm game if you are.'

Frida looked up at him sharply.

'You speak Dansk?' she asked.

He winked and held out a hand. She stared at it for a moment, then lifted her arm and wiggled her fingers. She took his help grudgingly, and he yanked her to her feet.

'So, tae show you I'm on your side, you'll see I've been busy. Now, I know 'tis no' as pretty as your dress, and maker knows 'tis too small for you, but I've found something a little more . . . well, see for yourself.'

He ducked into the cabin, before coming out with a garment in his hands. It was . . . a smock. The kind worn by old women, or widows. A stark contrast to the embroidered dress that by now was so ripped and sullied it looked like a sabretooth had taken its claws to it.

'Been stuffed up in my rafters for nigh on ten years – I used it tae plug up a draught. And here.'

He tossed a pair of thick, wool socks to Jai, then a pair of boots that Jai promptly dropped.

'Took these off a man who thought he'd test my patience with a bit o' robbery on my way home one night. Failed that test. He sure had fun showing up at the Phoenix with his twig and berries out.'

He nodded at Jai's bare feet.

'Checked your size when you were sleepin'.'

Jai could not help but grin. Though, as a musty scent filled his nostrils, he held the socks out at arm's length.

'Socks're mine though,' Rufus chuckled. 'My other pair. You'll need 'em if you expect the boots tae fit.'

He turned to Frida and dangled the smock tantalisingly, holding it up to his own chest and swaying his hips.

'You go get dressed, and I'll just have a chat with his majesty here.'

Frida looked at Jai, gauging him.

'I'll be OK,' Jai said. 'I bet you can't wait to get out of that thing. Go on, you're a shout away if he tries something.'

Rufus rolled his eyes at that.

'Oh, *aye*. There's me, hellbent on murderin' you, watchin' the two of you snoring away in my home. And I think to myself, why, best thing tae do is wake 'em, clothe 'em, and *then* do the murderin'. You've got me.'

Frida spat off to the side, then stomped by Rufus, snatching the dress as she passed.

'Good lass,' Rufus said, barely containing a grin.

Then he turned to Jai, and his smile faded.

'So, your *eminence*. You said you'd tell me the rest on the road. Well, I say the road starts here. Get talkin'.'

Chapter 58

The story took a surprisingly short time to recount. It was strange to sum up his life in a handful of breaths, but that was what he did.

He did not lie. He did not embellish. It felt wrong somehow. Despite this man's dubious provenance, Rufus had clearly been deeply wronged at Leonid's hands. Deeply enough to have become a drunk, despite his power, passing his days in the lowest pub in all the land. To lie to Rufus in the recounting of a life so intertwined with his own felt . . . dirty.

The words tumbled out of him like the tears on his cheeks; rushed and unplanned. It was as if he had been holding the story within him, the tale wound tight as a spring.

Rufus, to his credit, listened without interruption. Not even to clarify when Jai's words lost direction, nor when he mumbled or paused.

Only when Jai mentioned the killing of his brothers did Rufus stir. A simple gesture, a closing of his eyes and the lowering of his head. It was enough. Enough for Jai to know there was good in this man.

Rufus sniffed loudly as Jai ended his tale by confessing he

had not killed Leonid after all. The words petering out like the dregs of an upturned flask. And just like one, he felt empty. Purposeless.

'I had you pegged one way, lad. Not wrong, per se. But not right either. I've a trade tae offer. This one, I won't force on you. Refuse it, and I'll honour your decision.'

Jai looked up at him, his eyes burning from spent tears.

'You said you've read every book upon Leonid's shelves. But you don't know my name . . . or any like it?'

Jai nodded slowly.

'The book in yon bag. You say it's in Leonid's own hand. From the War of the Steppe, 'afore he had you and the priests transcribe 'em?'

Jai nodded slowly.

'Then I'll trade you for it. Just for the week, mind – I know you've plans tae read it yourself. I'll give it back when we part ways.'

This was unexpected. Jai wondered just how this man had known Leonid. Perhaps he had once been a Gryphon Guard. After all, following the execution of those ten traitor knights, Leonid had had every member's name wiped from history's pages. Maybe they had been Rufus's friends.

Or was he related, somehow, to the strange boudoir he had stumbled across? Perhaps the woman or child had been Rufus's wife. Or daughter.

Jai looked to the bag, where Frida had dumped it unceremoniously by the door. He knew he had to read the journal. But there was too much for him to cope with right now. It was hard enough keeping his brothers' faces from haunting his thoughts.

Had Rufus not asked for it, he might not have looked at it

for another month. He'd lend it for a hot meal, let alone whatever Rufus might give him, if he was sure he'd get it back.

Still, it was best to let Rufus tell him what he had to offer first. Jai hardly knew what more he could ask for beyond food, garb or simple tender. Or . . . arms.

'I'll trade it for Frida's blade,' Jai said, siezed by inspiration.

Rufus chuckled drily.

'Nay lad, that dagger's tae be my retirement. Saves me from having to sell *this* beauty.'

He stepped back and drew the weapon at his side, holding it up to the light. It was a slim, single-edged blade, made entirely of one solid piece of metal – hilt included. The sword was unusual in one other aspect, and it confirmed Jai's suspicions of Rufus's origin. The hilt took the shape of a gryphon's head, with its extended wings flaring into its crossguard. Jai knew it must have cost a fortune to forge it.

'Sometimes feel like I've been carryin' this longer than my own cock . . . and played with it more too.' Rufus gave Jai a wink, and slid it back into its simple scabbard.

To Jai's surprise, he bowed down, taking some dirt from the ground and muddying the exposed hilt.

'Never know who'll recognise the metal,' Rufus said, pulling his cloak over it once more. 'If'n I'd known Camilla had heard tell of them, I'd've been more careful. Rare things, they are.'

Jai chewed his lip, somewhat disappointed. Still, he had to get *something*. He wasn't sure if when Rufus had a few drinks, his sense of honour might give in to curiosity. The old warrior would read it anyway.

'So, what, then?' Jai said. 'Another week's protection? That'll only get us halfway to the border.'

He reached up, and scratched Winter absently beneath her

chin. She was hungry. He went to the bag to fetch her another carrot.

Rufus eyed him with a measured gaze.

'You've some knowledge,' he said. 'You can't've managed tae soulbreathe without Frida givin' you some pointers. Well, lemme tell you somethin' lad. I've lived a long life. Killed more men than I can remember, and then some more for bad measure. You can learn better parlour tricks, and more besides, from other sects out there. But none'll teach you tae kill like I can.'

Who *was* this man? His accent was an unusual one, now that Jai thought about it. He recognised it as Samarion, from the northern reaches, on the border where Frida's homeland met the northmost edge of the empire.

But stranger still was the way he spoke it. Most times he sounded like a common man, plainspoken. Yet other times, his verbiage seemed beyond it. As if he were someone born poor, and fallen into wealth and education. And if he spoke truly – and his Samarion tattoo said he did – he was a trained killer.

Jai tossed a carrot above his head with feigned nonchalance and heard the snap of Winter's beak. The pulse of revulsion moments later was so visceral, he almost pawed at his own tongue. The message was received. Not one of the little beast's favourites.

'Say I believe you,' Jai said, grimacing at the strange aftertaste in his dragon's mouth. 'What of it?'

Rufus splayed his hands, then brought them in to thump his chest.

'I'll train you up, lad. And more besides.'

Jai had to force himself to not blurt out in enthusiastic agreement.

'One week of soulbreathing advice?' he said casually, squatting on a stack of firewood and tugging on the slightly-too-loose boots. 'I think I can manage without it.'

Rufus held up his hands in surrender.

'There'll be more tae it than that. Wisdoms even your Frida can't share. She's a fifth-level soulbound, being generous.'

Jai considered the proposal. Rufus took Jai's silence for confusion, and went on:

'She's young, but she should be better'n that. Plus, them Dansk've always relied on the strength of their dragons. They know the simpler spells and charms, knowledge even the smallest sects have. Little more.'

Jai didn't have to force the scepticism in his face. He might have believed that about Ivar, but Frida was no illiterate ruffian. She'd have sought out every scrap of knowledge she could have if it would have allowed her to better protect her people.

But he *did* believe that there might be a few scraps to be had. And he was about to be offered a week's protection.

Rufus spoke again before Jai could accept.

'You think about it,' Rufus said. 'Take the day.'

Jai opened his mouth, and now Frida's voice called out from inside.

'Three weeks,' she called out. 'You protect us for three weeks. Fifty sesterii too, and lessons for me. We'll accept it then.'

She stomped out the door, giving Jai a look that told him any comments about her smock would be met with violence hitherto unimagined.

Jai was only a little annoyed that she'd negotiated on his behalf, especially for something that held such importance to him. But he supposed he'd done something similar in the tavern. She'd asked for more than he'd have thought to. A lifetime of coinless opulence was working against him.

'Deal,' Rufus uttered a little too quickly.

Already, he had his palm extended. Jai turned it into a hand-shake, gripping him at the wrist.

'Money and a safe place to sleep tonight first,' Frida said, as Rufus again reached out for the book. 'Just to be sure you're not distracted. Our first day will be our most dangerous.'

Rufus grumbled at that.

'Don't count on it,' he said.

Chapter 59

They did not head straight for the Kashmere Road – not least because they knew the legion would be ahead of them by now. Instead, Rufus led them down the back trails; ways known only to goatherds, bandits and the like.

It would take them longer, but they'd overtake the legion if they marched into the night. On a war footing – even on home territory – the legion threw up a short palisade each night that meant they stopped before sundown to cut stakes from the surrounding vegetation.

Already, the neat square fields of crops that made up the western empire were becoming less frequent and being replaced by scrubland and rocky ground.

To Jai's surprise, Frida expressed sadness at the change in scenery. She had taken a liking to the remnants of corn they'd scavenged, and this area only had the remains of headless wheat stalks.

The four of them walked in silence, much to Jai's chagrin, but he did not complain. Rufus had promised them a safe place to sleep that night, and a way to get ahead of the legion – that was enough for him. His sleep the night before had not felt like sleep, but like he'd closed his eyes for a second and time had moved forward when he wasn't looking.

Still, he was conscious enough to put one foot in front of the other until at midday they settled on a log beside the overgrown path and took the time to eat something.

Crunching down raw vegetables was quite unsatisfying, made more so by Rufus's own repast of buttered bread and salt pork. He grinned at their wolfish looks as he licked the oils from his fingers.

Only Winter received any pity from him, gulping down the rind of fat he had cut from the meat whole when he tossed it to her. She needed it – she was now refusing outright the carrots of the past days and roaming further and further afield as they walked, hunting for field mice in the brambles surrounding them.

'We'll get supplies tomorrow mornin'. And transport. Hell, you might just get a chance tae soulbreathe, Jai.'

Jai's ears perked up at that.

'You're going to teach me?' Jai asked.

Rufus sniffed.

'Soon as you give me the journal.'

Jai sighed and dug the journal from Frida's pack. He handed it over, but withheld it as Rufus reached out his hand.

'I want this back if you don't teach us something Frida doesn't already know. It has to be good.'

'It was good enough for half the Eyrie,' Rufus growled. 'Let alone a little upstart like . . .'

He stopped himself and nodded.

'Fine,' he said. 'Keep it till the evening. I'll teach you somethin'.'

Jai furrowed his brow.

'You taught at the Eyrie?' Jai asked.

Rufus stared at him.

'Aye,' he said. 'That I did.'

He looked at Jai, then Frida.

'I suppose there's no harm in tellin' you. It's not like you're gonna run off tae the Sabines and tell 'em my whereabouts. You're the enemy o' my enemy, no?'

Jai nodded, though the man was mostly talking to himself.

'I was a Gryphon Guard, once. Long time ago now.'

Jai's eyes boggled at that, even if he had suspected it before.

'I have never heard of you,' Jai said. 'Even if you were a rejected acolyte . . .'

Rufus interrupted with a laugh.

'Ain't no such thing as a reject. The Gryphon Guard is for life, whether you're a servant or a warrior. That, you must know.'

Jai sniffed. He *had* been testing him.

'So, you escaped, then. That's why you live in hiding.'

Rufus looked him dead in the eye.

'In a way lad. Now, do you wanna learn or no'?'

Jai nodded, biting back the many questions swirling around his head.

'All right,' Frida muttered. 'Teachings have been a bit thin on the ground so far. Perhaps we should make it a hundred sesterii.'

Rufus clapped his hands, sending Winter scuttling down Jai's shirt.

'Right. Now, I know you can enter the trance on your own. Good. Some acolytes take months tae master it.'

Jai allowed himself a small amount of pride.

'Now forget what you've been doin' so far. Long deep breaths, right?'

Jai gave a second, hesitant nod.

'Nay lad. You're a warrior, not some ink-faced scroll-squinter. Short, tight breaths. You enter a half-trance. You can walk, ride, even do it while you majick. 'Tis less effective, and you can't direct it. But it means you can keep on the move. You let the mana travel where it will – it'll reach your core eventually. You try, lad. Come on. We've a fair ways tae go yet.'

At this, even Frida listened.

'And for the higher levels?' she asked. 'Is it enough mana to make it worth doing?'

Rufus nodded.

'Not nearly as much as if you were soulbreathin' properly. But enough tae top you up when the fightin's fiercest and time's a luxury.'

As he spoke he was already walking.

For a few minutes, Jai trotted behind and simply tried to remember what it was like to enter the so-called *trance*. To do it while seated and breathing long, calming breaths was one thing. But with the wind, uneven ground, even the basic movement of his legs, it seemed impossible, fast breaths or not.

'You sure this is a thing?' Jai asked.

Rufus snorted.

'It's an advanced technique – we call it the *hummingbird*. We only teach it to knights, since the squires're better off doing it the usual way. Comes easy to some. Harder for others. Listen.'

Jai did, and heard short, rapid breaths that were more akin to a dog panting than normal human breathing. Still, he'd paid for this teaching. It might have been with coin he wasn't sure he'd ever spend, but it was a payment just the same.

So . . . he panted.

Chapter 60

Their journey passed in a blur, as Jai danced along the edge of the half-trance. It required a strange form of double think. To both focus and empty his mind at once. A few times, he caught glimpses of what the half-trance was. The edges of things seemed to shift, and eddies of golden light faded in and out of sight.

It was, to Jai's surprise, Winter that helped him finally break through. The dragon had returned with a full belly at dusk, when the torchlights of what counted for civilisation along the Kashmere Road came into view. She took what was becoming her customary place upon his shoulder, her swinging tail tickling his lower back.

In one of those rare moments where his hummingbird breaths settled into a semi-comfortable rhythm, he managed a glimpse of that world again. And in that moment, just as it escaped his mental grasp, a jolt of stubborn feeling pulsed down their connection.

It was distracting enough to empty his mind of his surroundings while also focusing his thoughts upon his core and connection. And for a few seconds, he found the mindset.

He felt the mana swirling within his lungs, felt his core compress and swell in tandem with his breathing . . . allowing that directionless mana to filter through his lungs. A golden, purifying light, permeating his being.

His surroundings were like ghosts. Opaque and blurred, as if he could walk right through them. And all the while, golden dust flowed around him, hanging in the air like a fine, dry mist.

Then, the feeling was gone. But once he'd achieved it the first time it was relatively easy to slip into that state again – made easier by listening to the vagaries of Winter's feelings. She communicated only sporadically, but if he sent her a feeling of his own, he found she reciprocated in kind. Mostly, she was worried.

She did not worry about anything specific. Rather, her feelings were a reflection of his own. Somehow, it was easier to understand himself from her perspective. He had ignored that sense of impending dread – partitioned it off in his mind. No longer. Now, he faced it. Fought it. And became stronger for it. He found there was more within him than despair. His life, hitherto limited to caring for an aging god, had moved on. His world was no longer confined to a wardrobe, or a chamber, or a palace. The few tastes he'd had of walking the city streets were nothing in comparison to the vast expanse of opportunity before him.

This was a freedom he hadn't even known he'd been denied. To walk an untamed land, each step a discovery, each moment ripe and vivid as the first bite of a new fruit. He revelled in it.

Jai practised the half-trance as he walked. It was strange to see the gold framework wash through the world, beyond what he could make out in the gloom. See the outline of trees, of rocks, of the topography itself, where the flowing motes of light were *not*. It was like seeing rocks in a rushing stream.

It was hard. With each snatched breath, the mana barely reached beyond his core, only following the natural eddies of his channels. Not to mention that breathing that way left him out of breath and dry-throated.

But it was useful. In the evenings, when he could enter the full trance, he would build up a reserve. During the day, he would slowly top up this mana with the hummingbird technique even as it drained away at the whims of his body.

When Rufus eventually led them to the gates of a town, Jai was glad of it. His clothing was sweat-stained and ragged, and he'd taken most of it off a corpse – albeit a fresh one.

Before they stepped through the gates, Jai turned back to look down the long, cobbled highway that made up the Kashmere Road. The legion was close behind. So close in fact, Jai would not have been surprised to see some officers in the tavern. He could see the lights of their camp no more than a brisk walk away.

Somewhere in the wilderness behind them, Jai sensed Winter had found shelter, and she was beginning to doze.

'Right,' Rufus growled. 'I've a friend who owes me a favour. He's a trader, but he doesn't travel the road much. Just buys wares from other traders who want tae turn back east and sells it to those who don't. At a mark-up, of course. You lovebirds stay here.'

The near-squawk of indignation from Frida only slightly dented Jai's ego. Still, it gave him the motivation to squat by a helpful rainwater-fed trough at a hitching shelter outside the gates and scrub at himself with wet straw.

It was somewhat freeing to be a wild man, roaming like an unwashed bandit away from the routine and drudgery of his previous existence. The romance of it all only occasionally faded behind the reality. Now was one of those times.

'You believe he is who he says?' Frida said.

Jai looked up from the handful of straw he'd been scrubbing

his neck with. A mule sipping further down the trough whinnied and stepped away, stretching her halter as far as it would go. He sighed and tossed the straw, admitting defeat.

'He is not mentioned in Leonid's books – but it's true that Leonid had the names of every Gryphon Guard struck from them after . . .'

His thoughts came in bursts, half-formed. He'd been so focused on soulbreathing, he'd hardly given Rufus's story any consideration. It had been foolish, in truth.

He stopped, considering what he knew.

'There were some of their knights executed, more than ten years ago. It was right before I entered Leonid's service. Perhaps . . . Rufus left them then?'

Frida sniffed, her eyes fixed on the torchlight of the legion's camp behind them.

'We are safer if he hates the Sabines,' she said. 'But it is strange. He has put us in mortal peril. He has tricked us several times over. Yet . . . I trust him. He is an honourable man . . . who acts as if he is not.'

Jai tried to wrap his mind around that one, but gave up as exhaustion set in. Then there was Rufus, beckoning them to follow, and a portly, bespectacled man peering nervously behind Rufus's bulky form.

'Honourable or not,' Jai said. 'He's all we've got.'

Chapter 61

They stayed in a stable that night, one belonging to Rufus's contact in the village. Jai had slept near the doors, away from the dark interior, for there was the animal stench of beasts, deeper within.

Straw was becoming Jai's friend. Itchy though it was, his straw bedding had allowed him to sleep almost all the way through the night, but for a brief interlude of soulbreathing when he'd woken to relieve himself.

He'd found it harder to soulbreathe while Winter was asleep, and the amount of mana he produced was far less than what he managed when she had been touching him. Even so, he'd made solid progress, building a small reserve he hoped he could keep throughout the day. He thanked the heavens Rufus had taught it to him. He'd waxed lyrical on the subject earlier that day, which resulted in Rufus claiming to have invented it, though a snort from Frida told Jai that of all things, *that* she didn't believe.

Jai wasn't so sure. At the least, the old guard had named it.

Now, he dozed in the relative warmth of the winter morning, curled beneath a potato sack. He listened absently to the hubbub of activity outside. He only wished Winter was here to cuddle.

He wouldn't mind Frida joining him for a cuddle either. He could almost feel that pair of soft lips nuzzling at his ear. Her hot breath . . . her . . . tongue?

Jai leaped up with a yelp and a great, furry form reared, lowing in surprise. The beast crashed back, its hooves thundering a tattoo on the ground. Before long, it was lost in the shadows.

Jai heard cackling, and turned to see Frida with her head thrown back, seated on a hay bale.

'You seemed to be enjoying that,' she chuckled.

Jai blushed hard, glad his trousers were loose. Before he could say anything, the stable doors were thrown open and Rufus stomped inside, his face a picture of mischief.

'I see you've met our new steed. She's an old girl, but she's sure o' foot and used tae the road. Come here, Lovely.'

He clicked his tongue and extended a wrinkled onion upon his palm. A mournful snuffling came from the stable's gloomy interior and then Jai watched as a khiro stomped into the dawn light.

Jai was amazed. Khiroi were rare in the west, for they were notoriously hard to tame, particularly the males. They also ate half their weight in grass each day, making them expensive beasts to keep when away from their native grasslands.

This did not seem a problem for her current owner. Even through the layer of shaggy, wiry fur, the outline of her ribs were as clear as the spars of a ship.

She was different to the great beast he had mercy-killed in the Sabine hunting grounds. Smaller, and with a horn not like the great mast he had seen on his late quarry, but so short and blunt as to be almost decorative. It was set above wide, puckered nostrils and framed by two conch-like ears. She was a greying, older specimen, but she still had the tri-toed hooves, barrel-belly and squat shape that made her kind the invaluable beasts of burden of the Great Steppe.

The khiro gave Jai a wide birth as she sniffed at the onion, then a long, leathery tongue lapped it from Rufus's hand like a dog snarfing up a treat. Her eyes, though small, were bright with intelligence, and she eyed him warily as she crunched through the pungent vegetable like it was the most decadent treat in the world.

'There you are, Navi,' Rufus said.

'I thought their horns were bigger,' Frida said.

'She's a female,' Rufus said. 'This is as big as theirs get. Now a male un' . . . that's a different kettle o' fish. Bigger, meaner . . . but the princeling here'll tell you all about that.'

Jai knew he could not, for what little he knew of them had been told him by Balbir when he was but a youngling. Still, there was something about the beast that drew him to her. Not least the Damantine steel armour he wore on his upper chest, which depicted her wilder male counterpart.

Rufus scratched Navi's snout, and she trumpeted in delight, leaning in closer and turning her head. Now that Jai looked closer, he saw the scarring upon her face. Strange lines, curling about her ears and cheeks. He felt rage stir within him as he realised it was the work of a whip or cane. He dreaded to think what other old wounds might be hidden beneath the shag of her coat.

'Where's her old owner?' Jai asked.

Rufus's eyes shifted away.

'Let's just say . . . he'd forgotten the favour he owed me. Thought lettin' you kip in his stables was enough. Had tae . . . convince him to part with 'er. Only a little forceful-like. But we'd best be off soon.'

Jai allowed himself a grin at that. That a beast which had been so abused still trusted enough to take food from the hand of a big man like Rufus was a testament to her good heart. He only wished he could risk an altercation with her former owner.

There were . . . not so much words . . . that he wished to exchange with him.

But the confrontation at the Phoenix had taught Jai his lesson. One group hunting them was enough. Taking her off the man's hands would have to do.

'You don't think a khiro will make Jai seem more . . . Steppe-like?' Frida asked.

Rufus shrugged.

'Maybe so. But it's all that's available, and a khiro'll walk all day and night, then ask for more. She'll haul you over rough ground and soft, road or track. You can ask for no finer work animal. Just need to make sure we feed her.'

Jai took a hesitant step towards Navi. Even a few days ago, approaching such a beast would have terrified him. Now . . . he was more scared of startling her.

'It's OK,' Jai whispered. 'I'm not here to hurt you.'

Her eyes. They were so expressive – almost human. He could see the distrust . . . and hope. Hope, that he might show her some kindness.

He extended his hand, and gently ran a finger beneath her chin. In his mind, he felt a twinge of jealousy from Winter.

'Don't you worry, Winter,' Jai whispered, smiling half to himself. 'There's room for more than one lady in my life.'

Frida's chuckle at that was only a little hurtful.

'Now you've got yourselves acquainted, come on outside,' Rufus said. 'See what else your sesterii bought you.'

He threw open the doors, ignoring Frida's garbled indignation at his apparent spending of the money he owed them.

But her protests fell silent at the wagon outside.

'You find this on the side of the road?' she grumbled.

It was a ragged thing. Navi's counterpart in every way, battered, old and scarred. The canvas awning that covered its wooden frame was so torn Jai could see right through it in places.

'She's got fine bones on her,' Rufus said, stomping forward and slapping the wheel. 'Ironwood frame, ironwood wheels. There's no worse thing than a broken-down wagon on the road, so that's what matters. Don't matter it weighs a ton when you've got a khiro pullin' it. We'll patch her up when we make camp tonight. No more stables for you. Or taverns, for that matter.'

He parted the open slit at the front, showing them the inside. There was a heavy layer of fresh straw there, as well as an enormous sack of what Jai assumed were more vegetables. There wasn't much else, but for a string of garlic and a thick leg of salt pork hanging from the wicker spars. Enough to last them the journey, at a pinch.

'Is there anything left?' Frida demanded. 'Or did you spend it all.'

Rufus grumbled and held out his ham-hock of a fist to drop a handful of coins into her palm.

'You should be payin' me, the deal I got. A khiro and wagon outta cost twice what I paid.'

Frida was unimpressed, instead transferring the sesterii to her purse and scanning their surroundings. The village was small; little more than a gated and walled market square with ramshackle huts studded along the walls. But there were wares to be had. Not just food but leathers, furs, spices, even tools.

'After today,' she said. 'I want to avoid the villages. So, we buy what we need here. All of it.'

Rufus rolled his eyes, but eventually allowed them a curt nod.

'It's your money. But we'd best set off soon; the legion'll be on the move within the hour and they're no' far off.'

Frida had already taken hold of Jai's arm. It seemed they were going shopping.

Chapter 62

Frida was in oddly good spirits as she strode about the market square peering from stall to stall, shop to shop. With enough vegetables and meat to keep them going for the foreseeable future they skirted the more crowded food stalls and went to the shops themselves.

The handmaiden seemed far too relaxed for Jai's liking, though she kept her stained hair covered. Even in her matronly smock, she drew glances from others. The dress was small for her and did little to hide her slim, feminine frame, nor did the shawl obscure her striking features. Her natural beauty was hard to disguise.

He had little to hide his own appearance, but he kept his head down and his fringe over his eyes. It would have to do. He suspected the general state of him made most give him a wide berth.

'This one,' Frida said. 'Hurry now.'

She pointed to a low shop entrance. Strangely, it had no symbol or sign to demonstrate the wares it had within, nor anything on display, for it had no window. Its only feature of merit was there seemed to be nobody in or near it. In fact, Jai was not even sure it was a shop at all and said so.

'Look there,' Frida said, nodding at the door lintel. 'See the symbol?'

Jai looked closely and made out a handprint there. It was hardly anything to look at, almost a child's finger painting.

'What is it?' Jai asked.

'It means this place sells items for the soulbound,' Frida said. 'It's a gallipot. A small one, but it'll have what we need.'

Jai furrowed his brow.

'I've never seen one in Latium,' Jai said.

Frida laughed at that.

'Nor would you. The Gryphon Guard have all they could ever want in their headquarters, I'm sure.'

'Why the secrecy?' he asked. 'Why hide it?'

Frida shook her head and gave Jai a pitying look that was only slightly patronising.

'A good soulgem is worth more than most people's homes. They prefer to stay hidden – keeps the bandits from their doors. Not that any in their right mind would rob one. Gallipots are usually owned by retired soulbound warriors, selling the wares they've gathered in their careers.'

Jai didn't get a chance to respond, for Frida disappeared into the shop's dark confines before he could digest what she had said. He followed her eagerly, though. This was something *new*.

Inside the shop, Jai was immediately struck by the herbaceous smell. With his slow-draining mana to boost his senses, it was overwhelming.

The space within was small and Jai hardly dared move for fear of knocking something over. A counter with a curtained doorway behind it took up the majority of the space, and Frida leaned against it, rapping her knuckles against the wood.

Jai was in no hurry, swivelling slowly with widening eyes. The walls were packed to the rafters with bottles, chests and boxes balanced precariously upon leaning shelves. Leaves, roots, bark, flowers and seeds were stored in baskets or hung in garlands from the ceiling.

Stoppered glass bottles and jars were everywhere, prefilled with liquids, tinctures, resins, salves and unguents, if the labels that adorned them spoke true. But strangest of all were the pills.

Jai had seen pills before, for Leonid's ailments, real and imagined, had demanded their use on occasion. Even Constantine had been rumoured to use questionable aphrodisiac pills, such that they had become nicknamed 'little emperors'.

But these . . . they amazed him in their numbers and colours. Some were hard, chalky pellets, hand-moulded and stored in baskets of sawdust. Others came in strange, rice-gum-wrapped capsules, piled high in their jars and urns.

Frida's knuckles rapped the counter again and Jai finally heard the sound of movement from upstairs. She turned and gave him a forced smile.

'It's not the best-stocked, but it will have what we need.'

Jai couldn't imagine what a well-stocked gallipot looked like, if this was not one. Nor could he imagine what item Frida could want. Looking closer, he could even see animal parts, pickling in yellow-green liquids on the shelves.

'What do you want?' a quavering voice called from behind the curtained-off interior.

'We've plenty of denarii and we intend to spend them all,' Frida called back.

There was a grunt of annoyance; then the curtains parted. A small, wrinkled old woman stepped into view; one so short and hunched that her small, black eyes hardly saw over the counter. It was not the woman who drew Jai's attention, though, but the beast that lowered itself from the rafters onto her shoulders.

It was monkey-like in some ways, complete with grasping

hands, a flat, simian face and bright, intelligent eyes. But in others it was like a squirrel, with an impossibly long and fluffy tail lashing above its tufted ears while somehow avoiding knocking anything over.

The woman took them in at a single glance, then chewed her lip.

'Gallipots take no sides,' she said. 'And true Samarions tell no lies. But a Dansk and a Steppeman . . . means trouble.'

Jai went to protest, but Frida caught his eye and shook her head.

'You refuse us, that's taking the Sabines' side,' she said. 'You're a shopkeep. So keep your shop.'

The old woman said nothing until Frida emptied her purse upon the counter. A coin rolled towards the edge and the old woman slapped down a hand upon it. She lifted it and handed it to her beast.

It sniffed it, then bit it, before letting out an animated chatter. The old woman stared at them for a moment longer, then gave a curt nod.

'You get caught, you've never been here. Understand?'

Jai found his mouth suddenly too dry to speak, so he nodded back.

'My pithecus here will get what you want if it's out o' reach. Just point at it and he'll bring it tae the counter.'

The vendor punctuated this with a groan as she eased herself onto a tall stool. The pithecus chattered excitedly and leaped into the rafters, watching them closely. It seemed stealing was out of the question. Not that Jai was tempted.

'We've need of soulbreathing pills,' Frida said, in her usual blunt way.

The old lady smiled at that.

'I guessed. Nothin' gets past old Kenna.'

She winked at Jai and waved a gnarled hand.

'I've pills for faster cleansin'. Pills for reachin' the trance easier. Pills for holding it longer. Pills to ease your breathin'. I've even pills that'll fill you with mana, but that'll cost more'n you've got.'

Jai looked at her curiously. Kenna's accent was like Rufus's – another Samarion then. Frida was oblivious, already rummaging through the shop's shelves, lifting things to the meagre light from the shop's single transom window for a better look.

Jai stood awkwardly and forced a smile. The old lady smiled back politely.

'Your beast . . . I've never seen its like before,' Jai said, wincing as Frida's search sent a pot-lid rolling along the paved floor.

'Oh, he's a rare one. Comes from a land across the Silver Seas and far beyond that, tae boot. Cost me half my store for him, truth be told. But when my direwolf died, I couldn't go without a companion.'

Jai had heard of direwolves. Larger and more powerful than their more common wolf and dog cousins, they made for excellent totems.

'Where's your khiro?' Kenna asked. 'The one outside seems a bit old for you.'

She noticed his surprised expression.

'I can smell it on the both of you,' she said. 'I can tell t'isn't far.'

Jai stopped for a minute, considering her. Could he trust her with the knowledge that he had a dragon?

'You say you're a Samarion,' he said. 'And you've an accent to match. But I hear hardly any of you are religious these days.'

She smiled, then cocked her head to the side, lifting the hair behind her ear. There, he saw the symbol of an open eye, tattooed in black. The same one Rufus had. She let her hair drop.

'One lie and my soul goes straight tae hellfire. Our word is our bond. 'Tis a dying religion now. But those who follow it thrive.'

Jai nodded politely, but her assurance did little to ease his worries. She could be lying right then for all he knew.

'I need a satchel,' Jai said. 'I know it's not quite what you sell here, but I'll pay a fair price if you have one spare.'

Her face split into a smile.

'I've just the thing. It's not cheap, mind.'

She disappeared behind the curtain once more, and Jai heard her slow stomping up the stairs. Above, the pithecus lowered itself by its tail, its black-and-white banded fur standing on end as it stared at him with large, placid eyes.

'Frida,' Jai hissed, unnerved by its gaze. 'What are you looking for?'

Still Frida rummaged.

'She has enough ingredients, but the readymade pills she's got are hardly worth swallowing. Stuff for acolytes still cleansing themselves.'

'Makes sense,' Jai said.

He was beginning to feel sick at the smell of the herbs, spices and heaven knew what else mouldering on the shelves. It was no wonder the shopkeeper preferred to stay upstairs.

Jai heard the tinkle of the curtain rings on their rail and turned to see Kenna holding up a leather satchel. It was little more than the same one that legionaries wore, but she opened it wordlessly at his dubious expression to show him the inside, where she had added pockets and netting to hold other items. Best of all, there was plenty of room for Winter, though the little dragon had grown an inch in the space of a few days. Before long, she'd not be so easy to keep out of sight.

'Five sesterii. And that's a fair price, before you ask for less,' she said.

Frida, strangely, did not argue. She counted out the coins, scraping each one across the table with a finger.

'I need . . .'

Frida began, but already the shopkeeper had placed a single, golden-coloured pill upon the table. Even in the gloom of the shop, it seemed to glow.

'This what you're looking for?'

Frida looked like she was practically salivating at the sight of the pill.

'It's a *third*-grade lustration pill, afore you get too excited,' Kenna said. 'But you couldn't afford first-grade quality anyway. This'll double your soulbreathing speed and purify your mana, for a time. Might even help you advance to the next level. I'll take ten sesterii for it. And before you ask again, I do think this is a fair price too.'

'Done,' Frida said.

Jai let out a small grunt of protest, but it was hardly audible over the jingle of coins as Frida counted them out. While this happened Jai looked hungrily at the pills around the shop.

It was not so much that they looked delicious – they most decidedly did not, especially when he could see the grislier ingredients that might have gone into them sitting on the shelf beside them.

Still, with the paltry remainder of their coins, he hoped they could buy *something* to help his own soulbound training. Kenna grinned at his expression, and her pithecus swung to a shelf and back. A little black hand opened in front of Jai's face, showing him a trio of black, encapsulated pills.

'Soulbreathing pills. Trash-grade. One sesterii. 'Tis a good deal for you. But I can see you need it.'

Chapter 63

Jai stared at the shaking canvas ceiling, trying to get used to the wood floor's rattling and jostling. They were laying low, for Rufus had seen some of the scout riders in the legion racing past, off to arrange supplies for the coming army. These men were some of the wealthier in the army, paid well to care for their horses, but they would still not hesitate to rob them blind, even if they didn't know they were fugitives.

The cart certainly protected them from the eyes of passing legionaries and sheltered them at night, but it came with its own dangers, too. There were the dreaded tax and excise officials of the empire, small men with sticky fingers who patrolled the road with legionaries in tow. Or at least, that was how Leonid had described them. Now that Jai and Frida were in a vehicle, there was a chance it would be searched on the road, or at one of the many tollgates ahead.

It had now been six nights since he and Frida had escaped the massacre. It would take another few weeks on this busy stretch to reach the point in the Kashmere Road where they would turn north, taking the dirt paths until those ended too and they would be forced to go on foot. In all, the journey might take them two months. Anything could happen.

The wagon was cramped, little more than a fruit cart with steam-bent spars and a canvas above it. He and Frida could just about fit laying side by side, top to tail of course. In that position, there was enough additional room for a single person, even one as large as Rufus, to sit cross-legged at the wagon's entrance . . . though they'd have to put up with garlands of garlic dangling in their face.

Since someone would need to keep watch through the night, this arrangement seemed like it would work well, and Jai had been glad to see Rufus had purchased supplies for their comfort too. These included a battered stew pot, water flasks, a small hanging lantern and even some horsehair blankets.

Realising the morning nap he so desired was not forthcoming, Jai sat up. He rummaged through his new pack, smiling to himself. Winter had taken no time at all to settle into the warm, fur-lined compartment within, though she kept the end of her snout poking out, to allow herself fresh air . . . such as she could get in the musty interior of the wagon.

Beside him, Frida sat cross-legged in the corner, the golden pill perched upon the centre of her palm. She stared at it, brow furrowed.

'Think she poisoned it?' Jai joked. 'She's a practising Samarion, you know. You needn't worry.'

He was only speaking to comfort her, but Frida cast him a withering look. Blue eyes full of disdain and pity.

'Samarions tell no lies . . . *if* they are true followers of the faith. The tattoo looked genuine, but some only pretend. Though if a true Samarion catches them, their religion permits them to kill the imposter in cold blood. For some scoundrels, the risk is worth it.'

Jai was confused. 'Why would anyone fake it?'

Frida shook her head. 'You know so little of this world, Jai. There are few true Samarions, but even in the Tundra they are known as trustworthy emissaries and messengers. Good traders too. You can rely on the quality of an anointed Samarion's goods and prices, most of the time. A conman might use the tattoo to trick you though.'

'Most of the time?' Jai asked.

In truth, he had met few anointed Samarions beyond Rufus, for the royals disdained their religion. If the few emissaries he had met were so, they had not announced it.

'Yes. Even a true Samarion can find ways to twist the truth. Kenna might tell me, for example, that this pill cost a fair price. But what if she has only convinced herself of that fact by inflating its value in her mind. Samarions become good at lying to themselves, so that they can do so to others. Still, she cannot blatantly rip us off, for even she cannot trick herself of that. And we had no other choice. These gallipots are rare. And if I cannot refill my mana quickly we'll have little protection when Rufus leaves us. No offence.'

Jai felt only a little sad at that, but realised he'd done little to show her otherwise. Though, he did think his little standoff in the Phoenix had been going pretty well until Rufus had stepped in.

'Take it, then,' he said. 'The time to doubt it was in the gallipot. Not now.'

Frida sniffed and pocketed the pill.

'Pills such as these are rare, and one of such a low grade will only work for a few hours. I should only soulbreathe under its influence when we settle for the night and the distractions of the road are gone. I suggest you do the same.'

Jai could practically feel the three pills burning a hole in his pocket, but he understood her logic.

'Now, soulbreathe or sleep, but leave me in peace. I need time to . . . think.'

'Jai,' Rufus called out. 'Come up here, lad. I'll not be your coachman the whole week, nor after. Best you learn how to handle her now, afore the road gets treacherous.'

Jai's teeth rattled as he scrambled to his feet, swaying slightly at the juddering of the wagon. He wondered if Rufus had been listening to them. Almost certainly. He was probably listening to the conversations of the wagon a dozen yards ahead of them too. Such was the advantage of being soulbound. No wonder Leonid had placed so many wards and charms in the walls of his room.

It was chilly outside the wagon, so Jai drew one of the itchy horsehair blankets around himself as he joined Rufus on the driver's perch. He blinked in the blue-grey light of the winter morning and gazed at the wilderness surrounding them.

So much land there. Untamed, yet ripe with trees and fertile soil. It seemed an impossibility, that the Sabines wanted more, and more again. Taking for the sake of taking, to move lines on a map. They had no need for the Huddite's farmlands. They had enough land here to triple their population, if they would just tame it. But the Huddite farms were already there.

Now, the legions would strike deep into Jai's peoples' heartlands. And for what? Steppefolk kept few treasures and bartered more than they used coin – he knew that much. There were no riches to be found in the slaughter of his people. Only fettered . . . and supposed glory. The Sabines had more than enough of those to spare too.

'Bet you're glad you don't have to wade through that, eh lad?' Rufus said, distracting Jai from his thoughts.

The bearded old warrior clicked his tongue and twitched the

reins. Navi edged to the right beneath her yoke in front of them, avoiding a large pothole in the road ahead.

'Flick the reins to start her off and pull on them to slow her. Tug on it to stop. Pull right to go right . . . and pull left to go . . .'

He let the words hang in the air.

'Left,' Jai said.

'And that's all there is tae it lad,' Rufus chuckled richly, slapping Jai on the back. 'You're a natural. Now ridin's not too different, save for stayin' on top of course. Not as easy as you'd think. I tell you, there's some whores back at the Phoenix could break a buckin' . . .'

A cleared throat from within the wagon cut his words short.

'Later I'll show you how to tie her up and hitch her to the wagon. Khiroi like tae roam. 'Tis in their blood. Bit like you Steppefolk, eh. You like being on the road?'

Jai grinned, suddenly noting Rufus's shallow breaths. The man was cultivating mana with such ease, he could talk at the same time.

'Did you read the journal?' Jai asked.

Rufus stared out at the road ahead, silent. There was little to look at, and after a while Jai thought the man would not answer. But finally he spoke.

'I have started it. But . . . I needed sleep.'

The man pulled a metal flask from inside his jacket and took a swig. Jai didn't need to be soulbound to smell the scent of hard liquor. Not wine this time. Something stronger.

Catching Jai's eye, Rufus cleared his throat and offered the flask to Jai, with a somewhat guilty expression.

'Put hair on your chest,' Rufus said.

'Plenty of that to come, if my older brothers were anything

to go by,' Jai said. He took a sip, and grimaced. Handed it back like a hot ember.

Jai felt a pang of loss, remembering his brothers, and had the sudden urge to cry. He allowed himself a tear but forced the rest back. Not from shame. But because he'd remembered his deal with Rufus. He had traded away a lot to allow himself this training. It was time to take advantage.

Chapter 64

Frida wanted to keep on through lunch and set a fire in a cooking pot inside the wagon itself. But Rufus insisted they stop by the side of a road to cook their midday meal, claiming he needed to stretch.

Jai did not mind the break for, as Frida prodded at the coals and watched the food bubble, Rufus led him further off the path and armed himself with a long stick, teaching as he went.

Jai was still losing nearly as much mana as he was soul-breathing, even with the hummingbird technique. Certainly not enough to burn his mana doing anything but using his heightened soulbound senses. Until he learned to contain enough of it to use as a weapon, some skill with a blade would not go amiss. Not to mention that if Frida saw him able to swing a sword, it wouldn't hurt. Might even help.

'Stand ready, lad,' Rufus said. 'I've the advantage.'

Jai scoffed a little at that. Rufus might be a powerful, soulbound warrior, but the stick he held in front of him was more like a riding crop than a club. Jai, on the other hand, held his rusted sword. Rusted, but sharp enough to chop through a carrot without too much effort. A soulbound's skin might be tough, but he could skewer Rufus with it if he wasn't careful.

'I'll try not to hurt you,' Jai said.

The chuckle from Frida only slightly hurt his feelings. He turned, and saw her gulp down her pill. No going back now.

'Have you mana, lad?' Rufus asked. 'Even a dreg'll do.'

Jai half-closed his eyes, quickening his breath. He slipped into the half-trance, giving the world a hazy overlay of his core. With each day, he could see more and more of it. It seemed so small, hanging in the void of his centre. Like a kernel.

A kernel with a small drip of mana within. All he'd managed to gather that morning . . . and more.

'I have mana,' Jai said. 'But it's more than I should have . . .'

Rufus nodded at that.

'You've a good beast, so you have,' he said. "Tis common for bonded beasts to give their mana tae you, but rarely so young and rarely much. They get little enough of it as it is, being unable tae soulbreathe themselves. It drips into them, slow-like – she must've spent all morning pushin' it your way. Takes a while for 'em to manage it at first, especially if you're far. Winter felt you needed it more'n she. Clever girl.'

He chuckled, though Jai did not see the joke.

Still, he sent a pulse of thanks to his beast, and felt a sleepy acknowledgement in return. He was getting better at communicating with her too. This . . . transfer of emotions. It was like another language.

'So when you're far from your beast . . .'

'Now lad. I'm loath tae waste it on trainin', but I can't well teach you tae manage your mana when you don't have any. Cultivatin's a lengthy process, and when your mana's low, you'll need other ways to protect yourself than external majickin'.'

Jai listened closely. Every sect, the Gryphon Guard included, taught their acolytes these lessons, often over years. He was going to have to pack everything into a week. Even learning the theory of a skill, even if he could not do it yet, would give him something to work towards when he finally ascended.

'Charms and spells are all well and good, but *internal* majicking is more efficient. Now, your body'll use plenty of mana on its own before you ascend – that's why you're almost empty. You'll use mana if you run beyond your natural ability or strike a blow harder than your muscles'd allow on their own. Your enhanced senses even, come at a price. But that's all subconscious-like. If you focus your mana, send it where 'tis needed, you can run even faster, should you wish. Strike harder. Even smell better and see farther.'

Jai's eyes widened at that. *This* was what he'd paid for.

'Shouldn't Frida be listening to this?' Jai asked. They were a fair way away from her, where the ground was a little more level.

Rufus grinned.

'This, even she will know. Though that's no' saying much. These Dansk, they never formed a sect. Kept their dragons amid their royals and such. Oh, they know some things. Shared knowledge, passed down from parent tae child. But they relied too much on the strength o' their beasts; cave bears, direwolves and the like. Beyond the mammoths of the far steppe, dragons are some of the largest beasts that can be bonded with.'

Jai shrugged.

'I've heard that too. But Frida . . .'

He stopped himself. He'd told Rufus as little as he could about Frida, for her secrets were not his to share. But Rufus seemed to know she had once been bonded to a dragon.

Rufus misunderstood him.

'Some Dansk nobility also ride dragons, true. Second sons and daughters o' previous generations o' royals, mostly, those

that married into nobility and carryin' on the tradition. Young
Frida's got a distant claim tae their throne, most likely.'

Jai nodded slowly. It wouldn't be unusual for the daughter
of a lesser noble family to serve as the princess's handmaiden.
Jai would ask her about it. For now, though, he needed to know
more.

'How does one safely . . . ascend?' Jai asked.

Rufus looked at him with raised brows.

'You don't know much, boy, do you?' he said.

Jai grimaced and inclined his head in agreement. 'In Latium,
the Gryphon Guard kept their practices secret. It was as if their
knowledge of majicking gave them leverage over the imperial
family. What I know, I know from my childhood *amah*, Balbir.
My nursemaid. That, overheard conversations, and what little
Leonid wrote of them. Or the old guards, speaking of the past
wars. Fragments.'

Rufus ruffled Jai's hair.

'Well, lad. Ascension's no' really somethin' you need tae worry
about.'

'Oh?' Jai asked.

'That's because there's nothin' tae be done about it,' Rufus
said, grinning. 'Once your core's grown and thickened enough,
it'll just happen on its own accord. Might survive it, might not.
Some folk can't take the strain of it.'

Jai stared at him, shocked.

'I've seen a man ascend while swimming in the ocean. Watched
him drown while doing it. Seen a couple ascend in battle, get
their throats slit. Even heard o' a woman who ascended while
twixt her lover's legs.'

He slapped Jai's back.

'Just need a strong heart. Or be too stubborn to die. I reckon
you've got the latter quality at least.'

Jai took a deep breath of fresh air.

'So, you said I can strike faster?'

Rufus blurred. He moved so quickly Jai hardly saw the blow coming. Rather, he felt the red flare of pain across his shoulders.

The big man danced back, flashing Jai a grin.

'That's tae . . . properly motivate you.'

Jai gritted his teeth, lifting his sword. The thing was so rusted and blunt, he had picked it up by the blade on more than one occasion.

It isn't that sharp, right?

He lunged forward, and practically felt the mana seep from his core as he gave the sword a wild slash. A swift slap from Rufus's branch spiked it into the ground, and Jai found himself staggering past the middle-aged man. The swift shove that followed sent him face first into the ground.

'We'll work on your technique another time. For now, let me teach you tae channel that blow. First time's the hardest. I need you tae focus on your core when you push your body beyond your natural abilities, be it a sprint or blow.'

Jai brushed himself off, pushing away his annoyance by reminding himself that he wouldn't have cared had Frida not been watching.

Indeed, looking at her now, she was no longer watching. Rather, she sat upon the wagon's footplate, cross-legged. She looked strange . . . in fact, her hair practically stood on its end, flaring up slightly around her as if she had rubbed her feet on a woollen rug. Whatever the lustration pill did, it packed quite a punch, it seemed.

Jai picked up his sword from where it lay and gripped it in both hands.

'I've got hardly any mana,' Jai said. 'So this one has to count. What do I do when I strike?'

Rufus jabbed the stick at Jai's chest.

'You squeeze your core as the mana leaves it. Push more through. It'll follow the same route to whatever limb you're using, there'll just be more of it.'

Jai closed his eyes.

'Not much use if you have tae close your eyes tae do it,' Rufus said.

'I'll figure that out later,' Jai muttered. 'I need to learn how to do it at all first. Now let me focus.'

'Not much use if you need quie—' Rufus chuckled, then held his hands up in peace when Jai flashed him a glare.

Jai closed his eyes once more. Drifted to the trance. Saw his core, floating in that abyss. He was loath to waste the precious mana that Winter had given him. But he needed to learn this.

He focused on the movement he was about to make. Rufus was just in front of him, and a little to his left. He needed to take a single step and cut to the side in a swift, short chop. He could feel the anticipatory twitch of the muscles. Knew where the mana would go.

Still, he waited. He let his mind drift to his core. He could almost feel its walls. They were as much part of him as the heart they resided in.

When he soulbreathed, he dilated to breathe *in*.

Now . . . he squeezed the core to push *out*. Like letting out a great gout of breath, pent up within him.

He let the mana rush through his body, roiling through him like fire in his veins. Swirling, waiting for where it would be willed. In that same moment, he made his move.

The air thrummed with the speed of the blow, and Jai felt himself spinning as his blade met nothing but air. He had not expected such force and his back muscles strained hard at the sudden twist of his body. There was a thud as his sword chopped a deep tuft of turf from the ground.

Jai saw Rufus a few feet away, pawing at his beard.

'Damn near gave me a trim, lad,' the portly old man cackled. 'You're a fast learner, I'll give you that. Terrible, terrible technique though. Now, square up. 'Tis time tae show you what swordplay really—'

Jai gave him no time to react, slashing once more with the last of his mana. Rufus's hand darted forward, latching like a vice upon Jai's wrist. He yanked, once, and butted his head forward. Jai felt the hard slam of Rufus' forehead, and his own nose squashing like overripe fruit.

Pain.

Jai did not realise he was on the ground until the world swam back into view. He snorted, and a rush of warm blood gushed from his nose, running down his face and into his ears.

'Ain't no airs and graces here, lad,' Rufus chuckled. 'Fightin's no sport. It ain't a dance. It's a brawl. That means 'tain't just a blade you'll be usin'.'

Jai gurgled incoherently, spitting the blood from a split lip. Rufus nudged him with a foot.

'On your feet. Again!'

Chapter 65

Jai gulped down as much of the stew as he could, groaning at the thick slurry of nutrition his body so desperately needed. Somehow, gnawing on some wrinkled raw vegetables in the days before meeting Rufus, had not done the job.

He made sure to leave the dregs for Winter, who gulped them down with her snout pointed to the darkening sky like a baby bird.

Jai winced as he put the bowl away. His body was a mass of welts and flowering bruises, not to mention the various muscles he'd pulled. Rufus had not been kind in their sparring. To his credit, though, he'd struck, parried and dodged no faster than a normal man might.

Swordplay, Jai now realised, was far more complicated than he'd thought. There was far too much to hold in his head at once. The positioning of his feet – something he'd never even thought might matter – seemed to be all Rufus talked about. That, and his balance, and where his weight was spread. It reminded him of his brothers' first attempt to teach him to ride a horse. Utterly strange to him, yet somehow made to look effortless by the teacher.

He'd hardly lifted his blade before Rufus was haranguing him about one thing or another. And even when he did manage to get it right, the next hundred things to think of were pointed out: the position of his opponent; the *stance* of his opponent; the length of his opponent's blade, the length of his own. And this before he'd even begun to think about striking.

Soon enough, he'd given up on getting things perfect, instead attempting to wipe Rufus's smirk from his face. In some ways, he'd brought the beating on himself.

'Cheer up, lad,' Rufus said. 'Might never happen.'

'What might?' Jai muttered.

'Just a sayin',' Rufus chuckled. 'But you've a dark look on your face that says you needed tae hear it.'

Frida had eaten her meal while they were sparring and now sat upon the wagon's footplate, cultivating. In this, Jai had at least some relief. His lesson with Rufus had been many things, but impressive was not one of them.

'I'll never learn to fight like you,' Jai said. 'I can't hold everything in my head at once.'

Rufus shook his head ruefully.

'You're no slower a study than most, I'll grant you. But I've seen dull-witted brutes fight better'n most too. Trainin' with a blade ain't learned from no book. It ain't earned with smarts neither. It's practice. Practisin' so your body remembers. Not your mind. Soon it'll feel like second nature. Like dancin'. Or fuckin'.'

Jai rubbed at a bruised shin.

'My body won't be forgetting that in a hurry.'

Rufus laughed.

A small, white snout nudged at Jai's elbow, and he made room for Winter to leap onto his lap. She looked up at him with wide, blue eyes and lapped at one of his bruises.

'Good girl,' Jai said, scratching her beneath her chin. She purred at that, and burrowed deeper before exposing her belly for a rub. It was pink-tinged, like a puppy's. Jai could not help but oblige her.

'So, lad,' Rufus said. 'What'd you do to convince our resident noble to let you have that hatchlin'? Or even bond with it? Gryphon Guard've been tryin' tae get hold of one for decades . . .'

Jai had no intention of sharing what he knew with the old Gryphon Guard, whether Titus knew the secret already or not. Rufus had his secrets. Jai would keep his own too.

'She didn't,' Jai said. 'I did it on my own. Just . . . happened.'

Rufus leaned closer, glancing at Frida. She pursed her lips, though her eyes remained closed.

'Go on,' Rufus urged.

'One more word, Jai, and those taps from Rufus you're nursing will feel like gentle kisses by the time I'm through with you.'

Frida's voice cut off Jai's chance to deny him, startling Winter with its loudness.

'I wasn't . . .'

'One. More. Word,' Frida snapped.

The girl remained cross-legged, with eyes closed. Even unable to meet her gaze, Jai sensed her fury.

'Fine,' Rufus muttered. 'Keep your secrets.'

They sat silent, waiting for the tension to ease from the air. Jai fiddled with his sword, testing its edge. He pulled his thumb away. It was still sharp enough to cut.

'Here,' Rufus said. 'Hand it over.'

Jai did so, and the grizzled warrior looked it over, flipping it one way and then the other, before testing it with a few swift jabs in the air.

'You took this off Tullia, right?' Rufus asked.

Jai nodded and held his hand out for the blade. Winter purred, and lapped his palm with a smooth, wet tongue.

''Tis a fine blade. Good balance. Looks like strong steel, probably a Damantine blend, forged local. Must've been her father's afore she let their estate run to ruin on drink and expensive tastes.'

Jai looked unconvinced.

'Here,' Rufus said. 'Watch.'

He cast about the clearing, scrabbling on hand and knee. Jai looked on, utterly confused. Soon enough, Rufus returned with a handful of pebbles.

'Carin' for your blade's important. Now, a whytblade'll keep better'n any steel, but you still gotta oil it; oil its scabbard too. I'll loan you some o' mine. But this one . . . needs sharpenin'.'

He held up a stone.

'There's better'n this out there, but it'll have to do. Quartz ain't a bad whetstone, as they go. See, you need a flat one. You take it and you . . .'

Rufus stuck his tongue between his teeth as he scraped it down the side of the blade. Rust fell away like stubble against a razor as Rufus dragged the stone along the full length of the sword.

'See, you do this for half the night and you'll have a sword that'll lop the heads off a dandelion. 'Course, if you don't keep sparrin' with me, that's all you'll be cuttin' with it. So, we train every lunchtime, till you've got the grasp o' it. Deal?'

Jai let out a long breath, wincing at the ache from the bruising along his ribs.

'Deal,' he said.

He already knew he was going to regret it.

Chapter 66

A hand clamped over Jai's mouth, silencing the yell that came unbidden. Rufus's bearded face filled his vision, a finger pressed to his lips.

Jai raised his hands in supplication and he was slowly released. He sat up, heart hammering, dizzied by the sudden rush of adrenaline, and confused by a deluge of fear from Winter.

Frida was crouched beside him, peering out from the wagon, her head turned to the heavens.

Rufus leaned close, until his whiskers tickled Jai's ear.

'Gryphon Guard,' he breathed. 'Hunting. They . . .'

He paused, cocking his ear to the sky, his fingers dancing along his earlobe. Rufus's eyes flashed white.

'They seek a Dansk girl.'

Jai hardly dared breathe. Winter rustled in the straw and Jai urged her silent with a thought.

So . . . they had found Frida's dragon. Seen where the soulgem had been cut from its chest, with a whytblade no less. They knew she was alive, and soulbound. On the run, with full knowledge of the coup at the palace.

Of course they were hunting her. How could they not be?

Rufus pulled Frida back from the entrance, practically hurling her into the back of the wagon. He let out a loud curse.

'Move your lazy bones, boy,' Rufus snapped. 'We have guests.'

Jai stared, even as Rufus rustled in his bags, pulling forth a manacle. Before Jai could say a word, the big man had snapped it onto his wrist, then tapped Jai's gorget. He nodded towards the doorway, before taking a bottle of liquor from his bags.

Frida furrowed her brow as he uncorked it, but rather than taking a swig, Rufus dashed most of it over Frida, and Winter too. Immediately, the acrid stench of booze filled the cart, and Rufus splashed liberally in his own beard for equal measure.

Jai hardly had time to pull off his father's armour before he was yanked by the scruff of his shirt and shoved bodily into the open air.

Outside, a man crouched beside the embers of their campfire, and even in the thin light of the crescent moon, Jai could see his golden armour glinting.

Jai opened and closed his mouth, unsure of what to say. Behind the first man, a pair of gryphons prowled back and forth, their yellow, eagle eyes firmly fixed upon him. Each was as large as Navi, and the khiro whickered nervously from where she had been haltered beside their wagon.

A second man dismounted, patting his totem. He joined the first, both looking at Jai with apparent bemusement. Then Jai was shoved aside as Rufus emerged from the wagon, rubbing his eyes. His shirt had been unbuttoned, revealing the Samarion tattoo beneath his collarbone.

'Forgive my lad,' Rufus mumbled, slurring his words. 'He's new. You might say he's dumb as rocks and twice as slow.'

The closest Gryphon Guard flared a glintlight with the flick of a hand, casting the clearing in ethereal light. They were some way off the road in the shadow of the forest. How had they been spotted?

The closer man was raven-haired, and slimmer than most Gryphon Guard. Behind, his companion was the exact opposite, blond, and broad as Magnus, though squat and round-faced.

'Your khiro,' said the guard. 'It's a rare beast in these parts. Thought we'd come see who you were. Plenty of Steppe-spies about in these dark times. We've stopped a fair few of their traders, running back to that wasteland they call home . . . it's been . . . illuminating.'

The bigger man let out a low guttural laugh: a *hur hur hur* that made Jai's stomach twist.

'Aye,' Rufus said, scratching his beard. 'I thought a Steppeman might know more'n I about trainin' 'em. More's the pity with this one.'

And it was then that Jai realised.

Rufus couldn't lie. Not directly. He was Samarion.

Jai felt the blood drain from his face, even as he sent Winter an order to be still. These men . . . they might well hear the straw rustle, if they didn't sniff the pair out first. It had been quick thinking, with the liquor. But they now walked a razor's edge.

The man raised a thin brow, the glintlight floating over toward Navi with a twitch of his fingers.

'She's been whipped proper,' Rufus grunted, prodding at Navi. 'Knows her place.'

The dark-haired man ran his eyes over Navi's thin frame, taking in the many scars that crisscrossed her fur. His eyes lingered on Rufus's chest, and he seemed to relax at the sight of the tattoo, his shoulders slumping a little.

Rufus stumbled forward, proffering them his hipflask and letting out an involuntary burp.

'Have a drink. Fine warriors such as yourselves . . . must have stories tae tell.'

The man raised his palms and wrinkled his nose.

'None for us. But we'll let our totems rest a while, for they've been on the wing all night. Come, sit with us by the fire. It's been a while since I've spoken with a true Samarion. I am Septimus, and this is Bolat.'

'Ru-uufus,' said Rufus, letting out another belch.

If Rufus had hoped to move them on with his apparent drunkenness, it had backfired. Apparently these soldiers would boast to anyone, even a winesop such as Rufus.

Septimus and his companion settled upon one of the rotted logs by the fire, where Jai and his companions had eaten but a few hours earlier. Rufus had no choice but to sit opposite. Jai hovered awkwardly until his 'master' turned to him.

'Fetch my guests some vittles, smart-like. Or I'll have your hide and yon beast's beside.'

Jai jumped to obey, scrambling back into the wagon, glad its entrance was angled in such a way that their new arrivals could not see within.

Inside, Jai scrambled to find their pot, where the vegetables and meat ready for the morrow's breakfast were waiting to be boiled.

A hand emerged from the straw, shoving it towards him. Frida peered out from where she had burrowed, and he saw Winter's tail poking out beside her.

They exchanged a terror-filled glance, but as Jai turned to go back, she seized his wrist. Her hand disappeared back into the straw, then returned with a fistful of salt. Their entire supply for the remainder of the journey.

She dumped it into the pot. Jai scrambled out before the others became suspicious.

'. . . begged. But Bolat has a way of wringing the truth out of them. Before he wrings their necks, of course.'

Rufus laughed uproariously, overlong and loud. Even Septimus winced at it, and leaned away from a spray of spittle. Bolat only glowered, his gaze almost hungry. He had not taken his eyes off Jai since he'd returned.

Jai was swift to dole out the broth, handing a bowl to each man. Septimus gave it a deep sniff, then touched the liquid with his tongue. He grimaced and set it aside. Bolat simply spat, ignoring Jai's proffered hand.

Poor company, worse food. What else would it take for these men to leave?

'But enough about us,' Septimus said. 'Tell us what brings a Samarion so far from his homeland.'

Rufus took a swig from his bottle, smacking his lips.

'Wine,' he burped. 'Women. War. Is there anything else worth having in this world?'

He waggled his eyebrows, but his vague answer seemed not to satisfy the guard.

'War?' Septimus asked.

Rufus shrugged.

'I go for trade. War always brings opportunity. A business venture, one that screws over Dansk and Steppeman alike.'

'Oh?' Septimus asked, his eyes lighting up at that.

'Aye,' Rufus said, swigging his flask again. Jai only hoped they did not notice it was already empty.

Septimus leaned closer and Jai began to panic.

'Sire,' Jai muttered, shuffling closer. 'If the food is not to your liking, I can make you something else.'

Jai did not even see the man's hand move – only felt the slap whip across his face, spinning him into the dirt. Septimus sniffed, and dashed the broth over Jai, as casually as if he were tipping a chamberpot.

'You've trained this one poorly,' he said. 'A fettered should not speak unless spoken to, you hear?'

He directed this at Jai, before turning back to Rufus.

'A firm hand is all a Steppeman ever understands.'

Jai crawled away on his belly, only for a hobnailed boot to press him into the mud.

'We can take 'im off your 'ands,' Bolat rumbled, grinding his foot down until Jai whimpered. 'Let the gryphons 'ave their fun with 'im. Be good to get 'em used to the taste of fresh Steppeman.'

Rufus let out a sniff.

'He's a poor cook and a worse servant,' he said. 'But I've use for the lad yet. Now I'd ask you tae release him, lest he shirk his duties on the morrow.'

Bolat released his foot, and Jai choked and spluttered, clutching his chest. Soulbound or not, it had felt as if his ribcage had been about to snap.

'Shame,' Bolat grunted.

Beyond, the man's gryphon let out a shriek of complaint, apparently disappointed at its lost meal.

'Maybe . . .' Bolat began.

'How goes the war?' Rufus asked. 'Legions are on the march. Do we take the Tundra first, or the steppe?'

Septimus raised his brows at that.

'What you ask is only known to the emperor,' he said. 'Why so curious?'

Rufus raised his hands.

'I go to the border, and no further. I only ask to know how safe it'll be, or if I should turn back sooner.'

Septimus let out a dry laugh and motioned at Rufus to lower his hands.

'You must have noticed the legion on your tail. Fresh from

the slaughter of the Dansk traitors – patriots all. None'll bother you if you stay close to them.'

Rufus nodded his thanks, staring off into the flames. Jai wheezed and tried to crawl until a kick from Bolat doubled him over. Jai clutched his belly, his mouth opening and closing breathlessly like a beached fish.

If Rufus noticed, he did not show it. Instead, he blinked a few times, letting his eyes half close. Septimus snapped his fingers in front of Rufus's face, until the old Samarion raised his head.

'Long day,' he muttered. 'My apologies.'

Septimus sighed, before slapping his knees and getting to his feet.

'This was a mistake,' he said. 'Come, Bolat. The legion will have better hospitality.'

'Please,' Rufus said. 'Stay a while longer. I've some homebrew somewhere, perhaps . . .'

Septimus held up a hand to silence him.

The gryphons prowled closer, apparently summoned with a thought, and Septimus and Bolat were mounted before Rufus had time to struggle to his feet.

'Oh, before we leave,' Septimus said, taking up his gryphon's reins. 'We might as well ask. Have you seen a Dansk girl in these parts?'

Rufus swayed on his feet.

'Why d'you ask?' he slurred. 'She a pretty one?'

Bolat's gryphon lifted its wings but Septimus held up a fist, stopping it in its tracks.

'Answer me, you drunken oaf. Have you seen a Dansk girl in your travels here?'

For a moment, time stood still. Jai lay there gasping, trying to summon his mana. Ready for a battle he was sure they could not win.

Rufus stared at Septimus, but the warrior did not blink.

Then Rufus sighed.

'Nay, sire, I have not,' he said. 'You warriors travel safe.'

Only when the gryphons were long gone did Jai dare let out a breath. Rufus sat by the fire, staring deep into the flames.

He crawled over to him, and pressed his back against the log, moaning from the pain. To move was agony.

'I am so sorry, Rufus,' Jai choked. 'You . . .'

He did not know what to say.

Rufus sniffed, but said nothing. Jai let the silence drag out a while longer, even as Frida and Winter scrambled out of the vehicle.

'You wily old dog,' Frida finally said, peering into the sky. 'That Samarion tattoo . . . it looks like the real thing.'

Rufus snorted.

'It is.'

Frida stared at him, confused.

'But then . . .'

'I am a Samarion,' Rufus said. 'By both blood and creed. Tae lie is tae condemn myself tae hellfire.'

Jai didn't understand. Surely . . . surely Rufus did not truly believe that?

'But you lied . . .' Jai said.

There was no other way of reading that question. Nor Rufus's answer.

Rufus remained motionless.

'I already know where I'm headed,' he whispered. 'There's no forgivin' my sins.'

For a moment, Jai thought he saw the shine of a tear on Rufus's face.

'To bed, all of you,' Rufus said, turning his head away. 'We shall nae speak of this again.'

And with that, the man was on his feet, striding off into the darkness. Jai might have followed him, if he could have borne standing. Instead, he gathered Winter into his arms, pressing her as tight as he dared to his chest.

Winter mewled in sympathy, lapping at his chest as if she could somehow soothe the pain within.

There was a crunch of gravel. Frida settled by Jai, prodding a branch into the fire.

'That man is more than he seems,' she said. 'Just when I think I understand him . . .'

She sighed, and then her fingers danced, running along Jai's spine. He felt a warmth suffuse him and caught Frida's glowing eyes as she let her healing hand fall away. The pain of his ribs receded enough for him to climb up into his seat.

For a moment they sat together.

'Tomorrow then,' Frida said.

Jai was left alone with Winter. Somewhere behind them, a legion slumbered. Beyond, their path stretched out with no end in sight.

And above . . . above, men hunted.

Chapter 67

Rufus kept his promise, and in the following days his training became even more painful. Jai's excitement at being taught by such a capable warrior had dulled along with the bruises on his face, which, thanks to his healing mana, were already beginning to fade.

Still, that did not stop him from raising his newly sharpened sword and giving Rufus all he had.

He was improving slowly. Or at least, that was what Rufus said. Pain was a powerful motivator, and on this day, Jai's frustration had been replaced by a healthy fear of the aging warrior's blurring branch. Yet by the end of the session, Rufus remained unharmed. Meanwhile Jai had bruises on his bruises, and a few fresh cuts to boot.

To add humiliation to injury, Rufus had spent the rest of the day shaping and polishing the very same stick with a knife, asking Jai whether this splinter or that one had come from bashing his dome.

If Rufus was worried about what had transpired with the Gryphon Guard, he did not mention it. Only the man's glances into the sky revealed he had not forgotten the event entirely.

Now, some two weeks after they had left the Phoenix, it was all feeling almost routine. The three had finally stopped for the night; Jai was wincing as he settled by the fire. Frida soulbreathed quietly beside him, while Rufus stoked the coals and stirred the pot.

'You OK lad?' Rufus asked softly. 'You've hardly said a word.'

Jai looked up, confused. He had been staring into the flames, his mind blank with exhaustion.

'You're a quicker learner'n before,' Rufus said. 'You keep this up, might even make a half-decent warrior of you someday.'

Jai felt his cheeks flush at the rare compliment and stuttered his thanks. Until that moment he had not known how much the man's grudging praise had meant to him.

'I . . .'

He paused, trying to phrase the question politely.

'I appreciate the training with the blade, truly. But I'll never become much of a warrior if I can't store my mana. I'm always using it up, whether I want to or not.'

Rufus grinned at him.

'Aye, that's a fact.'

'So how do I do it?' he asked.

Rufus let out a long sigh, then gave the pot a final stir and took it off the coals to cool.

'You close your eyes.'

Jai did so, trying not to let his excitement build too much. He took a long, deep breath, allowing his mind to drift to that ethereal state where the world turned to ghosts and gold and his inner being was laid bare to himself.

There was a deep pulse within. The heavy beat of his heart. Blood, rushing. And that hollowness at his centre, where his very soul, his core, resided.

It was there, floating. Empty, but for a tiny thimbleful of mana at its bottom.

'Bring in mana,' Rufus said.

His voice was slow . . . and almost seemed to echo. Jai surrendered to its instruction, sucking in a deep gulp of air. Then another, and another.

Slowly, mote by mote, the mana filtered through him. Following the paths, splitting and merging through him in a tumble of golden light. Turning to liquid, soothing as it flowed.

'Find a rhythm,' Rufus's voice boomed. 'Do not snatch the air. Breathe deep, slow, and regular. Dilate your core in tandem with each breath.'

Jai did so, and almost lost concentration in his amazement as the mana flowed faster. Such a simple thing. He listened as if Rufus's voice was that of the gods, yearning for more.

The first droplets of mana splashed upon his core, seeping through the translucent crystalline shell. As they passed, their light grew purer, beading into pinpricks and trickling down the inner walls to pool at the core's bottom.

'Now . . . concentrate. Do not break the trance.'

Jai almost lost it then and there. The advice sounded obvious. Then . . . pain. Sharp, burning pain, flaring up his forearm. Rufus was . . . hurting him.

The world shifted and Jai fought to regain composure. Just before he lost it completely, the burning receded, leaving a stinging in its place.

And within . . . Jai's mana leeched from his core, tendrils of it flicking away, rushing to his arm.

'Try to stop it.'

Rufus's instruction was like gospel, yet try as he might, Jai could do nothing. Only watch as more and more left his core.

'It's like holding your breath,' Rufus whispered. 'Come on. Try it.'

Jai focused. By now, he could manipulate his core without too much effort. He could dilate and contract it, like squeezing and releasing a sponge. But how did one stop the sponge from leaking?

Still, he tried. His mind boggled, attempting to manipulate the glowing orb within. It was like a phantom limb – he could feel it on the very edge of his control.

'Come on,' Rufus growled, his voice like a lash.

Jai gritted his teeth, willing his core to seal up.

Nothing.

'Imagine it,' Frida's voice said, and somehow her words soothed him. Slowed his thinking. 'Picture the core sealing itself. See it in its full detail. Make it all you see.'

Jai slowed his breathing even further. Let the ebb of mana steady. For a while it was all he did. Breathed. Focused on it.

And then . . . he forgot it. Let his body do the breathing. Emptied his mind of all.

The core. A glint in the dark, a *denarius* at the bottom of a well.

Closer.

Now, a lustrous gemstone. And that thin thread, connecting it to Winter, a spider's thread lost in the gloom.

Closer.

It filled his vision. Like a lantern of cut glass, wet with golden dew. And the glow of a candle within.

Closer.

The core filled his vision. And Jai *saw*. Saw the membrane within, as transparent as the jewelled surface it hid behind. Saw it flex with each breath. And the liquid, passing through. Beading on the crystal.

He seized the membrane. And *tightened*.

Something changed. Something . . . sealed.

And for a moment . . . or not even that . . . the flow of mana stopped. The pain of his arm . . . flared.

Jai lost it as soon as he had it, the sudden pain jarring him out of the trance. But as he opened his eyes, he knew he could do it again.

Rufus grinned at him, and Jai realised he was grinning too.

'I had it,' he whispered. 'By the gods, I sealed it.'

'I 'ain't no god,' Rufus said. 'Just a good teacher.'

Frida snorted, earning herself a glare from the red-bearded man.

'Well done,' Frida said, and Jai saw her wink. 'You've learned to hold it. Like a child at bedtime.'

She handed Jai a bowl and he smiled gratefully.

'Really,' she said. 'Well done. You're a third-level soulbound now. Not many manage it on their first try.'

She sighed, and reached into her pocket, handing Rufus a single *sesterii*.

'Told you so,' Rufus said.

He thought for a moment, then flicked the coin over to Jai.

'Buy yourself something pretty,' Rufus said.

Jai tried not to let that upset his mood. He was still buzzing with excitement. If he could do it once . . . he could do it again.

Jai took a sip and noticed the broth was lukewarm. Had it really been that long?

'How long was I out for?' Jai asked.

'Better part of half an hour,' Rufus said. 'Knew you'd make it, sticking with it that long.'

'What's next?' Jai asked. 'If I learn to seal it properly.'

Rufus tapped his nose.

'You fill that core to the brim,' he said. 'Then fill it some more. Then some more. Hurts like a bastard, but it'll make it bigger. Stretchin' it. Takes some a year or more to learn to bear the pain.'

Jai set his jaw and took another sip of the cooling stew. Pain. A price well worth paying.

Chapter 68

The Kashmere Road stretched endlessly in front of them, meandering, twisting, sometimes even going back on itself across the contours of the land, but continuing inexorably on to the eastern reaches of the empire and beyond.

It had been three weeks since they had fled the palace, and their time with Rufus was nearing its end. They had settled into a routine of sorts. Each night, they would pull their wagon off the road, usually sheltering in the lee of a tree and taking turns to keep watch throughout the night.

Frida had taken to sleeping outside with Navi, snuggled up against her belly like a piglet. Jai had wondered at that, until he remembered Jormun. Just as Winter curled up upon his chest at night, so too must Frida have done with her dragon.

He looked down into the little beast's turquoise eyes, comforted by her small weight on his chest. He could hardly imagine her being large enough to sleep on. And despite his dreams of flying . . . he wanted her to stay little for a while longer.

She grew heavier each day – which was unsurprising, since she spent every spare moment scoffing the small fauna of their surroundings. She had become adept at returning to the safety of their wagon, or staying hidden whenever they passed another traveller.

She was no longer the size of a housecat, but rather that of a runtish hound. If he squinted and was a little generous, he'd say she might even take on a chamrosh.

Rufus and Jai slept top to toe until Frida's watch was over. Then Jai would stay up through the early hours, soulbreathing occasionally with Winter pressed against his chest.

Rufus would replace him for the rest of the night, and then slept through the morning while Jai hitched Navi up and set the wagon on its course. There was little more to it than that. Jai would drape himself with a horsehair blanket, twitch the reins if Navi was headed for a pothole, and gather mana using the hummingbird technique until Rufus took over.

Lunch time was spent training. Usually it was swordplay, but sometimes Rufus spoke of the rare majicking and techniques that only the Gryphon Guard knew, and even Frida would listen, albeit with poorly feigned disinterest. Oftentimes, Frida would grill the man into the early hours. Much of what they spoke of went over Jai's head and he slept through most of it. He was glad that Frida was learning, so she could teach him in turn when the time came.

As for sealing his core, it had been slow going. Sealing it while in the trance was easy enough. Keeping it sealed throughout the day . . . well, he was still working on that. Just when he thought he'd mastered it, keeping his mana from being used by his body, he'd check his core and see he'd lost much of his mana, all used up on the bruises from his training with Rufus. It was as if he could track his failures by the speed at which the black-yellow flowers faded upon his flesh.

Still, with each day he improved until he could reliably keep more mana than he was using up.

He'd also taken two of his three pills. They were useful things, almost doubling the amount of mana he could gather each day. When he took them, everything was just that little bit easier . . . his mind clearer, his control of his core better. Even the mana flowed through his veins as if it were drawn to his centre. He might have thought he'd been imagining it . . . if he hadn't ended up with twice as much mana at the end of the day.

The only downside was they wreaked havoc on his stomach, and left him with a sour, hungover taste in his mouth the following morning. But even so, they were well worth it. His core was almost full.

The Kashmere Road had become wilder and narrower as the days had passed. The small towns and villages became scarcer, and today they'd seen nothing beyond a single inn, instead passing dozens of travellers camped out upon the side of the road.

These travellers too seemed different. There were more travelling together in caravans, and far fewer walked. This was where the Kashmere Road truly began. Where bandits roamed, legionaries patrolled, and taxmen prowled for traders to rinse. There were even rumours of packs of direwolves and other such rare and dangerous creatures.

Yet with the dust cloud of the legion on their heels, these rumoured beasts were the least of Jai's worries.

Still, Navi was a godsend, never letting the legion get any closer, and making good pace along the road. Rufus had been right about khiroi. She was tireless, and so long as she was kept fed and had a good back scratch, she was perfectly happy sleeping in a dustbath of her own making. Only when it rained did she look miserable, and spent half those evenings with her head poking inside the wagon. Nobody begrudged her that.

Tonight it rained again. Or rather, stormed. So much that Frida planted Jai's sword in the ground beside their wagon to deter lightning. Apparently lightning strikes were not an uncommon way to die for soulbound who rode winged beasts.

Tonight, Jai went out into the tumult, a yapping Winter in tow. It was the kind of rain that slapped you, hammering down as if the very sky wished to thrust him back inside. But there was something he had to do. He pushed on, forcing his way through, feeling his mana slowly seeping away as it protected him from the ice cold. He sealed it with no small effort, tripping over rocks and branches as his mind tried to do two things at once. In an instant, his body was chilled to the bone.

Jai headed for a hill amid the bracken and shrubs, climbing until he stood at its zenith, and stared out over the landscape. Winter, as full of vim as he'd ever seen her, sat upon his shoulder, barking at the sky. And her namesake answered her call.

The ice wind battered him and the heavens poured a sea onto the wild country around him. He stood in the light of the full moon and yelled wordlessly into the swirling gale. The cold would be his gauge. As long as he felt it, he knew his seal was strong. And it would have to be if he was to expand his core.

For tonight he would be filling it to overflowing. Blowing it up, like a ball made from a tied pig's bladder.

The water cleansed him. Washing away the fear, the regret, the past. Who needed the warmth and comfort of Leonid's chamber, or the food but a bell's ring away. He felt as if the wilds would keep him safe, so long as he loved them.

This was *freedom*. To go out into the world. To *live*.

Tonight was a special night. It was the first time he would attempt to expand his core, for it was filled to the brim. Tonight, he would no longer have to take from Winter in his haste to fill it, for she had little enough of it herself.

'Are you ready, Winter?' Jai asked.

The little beast chirred with encouragement and Jai settled

cross-legged upon the soaking ground. He sought out the trance, and watched as the mana flowed across the landscape, an ever-present haze.

It was strange, for the mana drifted of its own accord, as if the tumult hardly disturbed it. A golden mist, made up of as many glittering motes as there were stars in the heavens.

It drifted across the landscape as if propelled by a gentle breeze. As if the two plains of existence only grazed each other, and he could but glimpse where the two overlapped.

He closed his eyes, and let his mind seek out his core.

It glowed bright, like a floating sun. In the past few days, with the help of the pills, he had filled it to the brim.

Now, he would have his first chance at expanding it.

In his mind's eye, Jai sucked in deep breaths of mana, letting the substance coat his lungs. He heaved at his fledgling core, feeling its walls expanding. After so many days of constant soulbreathing, the pain was almost too much to bear. It was no wonder some soulbound took years to ascend.

The mana travelled down his channels, and more still trickled through his connection with Winter. The core's pressure grew with every droplet. Like a dam that needed only the smallest crack before it . . . Jai hoped it would not burst.

Slowly, ever so slowly, he let the mana pass into his core.

Pain.

Jai grunted with effort, almost losing the trance as a fresh deluge of rain battered him. Deep within him, Winter's cord pulsed, guiding him back to the trance. He forced himself on, gritting his teeth through the pain.

He gasped for air, for the deep pull of his core felt like holding his breath. Jai pushed on through it all. He was not a man on a hillside. His world was that dark warren within, and the golden light that flooded it.

The storm was his friend. It numbed his body – that endless distraction of emotion and sensation. Soon, he could not feel the rain or the cold. Just the mana, ebbing and flowing through his channels. And the pressure building. He could almost feel his core creaking against the strain. Mana pooled upon its surface, struggling to pass through to its pressurised interior.

He would succeed that day, or the storm would take him. The mana burned, and Jai screamed in a final, defiant heave of his core.

And then . . . he felt a shift. A release, as the pressure eased.

At first, Jai thought he had burst it, for the pain was like nothing he'd felt before. A thousand, thousand needles were stabbing at him. He had fallen over. Laying on his side, gasping like a beached fish.

Jai's core had seized up, but he didn't care. He'd done it.

His mana had all gone, but the core was a little bigger. Hardly more than the difference between a lime and a lemon. But enough.

Jai felt an exhaustion unlike any other he'd known, but knew he could not let unconsciousness take him. Not when his body was swiftly freezing. Already, his breath felt strained and shallow.

He gripped his core with every ounce of his being, forcing it to pull the mana once more. It hardly moved, and the action was so painful Jai almost passed out that very moment. The thing was fragile after what he'd put it through. He dared not break it now.

But it was enough. Enough for the first mote of mana to graze his core's surface. And like a snowflake upon a tongue, it dissolved into liquid, passing through the crystalline shell. Then another, and another.

He released all control of his core, letting his mana go where it willed, the golden droplet within instantly blazing out. He felt a flood of warmth, as sudden as if he'd been thrown into a bath.

After holding his mana back for so long, its effects were almost euphoric. The joy intermingled with his triumph.

All his life, he'd never considered himself good at much of anything. But this . . . this he could do.

As just a man, avenging his brothers was but a dream. But as a powerful soulbound . . .

Jai opened his eyes.

He stood in the windstorm, as steam billowed off him like great gouts of dragon breath. His skin practically sizzled, and he could suddenly breathe again.

Jai threw open his arms, lifting his voice to join Winter's howl of victory. Together, they bellowed their defiance across the wilds.

The storm raged. And they raged with it.

Chapter 69

Jai slept soundly in the wagon that night, wrapped in a ball by the entrance with only a horsehair blanket for covering. He shivered, but had no desire to waste his precious mana on keeping himself warm through the night.

With slow, concentrated effort the next day, and a not insubstantial amount of agony, he'd filled his tender core by perhaps a twentieth of its new capacity before lunch. He felt he could soulbreathe all week and not fill it.

For now, he warmed his hands by the fire. Winter had taken up her usual place, curled up close to it – so close that Jai was sure she'd burn, the first time she did it. He supposed dragons were known for their love of extreme cold or heat.

Winter was watching him protectively as he ate, as she did every meal.

'Come on girl,' Jai said. 'I know you're full. I can't eat with you watching me.'

Frida chuckled.

'Not many a man who'd complain that their best girl gazes at them in adoration,' she said. 'My Jormun would do the same at mealtimes. Then, and when . . .'

She reddened, and Jai stifled a grin. For once, he had the upper hand. He knew what she'd been about to say, because Winter had the same habit.

'And when you go to . . . ahem . . . drain the aqueduct?' Jai said.

Frida looked at him, confused.

'You know . . . lift a leg? Water the flowers?'

Frida let out a loud laugh.

It was a joy, to see her happy. Her cold, hard beauty dissolved into delight in a heartbeat. The harsh line of her mouth was softened by a warm smile, and a blush came to the porcelain of her newly dimpled cheeks.

Usually he glimpsed her softer side only when she played with Winter. Though even then she was reserved, knowing Jai could feel it all. The rest of the time she put up a hard front, one that even Rufus's constant joshing had barely made a dent in.

'She does that too? I thought it was Jormun's weird thing!' she laughed, tossing her hair. By now the ink had long been washed out, and Jai could not help but wish he had not chosen to sit so far from her tonight.

'Guess you don't know *everything* about dragons,' he said.

Their eyes met.

And then Rufus arrived, crashing down between them with a groan.

'I'm as hungry as a flight o' gryphons,' he said, scratching at the bush of his beard. 'Thanks for cookin', Frida.'

Frida grunted and slurped at the soup.

'Charmin'.'

Jai's belly rumbled, but as Balbir had taught him, he waited for his elder to begin his meal.

'So, lad,' Rufus said, prodding the fire with their training stick. 'You've grown your core. And in less than a few weeks, no less. Most acolytes take half a year afore they manage it. 'Course, some burst their cores when they try too early.'

'I could have burst it?' Jai asked, incredulous.

'Well . . . only the ones that lack the talent for it.'

Jai gave him a reluctant smile, feeling just a little proud.

'But then, they're bonded to chamroshes. Their initial cores'll have been smaller than yours, Jai, with thinner walls.'

Jai glanced up at him.

'Oh?'

Rufus ran a hand through his red beard, exasperated once more by the holes in Jai's knowledge.

'Size of your initial core depends on your totem. A dragon's bigger 'n' tougher than a gryphon, right? A gryphon's bigger 'n' tougher than a chamrosh, and so on. And the size of the initial core – the kernel, some call it – their soulbound get follows from that. Bigger, thicker core can store more mana, and pull mana more quickly. Won't find many powerful soulbound with weak totems. With a dragon . . . you've got an advantage.'

Jai felt only a little deflated at that.

'Took me a month,' Frida mumbled through a mouthful of stew. 'I wasn't training as much as him, but he did it faster than I thought. Give him some credit.'

Rufus grinned, turning to her, which allowed Jai to cover his own grin. Rare praise.

'Never helps to have a student with a big head, but yours started smaller'n most so we'll let you have this one.'

Rufus had taken to bringing the wooden stick he used to train with Jai along with him in the cart, purportedly lest they reach an area lacking appropriately sized sticks. Considering they were currently travelling through a wood, Jai was sure it was a reminder. As if the fresh set of welts on his body wasn't reminder enough.

Now, Rufus tossed the stick into the fire.

'Right lad. We've got a few days yet to learn the true tricks of the trade. I'll leave you and young Frida here with some spells, charms and wards even the Gryphon Guard don't know. Or've forgotten, anyway.'

Jai didn't rise to the bait. Rufus loved to dangle these secret majicking techniques in front of him, then tell him he was not ready. Even Frida was becoming annoyed at this point.

'You're not ready yet,' he said, right on cue. 'But you can learn the basics. How to form a spell. How to cast it. Principles are the same whether you're moving a few grains of rice or stopping a charging mammoth dead.'

Rufus caught Jai's amazed expression.

'First time I saw a mammoth rider fly,' he winked. 'One of the Mahmut tribe. Hopefully not a friend of yours.'

He laughed at his own joke and stuffed another spoonful into his mouth.

Jai shifted closer, despite the teasing.

'Now,' Rufus said. 'Everyone learns fire as their first spell. Even the Dansk, right?'

Frida nodded absently. She rarely listened in to Rufus's lessons unless he was talking about something very advanced.

'So, we're gonna do a little experiment,' Rufus went on. 'Jai here is going to restart our fire.'

He leaned out a foot and began kicking earth over the coals.

'Hey!' Frida protested. 'I was just warming up.'

Rufus flapped her objection away.

'Be serious girl, the cold won't bother you none, soulbound or not. I've been to your kingdom. I'd sooner dip my balls in a direwolf's mouth than spend the night camping out there.'

Even Jai grimaced at that one.

'Go on then,' Jai said. 'Show me how. Lunch's getting cold.'

Chapter 70

Winter sat up, noting Jai's excitement and the change from the drudgery of watching Rufus whacking at her master. The four of them sat around the smoking fire and Rufus piled some straw at its edge.

'There's your target,' he said.

Rufus extended a hand and contorted his fingers. He pressed his four fingertips together, each slightly crooked, with a curled thumb tucked into his palm.

'The fire gesture,' he said. 'The more mana you push through, the more flame you get.'

Jai lifted a hand, contorting it as Rufus had.

'Close your eyes,' Rufus said. 'Always helps, the first time.'

Jai did so, taking a deep breath. He entered the trance, opening up his inner world. He started, as always, at the core.

He could sense Winter's consciousness, shifting and echoing down the long cord that connected their souls. Her presence focused him, as it always did.

'When mana enters the core, it must travel through the channels – paths that trace alongside your veins and arteries. It goes out the same way.'

Rufus's words sounded distant.

'Now . . . you want tae push the mana out of your hand. Will it there, as you compress your core. Then *through*.'

Jai squeezed his fragile core and saw the liquid dissolve through the crystalline walls, flowing like sentient gold out of his heart's chamber. Moments later, he felt warmth along his right hand and a static buzz across his skin.

'Can you feel the resistance?'

Jai could feel it within his fingers; hot and fizzing, yet unable to pass. Something was . . . catching. Like a comb in tangled hair.

'Yes,' Jai breathed.

'Adjust your fingers,' Rufus said.

Jai did so, making ever so gentle movements. When he moved them one way, the resistance eased. Another, and it increased exponentially.

'Keep on,' now Jai heard Frida's voice. 'Until it feels right.'

Jai did the best he could, opening his eyes and realising he could still hold the spell at the ready.

'Now push the mana to your finger,' Rufus breathed. 'Not with your core, unless you want to use more mana. Push with your mind.'

Jai gritted his teeth . . . and pushed.

At the end of his finger, a tiny sphere of flame flowed into existence. Jai twisted his hand, gazing at it. He could feel the heat of it upon his face . . . and the warmth and static seeping from his hands.

It spun lazily in the air like a flickering, miniature sun, yet even as he marvelled it sputtered and shrank, for the paltry mana he had given it began to fade.

Jai could feel it still connected to his finger, as if held there by an invisible string.

'Now,' Rufus said. 'Push it at the fire. There's no way to teach it. You need to find the way in your mind.'

Jai pointed his finger, struggling and wincing as he attempted to somehow move something disconnected to his body. The flame remained stubbornly in place.

Within moments, the fire was gone, and with it almost all of Jai's mana. If he soulbreathed enough to fill his entire core, he might just have enough to actually defend himself.

'All that mana,' Jai said. 'For a few moments of flame?'

Rufus chuckled.

'Told you internal majickin' was more effective. Better tae hack a man in half usin' a few drops of mana than lightly toast his beard for the same.'

Jai was disappointed. He'd secretly hoped his flame would last far longer. Rufus must have caught his expression.

'Don't look so glum. Spells such as these have their uses, specially the four keystones. Lightning, flame, ice, air; they use less mana than most. And in different forms too. Bolts, blasts, even waves if you've the knack for it. I once knew a lass'd paint you a portrait made of flame in the air. Most soulbound you'll battle will use some combination of those four, if they've the mana and the trainin'.'

Jai sighed. It was all so tantalisingly close. Yet that mana he'd used on the flame could have had him running full-tilt for an hour. Practising was out of the question until he knew they were safe, or at the very least his core was almost full.

'Just wait until you learn wards,' Frida said, lifting a finger and crackling the fire back into life with a spurt of flame.

'Leonid's chamber had so many wards beneath the paint, you could almost hear it buzzing when the wind stilled,' Jai said. 'It must have been the most warded place in all the empire.'

Rufus snorted.

'Try the Eyrie,' he said. 'That thing wasn't built with cement. Ain't no material on this earth that could hold up all that water 'n' marble, no matter how much Leonid's engineers pulled their hair out.'

Jai had always wondered about that. It made sense, for the Gryphon Guard's tower stretched taller even than the steeple of Constantine's great cathedral.

'You know, there's nothing stopping you from teaching us these so-called rare spells now,' Jai said. 'You don't need to wait until the last day.'

Rufus grumbled beneath his breath. Jai was sure the lesson was coming. Just that Rufus was still working himself up to it.

'I'll tell you what,' Rufus sighed. 'I'll teach you one now.'

He held out his hand and contorted it into a knot of over-lapping fingers. This time Frida leaned in, even reaching out and tracing his interlaced digits with her hand.

Then he tugged his hand away and pointed it at Jai's boots. There was a rush of . . . something. A tremble in the air. A flicker.

And Jai's laces tightened. Knotted.

'The keep-fast charm,' he said. 'Good for your saddle, when you're riding. Armour straps, and yes, *laces*. Someone takes a knife to it, or snaps the rope or belt, it'll come away as any would. But that knot'll be tighter'n a Sabine priest's purse.'

Jai made a face. Not exactly the epic battle spell he'd been looking for.

'And on that note,' Jai said. 'I'm going to soulbreathe.'

Chapter 71

J ai did not soulbreathe within the wagon as he usually did, for today the sunset sky was clear and the low, tree-lined valley they had stopped at for the night seemed immune to the bitter chill of winter.

Jai sat cross-legged, as he had seen Rufus and Frida do. He'd created a nest for himself, deep among the trees. The scent of pine trees was rich in the air, and their needles made for a soft seat beneath him. The boughs of the tree above him created a soft if somewhat permeable ceiling, and the undergrowth was so thick around it that he was practically sealed in, but for the path he'd hacked through the brambles.

He intended to sleep here, so long as Winter woke him for his turn to keep watch. It felt . . . right. He'd never known how stale the air had been, back in Latium. He could smell the earth here. Feel the electric buzz. Hear true quiet, not that heavy, dusty silence within Leonid's chamber.

The air was still, and silent. Not even the soughing of the breeze disturbed him. As he entered the trance, he saw the world lit up in gold. Here, amid the vegetation . . . the air was alive with mana. And above, it poured into the sky, stretching high into a pillar of light.

Living things must be a source of mana. Billowing into the world, in that strange way it did. Pooling and flowing like liquid, yet rising and drifting like air. And within, those motes of glittering dust. He wished he could put out his tongue and taste them.

If there was ever a place to soulbreathe, it was here. No wonder so many soulbound eschewed sects and became hermits, living and training themselves in the wilderness. He could so easily become lost in this place.

There was beauty here. A life, even.

It was then that he realised it. He truly was *free*.

Until now, he'd only thought of his and Winter's survival. Yet in these past, peaceful days he was finally catching his breath. He had time to *think*. To understand what he had become.

He gathered Winter up into his arms, tracing the nubs of her horns with his fingers. She had grown larger of late. As large as a chamrosh, he'd wager. It looked like a diet of squirrels and bugs suited the young hatchling.

'Is this the right path, girl?' Jai asked.

He had no master. His life . . . it was his own. There was no Leonid to serve. No guards to fear, no hierarchy to eschew. He chose what mattered to him and what didn't.

Did he owe loyalty to the uncle who had signed away their lives? To a people he hardly knew? There was nobody waiting for him out there in the Great Steppe. Only danger.

Nobody would look for him in this wilderness. Not in this copse of pines half a mile from an empty stretch of the Kashmere Road. He had spent his whole life stuck in a room. Would it not be bliss to live in nature, beneath the open sky? He could pass a few years here, watching Winter grow. Wait out the war, until Winter could fly him wherever their wills took them.

Jai allowed himself that fantasy for a moment. It was only when Samar's face flashed through his mind that he shook it from his thoughts. Instead, he thought of Arjun. Balbir. Their courage in the face of death.

He stiffened his resolve. His people lived beneath as wide and open a sky as any, in a wilderness far vaster than anything here. He would not go quietly into obscurity. He owed it to his brothers. He owed it to Balbir, who had loved their people with all her heart. He owed it to himself.

He would claim his birthright. No matter how far he'd travel, no matter how much hardship he endured. He was the son of Rohan. He was rightful heir to the Kidara clan. Not some wild hermit living off river fish and squirrel meat.

And the first step was to become more powerful. To ascend and take the first true step as a soulbound warrior.

Jai closed his eyes and began to breathe rhythmically.

Cultivating mana was still like trying to run while breathing through a straw. Difficult enough, without the temptation of sleep. He'd heard of soulbound soulbreathing while sat upon beds of nails and thought them quite mad. Now . . . he kind of understood.

Time passed excruciatingly slowly, as each drip of gold filtered into his core. By the time his core could bear the strain no longer, what little sunlight there had been was long gone.

The whole process left him exhausted, and with little more to show for it than recovering what he had lost that afternoon.

With the moon high in the sky and the remnants of what must have been *another* pot of stew waiting for him back at camp, Jai was ready to turn in. And then . . . he heard it.

The snapping of twigs. Soft footsteps, treading with care.

But he knew who it was. Winter could smell her. Frida.

Jai waited in the shadows, wondering if she was looking for

him or going on her own night-time wander. When she ducked into his cave Jai gave her a hesitant greeting, for her face was dark with foreboding.

'What's wrong?' he asked as Frida motioned for him to remain seated, and sat cross-legged in front of him. For a moment she listened intently and Jai could tell she was using mana.

'He's snoring,' she said. 'We can talk.'

'Who?' Jai asked. 'Rufus? What do you care if he hears?'

Frida chewed her lip, appraising Jai. She nearly spoke, then hesitated. Chewed her lip some more.

'I think we should leave,' she said finally.

Jai stared at her, confused.

'What, now? Did the legion catch up to us? Or are their scouts on the move again?'

Frida shook her head.

'No nothing like that. Listen . . .'

She stopped again.

'I . . . I can't give him my blade,' she stuttered, avoiding his eyes. 'It's all I have left of my mother. And you heard him today. He's never going to teach us anything useful. In two days he leaves and takes my whytblade with him.'

For a moment, Jai didn't know what to say.

Then: 'Say we went ahead with Navi and Winter while he was asleep . . . he'd catch us in minutes after he woke up. He's soulbound.'

'So we leave the road,' Frida said, crossing her arms.

'It'll take us twice as long to get there,' Jai said.

'No,' Frida said. 'In a few days we leave the road anyway, head north-east to the mountain pass where the borders of our lands meet. We never told Rufus exactly where we were headed. It might cost us a few days, but we've travelled most of the way we needed to on the Kashmere Road.'

Jai stared at her. Saw the set of her jaw and the flint of her eyes.

This was . . . he hadn't even considered leaving.

'We made a deal,' he said slowly, speaking his thoughts aloud.

'Do you remember how that deal was made?' Frida growled. 'If he hadn't spoken up, we'd have gotten away.'

'And we'd have had Camilla's gang of cutthroats chasing us to the ends of the earth,' Jai retorted.

'Have they caught up to us yet?' Frida demanded. 'One night's soulbreathing and I could have taken on anyone they sent our way.'

'Even another soulbound?' Jai asked. 'With a totem of their own? Maybe the fact they know Rufus is with us is the only reason they didn't follow us. *If* they didn't.'

Frida wrung her hands, and Jai saw tears of anger shine upon her cheeks.

'I can't give it to him,' she whispered, seizing his hand. 'I won't. Come with me, Jai. I can't do it alone.'

'Look, even if we leave him, he'll track us through the forest,' Jai said. 'I've yet to see him angry and much as I like the man, I don't think I'd want to. Now for Winter's sake, drop this mad idea. We've been dealt a shitty hand. We need to learn to live with it until we can change the odds.'

Frida spat derisively and threw his hand aside.

'You're a coward,' she said, pushing herself to her feet. 'I should have known.'

And with that . . . she was gone.

Chapter 72

Rufus was half-asleep when Jai returned in the early hours of the morning to take his watch, and gave him little more than a grunt of acknowledgement before disappearing into the back of the wagon. He could see that Frida had returned ahead of him and was lying inside, her shoulder blades hunched and her face turned away from the door.

It was with some awkwardness that Jai found himself riding on the driver's bench alongside her the next day.

Only . . . she was not unkind to him. With a little softness, she asked him how he had slept, and even prepared a tea. He could see it in her eyes. That she was sorry for how she had spoken to him.

When they resumed the journey after the tea, she settled back. And taking a deep breath, she spoke.

Spoke more than she ever had before, the words pouring from her as if she had kept them pent up inside. As if sharing that secret part of herself was her way of apologising.

She spoke of home. Of the music and song of the Dansk *skalds*, travelling bards who sang tales of the happenings that year. She'd sneak out of the palace to the mead halls, just to hear them.

She'd had to, for even in the rough-hewn halls of the Dansk Kingdom, where queens were as powerful as kings and shield-maidens fought alongside their husbands, a princess and her entourage were not permitted to hear the ribald tales that were so often the most popular.

What Jai learned, more than anything, was that Frida was in love. Not with him of course, nor anyone else for that matter. But rather, with her people.

She thought about them constantly. It was as if she felt responsible. Jai could not understand why she took on that great weight. He supposed he was not so dissimilar, but he had a birthright to go along with that duty.

What was clearer still was that Frida was in mourning. The relationship she'd had with the king and his daughter was a subject she avoided, but she mourned them as much as Jormun.

Jai was happy to wait to broach the subject, considering their fledgling . . . friendship?

He did not know what they were. Only that when Rufus finally did emerge from the wagon, scratching at his bald pate, she drew away from him.

He felt . . . something, at that. Almost annoyed. What did she care what the old sot thought? He distracted himself with further cultivating, filling his core a little bit more. It was almost a tenth full – with a bit of practice, he might just manage to accidentally set himself on fire.

By the time they made camp for the evening. Jai was becoming nervous.

Since all she had shared that morning Frida had hardly said a word to him outside of their usual polite repartee. Did she regret what she had told him? The very thought burned him, and he had to shake it from his head.

Now, they sat around a campfire, cooking up more stew.

Somehow, Jai had not grown sick of it. Only Winter turned her nose up at it, preferring to hunt in the wilderness until the early hours of the morning.

Rufus was drinking. What little sleep Rufus had had the night before had been spent tossing and turning, and he had slept fitfully through the morning. Then Jai had noticed the older man finally reading Leonid's journal after lunch.

'Lil' more?' Rufus asked, stretching out his bowl. 'In my day, wouldn'a asked. Wouldn'a *had* to ask. My day. My bloody day.'

He slurred his words as he spoke, stew slopping over the edge of the bowl. Frida had told him it took a lot more alcohol to get a soulbound drunk than it would for a normal man. Jai wasn't sure *where* in the wagon Rufus had stashed his booze, but he must have guzzled more than his flask could contain.

'You wanna know, huh,' he grumbled. 'It being the last night 'n' all.'

He stabbed a finger at Jai.

'Tit for tat, tit for tat. That's what Leonid used tae say. An empire for his friendship. That's what I traded him. And he *spat* on . . . pissed . . . pissed on . . .'

He slumped lower on the log he'd sat upon, his finger swaying in the air. For a moment, his ranting slowed as he glowered into the flames.

Frida looked particularly worried. Jai leaned close to her, waiting until Rufus was distracted, scraping at the bottom of his bowl.

'He'll be right by morning. We won't slow.'

Frida shook her head. 'Ivar used to get like this. He got . . . *mean*. You don't want to know what a drunk, mean soulbound is capable of.'

Jai winced at her words, seeing the truth in them.

'Conspiracy!' Rufus announced, holding up a finger. 'You're at it. I can hear it. See? You see?'

He straightened, a fresh bout of bitter rage stirring him from his stupor.

'That's what . . . they called it. She was just a girl, you know.'

He let out a long, fluttering breath.

'I should've known,' he whispered. 'Should've known, should've known.'

He gave a nervous scratch at his beard, eyes dancing. It had happened so quickly. Like the man had just guzzled half a barrel of beer.

'Hemlock,' Frida cursed. 'The fool. He's spiked his drink with it, so he can get drunk without the mana burning away the booze. Ivar used to drink a full barrel of beer before daybreak, and Rufus can't have stashed that much. He'll be no use tomorrow.'

'So . . . I . . . can forget,' Rufus said, holding up an indignant finger.

The man's mood was all over the place. But Jai couldn't help it, the need to know more almost pulling on his tongue.

'Forget what, Rufus?' Jai asked.

The question just slipped out. He knew it wouldn't change anything. Knew it would do nothing but rile the drunk man further.

At least Rufus's self-poisoning had left his power suppressed. He'd not be blasting them to pieces any time soon.

But if the man had heard Jai's question, he didn't react. Instead, he slumped all the way down, pushing his feet toward the fire. A soft snore followed. Then a louder one.

Frida sniffed.

'I've seen what drink can do to men. Whatever happened to him, he's been taking the hemlock for some time. Only way we soulbound can get blind drunk.'

Jai was silent, watching the wreck of the older man's face. He wondered how old he was. Everyone knew that soulbound lived longer than others, rarely falling ill and living long lives. But Rufus . . . he'd been a powerful practitioner his whole life, it seemed. To look so craggy, so ruined by the wear of the world . . . he could be older than Leonid had ever been, in this moment.

Rufus had finally revealed something of his past, though. Could the girl he had mentioned be the same one in Leonid's secret chamber?

'Did you know Ivar, as a child?' Jai asked, keeping his voice quiet.

For a moment, there was nothing but the crackle of the flames. Then, Frida sighed and spoke a single word.

'Yes.'

'So . . .'

'You don't need to know about that,' Frida said, shaking her head. 'I . . . I've been thinking. I've said too much. Everything I tell you is one more the Sabines' torturers will hear if we're captured. I'm ascended – I can take their tortures. But you? You'll break.'

'I'd die first,' Jai said, indignant.

'Really?' Frida said. 'You'd die to keep Ivar's great love of beer a secret?'

'Well, no,' Jai admitted.

'That's how it starts,' Frida said. 'Then you say a little more, then more, and more.'

'But . . .'

He never finished his thought. For a voice interrupted him. One that emerged from the trees behind them.

'*We'll* keep it secret; don't you worry about that.'

Jai's head snapped around so fast he almost broke his neck.

Two men stood just beyond the treeline. No . . . two boys, shrouded in shadow. They were younger than him. One only by a year or so, the other whose balls had hardly dropped, if the crack in his voice was any indication.

'How did you . . .'

Jai fell silent as he saw the beasts prowling beside them. Even in the darkness, he could tell what they were.

Chamroshes.

Chapter 73

'This may just be the easiest gig I've ever had,' said the older boy.

'Don't count on it,' Frida snarled.

She stood, awkward in her sack-cloth smock, with a hand close to her side.

'Oh, you can pull your blade, Dansk girl,' the younger one said. 'We know you have a whytblade.'

Jai could almost feel the rage pouring from Frida. She yanked her dagger free, and their surroundings were immediately lit by the weapon's glow.

'Ooo,' the older boy said, holding his hands up in mock horror. 'Little Dansk girl has a fancy toy.'

To Jai's shock, he recognised him. It was the same boy who had guided the royal hunting party to the khiro. Silas.

Frida cursed beneath her breath, then kicked out at Rufus. The man grunted and a dribble of vomit fell from his lips. Nothing more.

Jai reached into his pocket and gulped down the last pill he'd been saving, though he suspected it would not help much. Either way . . . this was bad. Though these boys did not wear the garb of Gryphon Guard squires or acolytes, the chamroshes by their sides were telling.

'If you know my blade, then Camilla hired you,' Frida spat. 'Come, take what you're here for. I've always wanted to kill a Gryphon Guard.'

The younger boy grinned at that. Then he did something strange. He bowed.

'Camilla is a craven cunt who can be no less trusted than a common thief. We, however, are guildsmen today. So, we must keep our word, more's the pity.'

Frida cursed some more.

Guildsmen. Jai felt only a slight rush of relief. He knew something of this group, not least because Constantine had complained of their existence to Leonid on more than one occasion.

They were a mercenary sect that existed within the empire's borders and beyond. They hired themselves to petty kings and warlords, joining armies as scouts, spies and more. With the Gryphon Guard at his beck and call, Constantine had no need of their services. Only his enemies did.

Beyond that, Jai knew little of their practices. He only knew that the Gryphon Guard allowed their acolytes and squires to leave for one year of their choosing and many hired themselves out to the Guild for the duration. It was a rite of passage, one that allowed young guards to learn new techniques and earn some of their own money. Most tended to travel well beyond the borders of the empire so they could easily wash the blood from their hands upon their return.

'You *are* Gryphon Guard,' Jai said bluntly, letting his hand stray to the sword at his hip. 'Your sect is at war. You've no business working for the Guild right now.'

The younger boy grinned but said nothing. He was likely an

acolyte, still wet behind the ears. But Silas . . . he was a squire. Ascended if what Rufus had told him was true, perhaps even a high-level soulbound.

Beside him, his chamrosh let out a low cluck. It was a young beast, but still larger than Winter by a few inches. It stared at them with piercing yellow eyes.

As for the other chamrosh, it paced back and forth behind the soulbound pair, protecting their rear. Despite their casual introduction, Jai made no mistake. These boys were ready for a fight.

Somewhere inside the wagon, Winter stirred. Jai forced a message through to her, one with enough feeling that she'd listen. To *stay*. The sight of her would put them in far more danger than she could prevent.

So far, they likely thought Frida an escaped Dansk noble, and he her indentured servant or fettered. There had been no flicker of recognition from Silas. Clearly he had not been paying much attention to Jai or his brothers.

'Come on,' Frida snarled. 'Let's do this. I've a full core and it's *itching*.'

The older boy snorted at that.

'We've no desire to fight. We'd have ambushed you if we wanted to do that. No, you're going to come peacefully. You and your pet Steppeman.'

Frida scoffed at that. But then . . . something strange happened. Her blade's glow began to falter. Its light sputtered, then faded to its usual white sheen.

Their surroundings were cast in darkness once more and Jai allowed some mana to seep from his precious store, to allow his eyes to see better in the dark.

The acolyte sucked his teeth, then reached into his pocket and handed something to his elder. Jai heard coins jingle.

'Early,' he grumbled. 'Very early.'

The squire shrugged.

'Belly works faster on the road,' he said. 'Took a good an hour at the wedding rehearsal, I'm told.'

Frida was unusually silent. Her eyes bulged from her head. This was more than anger. It was . . . something else.

And now Jai was feeling strange. There was a roiling in his belly to match the hammer of his heart.

Beside him, Frida vomited.

'Poison,' Frida moaned. 'Run. Run!'

Jai ran.

THERE WAS NO TIME to look back. Not even to call Winter to his side. He was already haring through the forest, forcing his legs to push on.

He knew what had happened. He'd seen it before, just a few weeks ago. It seemed word of the poisonings at the wedding rehearsal had spread. Spawned ideas.

Already, he was feeling weaker. His legs did not want to obey, and twice he tripped over his own feet. He'd eaten as much as Frida had, a few spoonfuls before they'd been distracted by Rufus's raving. For now he was still able to move, but he knew it wouldn't last. His only chance was to hide.

He entered the half-trance as he ran and saw the poison in his mind's eye. It was like a red leech in his belly, sucking out the mana that rushed to hold the toxin at bay.

Only . . . some mana still remained. The hemlock's pull was struggling with the mana he had let out to suffuse his body, spreading more slowly where it met the circulating, golden light. And the pill, too, acted against it, its fizzing presence in his stomach slowing the poison's pull.

Mana seeped from his core no matter whether he tried to seal it or not, drifting down his channels to fight the hemlock. It was slow, but sure. Before long, he'd have none left to use.

Behind him, Jai heard the crackle of branches. He stopped, knowing his chance to hide was gone. Instead, he drew his blade, facing the way he'd come. Moments later the acolyte emerged and behind him, the chamrosh followed.

It hissed, pawing the ground like a bull. The black-tipped beak was hooked and sharp, while its muscled canine body was rangy and covered in a thick meld of fur and feather.

'Come now,' the boy laughed. 'You can't beat a soulbound, especially poisoned as you are. You can keep your life if you last the night — I want to sell it, not end it.'

His face was cherubic, portraying an innocence and youth belied by the cruel words that came with the smile.

But the boy had made a mistake. He didn't know Jai was soulbound. Perhaps Camilla had lied about it to reduce their price. Or perhaps Camilla had thought Jai was bluffing.

It did not matter. In a few minutes, Jai might as well not be soulbound. He had to use his mana, fast.

Jai lifted his blade and squared up.

'Come get it.'

Chapter 74

The acolyte laughed. He did not even bother to draw the sword at his waist. Instead, he lifted a threatening hand.

Jai ignored it. At his age, this boy was no more capable of serious majicking than Jai was.

'Don't make me burn you, savage,' the boy said tauntingly.

'Burn away,' Jai snarled, squeezing his core.

He struck with all the speed and mana he could summon, forcing it through his body in a rush of terror.

His arm lanced forward, just as Rufus had showed him. But the acolyte spun away with unexpected speed.

The blade grazed him, slicing above the hip and past, bursting through a tree in an explosion of splinters. Then the chamrosh was on Jai, launching itself in a spray of drool and fury.

It was all Jai could do to leap back, tumbling through thorn and briar. The beast was relentless, snapping and snarling, its beak slicing his arms to ribbons as his next blow went wide.

Sobbing in pain, Jai managed to force his blade between him and its darting beak, keeping it from his face as it slobbered at him. Saliva dripped into his eyes, and he kicked out in a mana-infused burst of desperation.

The chamrosh erupted into the air, feathers billowing, but was on him in a matter of moments, swooping back in a flurry of scrabbling paws and stabbing beak. The blade was gone – Jai hadn't even realised he'd dropped it.

All he could do was grasp the beast by the neck, his mana slowly seeping away as it squawked and slavered. Its paws scratched at his chest, as if it could dig its way to his heart.

With every second, it inched closer to his face, and he could smell its animal breath. Blood dribbled from his arms, coating his torn sleeves in blood.

There was a screech somewhere close by, and the chamrosh slammed to the side, a white flash of whirling claws knocking it into the underbrush. *Winter.*

Jai sobbed at the hatchling's pain as the two ripped into each other, but there was no time to help. In the swirl of drifting feathers, the boy rushed at him with blade held high.

Twice, Jai launched himself aside as the sword chopped down without thinking where the movement was taking him. Soon he found his back to a thicket, thorns ripping his shirt.

Instinct took him as the third wild swing came down. He stepped into the boy's guard, too close for the blow to land.

For a moment, they were face to face, heaving against each other. Jai could smell the acolyte's fear as they grappled, the blade clutched above their heads, inching back and forth.

In his mind's eye, he could feel the last dregs of his mana sapping away. He had but seconds to make a move.

Their eyes met and Jai launched his head forward. Saw *stars.*

He staggered away, dizzied, the world a blur. Any moment, he expected a sword to punch through his chest. Instead, there was . . . nothing. Only the desperate agony of Winter's battle, somewhere out of sight.

In front of Jai, the acolyte twitched unconscious upon the ground, his blade forgotten.

Jai leaped for it, snatching the weapon with frantic hands. Raised it, still dazed, and stabbed down once. Twice.

Then again and again, screaming with rage and fear. He did not look at what he was doing. Even closed his eyes, forcing himself to hack until the gurgling stopped.

He heard the crack of a branch and spun. Only to see Winter there, mewling. She limped to him and lapped at his injured arms and wrists.

'Come here, girl,' Jai whispered, gathering her up into his arms.

He could feel her pain. Even sensed where it was; where the chamrosh had bitten deep into her neck and shoulders. She was injured . . . and badly. He needed to help her.

First, he searched the boy's pockets. He wore little and must not have brought his valuables with him from wherever they were camped. There was nothing beyond the sword and a pouch of tobacco leaf and paper. Jai could do no more than rip strips from the corpse's shirt hem and bandage Winter as best he could. He did the same to his wrists, glad that the cuts were mostly superficial.

By the time he was finished, the place was eerily quiet.

Jai listened, but his mana was all gone. Still, he knew if Frida had been captured, she'd be close. Probably the way they'd come. He cast about, averting his eyes from the dead boy, and saw the dead chamrosh.

It lay, tongue protruding from its beak, a deep rent in its neck where Winter had ripped out its throat. She was small, but there was a reason the Dansk guarded their dragons so closely. Even as a hatchling, she could defeat a chamrosh.

A realisation came to him then.

Jai scrambled on his hands and knees to where his blade had fallen. He took it and made his way over to the chamrosh's corpse.

Up close, he could smell it, even without the mana to enhance his senses. It was a heavy, animal scent, with a coppery edge of blood.

He didn't have time to hesitate. Jai stabbed down, sliding the blade through plumage and ribs, then began sawing into the beast's chest.

Without mana to aide him it was hard work. Twice, panic forced him to stop and listen to the silent woods, his heart pounding in his ears. But nothing came and soon he had cut a rent deep enough that allowed him to push a hand into the beast's chest cavity and seek out the strange stone that Frida had removed from her dragon all those days ago.

At first he found only hot entrails, but then he felt his hand wrap around what he thought was the beast's heart. It was large and rubbery, but he could feel something hard within when he palpated it. After some awkward stabbing, he managed to cut open a hole and rummage within.

Jai jerked his hand free and held it to the moonlight, sifting through the wad of clotted blood in his palm. Something . . . glowed.

The soulgem looked for all the world like a large marble, but one that was hollow and filled with a liquid light. *This* was what the core looked like. Or at least, what the core became when the totem had died.

Jai retched. Nausea was beginning to take hold. Whether it was the adrenaline, the poison, the sight of blood or his own exhaustion, he had no idea. Who knew how much hemlock he had consumed? Enough of it would kill him, soulbound or no, and whatever the mana had been doing to protect him had faded.

He could feel a numbness spreading through him. Breathing was becoming more difficult. He *needed* mana.

Jai could hardly remember what Frida had said of soulgems, but he knew it would help him somehow. As the last of his strength began to leave his body, Jai pushed it between his lips and forced a gulp.

It was not a moment too soon, for he slumped forward, face half-buried in the mulch. He could feel Winter desperately trying to send him mana. But their connection was too tenuous, and her own mana was almost all spent.

The light of the world faded . . . and Jai was gone.

Chapter 75

There was no world beyond the one within him. And the one within him was at war.

He could feel the poison like a red, caustic infection spreading through his insides. But at its centre was the soulgem, fizzing within his burning belly.

Jai tried to soulbreathe. Tried to force his lungs to obey. But he had left it too late. His lungs no longer responded to him. Nothing did.

He was a prisoner within the shell of his own body. An observer of his own demise.

And then . . . a light. Erupting in the centre of his being.

At first it was but a sputter, a spark in a spreading sea of red. But soon, more poured forth. It was not much, but the red seemed to dissolve at its touch. As if the mana was cleansing the poison, just as it had cleansed the blockages in his channels.

The golden light spread, raging through his belly like a wildfire. And then . . . it was gone. Used up like a match.

The red remained, but now, it was a slow pain, spread across his extremities.

He gulped in a deep breath. Groaned.

There was a warm hand upon his brow. This was . . . somewhere else. But no matter what he did, he could not open his eyes. Nor could he hear anything.

He hung in an abyss, caught between his inner world and the one without. Fragments of feeling pulsed, but nothing more.

Jai arched, feeling his body spasm, the poison wracking him once more. Now, he had nothing left. What little mana the tiny soulgem had given him had bought him time, but already the poison was taking hold once more.

He had to soulbreathe.

Jai forced another breath, almost swallowing it down. Then another, and another.

> *The lungs, the bellows*
> *The heart, the hearth.*
> *The stomach, the cauldron.*
> *The blood, the filter.*
> *The core, the cast.*

Balbir's mantra echoed through his mind as he pushed his numbed lungs to work. Tiny dregs of mana passed through him, entering and emerging from the core almost in the same moment. His body sent mana to where it was needed.

With each foothold the poison seemed to take, the mana pushed it back. A war of attrition, endless and exhausting.

But Jai persevered. Forced each breath, over and over. He did not know if time was his enemy or his ally. He only knew one thing. To soulbreathe.

*   *   *

JAI COULD FEEL THE edges of himself once more. He was . . . warm. He was lying on something hard – no longer the forest floor.

He had been dreaming, a moment before. Already, it was half-forgotten. Imaginings of the Eyrie. Of meditating in their temple. Sparring on the marble causeway.

So strange. He pushed the images from his mind.

It was a slow awakening. An ebb and flow of consciousness, made up of fragments of sensation, smells and sounds. He did not know how many days passed. All blended into one.

A cool finger lifted and lowered his eyelid, and he saw the soft blur of Frida's face, deep in shadow. There was her voice, and that of another. Water being sponge-dripped into his mouth. The scent of cooking. And the shame as he felt cool air upon his nethers as he was stripped, wiped and clothed.

The battle with the poison within him seemed never-ending. There were times when he thought it would overwhelm him, when he slept and woke to find the poison seizing up his lungs once more. Only Winter, kind, loyal creature, kept him from death. For while he slept, he knew she fed him what little mana she had. He could feel it sustaining him. Keeping him alive.

A few times he thought he'd quashed the poison entirely. Times where he felt just a little longer, and he'd be well again – only for the red infection to spread out from his guts once more. But each time, the roots of it seemed to shrivel. With each resurgence, it came back a little less.

IT WAS PAIN THAT woke him. The stomach-dropping feel of falling and the hard crash of his body upon a stone floor.

That, and the shock of cold water, splashing across his face and driving him back to the floor as he attempted to sit up.

'Wake up, sonny boy,' a harsh voice said.

Jai shuddered as he opened his eyes; the ground beneath him was cold as ice.

He was in a dank, stone room, one with bars upon the single window. It was hardly larger than his wardrobe at the palace.

He turned groggily, but there was no time to see his captor. The thick, barred door had already slammed closed.

'Faking it,' the voice chuckled. 'Told you.'

The sound was faint, but some small remainder of mana allowed Jai to hear it if he strained his ears.

'Just give me my coin and I'll be on my way.'

The second voice was . . . familiar. It had to be the older guildsman. Silas.

That realisation hit Jai so hard he almost passed out again. These past few days, he'd felt . . . safe. Cared for. All the while he had been in that bastard's clutches. Jai felt sick.

'How much did we say, Silas?' the voice said. 'Ten for the boy, a hundred for the girl?'

'Two hundred for the girl,' Silas said. 'And it'll be three if you try that again, Aurelius.'

'You have any idea how much I risk keeping her here?' Aurelius snapped. 'We've already received word that there's a bounty out for a young Dansk woman escaped from the palace. She might be the one they're looking for.'

'Do you have any idea how much she's worth if you can break her?' Silas retorted. 'That's why the Guild sent her to you – this is the perfect place to try it. She's a noble. With a dragon too, if I had to guess. Think what she might know. Mayhap the secret to bonding with dragons.'

'One fifty.'

'I lost my partner, you thick cunt,' Silas snapped.

'One. Fifty.'

'You want to renege on a deal with the Guild, you go right ahead. They'll send a crew here to beat your hide just for the principle.'

'Fucking Guild,' Aurelius groaned. 'I'm supposed to be their business partner.'

'You're *lucky* I'm here on Guild business,' Silas muttered. 'She'd be sent right back to the Sabines if I was still with the Gryphon Guard. Just remember, if you break her, you come to the Guild first. That's the deal.'

'You've got a great deal already,' Aurelius snapped. 'They're the richest sect in all the world. What's fifty more denarii to them.'

Jai could feel the last vestiges of warmth seeping from him into the stone floor, and he willed himself to move. He sat up with a groan, straining his eyes in the dark. But he could see very little, only smell damp straw somewhere in the room.

He needed to know where Frida was. He tried to speak, but all that came out was a wheeze.

'I remind you, I'm only with the Guild a year. Nothing stopping me from coming back here when I've rejoined the Gryphon Guard, if you try me further.'

There was a sigh, and then the rattle of coins. Jai had no idea how he was alive. Had forgiving his murder of the acolyte truly been worth ten sesterii, on top of all the hassle of bringing him here?

'You keep that Dansk whore fed on one cup of hemlock tea a day, she'll be docile as a lamb,' Silas said. 'Just enough to keep her incapable of filling her core as she battles the poison.'

'Hemlock,' Aurelius spat derisively. 'I'd more likely kill her. My father tried using it to keep the soulbound docile, back when he ran this place. Killed most of them.'

'How'd you think I got her?' Silas snapped. 'One of our beasts dropped a ball of leaves in their stew from above. Oldest trick in the book. That savage is lucky he lived – must've only had half a spoonful.'

'You better be right,' Aurelius grumbled. 'She looked half-dead when you brought her in. The boy too.'

'Or what?' Silas laughed without humour. 'You'll set your thugs on me? Wasn't my first choice to bring her here, but the Guild want the secret to dragon bonding. That, and they've no love lost for the Sabines. Only place that won't hire them, so why should they help the royal cunts out?'

'And I'll sell it to them. If the price is right.'

Silas laughed aloud at that.

'The Guild know it's a long shot. Might not have a dragon at all.'

'I thought you said you thought she had a dragon,' Aurelius said.

'That was before I had the coin in my hand,' Silas said.

Aurelius cursed, long and hard.

'If she knows, I'll wring it out of her,' Aurelius said, lamely.

'Good luck,' Silas laughed. 'A soulbound can retreat into themselves, even let their body be ravaged, and feel nothing. It's been tried before. You should know that – your father did run a prison for low-level soulbound after all.'

He jingled the coins.

'Too late to back out now though,' he laughed.

'There's other ways,' Aurelius said.

Jai heard Silas spit. Then footsteps and the sound of a door slamming.

'Fucking soulbound,' Aurelius muttered.

Jai took a shuddering breath and made a monumental effort to move again. His arms moved sluggishly, enough to dig his nails into the rough-hewn surface and haul himself to his feet. The world spun and he almost collapsed, but he managed to topple closer to the door. Footsteps began to recede as he caught his breath.

'Wait!' Jai croaked. 'Tell me where I am.'

The footsteps stopped. Then continued.

Jai was alone.

Chapter 76

Jai was starving, but there was nothing in the room except a bucket of water in the corner beside the drain that was his toilet.

He crawled there and plunged his face beneath its surface. The water was cold and he broke through a thin layer of ice at its rim, but it was a small price to pay for the *sensation* he felt once more.

It must have been days that he had been trapped within his body, fighting a private war against the poison. To feel anything external, even that icy shock, was a sudden blessing.

His mind raced, even as he gulped down water, sating a raging thirst he had not fully comprehended until that moment.

It felt like a full minute before he emerged, gasping for air, water sloshing in his belly. For now, his stomach was sated, if falsely. He threw his head back, panting and letting water fall from his hair.

'Frida!' he bellowed.

There was no reply. She was here, he knew that at least.

Silas must have come upon his dead compatriot and seen what Jai had done to him. Seen his dead chamrosh with its throat ripped out and thought that Frida's beast was still alive and coming for him.

Silas must have grabbed his and Frida's paralysed bodies, leaving an injured Winter and an unconscious Rufus behind. Jai doubted the old drunk would have been able to pick up their trail when he finally awoke, for Rufus would have been left in as bad a state as Jai had been. If he'd want to rescue them at all.

It must have been Frida that had cared for Jai, even while enfeebled from hemlock herself. He knew from the bandages on his arms that he'd not just been chucked in the back of a wagon and left to rot all the way here.

And now Frida was to be tortured for the secret of dragon bonding. Dosed with hemlock, she must be trapped within her own body just as he had been. All that time she'd held information back from him for fear of capture and torture. And he'd resented her for it. What a fool he'd been. She had been right all along.

What would she be forced to endure in this cruel, sterile place? Pain? Or worse.

He felt rage. Rage at the unfairness of it all. To have made it so far . . . only to . . . he let out an angry sob and slammed a fist to the ground. It hurt.

Enough to jar him from his stupor, as he examined himself for the first time.

Jai lifted the rough-spun cloth that wrapped tight around his wrists, to see heavy black scabs there. Some had even peeled away, leaving pink skin in its place. Jai's eyes widened. He must have been out for *days*. That, or he'd had mana to spare for healing. Unlikely.

Where was Winter? He closed his eyes, seeking her out. He could sense her. That was good – she was still alive. But she was . . . sleeping. And their connection felt faded. Distant.

No clues to her whereabouts there. Why was she sleeping?

Jai looked up at the tiny, barred window and saw the sulking blue light of early morning. He could hear birds outside, but the window was too high to reach.

It was set deep into the wall. Indeed, the walls looked thick, made of large, weighty stones. There was not even mortar between them, only their great weight holding them in place. Even with a full core of mana, there would be little he could do to get out of here.

No, he would not tunnel out of this place. His only exit was the barred door. Jai looked down at his fists, then the bucket. There was no way he could batter the door down, soulbound or not. It was ironwood and Damantine steel by the blue sheen of it.

He would remain until someone came for him. There was nothing to do but drink, piss and shit. And soulbreathe.

Jai settled cross-legged upon the cold floor. Entered the trance.

It was so *easy*, like slipping into a warm bath. His inner being had become familiar during those days of training. His body felt . . . like a friend.

He could see so much more clearly. Every channel, every organ, every crevice of his being. It was all laid out before him, in all its pulsing, gurgling harmony.

That soulgem had done its work, holding back the poison. But moreover, his constant soulbreathing in the past weeks seemed to have strengthened his core somehow. As if he had strengthened the membrane that allowed him to flex his core like a muscle.

Even his channels seemed pinker, wider and more flexible. He could only imagine some combination of practice, the soulgem and the pill had left him far better at soulbreathing than some weeks ago.

It was a pity the gem had come from such a young beast, and one so small and relatively weak.

He took a deep breath and let mana fill his lungs. Again, it felt *easy*. It was those hours upon hours, cultivating to save his own life. Pushing through paralysed lungs, forcing mana where it was needed. It had damn-near killed him, but he was far stronger for it.

Silas's assumption that he could not be soulbound had saved him once, allowing him to defeat the acolyte. Perhaps it would again. In fact, that secret was likely his only advantage in this godforsaken place.

He could not, however, be complacent. Every day that Frida remained here was another she would be tortured.

The very thought of it made him sick. He knew the cruelty that bad men were capable of. Knew what many might do to a beautiful young woman such as Frida. It was all he could do not to throw away his mana attempting to burn the door down with the last dregs of it.

Still, what Silas had said was true. Or at least, what he'd said once the coin was in his pocket. To break a soulbound would be hard if the secret they kept was one they wished to take to their grave. And Frida *was* stubborn enough for that – of that he was sure. But equally, the squire was wrong. Frida might be a lesser noble, but she knew the secret that her people had harboured for so long.

Dragons might not have been what kept the Sabines from their door, but they kept rival sects out of their skies. With the secret to their bonding likely given away by poor Erica, Titus and Magnus likely already knew it.

But they would keep that secret for themselves. If the Guild found out too . . . there'd be hundreds of their members crossing into the Northern Tundra, seeking dragons of their own.

Jai would not waste his time alone in this room however – he would fill his core. Right now, it was the only advantage he had.

Gritting his teeth, he settled upon the cold stone floor, lying as if asleep rather than sitting in case someone looked through the door's barred upper slot. In truth, he *wanted* to sleep. His last few days had been sleepless, for every minute he had slept was one where he'd stopped cultivating and the poison could spread freely.

He was exhausted, both in mind and body. But he did not know what was coming his way, or what opportunity might arise when they transferred him from this apparent holding cell. He had to be ready.

Chapter 77

Jai woke to the sound of the door rattling open. He did not remember falling asleep.

He stared at the woman in the doorway, blinking in a daze. She looked at him curiously, then sniffed the air.

'They weren't wrong. You savages stink worse than the Huddites.'

Jai felt his hackles rise. The warden was a sallow, pock-marked woman with long locks of greasy grey hair. She was buck-toothed and had sunken, dark-circled eyes. From the coiled whip in her hand, he knew she was cruel too.

'You speak Imperial?' the woman asked, snapping her fingers at Jai.

Jai remained silent. Stared as stupidly as he could.

She muttered. 'Thick fuckers too.'

The warden motioned at Jai to get up, and he did so. He eyed the whip. The thing could take out an eye, soulbound or not.

'Yeah, you know what this is, don't you?' she said, grinning. 'Now move your arse before I cut the cloth that hides it.'

She punctuated her last words with a shake of the coiled whip.

Jai was quick to obey, if only to get out of the freezing room. For effect he rubbed his hands together, though his mana – little though he had of it – had kept him warm through the day.

Outside the room, Jai found himself emerging from one of many doors down a long, low corridor. There was no natural light but for a lone source at the corridor's very end.

He wondered if one of the cells contained Frida, but as he moved to look closer, a hand seized his collar and yanked him back.

'Come on,' the woman said. 'Follow old Beverlai. There's a good boy.'

She spoke to Jai as if to a dog or young child. To be under-estimated was a good thing. Jai leaned into it.

'Dansk?' Jai asked. 'Here?'

Beverlai grinned.

'Oh, I bet you've been pulling your piddle raw thinking of that hellcat. You can say goodbye to that one. She won't last long with Aurelius working her, feisty though she is.'

She stopped, then pressed Jai up against the wall.

'You no talk about the Dansk. You get that, savage?'

She was strong for an old lady. Unusually so. Could she be soulbound? Or had he become so frail?

Beverlai lifted a finger to her lips.

'No talk,' Jai repeated. 'No talk Dansk.'

Beverlai slapped Jai hard across the face. Jai was lucky he had seen it coming and was quick to loosen his neck and fall to the ground. He rubbed his cheek – the blow had stung.

'Good boy,' Beverlai snapped. 'Come on. I've a bed to get to.'

She kicked Jai forward, nudging him down the corridor with her boot until he had scrambled to some stairs with a gate at its end. Light streamed through its rusted bars and Jai could practically taste the fresh air.

Beverlai whistled and a hand reached out to open the gates. Jai clambered into the light, sucking in air. He had never been scared of tight spaces but the place behind him had a bad feeling to it. Even out here it was not much better.

The ground was gravelled. Not even grass grew here, only puddles slowly being filled by the fine drizzle from the dark sky above. Behind him and in front of him, canyon walls cast a long shadow over the prison encampment, keeping even the moonlight at bay. The cells had been built into the very rock itself.

'Up you come,' Beverlai said, yanking Jai to his feet.

There were other wardens there. Men in leather helmets and armour, with long spears and whips at their hips. Some walked upon the walls that bisected the canyon on either side of him. These were made of simple rubble and mortar but were as high and thick as any Jai had seen bar those of Latium itself.

Jai half expected to be pushed towards one of the large metal gates set within the walls but instead was directed along the cliff-side.

The cliff was high and sheer, not dissimilar to that of the plague pits. The difference here was that the rock face was pocked with as many caves as there were holes on Beverlai's face.

These caves were protected by rusted metal bars, too. But unlike the one Jai had come out of, these had men pressed up against the grilles. Faces – more than should fit – peering out at him, and a forest of hands outstretched with bowls as they tried to catch the rain. Beverlai pushed him to his knees with a foot, and Jai went willingly enough. Even with the little mana he had, there was no chance of escape right now.

'Tell me, lad,' Beverlai said, her voice suddenly friendly. 'Who is the girl?'

Jai paused and turned, his hands raised. Beverlai stopped belabouring him, instead crouching down to meet Jai's gaze.

'What's Aurelius hiding?' she asked, half to herself.

Jai stared, keeping the dull, cow-eyed gaze that Beverlai expected of him.

Beverlai raised her hand threateningly and Jai shied away.

'Wasting my time with you. You crawl now, understand?'

She kicked Jai on and he had no choice but to move upon his hands and knees. He could hear jeers from both prisoner and guard alike.

Soon enough, he was at the entrance to one of the cells, stumbling by two others on his way down the pass.

For that was what this was. A mountain pass. But this was strange. There were few mountainous regions in the empire, which was coveted by its rivals for its undulating, fertile lands. How far had he travelled while he'd battled the poison?

'Back up, back up!' Beverlai snarled, unfurling her whip.

The men in the cave backed away from the bars and Beverlai tugged free a rusted key. Soon enough the gate had screeched open.

'Here, boy,' Beverlai chuckled.

She tossed Jai something from her pocket. It was a hunk of bread, little more than the size of a fist. Jai didn't even wait until he was inside before ripping off a hunk with his mouth.

'In you go.'

Another kick to his back sent Jai sprawling into the cell. The gates slammed shut behind him and Jai lay there, waiting for the sound of Beverlai walking away. But it did not come. Jai looked back to see Beverlai watching, a cruel smile upon her face.

And then they came. A mass of ripping, snatching hands, ramming his head into the ground. Fingers gripped his closed fist, forcing it open to take the bread within.

Even his mouth was plundered, though he managed to swallow some before a finger hooked its contents from his mouth.

Jai could do nothing. Only take a beating for fear of revealing himself. The blows seemed endless, his pockets ripped out by the seams, boots twisted away. He was lucky to keep the filthy shirt upon his back.

Blessed relief only came when the fight for the bread moved deeper into the cavern, leaving him dazed in the paltry light from outside.

Jai crawled towards the gate, if only to haul himself to his feet. He felt a glob of spit spatter across his face as his hands found the first rung. Beverlai cackled and wiped her mouth.

'Welcome to Porticus.'

Chapter 78

J ai lay crumpled beside the gate, gasping for air. He was alone in the darkness, pressed against the damp where the rain had seeped through. For now, at least, the prisoners had taken all they'd wanted from him.

His body was a mass of welts and bruises, and one eye was blurred from where a fingernail had scratched it. He was in agony, with his lips split in so many places it hurt when he opened his mouth to groan.

Jai had endured many a beating from the palace guards, but those had been nothing compared to this. This was a desperate, brutal place.

The cell's interior was not the same as the long corridor he had emerged from moments ago. These walls were rough and uneven, hacked into the rock in a long tunnel that disappeared into darkness. Jai allowed some mana to seep out, so that he could see all the way to the dead end in the cave's deepest recesses.

Men huddled together upon a thin pile of wood chips, skinny as rakes. There were a score or more, packed into a space no larger than Leonid's chamber. All were swarthy men, sporting beards and even darker skin than Jai. These were not Steppefolk, nor Dansk.

'It was a mine once,' someone said. 'If that was what you were wondering. Then a prison.'

A bare-chested man sat a few paces away from Jai, cross-legged. He was dark-eyed and black-bearded, with a wiry pelt of hair covering his torso. Even from here, Jai could see the deep slashes along the man's back, and a poultice that had been applied over them. He had been beaten too, and recently. His face was a mess of yellowing welts.

Jai attempted to speak but only managed a pained croak.

'You'll forgive them, in time,' the man said. 'They've not eaten in days. If you'd given up the bread faster, they'd've left you alone.'

Jai could not think of anything to say. He was not in the most forgiving of moods.

'Bastard wardens'll starve us to death before long,' the man said, half to himself.

Jai suspected even water was scarce here, if the bowls he'd seen the men holding through the bars earlier to catch the drizzle had been any indication. He would be lucky to survive this place, let alone escape.

It made him worry for Frida. If this was how their gaolers treated their fettered . . . how would they treat her? Would they feed her? Or even clothe her?

'Where are we?' Jai asked.

His words came thick and garbled, but the man understood easily enough.

'We are in the Petrus, my boy.'

Jai swallowed at that. He had travelled across half the empire while he battled the poison, perhaps as long as two weeks. At the very least, it was in the right direction.

'Nothing near here but wilderness, tundra and the Great Steppe,' the man went on. 'Put escape from your mind. I know you're thinking on it. We all do.'

Jai blurted a question.

'Why?'

'Direwolf'll get you, if Beverlai doesn't first.'

Jai stared.

The man looked dead ahead with tired eyes.

'She's soulbound with a direwolf. Few've made a run for it without that slavering beast bringing them right back.'

Only now did Jai realise how lucky he was to have been able to hide his powers. If not, he'd likely have been tortured for what secrets he might know, too. Instead, they'd assumed him a dumb fettered or servant, vulnerable and on the run like so many of his people must be.

'Most anyone's managed is a few days,' the man went on. 'Of course, better to die running than . . .'

He nodded out the gate and Jai peered through the drizzle, unwilling to move from where he was huddled. For a moment he stared, letting his eyes adjust.

Jai let out a stuttering breath. Across from their cell there were thick poles, arrayed in neat rows upon the canyon wall opposite. He'd thought them scaffolding, or the remains of an old building. But they were no such thing.

There were men there. Tied at the very top, hung from their wrists and left bare to the elements. He could not tell if some were still alive, for they were motionless, heads bowed beneath the wind and rain. The rest he knew were dead – mere skeletons held together by stubborn sinew and cloth. Jai could even smell the rot. With all the stench of the cave and the men trapped within, he had almost missed it.

'They last a day, maybe two,' the man whispered. 'They drown in their own lung fluid, held like that. If the cold doesn't take them first.'

'All runaways?' Jai managed.

'Some,' the man said. 'Others were turned in.'

He motioned Jai to come closer, then on second thought shuffled over himself.

'They've got spies in here. Cowards and the desperate, who'll trade a friend's life for a scrap of food. Trust no one here.'

'Not even you?' Jai asked, forcing a dry smile. He immediately regretted it as the fresh scabs on his lips reopened.

'I am Milkar,' the man said, proffering a hand. 'Son of Baal. What is your name?'

Jai hesitated. His first name was common enough among the Steppefolk.

'Jai,' he said, taking the man's hand. 'You are . . . a Huddite?' he asked, recognising the name.

The man had that look about him. Swarthy and bearded, with dark skin not dissimilar to his own.

Milkar nodded.

'So I am. We all are. They marched us across half the empire after that . . . second defeat.'

He spoke bitterly.

'We've been repairing those walls out there since our surrender. They work us to death carrying out a pointless task.'

Jai could hardly believe it. These were some of the Huddites from the battle he had witnessed. The folk who had refused to bow beneath the Sabine yoke. Reduced . . . to this.

'Not pointless,' Jai said. 'You did not hear?'

Milkar leaned closer.

'Hear what?'

'War,' Jai said. 'With the Steppefolk, and the Dansk.'

Milkar closed his eyes. 'So . . . our lands were not enough

for them. The Sabines are a cancer.' He settled back against the wall as if to sleep. It seemed the man hardly cared what happened beyond this evil place. Perhaps Jai should not either. Surviving another week would be challenge enough.

Worse, soulbreathing in this place, with its tight confines and desperate spies, would be risky. If he was caught . . . what would happen to him?

He would be considered too dangerous to keep with the others. At best, he would be thrown into solitary confinement, shackled by Damantine steel and locked behind a door even Magnus could not easily break. At worst, he'd be hung on the poles with the others.

Was that to be Frida's fate, if she kept resisting? Left on the poles to rot, or give away her secrets? Perhaps it would be their last resort.

Jai had no choice but to wait once more. He sat up, resting his back against the wall. Then closed his eyes.

Already, Jai could feel the mana seeping through his body, helping his injuries heal. For now, he would let it, but he would have to keep a close eye. If he healed too quickly . . . someone might notice. Luckily, most of the damage was hidden by his clothing.

In his rush to soulbreathe back in his cell, Jai had not allowed himself to feel. To consider these new circumstances, or his emotions. As he pressed his head against the rough wall, Jai felt the first tear run hot down his face. Then another, and another.

It was all he could do not to sob. There was no Frida here. No Winter, not even Rufus or Navi. Just him and these men, reduced to their most primal needs.

His friends were lost. In danger. And he could do nothing to help them. He could hardly help himself.

Winter. Where was she? Was she safe?

Jai reached out to his core, and gently explored the umbilical between him and Winter, sending her a tentative jolt of concern. So much had happened, he'd not yet had a chance to check if she had awoken since he last checked their connection.

And she had. But something was different. *Distant.* The feelings he received from her were garbled, as if they had echoed down the umbilical cord and lost meaning.

He felt . . . she was worried for him, but not scared for herself. Even over their confused connection, he felt faint pulses of joy. Joy that he was awake and conscious enough to send feelings of his own.

It gave him hope. Suddenly, he was not alone. Even if he could not speak to Winter; even if he didn't know where she was, she was there for him. Sending him encouragement. Love.

He had to get to Frida.

Chapter 79

They came in the morning. Wardens in leather helmets that obscured their faces. Not that Jai needed to see them. He was much more focused on the array of spear-points that corralled him and the other prisoners towards the southern gates.

It seemed the prison was sandwiched between two walls bisecting the canyon, with the southern wall leading back to the empire as yet unfinished.

Perhaps it was to keep the fettered from escaping, or had been started to defend against attack from the rear, back when Huddite lands lay only a few days' ride west. Whatever the reason, it was not yet finished. Jai could see the hole in the canyon side where boulders had been chiselled free and piled beside it.

For a moment Jai was excited, for it seemed an easy avenue of escape. But . . . that way led toward the empire. He wanted to go the other way.

Jai turned to the north wall, but there was nothing to see of his homeland, tantalisingly close though it was. Just the great heights of the canyon, fading into mist, and the wide barrier blocking his view.

Beyond that wall was where freedom lay. That was enemy territory for the Sabines. Perhaps they would not follow him there at all for fear of his so called 'savage' brethren.

Yet he could not leave. Not without Frida. And right now, he didn't even know where she was. He could give no thought to escape until he knew how to bring her with him. As for Winter . . . he could only hope she could sneak through the pass and catch up to them. At least the little dragon was safe . . . for now.

A spearpoint jabbed Jai from behind, pushing him on. He was at the back of the mass of men, but ahead he could see the Huddites from the other cells carrying rocks and mixing mortar in pits. Others stacked the walls, perched on precarious frames of timber and rope.

But Jai and his group were not being shepherded to the far edge of the west wall where the gap remained and the work continued. Rather, they were being taken to the black gates at the unfinished wall's centre.

Soon, they were walking beneath a great portcullis and looking down the dirt road that led away from it. This place was not on the Kashmere Road. If Jai's memory served him, the Petrus mountains were spread across the north-east, creating a natural barrier between the Great Steppe and the empire.

Further west and to the north, the mountains ended at the cusp of the Northern Tundra, whose border was determined more by its weather than anything else. Some said you only knew when you were in Dansk territory when your piss froze before it hit the ground.

The thought reminded him of Frida. Jai cursed beneath his breath, staring at the barred gates in the cliff-side that Beverlai had taken him from. Somewhere within, he was sure Frida was stuck.

Outside, there were more fettered working. All Huddites clad in loincloths, stripping the branches from felled trees. Jai's group were marched on. Down the path, past the working men. Deeper into the woodland.

And then, they abruptly stopped.

'Axes!' a warden shouted.

One of the leather-clad men dropped a bundle of cloth, tugging it open to reveal the tools there. Jai's eyes widened at the sight, for there were more Huddites here to wield these makeshift weapons than there were wardens – one for every two of them. But the fettered collected them without expression, and Jai followed suit.

Then a whistle caught his attention. Beverlai emerged from the forest, waving them to follow. And beside her . . . was her direwolf.

Jai would have known it was a direwolf, even if Milkar had not told him of it. This was no mere dog. Twice the height of even Titus's largest hunting dogs, this beast could tear out a man's throat without even having to leap, for its head was level with Jai's sternum.

The direwolf had paws that were as large as a lion's, and teeth to match. It could have eaten Winter in one bite and still had room for seconds.

It was no wonder the Huddites didn't try to escape, let alone attempt to take the prison for themselves. The thought of this beast ripping through the foliage behind them was threat enough.

They all followed Beverlai obediently, under the watchful eye of the great wolf. In its presence, the wardens seemed to drop their guard, many raising their spears or stopping to smoke clay pipes.

'All right,' Beverlai announced. 'Since there's a newcomer I'll remind you of the rules. I expect ten ironwood trees felled by nightfall. The next team'll come haul them out for processing tomorrow. Work in pairs, work in tens, I don't care. Ten trees, and you eat tonight.'

The Huddites moved with practised purpose. Most divided into pairs, leaving Jai on his own. Only Milkar lingered, looking at Jai with what looked like hope in his eyes.

'One tree?' Milkar asked.

Jai nodded and followed the man deeper into the forest. The wardens remained on the path, some even starting a fire and removing cooking utensils from their packs. Beverlai walked among them like a queen, her direwolf seated further up the track, surveying them all with yellow eyes. Jai was glad to leave them behind him, as he and Milkar pushed their way through the underbrush.

Here, the trees were shorter than in the Black Forest, but no less daunting. These were still ironwoods, just younger. The forest smelled of pine and the comforting musk of fallen leaves, and Jai took a deep sniff, trying to quell his racing heart.

'What do they need the trees for?' he asked. 'The wall?'

Milkar shook his head and beckoned Jai to follow.

'They have us stockpiling wood beyond the outer wall,' he said. 'We don't know why. But if there is war coming . . . it must be for the war effort.'

Jai bit his lip, thinking on it. This prison would likely have once been an outpost in the old war between Jai's father and the Sabines, for Leonid had garrisoned all the mountain passes when the War of the Steppe had started. Since the Sabines' victory it had likely changed its use to a fettered camp.

And though the two territories shared hundreds of miles of open country further south, this mountain pass was one of a handful that allowed easy passage through the northernmost border. Indeed, even the eastern edge of the Dansk border was likely no more than a day's ride beyond the north wall of the prison. Some brave Dansk raiders might well come that way too.

Either the logs were going to reinforce the east wall or they were to be sent deeper into the Great Steppe. It did not matter. Jai's stomach had never felt so empty, and he could not afford the draining effect this had on his mana. He needed to eat tonight, so it was time to chop.

They were in a basin of sorts, where the terrain opened up and sloped away from the canyon. No longer were the mountaintops visible on either side. It amazed Jai how far they could range without being stopped by the Wardens. But, he supposed, the terrain *was* the prison. Precious little food or shelter for miles, and the ground froze at night this far north. They didn't even have horses here – only a few pack donkeys, by the looks of it. For what need did they have of horses when the direwolf would hunt down anyone that escaped this place.

As a soulbound, he might have a chance if he stored up enough mana for the journey. Without it . . . he had no hope.

Milkar led Jai to a tree deeper into the woods, so far off the trail Jai could no longer hear the voices of the wardens.

He had to find a safe place to soulbreathe . . . and drink some water. It was the only way he'd have a chance at saving Frida or seeing Winter once again.

That morning, he had tried to feel his little dragon out. But she had been asleep, and he had not the heart, or perhaps even the ability, to wake her. Their connection stretched out into nothing, like a deep-sea fisherman's line; lost in a great void.

'Milkar . . .' Jai said, trying not to dwell. 'Is there somewhere private near here? Somewhere I can be alone and recuperate?'

Milkar looked at him strangely.

'If you want water, the wardens have a barrel and ladle. Be

sure to drink enough before we return, because there's nothing but a hole for piss and shit in the cells.'

Jai nodded.

'I don't need to drink. I need to be alone.'

Milkar stared at him as if he was an idiot.

'You have much more to worry about than being alone with your thoughts, Jai,' Milkar said. 'If the rest of our cell cuts nine trees and we don't, we won't live through the night.'

'Too right you won't.'

Jai had not heard them approach. Five Huddites, following behind them.

The speaker was the largest of them, and the biggest. The ringleader, if Jai had to guess. A hard-faced man, swarthy and bearded, like the rest of them.

They did not walk but prowled. Spreading to their sides, to their backs, weight on their front feet. Surrounding them.

'We needed that bread more than you,' the ringleader growled. 'You're a fat pup. But you'll learn soon enough.'

'Hanebal,' Milkar said, dropping his axe. 'I am no spy, I swear it.'

He raised his hands and Jai cursed internally. It had gone from two against five to one against five.

'Too many of our friends have gone to the poles,' Hanebal hissed. 'And all after they spoke with you.'

'You kill us now, you'll be on the poles as well,' Jai snapped.

His words had an effect, if the exchanged glances between the men was any indication. What he had said must be true.

'Mayhap the plainsboy's axe slipped,' one of the Huddites said. 'Cut his head clean off. We all saw it.'

Jai stabbed a finger in Hanebal's direction.

'Why now?' Jai asked. 'Why not kill him last night.'

'We made him watch,' Hanebal growled. 'He needed to see

what he'd done. He didn't shed one tear when our comrades choked to their end under the weight of their own bodies.'

Milkar wrung his hands.

'What can I do to prove my innocence?' he wailed.

'Step aside, boy,' Hanebal said. 'This is rough justice, but we have nothing else.'

Jai stood his ground.

'I'm eating tonight,' he said. 'And we won't cut enough trees with my partner dead. You want him, you take him when my belly's full.'

Hanebal gritted his teeth, shifting his balance to his back foot. Jai raised his axe in return, meeting the man's gaze with his own.

'I'm nobody's scapegoat,' Jai growled.

There was the crackle of a branch behind. The direwolf, padding closer.

That was all it took. The men were already moving, deeper into the woods. For a moment, Hanebal stood firm. Then he raised a trembling finger.

'This isn't over.'

Chapter 80

It was not safe to soulbreathe now – not properly. To do so, he had to block out the rest of the world. It was why the hummingbird technique existed – to give soulbound a way to cultivate mana without falling from their saddles, or having their throats slit.

And with Hanebal's crew nearby, the latter was a real possibility. Jai had no choice but to cut down a tree with Milkar while using the hummingbird to suck up what dregs of mana he could.

As he did so, his connection to Winter twitched. He could feel her. He called out, such as he could with his mind, and felt her return the call with twice the urgency. It was hard to discern much.

But what he did receive was mana. Mote by mote, drifting down their connection. Jai could hardly imagine the effort it must have cost Winter to send it to him from so far away. But she must have begun sending it hours ago for it to reach him here now.

He immersed himself in the feeling of gratitude that welled up in his chest at the thought of her trying so hard to help, and pulsed the feeling in Winter's direction. He knew not if she felt it.

The mana travelled through his channels as smooth as hot butter, and each lungful seemed to capture more too, despite his separation from Winter. His body had become accustomed to it. Demanded it even.

Before he'd been poisoned, things had been different. Somehow, those weeks soulbreathing constantly to keep himself alive – alongside the benefits of the pills and the soulgem – had primed his body for cultivating. His core was small but . . . he was proud of himself.

And glad that he would have a better chance of saving Frida . . . or even surviving this so he could see Winter again.

A bell sounded, close by. He heard the calls of the wardens summoning him back.

The fettered were marched back to the unfinished wall, prodded along by spear butts, or tips if they did not move fast enough.

Before they passed through the gates, Beverlai was waiting for them.

Her direwolf sat upon its haunches, sniffing each as they entered. Already, Beverlai had a pile of contraband in a cart beside her, mostly berries, roots and nuts, and two men kneeling nearby.

Jai tried to stay at the edge of their group, but Beverlai clicked her tongue and sent her beast padding towards them. Within seconds it was snorting at Jai's pockets and feet.

He could smell its raw, animal scent, a combination of wet dog and mulch. He could even smell the meat upon its breath. The beast was so large that its head was close to the size of his entire torso.

Jai tried to slow his beating heart, praying to any god that would listen that the beast would not sense his fear. He could feel a cold sweat upon the back of his neck, pooling in the hollow of his back.

The direwolf froze. Then sat, its thick muzzle pointed at Jai's chest. Moments later, wardens were shoving Jai to the front of the group.

'New fish,' Beverlai chuckled. 'It's good you'll learn your lesson early. Turn out your pockets.'

Jai did so. Indeed, the pockets were not just empty, but ripped entirely from their stitching after the assault Jai had received the night before. Beverlai tutted impatiently, her hands lifting Jai's shirt, then pulling down his trousers, to Jai's shock. Still nothing.

'He's got two berries and a twig in there, Beverlai,' one of the wardens chuckled. 'Why don't you reach in and grab a handful?'

Beverlai let out a forced laugh, then shoved Jai away. Jai fell, tangling in the trousers bunched at his ankles. The direwolf growled low, crouching over him

'He doesn't like you,' Beverlai hissed down at Jai. 'You smell *suspicious.*'

She crouched down and grasped a handful of Jai's hair, yanking him close. She took a deep sniff, her long nose scraping up the side of Jai's cheek.

'Beverlai!' a warden called.

The woman released Jai, letting him fall back upon the damp earth.

'Aurelius wants you.'

Beverlai let out a frustrated sigh. She stabbed a finger at Jai. 'This one gets nothing tonight.'

She stalked away, leaving Jai in the dirt.

* * *

THE CELL'S INTERIOR SEEMED somehow smaller as the key rattled in its lock behind him. Jai settled at its entrance, if only to keep the wardens within earshot and prevent Hanebal's crew from surrounding him.

Outside, Jai could hear the crack of Beverlai's whip. Some of her victims screamed with each blow. Others wailed like children. But Beverlai never relented, punctuating each swing with excited, panting breaths.

Jai struggled to keep calm as the sounds of human misery echoed through the pass. It was all he could do to stop himself flinching with every whip-crack.

The men were locked in wooden stocks by their arms and necks. In Latium, the stocks had been used to shame petty criminals. They'd been designed to allow pelting with rotten fruit, while the guards looked on with amusement. Here, they were to keep the fettered still and helpless so Beverlai could paint the canvas of their backs red.

Milkar sat nearby. Since their encounter in the woods, the man had become timid. As if Jai's presence were all that kept him from death, and one wrong word could lose Jai's favour.

Now, in the dark confines of the cell, Jai was not so sure protecting Milkar had been the right move. The kindness the man had shown him was clearly rife with ulterior motives.

He needed the Huddite for information, true, but he could have had Hanebal as his ally had he not stepped in. Then again, Hanebal's plan had been to frame Jai for Milkar's murder, so he hadn't exactly been left much choice.

Jai hated thinking in this cold, calculating way. But it was the only way to survive in a place like this. Let alone escape with Frida in tow.

The cells were as dank as they had been the first night, rain or no. There was no warmth here. Just a rough-hewn hole, full of starving, dead-eyed men, who had hardly the energy to do anything but lie there.

Jai could smell the scent of human misery.

'What happens to them if they kill you?' Jai asked.

He did not need to specify who *they* were. It was clear who was on Milkar's mind.

'They get strung up,' Milkar said dully. 'And they get whipped if they beat someone so hard that they can't work.'

Jai relaxed a little then. Given the beating he'd received yesterday and the yellowing bruises on Milkar's face, it was unlikely they would be beaten again.

Milkar went on.

'But Beverlai will whip you half to death for a dirty look. And don't mutter under your breath – she hears it all. Learned that the hard way.'

He motioned at his back, where dark scabs had formed.

Finally, Jai had a sense of the rules here. That, and the routine. But beyond a risky opportunity to soulbreathe, there was little chance of escape here. He needed to plot. To scheme.

'What was the escape plan for the . . . the ones who ended up on the poles?' Jai asked.

Milkar hesitated. He cast his gaze further down the tunnel to where the majority of the Huddites were huddled for warmth – away from the draught of the gates.

'Freedom lies beyond the east wall,' Milkar whispered. 'There's nowhere to run for a Huddite in the empire. Nor for you, it seems.'

Jai nodded in agreement.

'The wardens have begun to keep watch there, putting sentries on the wall, looking out over the steppe – I did not know why until you told me of the war. They fear your people . . . as do we – there is no love lost between the

Steppefolk and the Huddites. But the others knew if they could avoid your war bands and raiders, they might reach the Kashmere Road and join a trade caravan. Start a new life in the Phoenix Empire.'

'As good a plan as any,' Jai said. And he believed it too. Were he not a Steppeman, it might well be what he would have done. Continued on to start a new life. Away from the war that would inevitably swallow the west.

Milkar said no more, and Jai prodded him.

'Speaking of escape cannot be all they did. How did they plan to get beyond the east wall?'

Milkar sighed and closed his eyes.

'To go beyond the east wall we have to be with the crew that strips the branches from the trunks and carries them to the stockpile there.'

Jai thought for a moment.

'Why do they pile them there?' Jai asked. 'Why not within? If a warband came, they would set it afire.'

'You are asking the wrong person,' Milkar said. 'Perhaps they plan to take it out east, into the steppe.'

Jai grimaced, pondering this. Whatever their reason, it did not matter. Jai might well get beyond the wall, perhaps even run fast enough to escape the direwolf. But there was no way he could bring Frida with him as things stood.

'What else did the others plan?' Jai asked.

'Does it matter?' Milkar replied. 'We're never leaving this place.'

He caught Jai's expression and inclined his head.

'They bribed a guard to change us over to tree transport. Then they planned to hide among the supplies, and the guard would miscount the prisoners when they were called back. Then they'd make a run for it in the night.'

Jai's eyes widened.

'Which guard?' Jai demanded.

Milkar pointed outside, to a forlorn figure hanging from one of the poles.

'That one.'

Chapter 81

Jai asked Milkar little else that evening. He did find out that the nearest woman, beyond that crone Beverlai, would be in a brothel a day's ride from the camp. Clearly, Milkar had not seen Frida.

She was here, somewhere. Likely in a cell not far from where he had awoken yesterday morn, deeper down the corridor. Its gated entrance was but a stone's throw from Jai's own, and if he stuck his head through the gate's bars, he could see a warden stationed outside.

This, if anything, told Jai all he needed to know. For of all the cells, it was the only one with a guard. The rest were left locked, but there were no wardens to be seen. They were busy carousing, in the barracks beneath the east wall's gatehouse. Jai didn't need mana to hear that commotion.

The warden might be there to keep Frida from escaping, but Jai suspected it was to keep other wardens away too.

The Sabines would still be hunting for her, and would come looking if they found out there was a beautiful Dansk noble held here. Not what Aurelius would want, given he wished to torture the secret of dragon-bonding out of her and sell it back to the Guild.

As for Winter, Jai attempted contact twice. Both times, their connection was stronger than the last. As if . . . she were drawing closer.

She could sense his pain, and his misery. In turn, he could sense hers. But hers was an echo of his own, stemming from concern for his wellbeing. He could tell she was fed, and safe, but he could not glean more. The distance between them was too great, leaving whatever understanding they tried to get from each other garbled and faint.

Outside, Jai heard the trudge of feet upon gravel. He smelled her before he saw her, a musk of body odour and direwolf. Jai shuffled back into the gloom as deep as he dared. It helped not a jot, for Beverlai pressed her face to the bars, and gave Jai a yellow-toothed grin.

'Hello sonny boy. You're coming with me.'

JAI KNELT OUTSIDE THE cell, listening as intently as he could. Beverlai stood next to him, a hand resting upon Jai's head.

She had taken him back to where he had first awoken in this god-forsaken place. Only a little deeper down the corridor, further from where his own cell had been. His breath quickened, half from fear, half anticipation. Surely Frida would be close by.

'You will wake, damn you, or I'll start cutting pieces off.'

It was a low snarl, but the voice was unmistakeable. Aurelius.

Beverlai sniffed and leaned forward, rapping her knuckles upon the door. Aurelius cursed, then called for them to enter. Beverlai rattled her key in the lock, and the door was pushed open.

'Get him in here before someone sees,' Aurelius snapped.

Jai waited for Beverlai to shove him in, noticing the hoop of keys attached to the woman's belt. This facade of savage idiocy was clearly working to his advantage, and he was not about to give away his understanding of High Imperial.

Within the cell, he saw nothing to begin with. Then, he saw her. Chained in the corner, curled up on the floor. Frida.

He had hardly a second to look at her before Aurelius's face filled his view. A hand yanked him up by his shirt collar.

The man had watery, red-rimmed eyes and a jowled face that put Jai in mind of a bear-fighting dog. Indeed, he seemed like a once-burly man that had gone to fat, full-framed and beefy as they came. In many ways, he was Rufus's twin, in body if not in face.

'Here boy, you try.'

He spun Jai around and booted him in a sprawl beside Frida. Jai made sure to look as confused as possible, stroking Frida's hair from her eyes, as if he had understood he was to care for her.

'Wake her, damn your eyes,' Aurelius snarled, kicking out at Jai and almost losing his balance.

Jai scrambled to the corner, clutching his knees to his chest.

'Is she ascended, boy?' Aurelius asked, a sudden, fake smile upon his face. He reached into his pocket and withdrew a crust of bread. 'Go on. I'm not going to hurt you.'

'I told you,' Beverlai sneered. 'He hardly speaks a word of High Imperial. You'll be better off waiting till she's awake and using him as leverage. Maybe she cares for the boy? Find out. Start cutting pieces off.'

Jai only just managed to resist the abject terror he knew had almost been stamped across his face. The suffering here was sickening enough, let alone *that*.

Aurelius spat off to the side, then crouched with some difficulty and grasped Frida's shoulders, shaking her violently.

'See, boy. Awake. Make her wake.'

Jai scrambled further back as if in terror. He did not need to act much. These two . . . there was a dark cloud over them. As if this small horror was but a drop in the ocean of misery they ruled.

To rise in the ranks of a fettered colony such as this was only possible for the most heartless, from a bad bunch to begin with.

Aurelius let Frida fall back into the straw, clicking his fingers at Beverlai to help him to his feet.

Jai took the opportunity to look Frida over. There were no visible signs of injury, but he knew she could only last so long without water or sustenance. Only the highest level soulbound could live on mana alone, or so Rufus had told him. He knew only too well, for his stomach was practically eating itself.

Either way, Jai was glad to see she was in the same state he had been in since they had arrived. He rested a hand on Frida's leg, wishing he could will some of his mana into her somehow. She would need every bit of it, fighting the poison they must be feeding her.

He almost withdrew his hand in shock. Her skin was ice cold. So cold that only the faint lift and fall of her chest told him she was not a corpse.

He tried to contain his rage as the cruel fetterers bickered above him. If he were only practised enough in casting spells . . . he might have had enough to take them by surprise.

'The guildsman did warn you,' Beverlai said. 'Ascended or not, soulbound make for poor captives. Hard to keep 'em, hard to break 'em.'

Aurelius hissed a breath in frustration.

'You think I don't know that? My father did it for years before Leonid hung up his sword.'

Jai's ears pricked at that. So . . . this prison had once housed soulbound captives. Prisoners from Leonid's various wars, he imagined. No wonder some of the cells were locked by Damantine steel.

Beverlai grunted, and the pair stood in silence for a while, staring at Frida. As if some answer would jump out at them.

'The Sabines'll pay you most of what she cost, if you can get word to them,' Beverlai said. 'Maybe more. Only reason the Guild sold her to you first is they don't deal with the Sabines. I bet they knew you'd sell her on eventually. These so-called secrets were just a way to get the price up.'

Aurelius ignored her. 'I can't sell them damaged goods. But I'll have to damage her if I want to break her.'

Beverlai had no answer for that.

Jai felt sick, and not just from the hunger. To free Frida from here seemed impossible. It was the last cell in the corridor, and did not even have a window. To reach her from his own cell he would have to come through the single, gated entrance, in open view of the sentries on the east wall, not to mention the warden stationed outside and the other prisoners in the caves.

Not only that, but he had only days to do it. Soon enough, Aurelius might well decide the risk was worth the reward and begin to hurt Frida. Either that, or she would die from starvation and thirst.

Aurelius launched a kick into Frida's side and even Beverlai winced at the violence. Frida rose and fell with the force of it, utterly silent.

Jai needed to be brought back here. He needed to be . . . useful. If he could get Aurelius alone, he might take him hostage. But what could he do with Frida lying so limp and still? Carry her upon his back while holding a knife to Aurelius's throat?

There was no easy answer. He only knew that being close to Frida was a step in the right direction. Jai leaned close to her, lifting her head into his lap. Her face was serene, though dusted with straw and grime. Flawless, as always, but for a bruise flowering on her sun-freckled cheek.

He closed his eyes and began to hum a half-remembered lullaby. One that Balbir had sung to him, all those years ago. He only knew the tune, but it was enough.

Aurelius and Beverlai said nothing, and Jai rocked Frida back and forth. He did not wish to wake her. Only to give her comfort, deep within. And one other reason.

For all the while, Jai was pressing his fingers into her back, tracing the letters of an instruction to her.

'T W I T C H'

Time moved slowly in those moments. The song echoed through the chamber, rising and falling. It was a lilting, mournful song. One that Jai remembered meant longing, and missing home.

'All right, your little song isn't working, plainscunt,' Aurelius snapped. 'Shut your stinking hole.'

Jai paused, looking at him with an affected expression of confusion.

It was only when Aurelius cleared his throat to speak that it happened.

'She moved!' Beverlai cackled. 'Look, her hand.'

'What?' Aurelius demanded. 'I didn't see.'

'On, my life, Aurelius.'

Jai went on, singing where he remembered, humming where he did not. He took her limp hand in his own, as if it might encourage her to move it again. And within his cupped fingers, a thumb danced upon his palm. Tracing a pattern.

Jai had only a few moments to digest it, until a bark from Aurelius shut him up.

'That's more'n either of us got out of her,' Beverlai said. 'Mayhap this boy's not her servant. Mayhap he's her lover.'

Aurelius scoffed.

'Even the Dansk know what savages these folk are, nobles especially. They'd sooner tup an ox.'

'Wouldn't put it past them,' Beverlai chuckled, then yanked at Jai's shoulder.

'Come on, savage. We'll try this again tomorrow. Can't have you crooning your love songs all night.'

It was a relief to know she was still conscious, somewhere deep in the recesses of her mind. It was all he'd wanted, yet she'd given him even more.

Jai let the hand fall, trying to burn the pattern into his memory. Already, he had the first letters. Later, when he was shoved into the cave once more, he figured out the rest. A single word.

He had to check it again and again, tracing the patterns upon his palm. It made no sense. What possible reason could she have to write the word 'mouth'?

Chapter 82

Jai wished to soulbreathe through the night, but Beverlai's visit had drawn far too much scrutiny. Every eye in the cavern was upon him, and he didn't need his enhanced senses to know they suspected him of spying.

It did not surprise Jai when Hanebal sidled up to him. Milkar slept nearby, but Hanebal left him alone. Apparently, the pair of them were not due for another beating just yet.

At first Hanebal simply sat there, looking at Jai with searching eyes. He was haggard, yet Jai could still see where the man had once been handsome, before starvation and defeat had sucked the flesh from his face and left but the skin and grizzled beard behind.

'What did Beverlai want with you?'

'She wanted to search me again,' Jai said, the lie tripping smoothly from his tongue. These days, he was getting better at subterfuge.

'For nuts and berries?' Hanebal demanded. 'She wouldn't waste her time with that.'

Jai shrugged.

'All I know is the direwolf smells something wrong about me.

Could just be he's not smelled a Steppeman before. Maybe he's used to Huddites.'

Hanebal scoffed at that.

'Misery smells the same, race or creed got nothing to do with it.'

He looked over at Milkar, noting the soft rise and fall of the man's chest. Satisfied, he shuffled closer to Jai.

'You don't have to go tattling to Beverlai – we'll not harm you. We came down hard this morn, I'll grant you that. But when you watch a comrade choking and gasping to his end . . . you tell me you wouldn't want justice.'

'Justice?' Jai said. 'Justice is every one of these wardens on those poles. Not beating a brother to death because you reckon he might've said something.'

Hanebal grunted, though Jai was not sure if it was in agreement.

'They were the best of us. All fought alongside me in the Battle of the Three Armies. And the one before that too.'

Hanebal caught Jai's confused expression and shrugged.

'Wasn't much of a battle. We were going to fight to the bitter end, but then the fucking Dansk came from nowhere with their stinking dragons. Had hardly started before it was over.'

So. These men had been on the ridge that day too, when the Dansk had arrived for the wedding. Jai had wondered what became of them.

Jai looked out from their cavern. Without the rain, he could see the pitiful remains of the supposed escapee still there, rotting among the other corpses.

'Had you ever thought Beverlai might have overheard?' Jai asked. 'The soulbound can hear better than others. Much better, if they focus. Smell's sharper too. Sight.'

Hanebal shrugged, keeping silent. He too, was staring at the men on the poles. It was a fate they all might face, eventually.

'Can you smell it, lad? Almost sweet, isn't it?' Hanebal said.

At first, Jai thought he was speaking of the distant poles, but when Jai turned to him, he saw the long, skinny finger of the man pointed deeper into the cavern.

He had read about it in Leonid's diaries, when the old emperor had laid siege to cities. He had never believed it; that when a person starves and their body begins to feed on itself . . . they give off a sickly-sweet scent. Like fruit, just beginning to turn.

It made him feel sick.

'That's the smell of famine. Starvation, boy, when the body eats itself. Your breath smells like sugar. Strawberries, some say. We've collected food enough, though the poor bastards outside won't live to taste it. Might get us through winter, when the snows start to settle. Won't be long now.'

Jai could not imagine the discipline these men must have, to ration their foraged food as they starved. Hanebal nodded, as if he had read Jai's mind.

'We Huddites are no strangers to starving. Even before the Sabines cut us off from trading with the rest of the world. Blocked our only route to the Kashmere Road, sent patrols along our borders to kill any trade caravan that dared defy their decree. We weren't farmers till that cunt Leonid forced us to be. Thousands of proud warriors, breaking their backs on their land for a crust. Until we were weak enough for plucking.'

Jai felt sick at Hanebal's words. It was easy to think only of himself and his own in a place like this. Where the misery of strangers seemed to skid across his conscience like a pebble on a frozen lake. He wanted to help these Huddites.

But of course, Frida came first. Still, the two were not opposing aims.

'Would you risk escape, if you had a plan that might work?' Jai asked.

Hanebal gave Jai a level look. His eyes were dark, but they had lost none of their fire. There was intelligence behind those eyes. And a stubborn courage, if Jai was any judge of character.

'We all would,' he said. 'What are another few months of life? That is all we risk. That and a cruel end. But I'd slit my own throat before letting them take me.'

Jai believed him. He put his head back and let the exhaustion he'd been holding at bay wash over him.

'The Sabines are at war with the Steppefolk,' Jai said. 'Dansk too.'

Hanebal let out a bitter laugh.

'Serves those treacherous bastards right. Not you sav—'

He trailed off.

'We get to my people, I can protect you,' Jai said. 'We share a common enemy now.'

Hanebal stared at Jai, understanding dawning on his careworn face.

'We always thought the Steppefolk'd sell us back to the Sabines for a few cion. But if they're at war with . . .'

He shook his head.

'The direwolf'll get us long before we reach your people, even if you could vouch for us.'

Jai closed his eyes, whispering his thoughts aloud.

'We don't escape in ones and twos. We all go – the whole cave. Let the wolf try to bring us back then – it can't take us all on. Without it, they'll never catch us. They have no horses here. We move fast enough and with enough of a head start, we'll make it.'

Hanebal was silent.

'You come to me with a plan, boy, I'll be all ears.'

Jai held up a hand as he heard the man begin to shuffle away. 'You leave Milkar be, I'll help you on the other side. That's my price.'

Silence. Then a grunt.

It would have to do.

Chapter 83

For most of that evening, Jai stared at the broken men in their stocks, hanging limp and unconscious. As the whipping had gone on, the sentries on the east wall had turned their backs, and some even retreated to their barracks with the others in the east wall's gatehouse. Cruel men they must be, to work in this place. But even they were sickened by the sight and sounds of Beverlai's sadism.

Jai knew already that he needed keys to break into Frida's cell – even if he had been a fully ascended, fifth-level soulbound, the door was far too thick for him to force entry.

The same might not be true of the gates that barred his cave, and those at the entry to the jail that housed Frida. For they were far older than those doors.

The bars were deep set, but heavily rusted. Jai had already run his hands along their exterior and scratched at them with his fingernails. A normal man could never break or bend them. But he knew, at least, what a Gryphon Guard could do. He'd seen them perform feats of strength in Latium's amphitheatre, to celebrate Constantine's tenth year of rule.

They'd bent swords in their bare hands, lifted horses upon

their backs. Even executed prisoners, crushing their skulls between their hands like overripe grapefruit.

Jai knew that with enough mana he could bend the bars.

The bars were just too narrow for a man to slip their head through. With a little work, that could change. The same was the case for the gates that kept him from Frida's cell.

Where did that leave them? Outside the gates, but with a high wall to somehow pass through, undetected by the sentries that patrolled its top. And with Frida still to rescue.

As for food, weapons and supplies, those were out of the question – they could only take what Hanebal's men had gathered for winter. They'd have to simply hope that they would encounter Steppefolk quickly.

None of this helped Jai with Frida, either. He needed to get Beverlai, alone. Surprise her, take the keys. Break out Frida, break out the Huddites. Then charge the eastern wall, lift the bar that held the great doors closed . . . and run.

As for Winter . . . he'd have to find her later.

He sought out Winter once more. It was strange not to have her in his head as she had once been.

In truth, Jai felt guilty for not having spent more time trying to communicate with her, despite the difficulties. What was encouraging, though, was she was growing nearer. Her feelings were more purposeful, and louder too. She was seeking him out, that was for sure. Drawing closer.

And she never seemed alone. She seemed warm and well fed, with his absence and misery the only source of her distress.

The question remained if Winter would arrive to join Jai in his escape – perhaps even help him do so. She could be halfway across the empire, or a day's ride away. It was impossible to say. He didn't have time to wait and see.

So, Jai closed his eyes . . . and began.

As before, he saw his core. Throughout the day, it had gathered more mana. A consequence of Winter's gift – trickling every bit of mana she had to him while he slept.

Jai was desperate to use some, just to soothe his aches and pains.

If only. Wasting it was not an option. He needed every drop for the breakout.

He had spent two days in this place now. He imagined Frida had drawn into herself the moment she had arrived at the prison. Even if they were dabbing at her lips with a wet sponge, as she had done for him . . . he dared not risk another night.

Jai wished he had time to ascend.

He would finally have a core large enough to sustain more than a handful of fireballs. Hell, he might even have a real chance at beating Beverlai in a fair fight.

He gritted his teeth and sucked in another breath. That evening, he would fill his core as much as he could. Tonight? Death, or freedom.

Chapter 84

As the moon rose in the sky, Jai had less mana than he would have liked. His core was but a quarter full.

Two had died on the stocks that evening. Their bodies were still there, heads lolling, tongues protruding from their blue lips. Jai had not believed it was possible to whip a man to death.

But of course Beverlai was soulbound. Whether she was ascended or not, Jai had no idea. Even the weakest soulbound could peel a man's skin from his spine if she put her mana into the blow.

Beverlai was in a good mood, whistling to herself like a sailor on leave. She seemed to take pleasure in checking the stocks, prodding her victims to see if they were still alive.

It was a strange feeling, to have the threat of cruel death hanging over him. Hanging so close he could almost taste it. Escape seemed equal parts the last thing one of them should try . . . and the only thing.

Still, his observation had yielded crucial information. While the forty-odd wardens in the prison slept mostly together in the larger, eastern gatehouse, Beverlai had much of the newly constructed west wall's gatehouse to herself – with Aurelius living in its upper storey.

Being Aurelius's right-hand woman had some privileges. Jai suspected the presence of the direwolf, kennelled beside the door in a cavernous alcove, also had something to do with Beverlai's housing. It would protect both of them.

And in the rare instance of a fettered uprising . . . well, it was the one place they would avoid – they were far more likely to charge the east wall and escape into the Great Steppe than that of the west, back into enemy territory. There was no home waiting for them back there.

No wardens watched the cells tonight, for the cold was bitter. Only the sentries remained on the walls, looking out towards the steppe. Jai wished the wall did not block his view. He wondered just how much further they'd have to travel before they reached his homeland.

One more day of soulbreathing would be far safer. Winter felt closer every hour too. But Frida . . . she could not afford another night. For even if he succeeded in freeing her, the girl would be fighting the hemlock that the bastards were no doubt forcing down her throat; dying of thirst, and half-starved. She might not survive the journey *that* night, let alone the next.

Jai pressed himself against the bars. It was misty that evening. Just enough to make the sentries hazy figures, drifting in and out of view as a chill draught billowed through the canyon.

With as much quiet as he could muster, he heaved on the bars. Gritted his teeth and let the mana flow freely.

Sweat burst on his forehead at the effort and he felt his body sing with mana. Every muscle in his body was taut as a bowstring, and Jai forced half of his meagre supply of mana out, pushing his muscles to strain to greater heights.

Yet . . . the bars did not bend. Nor did they shift in their deep seating within the stone. Even as Jai hissed out a breath, making one last-ditch effort, he succeeded in doing nothing more than eliciting a creak.

He collapsed back, careless of who saw it. Soulbound or not, he'd made little impression.

'Damantine steel,' a voice called out. 'Only the surface is rusted. And little at that. You won't find a weakness there, boy.'

Jai turned to see Hanebal approach.

'I thought Damantine steel was for soulbound,' Jai said, hardly believing the man's words. 'Why waste such metal on us?'

Hanebal snorted.

'Who do you think carved out this passage?' he asked. 'Fettered soulbound, with soulbound wardens to watch them. Their beasts were kept in cages with wood ready to set fire beneath them. Poor bastards chipped this out long before the War of the Steppe, back when the Corvin and Blacktree kingdoms blocked the empire's trade route to the Kashmere Road. This was to be Leonid's way around them. Guess he defeated them soon after it was completed.'

Jai could hardly imagine a fettered soulbound. But then . . . was he not being used as one? He spoke, half to himself.

'So this cave . . .'

'It is where they kept them,' Hanebal said. 'Or the weaker ones anyway. Stronger ones were kept down there.'

He nodded his head at the far wall, toward where Frida's cell lay.

Jai tried not to curse aloud. It was no wonder Frida had been brought here. The Guild had found the perfect buyer for her in Aurelius. Hell, he wouldn't be surprised if the Sabines had sent her here anyway, had they been the ones to capture them, if they hadn't skipped the torture altogether and just killed them outright.

He had thought his strength might be the key to his escape. Now, he knew it could not be.

But he had to get outside. There were only two places Jai had seen where prisoners were left outside. The poles . . . and the stocks.

Chapter 85

C an your men be ready to leave tonight?' Jai asked.
Hanebal looked at him with what little amusement could be mustered in a grim place like this.

'Ready with what?' he said. 'We've two bags of vittles, and a single knife. You get us out of here, we'll rush the east gate. We've been waiting for a chance. Just put one in front of us.'

It was all Jai needed to hear.

'Tell them to be ready,' Jai said, getting to his feet. 'We leave tonight.'

He knew what he had to do. He just didn't know if he had the courage to do it. In the shadows, Milkar looked at him with fearful eyes.

'You want to prove your innocence?' Jai asked.

Milkar nodded meekly.

'Then you'll be in the front line when we rush the east gate,' Jai said. 'Show your people you fight for them. Hanebal, if he does this, do you guarantee his safety on the other side?'

Hanebal was silent for a while. Then he gave a curt nod. 'So be it.'

Jai strode to the barred door of the cave and pressed his face up against the metal. He could feel the bars against his skin, cool and damp from the mist. What he was about to do would likely kill him. But death was a guarantee in Porticus. At least this way, he could choose the manner of it.

'Beverlai!' Jai screamed. 'Beverlai! You wolf-piss stinking crone! Stop humping your beast's leg and face me, you coward!'

SOME TRIED TO SILENCE him. Hanebal even clamped his hand over Jai's mouth. But the damage was done. With her soulbound hearing, the old woman was already striding out of the eastern gatehouse before the first Huddites managed to tackle Jai to the ground.

He let them. They scattered soon enough when Beverlai's feet crunched the gravel outside.

'Who called me?' Beverlai asked.

If she was angry, she did not show it. Rather, she seemed bemused. Almost excited at an excuse for the violence to come.

'I did,' Jai said.

He did not bother with his act now. It no longer served a purpose.

Beverlai stared at him with surprise. For a moment, her brows furrowed in suspicion, setting Jai's heart apace. Then she let out a cruel laugh, one that went on for just a little too long.

'So, the savage has a tongue,' she chuckled. 'You pulled the wool over old Beverlai's eyes, I'll give you that. Or did one of these Huddite bastards teach you some new words?'

Jai remained silent. Beverlai seemed not to mind, instead opening the gate with a wry smile. She beckoned Jai to leave the cave.

'You know what the punishment is for insulting me?'

Beverlai asked, as casually as if she were commenting on the weather.

Jai shrugged, stepping out into the air. For just a moment he considered rushing Beverlai. Certainly, the direwolf was nowhere to be seen; likely prowling the woods as it was wont to do at night. But screaming insults at a woman as cruel as Beverlai had of course drawn the attention of the sentries. Even in the dark and mist, he could see the slits of their helmets turned towards him.

The decision was sealed when Beverlai locked the gates behind him. He would have to stick to the plan.

'If you want to die, there are better ways,' Beverlai said, still as cheerful as she had been that morning. 'I'll give you one chance. Give me something I can take to Aurelius about the girl, and you can go back inside with only the hiding of your life. Otherwise . . .'

She let her hand wander down to her whip.

Jai lifted his chin, giving Beverlai a level look.

'I thought I'd take the air,' Jai said. 'It stinks in there. Only a little worse than you. And they don't like me much.'

Beverlai's smile widened to a grin. She touched Jai's face, where the bruises from the stolen bread were already yellowing. Healing a little faster than they should – but Beverlai didn't know just how badly he'd been beaten.

'You savages are as strange as they say you are. You think it's safer in the stocks than in there with them? Their ministrations will feel like a whore's soft hands when I'm done.'

She gripped Jai by the neck, her fingers like twin clamps of steel. She practically carried Jai forward. It was impossible to say if Beverlai had ascended, but from that strength alone, he suspected she was. After all, a direwolf was a powerful beast, and she'd had many years to progress down the path.

Jai let it happen, resigned to his fate as his heels dragged in the mud and gravel. There was no avoiding this. He could only endure it.

He was as meek as a lamb as he lowered his head and hands into the open half of the wooden stocks. Didn't even yell out when it was slammed closed so tight he could hardly breathe.

But he did wince when he heard the leathery thud of the whip being unravelled. And when the shirt was ripped from his back in a single yank, like so much rice paper.

'Take a deep breath,' Beverlai hissed. 'I like to hear the screams.'

He heard the first blow before he felt it. A thrum that became a hiss. Then pain. Like a white-hot whytblade had sliced him from hip to shoulder.

Jai screamed until he had no breath in his lungs, croaking as an acid vomit dribbled from his mouth. The next blow came and he could only choke out more bile, gurgling at the agony of it.

Then another, and another, the hiss of the whip and Beverlai's grunting an awful harmony of sadistic glee.

Jai wanted to recede into himself, as Frida had. Let his body bear the brunt, while his mind lived within his eternal world. But even if it might be taken for unconsciousness, Jai had to bear the pain. For it was his screams that turned the eyes of the sentinels away, and kept the other wardens in their barracks. Few men desired to observe such horror.

The whip cracked again. And again, and again. Jai screamed until his voice was lost. Screamed as the blood ran down his legs, and the ribs of his back were exposed to the night sky.

He screamed until unconsciousness took him. A blessed darkness, one he wished that he would never wake from.

Chapter 86

Jai did not know the hour when the world faded into view once more. Only that it was still dark, and silent as a grave. Only the stain of sun on the horizon told him that dawn was not far off. Time was against him.

He entered the half-trance. And nearly vomited again at the sight of his mana. It was all but gone. Used up to keep him alive, to replace the blood that had painted his trousers red.

Jai knew his body now. He could feel the great rents in his back, already scabbing closed over exposed ribs. The bleeding had even stopped.

He was weak, but death would not take him that night. Not yet, anyway.

Jai had to act quickly – before long, the wardens would ring the morning bell. He closed his eyes, feeling the muscles of his shoulders and arms. He heaved, and pulsed the last ounce of mana he had after it.

Wood groaned beneath the strain, splintering and crackling . . . until the rusted steel hinge pinged free from its seating in the ironwood. Jai collapsed to his knees, pressing his forehead against the stock's post.

He could hardly stand. Beverlai had meant to kill him. Had left him for dead, to freeze in the night. Jai shivered, the cool mist that shrouded him sucking the warmth from his very bones.

He had traded all his mana and the very skin off his back to get to the other side of the gate. Now, he was on his own. No advantage. Just his broken body and a half-baked plan.

The stocks were not far from the west gatehouse, nor indeed from the secure cells. It was for this reason that Jai had chosen to be put in the stocks, rather than fake an escape attempt and be put on the poles.

Now, Jai crawled toward the door set in the wall that he had seen Beverlai disappear into twice before. Every inch he shifted was agony, his back and shoulders flaring as he pulled himself over the gravel.

When he reached the door, he used the handle to lift himself, and gasped in relief as his weight pushed the door open. It had always been a risk, this plan. Jai had seen no keyhole in the door, but the woman still might have barred it from the inside.

Pride was to be Beverlai's downfall. What fettered would dare enter her chambers? Luck was on Jai's side too, for the direwolf was not sleeping in its alcove either. Milkar had told him it slept little, prowling the western forest in the night. Nevertheless, it had been a wild gamble.

Jai wriggled into the doorway, wincing as the scabs on his back cracked at the movement. The chamber was dark, and he could hear the soft breaths of Beverlai somewhere in the room. Without mana, he could hardly see in front of his face. He fumbled in the darkness, finding nothing but wooden furniture with his hands.

And then, as his eyes adjusted to the gloom . . . he saw it.

Beverlai had not bothered to remove her clothing. Rather, she lay in her cot, fully clothed. The room was small – Jai could practically reach out and touch her.

Jai did not hesitate. Every second was another he might be discovered. He crawled upon his belly, then rolled beneath Beverlai's sightline, stifling a whimper as his raw back pressed against the dirty cobbles.

Above, Jai could see the woman's sallow face. The cruelty etched into her visage, like laugh lines in reverse. Even in slumber, a sardonic sneer curled the edges of her lips.

Jai reached out with trembling hand, unclipping the keyhoop at Beverlai's belt.

The keys jingled like wind chimes, and the soft breathing paused. Jai held his breath, suddenly wishing that he could find a blade in the room. If Jai had, he'd cut the woman's throat in cold blood. Though he hardly had the energy to grip the keys tight enough to keep them silent.

One-handed, he dragged himself from the room once more. Nausea gripped his belly, and he forced back a mouthful of bile. Adrenaline had gotten him this far, but it was fast fading.

His heart was pounding, and the room spun. He could hear Beverlai's hoarse breaths, and for a moment he forgot where he was. For a moment, he was in Leonid's chamber's once more, sleeping at the foot of his bed when the old man was sick. Listening to his breaths, counting the seconds until morning.

Only the pain, throbbing through his body, brought him back to the present.

Jai forced his body on, knowing at any moment, a sentry upon the east wall might turn and see him. He was lucky the mist had persisted through the night, coming in from the mountains to settle heavy in the canyon like oil on water.

He could see their silhouettes, a half-dozen men staring into enemy territory. Half a dozen crossbows, to shoot into his back. Darkness, fog and surprise would be his only defence . . . he had to move.

Twice, Jai had to stop, gulping air like a beached fish. He was weak as a newborn, hardly able to hold himself up by his elbows.

After what felt like an age and enormous effort, Jai reached the gates. The key here, at least, was one he recognised – longer and thinner than the others. It rattled in the lock as he stretched a trembling hand, and the other keys clinked merrily. Sound carried in this place, but Jai did not look over his shoulder as the gate swung open. Either the sentries had noticed it, or they hadn't. Either way, there was only one path ahead of him.

He let himself roll down the steps, into the dank corridor. His hissed in pain as he hit the ground, feeling the chill stone sucking heat from his body.

Jai forced himself on when he'd caught his breath. Frida's chamber was at the very end of the passageway. He pulled himself there by his fingernails.

Hand after hand, breath after breath. It felt like an hour before he reached the dead end, and the last barred doors on either side of it.

He hardly had the strength to lift the keys to the keyhole, let alone trial and error. But he did so anyway, trying the first key on the chain. And then . . . to Jai's surprise, the door swung open from the soft pressure of the key.

And inside . . . a growl.

No Frida.

Only a direwolf, saliva dripping from its jowls. He yanked

back on the door, only for a hand to grip its edge, holding it open.

Jai choked a gasp of horror as Aurelius's figure emerged from the darkness.

'Hello, savage.'

Chapter 87

J ai lay upon the cold slabs of Frida's cell, trussed like a pig for roasting. The kicking Aurelius gave him had left his bruised face so swollen, he could hardly see out of his eyes.

Despair had seized Jai's heart, making it heavy as a stone. He had never known such misery. Nor felt so hopeless. He sought out Winter's connection. Seized it like a lifeline. Perhaps it was . . . for he could feel the blood from the cuts on his back, pooling, warm beneath him.

The man crouched beside him, fingering a lock of Jai's hair.

'They say a Steppeman never cuts his pelt. You're no fresh savage, fooled though you had us. You're *civilised*. Who are you, boy?'

Jai had no response. It was hard enough to breathe through the pulped mess of his nose. Time seemed to fade in and out of existence.

Death was the only escape now. He only wished he had the mana to take some of them with him.

'I was going to have Milkar whipped for wasting my time tonight,' Aurelius chuckled. 'But the bastard never lets me down. I was already working the girl over, so all I had to do was move her cell next door, and leave Ulf waiting for you. Shame though. A boy of your talents . . . you'd make quite the work-horse.'

Jai felt the tears run down his face, cutting channels through the blood that had dried there. Of course – the direwolf had not been prowling outside. He had been protecting Aurelius in case Frida woke.

A new voice spoke.

'What a pretty picture you make,' Beverlai chuckled. 'All the yellows, purples and reds. I wonder what shade of green you'll turn after a few days on the poles.'

Jai had not heard her arrive. But he could hear the direwolf, panting in the corner. A hand slapped at Jai's face, mashing at his lips. Jai groaned, his breath coming out in a splutter, and Beverlai cackled.

'How did we not know he was soulbound?' Aurelius asked with low rage. 'That guildsman fucked us good and proper.'

Beverlai sniffed.

'I should have caught it when my Ulf became suspicious – he could probably smell the stink of the savage's totem. But he's hardly a soulbound. Likely bonded to a common khiroi. Didn't the guildsman say they had one when they were captured?'

'Well, you're lucky he didn't kill you where you slept,' Aurelius snapped. 'More's the pity. Milkar only whispered it through the spyhole an hour ago.'

Jai could hardly believe what he was hearing. Milkar? How right Hanebal had been. Jai had no strength left for anger. Only bitter tears.

Aurelius grunted, and Jai made out his figure leaning close.

'Now, boy. You have one chance to live. Oh, we'll beat you to the bone, but you'll live. You help us with the girl. Who is she to you?'

Jai moaned, spitting blood upon the flagstones. He had never known such pain. He could hardly think.

A blow near-lifted him from the floor and sent him sprawling.

'Good-for-nothing savage,' Beverlai snarled. 'You came into my *chamber*s. You laid *hands* on *me*.'

Another kick landed him against the wall and Jai felt ribs snap. He dry-heaved, and Beverlai cackled once more.

'Getting my money's worth with this one.'

'He's probably her servant,' Aurelius said. 'One of the orphans from the War of the Steppe, bonded with a beast of burden so he can better serve her. But he'll know who she is, at least. Mayhap what level soulbound she is.'

Jai felt himself being lifted by his neck, and felt Beverlai's hot breath in his swollen ear. Consciousness was a fickle thing, slipping in and out of his grasp.

'You tell us, or I'll take the skin off your hide again.'

'Hold it,' Aurelius snapped. 'I'll not have the boy die on me. It's a miracle he lived through the night. I want him to go slow – give him a chance to speak his mind if he breaks. A couple days out there might do it. If pain won't convince him, perhaps the elements might. It's always good to have a live one on the poles anyway. Keeps the Huddites docile.'

Beverlai pulled Jai close and took a deep sniff.

'He only survived because his mana healed him up. He's not got much now I'll wager, but you leave him on the poles, he'll soulbreathe. Break free again.'

Aurelius laughed at that.

'The poles were here long before you joined us, Beverlai, even if the stocks weren't. We've kept soulbound on them before, back when my father ran this place. Takes them longer to die, but they can't wriggle free with Damantine steel locked about their wrists. Or at least, not those that are yet to ascend.'

Beverlai released him and Jai collapsed to the ground, pawing at his neck.

'I'll fetch the manacles,' Aurelius said. 'You get him on the poles.'

Jai spluttered, trying to speak. He saw the hazy silhouette of Aurelius lifting a hand for Beverlai to wait.

'Mil . . . kar,' was all Jai managed.

Aurelius let out a cruel laugh.

'It is not cowardice that makes men turn on their brothers. It's love. His wife was made a whore in my brothel down south. I told him every man he turns in . . . well, it's another couple months I let her live. Funny thing is, she died a week after she got there.'

He laughed again and Jai felt nausea roll over him.

'Now . . . I've shown you mine. Show me yours. Tell me about the girl.'

Jai lay on his back, wishing the floor would swallow him up. There was nothing to be gained from talking. He was destined to die on the poles, drowning in his own lungs.

Whether Aurelius had expected an answer, Jai did not know. Certainly, the man did not wait long before spitting on him and leaving the room. Only then did he feel Beverlai take a handful of his hair and drag him out of the cell.

Jai writhed, if only to deny Beverlai the satisfaction of having broken him. The woman stopped. Grinned. Then slammed his head into the wall.

Chapter 88

Unconsciousness was a friend, now. Jai could not remember being lifted onto the pole, nor the Damantine steel being locked to his hands.

His body was suspended by his wrists alone, and blood ran down his arms where the steel dug close to the bone.

He could hardly breathe already, his nose broken beyond use. Only short gasps through his mouth were possible.

In some ways it was a relief, for he could practically taste the stench of the bodies that rotted nearby. Hanging from their arms like poorly cured meat.

The sun was already out, meagre though its rays were in the shadows of the mountain. He had been out for a while. The Huddites were working away, swarming the west wall, while others dragged the great tree trunks to the east gate and beyond.

Jai knew he would die if he did not soulbreathe. By all rights, he should be dead already. He would not give his captors the satisfaction of his death just yet.

Rage was a sentiment Jai hardly ever felt. His life had been one of fear. Now, he raged. Raged in helpless abandon, crying bitter tears.

He had thought he hated Titus, but that had not been hate. *This* was hate. It consumed him. A fire had been set in his soul, and he would not let it go out until he had righted this wrong.

It was this hate that forced his slow-filling lungs to gulp down breath after breath. It was rage that kept his heart beating.

Jai forced the mana into his core, drip by drip, even as more mana drifted from Winter. Every dribble of the liquid energy was instantly snatched away to another part of his body. Soon enough the wounds on his wrists had scabbed closed.

With every pulse of mana, his pain receded, bit by bit. It was nowhere near as fast as the healing spell that Frida had used upon him, in what felt like a lifetime ago. Even if he were cut down and allowed to rest this very moment, it would take him days to recover . . . if that was even possible. Jai had no idea what state his body was in. He only knew that he'd have died within the hour had the mana not saved him.

Jai may have been in pain, but it was his breathing that was causing him the most suffering. In many ways, this was the perfect method of executing a soulbound, for soulbreathing was made far harder. Each breath was a strain, and with every passing moment, his lungs filled with fluid. It was like filling the bottom of an hourglass . . . and the sands of time were moving far too quickly.

Already, he could hear the bubbling in his lungs and, despite the agony of his broken ribs, he forced out a cough to clear them. He almost fainted from the pain, but he breathed a little better for a few moments more.

This was not to be a quick death. He would choke and splutter until he could do so no more. Then he'd hang here to rot away like the others.

His wrists were the worst of the pain he felt, but there was a close second. All his weight hung on the joints of his shoulders, and at that moment, it felt like they were being slowly pulled from their sockets. Only by lifting himself could he give them some relief.

He did so every minute, allowing himself to take an easier gulp of air. These little hits of mana were heavenly, dulling his pain ever so slightly. But the mana came and went like a spendthrift's coin.

Rescue . . . was it possible? The miracle of a Steppefolk warband coming to free the prisoners. But Aurelius had been smart, taking only Huddites. A warrior of the steppe was far less likely to risk his life to liberate those of another people, especially one they had warred with in the past.

It was his only hope. Even if he forced himself to store some mana, he'd never break through the Damantine steel. If only he had ascended, he might have been able to – he could feel the rough rust upon them.

A sound distracted Jai from his thoughts. It swam through the mess of pain, focus and asphyxiation, and was so strange, Jai thought he had imagined it. No . . . this was real.

He heard the sound again and this time it was unmistakeable. A brassy trumpet call, echoing through the canyon. Jai might have found it beautiful, had the sound not filled him with dread. For he recognised what had made the sound. The imperial cornu, beloved of the legions. When they had travelled to do battle with the Huddites, Jai had been woken by that very noise in the legion's morning reveille.

But surely . . . could there truly be a legion outside the gates?

Jai forced open gummed-up eyes, staring at the western gate as it creaked open. Riders entered, their scarlet cloaks giving them away even through Jai's blurred vision. Imperial scouts. And behind them . . . a legion.

Men dressed in leather, red cloth and burnished steel, marching through the gates in tight formation. They lined up under the red-faced screams of centurions and optiones, somehow ignoring the spittle that sprayed their faces.

This was no veteran legion. These were young boys, fresh-faced and terrified. A newly conscripted army, summoned to bring war to the Steppefolk.

Jai almost laughed aloud. Had they escaped, they would have had an entire legion coming after them. What a genius plan he'd had.

He had been given so much in his life. A dragon of his own, and the blood of a king. Good health and his freedom. All squandered. The last of Rohan's line, left to rot. He had but delayed the inevitable.

Jai would not be surprised if this was the same legion that had followed in their footsteps all the way down the Kashmere Road. Yet, something gave him pause.

A familiar figure, broad as a bear, striding like a giant between the ranks. For a moment, Jai thought it was Rufus. Then the eagle-crested helm turned toward him . . . and his gorge rose.

Magnus.

Chapter 89

Jai had given up hope of surviving this hours ago. Despair had taken him, and it sat like a heavy cloud on his mind. Tears ran and dried, unbidden by his thoughts.

It was all he could do to breathe. And repeat.

He was dead anyway. The sight of Magnus . . . it brought him no fear for himself. Hell, he'd probably die quicker. Anger . . . it was there, but a distant, shrivelled thing. Instead, his mind turned to Frida.

Magnus would recognise her. Whatever abuses she received here from Aurelius would be nothing compared to if the Sabine torturers got hold of her.

Jai watched as Aurelius scurried from the western gatehouse toward Magnus, flapping his hands like an escaped chicken. Behind him, Beverlai slunk closer. She seemed almost annoyed at Magnus's presence, and Jai was not surprised. The old woman was used to being the most dangerous person in the prison even if Aurelius, as the governor, was more powerful.

The three converged at the front of the legion, whose final ranks were still threading their way through the western gates.

Jai tried to ignore them, focusing on his breathing. Every thimbleful of mana would keep him alive a little longer.

But he could not enter the trance. Not with all that was happening now. It was as if his mind had been seized by equal parts curiosity and despair.

If there had been any chance of a warband from the steppe rescuing him, it was now gone. While the veteran legions usually contained only a half complement of men, their numbers reduced over the years by death and retirement, this looked to be a full legion, if a little green about the gills. Five thousand men. They crowded into the space between the walls, ignoring the hateful looks of the Huddites watching them from the west wall's rubble.

Jai's heart jumped into his throat as Magnus fixed his gaze upon him. He lowered his head and was glad that his face was swollen to the point he could hardly see.

Magnus pointed . . . and nudged his horse toward the poles. He did so with a casual air, the fetterers running their mouths behind him. Soon enough, Jai could hear it.

'. . . sign of a single Steppeman or warband of any sort,' Aurelius said. 'You've nothing to fear in the immediate area.'

'I fear only that you've not gathered the materials we need for our fort. The lads'll sleep easier with a foot of wood twixt them and the savages,' Magnus said.

'Enough for the greatest fort in all the land,' Aurelius announced.

Magnus stopped his horse at the base of Jai's pole, his ruddy face staring up at him.

'No sign of a Steppeman, you say? What's this then?'

Jai felt like he would vomit, for he knew the cruelty of the man below. For while Beverlai enjoyed inflicting pain on any man, woman or child, Jai knew the hate Magnus held for Jai's

people. He could peel Jai's skin from his body with his fingernails, and enjoy every second of it.

'Oh, this is just a mutt,' Beverlai said, looking at Jai with
warning in her eyes. 'See, his hair is not even braided as the
other savages' is. We caught him trying to cross the border. Made
an example of him to the others.'

'Hold!' Magnus bellowed suddenly.

Jai winced at the sound of it. Magnus's voice was enhanced
with mana, for it echoed about the canyon far louder than the
cornu had. Silence reigned and not a single legionary moved,
such was the awe they felt for the man.

Magnus stepped closer, narrowing his eyes at Jai. He cocked
his head.

'He looks Steppeman enough.'

Jai thanked whatever gods might exist. His bruises were as
good a mask as any . . . if Magnus could even tell one Steppeman
from another in the first place. Jai had heard from his brothers that
the man could never tell them apart when he joined their hunts.

Magnus lifted a hand, beckoning with a closed fist. What
must have been fifty men emerged from the legion. Men with
horsehair crests crosswise upon their helms and far more ornate
armour than the others. Centurions.

They gathered close and Magnus addressed them in a low
voice.

'Have the men parade past this savage before they pass
through the gate. Let them see one for themselves. Half our lads
are fresh farm boys – most have never seen one before. I hear
the whispering in their tents at night. They fear the wild men
of the steppe. They've heard the rumours of the . . .'

He snipped at the air with his fingers, earning a chuckle from
the assembled men. Magnus dismissed them with a wave of his
hand and turned his gaze up to Jai once more.

'A shame. My gryphon used to love dining on the steaming liver of a Steppeman. Can't say fresher than this one. Wrapped up nicely for her.'

Beverlai chuckled cruelly at that.

Magnus's gaze turned to the other poles, where the corpses lay. He pointed at one. This one, to Jai's surprise, was a woman.

'Tell me. You have Huddites here, yet there is a Steppeman on the poles. Tell me, have any Dansk tried to pass? Perhaps a girl?'

Aurelius and Beverlai were lucky Magnus's eyes were fixed elsewhere, for the glance they exchanged was telling.

'None, Lord Commander,' Beverlai said, the lie smooth on her tongue. 'Why do you ask?'

Magnus grunted.

'One of the Dansk that poisoned Emperor Constantine has yet to be found. Every prison and fettered-camp in the empire is to keep an eye out for her – I'm surprised word has not reached you by now. There are faster ways to the border from the empire, but we heard rumours of sightings on the Kashmere Road. Should you find her, send a rider for me immediately. There's good coin in it for you, whether the one you've found is the right girl or not.'

Jai took a gasping breath and could not help but feel some satisfaction at the sudden look of fear upon Aurelius and Beverlai's faces. They thought he would tell Magnus about Frida. Of course, they had no idea that Jai would never do such a thing, but it gave him some small satisfaction.

'He's lucky we didn't let my direwolf have him,' Beverlai said, her voice pointed. 'Always talking back. If he runs his mouth, that's where he'll end up. In pieces, in Ulf's belly. Hear that, savage?'

Jai kept his mouth shut and closed his eyes. He could hardly breathe, let alone speak.

'Where is your beast, Lord Commander?' Aurelius asked. 'If it is not impolite to ask.'

Magnus sighed.

'We've got every gryphon and chamrosh in the Gryphon Guard scouting our frontiers and beyond. We cannot garrison every border town, nor blockade every port. With war upon us, our enemies will attack us with a thousand raids, as Rohan once did. But with our eyes in the sky . . . well, we can move the right pieces to the right places before they ever cross into our territory.'

He began nudging his horse around with his knees and clucking it on towards the western gate.

'Our young emperor leads by example and I must do the same. So, I ride this horse. Now, I will stay here a few days, while the men build the camp. My scouts will need rooms too, for their horses need rest. I trust you have refreshments prepared.'

Aurelius fixed a smile upon his face.

'You may have my quarters, of course. And the scouts can have the garrison. I am told the brothel is not too . . .'

They moved out of earshot and Jai let out a shuddering breath of relief. Already, the centurions were gathering their charges, marching them in ten-deep files past him and on through the east gates. Few looked up at him.

These were boys, many even younger than he was. Conscripts, most likely, not even given a choice to fight. He held no hate in his heart for them.

Jai closed his eyes, finally allowing himself to enter the trance. To take in those difficult breaths, borrow time from the mana within.

As minutes turned to hours, Jai clawed back enough mana to push back the pain, and to turn the scarlet bruises blossoming across his body yellow. He was deathly thirsty.

And then . . . he sensed it.

He had gone so long hearing only the garbled echoes of Winter's feelings that he had almost perfected the ability to ignore them. But now there was a pulse of . . . something clearer.

Jai let the pulses wash over him, seizing the connection like a lifeline. If only to say goodbye.

Winter was exhausted, in both body and soul. She was alone, cold and hungry, and moving with an urgency he had not sensed before. He could smell the forest . . . and sense the fatigue in her limbs.

He could *feel* it all. As if she were but a stone's throw away from him, as she had once been before.

Jai urged her to turn back. He would be dead long before she could do anything to help him. Even if she could sneak past the prowling direwolf her teeth could not break damantine steel. All she would do was put herself in danger.

If she heard him, she did not acknowledge it. If anything, she renewed her efforts.

Jai could do nothing to stop her.

Chapter 90

J ai soulbreathed with single-minded focus. He did not open his eyes until the sun had finally set and the entire legion had passed through the eastern gates.

When he opened his eyes again, it was quieter. Only the horses and their scouts remained within the prison, for it seemed they had taken over the garrison. Jai heard the wardens complaining as they carried their straw-filled mattresses over to the prison cells where Frida was kept. The rest were camped in the lee of the wall, their canvas tents scattered among the piled logs.

Lifting his eyes above the men who moved back and forth across the prison yard, Jai realised that from up here on the poles he could finally see what lay beyond the walls.

The canyon continued but a few hundred yards before opening up into the Great Steppe. Now, panting with the pain of lifting his head, Jai saw his homeland for what felt like the first time.

An ocean of land stretching beyond the horizon, yet flat and placid as a lake. It was still and silent, but for when wind swirled across the open prairie, dancing patterns in the grass. He could smell the grasslands. It was a rich, earthy scent, like upturned loam in the palace pleasure gardens. It smelled of . . . home.

And it called to him. He was so close it was almost as if he could reach out and touch it. Yet now he never would.

In his despair, Jai turned away from the east, and looked west. Back to the near-finished wall and the chopped woods that had denuded the hillside. Back to where he had come from.

His whole life he had been trapped between the two worlds. It was fitting, then, that he would die between them too.

It was in that moment that Winter called to him. A pulse of urgency, demanding his attention. To look closer. To look . . . lower.

And he saw her. Crouched like a gargoyle amid the crenelations of the west wall, a forlorn, scrawny figure, staring at him with bright blue eyes. They bored into him like chips of ice, cast in cloud-shadowed moonlight.

The sight of her sprung tears. He could not imagine what the hatchling had endured crossing the wild lands to reach him. And now she risked everything to be here for him. Even if it would be all for naught.

Jai urged her to return to the forest, but received nothing but stubborn fury back. He sensed something then. An emotion he had never felt from her before. Perhaps, it was the first time she had ever felt it.

Shame. She was ashamed of him. That he would give up now, when she was so close. That he refused help when it was offered.

The emotion was complex, but her meaning was clear. And yet Jai could not speak back to her. How could he tell her that she couldn't help him? That she could not break the chains that bound him, and that he did not even know where the keys to them lay. That even if she could free him he was half dead in the centre of a prison, surrounded by a legion and two soulbound that could rip him to shreds without even breaking a sweat.

The only response he could send her was one that balled up

all that complex detail into a feeling of futility despite his desire to escape. Whether she had understood him, he did not know, but he saw the little beast scramble down the wall, hugging the flank of the canyon until he lost sight of her.

The sentinels on the east wall had turned in for the night as the legion's presence made a raid all but impossible. Their disappearance was a thin silver lining, but Jai was thankful for it.

It was only when he heard the scrape of claws on wood that he knew she had reached him and crawled to the pole's top. He felt her hot snout upon his wrists as she gnawed at the manacles above him. They held his hands together and were set in a ring of the same steel, buried deep into the wood.

With time, she might scratch the ring free from its deep seating in the pole, but it would do little to help him. The same ring was attached to a steel chain, one that ran all the way to a bracket in the east wall. Jai suspected that more powerful soulbound had been held here than he. Only one who was ascended would have a hope of breaking free. Otherwise, a key was the only way out.

Jai waited until Winter had given up. He smiled through his tears when he felt her settle upon his shoulder. She was heavier than she had been before.

The little dragon had grown in the days and nights they had spent apart. She was the size of a hunting dog now. She would have reached his chest if she stood on her hind legs, and had to curl her smooth, warm belly around his neck and shoulders to fit.

He pressed his cheek against hers, holding back sobbing breaths. She was his truest friend. Perhaps the only true friend he had ever had. And now she was risking everything just to be close to him.

Jai had never felt such love for another living being – perhaps not even himself. He wished he could wrap her in his arms and hold her close. Tell her how grateful he was for her very exist-ence. To not be alone.

It was enough to give him hope.

Here was something that Beverlai and Aurelius had not planned for. They thought him soulbound to a distant khiro, not a dragon that could climb and slink and sneak. And they certainly didn't think his beast was anywhere near here.

Jai tried to think. It was not safe for Winter to stay with him much longer. It would take but a single glance from Milkar, a warden or even any other fettered to see Jai was not alone on the pole, dark though it was that night.

Jai could hear, if he listened closely, the sound of female voices from the west wall's gatehouse. Likely courtesans, brought in from the brothel nearby. He had overheard from passing guards that Aurelius, Beverlai and Magnus were within, as well as the scouts and high ranking officers in the legion.

It appeared they were having one last night with the fairer sex before their lonely war in the empty expanse of the Great Steppe.

Aurelius and Beverlai might have the keys to his chains, but they would likely be up all night. No chance of Winter stealing those keys.

Jai had to ascend. Somehow. Despite having hardly grown his core; hardly worked magick. He had to.

But the only way he'd been able to grow his core even a little had been the soulgem he had ripped from the chamrosh's chest. If he had another of those he might manage to grow it again. Perhaps enough to ascend. But he didn't have one. The only other item that might help would be one of those golden pills that Frida had used before.

He supposed that was what Frida had meant by 'mouth'. She had wanted the pill he'd bought at the gallipot, but he'd taken it before his fight with the acolyte. That was all it could be, right?

Or maybe . . . she didn't want him to place the pill in her mouth, but rather . . . to take something from it.

What could it be? He knew she'd already taken the lustration pill.

The realisation hit Jai hard and for a moment his mind reeled. It was not a pill at all. It was the soulgem. Her *dragon's* soulgem.

This was no stone from a newly-bonded chamrosh either. This would be far more potent.

Why Frida had not swallowed the soulgem for herself yet was a mystery to Jai. Unless . . . she had held it back for this very reason. For she could not break through the doors designed to house an ascended soulbound. But Jai might be able to break her out.

There was a chance she might have given up and swallowed it by now. But Aurelius had moved her to a cell with a small window. Too small for Winter to squeeze into . . . but large enough for Frida to pass the soulgem through. It was a chance.

Jai turned his head to Winter and whispered.

'All right, girl. You've convinced me. We're not dead yet.'

Chapter 91

Jai did not know Winter had succeeded until he felt the pulse of triumph through their connection. It had been hard to explain to her what she needed to do until he realised he could see the window to Frida's cell.

It was the furthest along, closest to the western wall. He directed Winter there and instructed her to chirr loudly until Frida gave her the soulgem.

The entire process had consumed the better part of an hour. Frida had been slow to emerge from her trance – perhaps she had suspected Winter's chirring to be a trap. He could only interpret the situation through Winter's emotions – her frustration, her fear, and finally, her triumph.

In that time, the sky above had darkened. It was filled with a cloudscape that seemed to swirl on the wind, caught in the unnatural funnel of the deep-carved canyon. Snow fell, settling instantly on the chill soil. The horses gathered for warmth and Jai shuddered and twitched as the first flakes sucked the warmth from his bones.

Now, he was left hoping that Frida would remain conscious. He didn't have a concrete plan yet, but he knew one thing for certain – whatever was going to happen, it would happen tonight.

And the odds were stacked against him. He still had to ascend, break the manacles, and somehow liberate Frida from a prison designed to hold soulbound.

He could see Winter scampering back, slinking close to the wall. Jai's heart nearly beat out of his chest when she passed the direwolf's kennel, but the beast was patrolling beyond the west wall once more.

Soon enough, Winter was crawling up the pole, and Jai winced as her claws dug into his battered flesh. She had no choice but to clamber up his chest, in order to drop the stone into his mouth.

Jai had but a second to glimpse it. It was like a diamond, or a misshapen vial of perfume. Opaque, with glowing liquid within. Jai was quick to close his mouth before someone noticed the light.

It was larger than the last, almost the size of a tangerine. It was with some effort that he swallowed it whole, the lump almost choking him as he forced it down his throat. He dared not crunch down on it, for he had no idea if that would limit its effects.

He urged Winter to retreat out of sight, but the little beast refused. Instead, she pressed close and pulsed mana down their connection. She knew this was his last chance, and his heart almost broke as she pushed everything she had to him.

Jai entered the trance, knowing his stomach would soon break down the walls of the soulgem. Soon the liquid would pour through – it was up to him to direct the purified mana through his channels and into his core before it was all used up.

In his younger years, Jai had been forced to test out the medicines prescribed to Leonid, for fear of poisoning or ill-effects.

One, designed to rid Leonid of malaise, had made him heady and drunk. Crushed poppy.

The feeling that hit Jai was the same as when he had tasted the poppy tincture. A powerful rush of pleasure and joy as mana poured out from his core, rushing to his extremities, healing and reinvigorating wherever it went.

There was so much of it. His mind boggled at the sheer scale of the mana jetting forth, as if the vessel had compressed a raging ocean.

Jai's body reacted instinctively, rushing to heal his broken flesh. Jai allowed it to do so. Bruises wiped away as if by a wet cloth, and he could feel his very ribs knitting together once more.

The mana was almost impossible to contain, let alone control. It went where it willed and only stopped when Jai near-broke his mind forcing it to bend to his will.

Now, everything Jai had learned while he had fought the poison came to the fore. Where once his channels had been a mystery, he now knew each and every one like old friends.

Time lost all meaning. There was nothing but the tempest within him, and he revelled in it. He did not fight the wild floods within, but rather shaped and guided them – closing some passages, and opening others.

And still, the mana jetted forth. Scouring his body, healing the battered wounds.

It would be so easy to let the mana work on its own. But Jai knew he must ascend. He had to grow his core. Gain the strength to break his chains.

Every so often, Jai was forced to surface from his trance to clear his lungs, losing precious mana in the process. But each time Winter's presence steadied him as she rumbled deep breaths against the back of his neck, giving him the strength to go back under.

Already, his core was at its fullest. Now he forced the mana to stay in his innermost channels, blocking the routes to his extremities now the worst of his injuries were healed. He needed every drop of mana.

And now his very channels were overfilling. It was time. He had to force more into his core.

He gulped a deep breath . . . and pushed.

Pain.

Yet it was no worse than what he had endured under Beverlai's whip. Almost an old friend. Jai strained as his core bulged and stretched.

Now agony. It was all he could do not to scream. It was as if a thousand needles were stabbing his very soul; as if the walls of his being were stretched and contorted. But still he pushed.

His core grew. And grew again.

The walls grew thinner with each expansion. Spider-cracks formed along its surface, yet Jai could not afford to stop.

He would ascend now or die trying. His core would ascend . . . or shatter.

In truth, Jai had wasted much of the mana. It was simply too much to store, too much to control. Too much had burned out of his lungs and into the air. When he pushed more of the mana to his core, more still poured out into him.

If he did not succeed soon, he would be empty by morning. And then . . . he would die.

Hope was fading fast.

Ascension was out of his control, or so Rufus had said. It could happen now, or take weeks. Years.

Jai tried to focus. Compressed his core, then expanded it. Seized upon his connection with Winter.

Nothing worked.

And finally . . . the soulgem ran out of mana. Dissolved to nothing in his belly, leaving his channels suffused with mana.

Again, Jai filled his core. Whimpered as he forced more mana through its walls. And within . . . he manipulated the delicate membrane within his core. Pulsed it so it swirled the mana within, washing the cracked walls of his inner being. Salving them . . . repairing them. Soon enough, the fractures were gone.

But he had lost his focus, and all the while mana leaked from his lungs. Rushed to his wounds. Wasted.

Jai pushed all that he had left in his channels. Gurgled through the pain, even as Winter lapped the tears from his face. And his core . . . *grew*. The walls thickened, the space within far more than what it had once been.

But now his lungs were so full he could no longer draw in mana. Only choke and gasp and splutter. Winter whimpered in his ear, scratching at his chest until she drew blood. Trying to force him to breathe on.

But Jai's mana was all gone. He had done all he could.

Time passed, measured only by the slow filling of Jai's lungs. The edges of his vision darkened and he could no longer speak. Instead, he kissed Winter's neck. He wanted to tell her this was not her fault. That she had done everything she could and more.

Jai took his final gurgling breath, entering the trance for a last time. Deep within himself, he latched to the cord that bound them. He wished he could sever it. Spare Winter the agony of his loss.

Grasping their bond, he sent her what lay within his heart. He let go of the hate. Let go of the rage. He wanted her to remember him in only one way.

With love.

Chapter 92

Jai's world shrank. He hardly felt his body . . . nor even the channels within. He was but a spark within his core, holding the dragon's cord with every ounce of his being.

The deep throb within him was slowing. The ebb and flow of his chamber, now little more than a slow tide. His heart was barely beating.

His lungs convulsed, somewhere inside him. They seemed so far away. Soon, he would no longer feel them.

With each second left to him, Jai told Winter how much he loved her. How good, and loyal she was, how proud he was to have been her bonded companion. Without the distraction of a physical body, Jai had never felt so connected to her.

Her mind had always been as if behind a warped mirror, one shrouded in smoke. Her feelings, thoughts, desires, had always been reduced to their simplest form. Now, she was as behind a pane of glass. He could see the grace of her soul. The kindness, the courage.

Such beauty. If it was to be his last sight, he could not ask for better.

Darkness.

It enveloped him like a warm blanket.

JAI'S CORE CONVULSED. WAS this death?

Pain, then.

The core surrounding him trembled. *Stretched.*

A structure was forming on the crystalline wall. A pattern, like the interlocking scales on Winter's back. Honeycomb, then a snail spiral, then the helix of a sunflower. A snowflake; the petals of a rose. Somehow all of these at once and then none at all.

A thousand patterns, assembling and dissolving, symphonic in its rhythms. The patterns of the secret language that governed the universe. It was like staring into infinity. Staring into the face of a god.

And then . . . light. So pure and blinding that Jai did not know where it began and he ended. He was his core. He was his body. He was the mana that flowed within. The flesh and the blood and the hidden channels ghostly beneath.

Agony and ecstasy were in harmony, blended in one. His bones shattered and knitted, skin sloughed and thickened. Flesh, sinew, cartilage. All renewed. Reborn.

He could *feel* his body rippling. *Becoming.* It was *alive.* Hot and hard as embers, pulsing and roiling and seething in all its organic glory. He was himself and more.

And then, as soon as it had begun, the world snapped back into focus. His trance, once all he knew, was ended like a slap across the face.

Within, he *saw.* Saw his core, sitting grey and empty. But so much larger, and its walls so thick and opaque he could hardly see within. This was what it was to be ascended. This was no kernel.

Jai gulped a breath. Then another and another. Cultivating blindly until the first motes of mana grazed his core's surface. And like a snowflake upon a tongue, they dissolved into liquid, passing through the crystalline shell.

Jai opened his eyes. The world was white with snow, but his very body steamed. His lungs, once filled, now vomited liquid, copious and frothing from his throat. Black filth dripped from him, boiled from his very bones, sizzling in the snow beneath, melted by a feverish heat that seemed it might set the very wood afire.

Jai wanted to scream. To bellow into the sky in triumphant abandon. Instead, he sobbed, once. Let the tears flow down his face, as the sheer relief of survival overcame him. Winter nuzzled him, her tongue lapping at his tears as if she wished to share in his pain. To shoulder more of the burden than she already had.

'Go,' Jai whispered. 'You've done all you can.'

No.

Jai did not hear the word. But he *felt* its sentiment. Something had changed between them. This was no longer the whispered echo of emotion. It was something deeper.

Jai squeezed his eyes closed one more time. He pulled himself up, as easily as if his body weighed nothing at all. Held himself by the strength of his arms, the chain between his manacles stretched taught behind his neck. Winter sat upon the pole's top, her teeth latched upon the links. For all the good it did.

But at least, Jai knew, this was no mana-infused strength. It was his body alone. His muscle and sinew. He had *ascended*.

Jai pulled, hard. Whimpered as the cold metal dug into his flesh, pressing to the bone. He had imagined, once ascended, he would pop the links like daisy-chains.

As the first hint of blue dawn blushed the western horizon, Jai knew he had not long to spare. He strained against the metal, sobbing from the pain as the steel cut into his flesh. He gripped the manacles as best he could, and felt the blood run down his arms and into the gutters of his hips.

'Winter,' Jai croaked. 'Go.'

No. Fight.

Sentiment replaced feeling. Meaning replaced emotion. Jai knew, now, that Winter had tied their fates. And he had no choice but to do his part.

He set his teeth. Entered the half-trance, gripping his strange new core. It was larger now, more uniform. But he had no time to examine it closely. Instead, he squeezed out every drop of mana, even as Winter pulsed the last of hers into his core.

Jai *pulled.*

Above, he felt the steel scrape down his bone, peeling the flesh. Winter chirred with excitement.

Almost.

She could feel a link, stretching wide upon her tongue.

Jai sobbed. And pulled so hard, he felt his very teeth would shatter in his mouth.

His hands flew apart, a broken link pinging free like a fallen coin. He landed in a wet thud, his face messed with mud and slurried snow.

The world spun. Shrank and expanded as his vision blurred. Blood pulsed from his wrists, even as his last dregs of mana rushed to heal them, doing little. He could but press his hands to his chest, attempting to stem the flow.

Winter leaped from above, landing in a scattering of white powder. She did not wait for him, instead haring toward the opening in the west wall.

Jai called to her in his mind, begging her to slow. No response. Just urgency. Frustration. She was leading him to something.

He stumbled after her, taking sobbing breath after breath. He had no shoes upon his feet, yet he felt no cold. Any moment he expected a shout, or the ringing of a bell. Yet none came.

No fettered watched from the cave bars. No wardens manned the walls, nor patrolled the ground of Porticus. The cold and the presence of the legion had sped his doom. Now, they were his salvation.

Jai watched as Winter disappeared through the unfinished wall. He looked to the gates that held Frida in the cells within. Knew even if he had mana to spare, he could never batter through her barred door, for it was designed to keep even the ascended within.

He knew he could not fight Beverlai for the keys, even as the cruel woman drunkenly caroused but a stone's throw away in the gatehouse.

If he stayed, he would die. If he left, he was a coward. But at least a living one. One who might yet find a way to free her. His way east was blocked by a legion, sleeping before their long march into the steppe. West, lay Winter. Forests to hide in, and food to forage.

Jai had no choice. He ran.

Ran with all the strength his legs could muster, leaping and bounding with all the fear he had buried in those last few hours.

He scrambled over rubble, ignoring the blood that left a crimson trail in his wake. Ignored the thorns that ripped at him as he tore through the forest, chasing Winter's retreating form.

And behind him . . . a crashing, enormous thing. Gaining on him, with a speed Jai could not match. He skidded to a stop in a spray of fallen leaves and topsoil, facing his pursuer.

The pursuer slowed. Branches crackled and a dark form

stepped out from the murk. Not a wolf, but a man. A tall man, broad as the trunk he had stepped out from behind.

Jai felt despair. Of course. The distraction of the courtesans had not been enough. Magnus had heard him. Perhaps some charm or majicking had alerted him. Either way, he had followed him here.

'Come on,' Jai coughed, still hawking up liquid from his lungs. 'Get it . . . over with.'

He lifted his fists and the shape lumbered closer. Stopped, still shrouded in shadow.

'I said come on!' Jai hissed. 'Let me show you how a Steppeman really dies.'

The figure stepped forward and spread his hands.

'Now lad,' Rufus said. 'Better put those down, afore you hurt someone.'

Chapter 93

Jai felt his knees hit the ground. Was it relief, that stole the strength from him? Or his blood, melting the snow?

Arms gathered him up like a bundle of firewood and sudden wind tousled his hair as they moved at speed.

Sleep stole his consciousness then. That blessed darkness. But Jai did not drift. He dreamed.

Images danced across his mind's eye. Of snow and ice.

Of bearded men, cheering him. Men with blond and ginger beards, lifting axes to the sky. Haggard men, dressed in furs. Dansk warriors. Raiders.

He saw longships, their great dragon-headed prows lifting and dipping with wind and waves. Saw them close, and from far above. Bloodied men and women, unloading grain and cattle at a crowded dock, as outstretched hands begged for a share in the bounty.

Jai could feel the wind in his long hair. That and the wild, ecstatic joy of flying. Of being free to go where his will took him.

Suddenly, Ivar's face. The king's rough hands cupping his chin. A kiss, fatherly and kind, upon Jai's soft cheek. No . . . not Jai's cheek. Frida's.

In this dream Jai was not a handmaid. For he wore jewels upon slender fingers, even while eating alone or sleeping.

No. Not alone. There was a girl, round-faced and timid, who combed out his long, golden tresses. Erica? The princess wore the fine but simple clothes of a Dansk servant. The same Frida had worn when Jai first saw her.

He read books in the light of day. Walked the ramparts of rough-hewn castles. Waved at watching crowds below.

Amid the images, scents, sounds and tastes, there was something greater. Jai felt . . . responsibility. A great duty, so heavy it might suffocate him. He wanted to wake from this dream.

Instead, he flew. On, over the oceans. Past icebergs and great sheets floating in dark waters. He flew to escape the crushing weight of it all.

But he always turned back. Always.

JAI DID NOT REMEMBER collapsing or falling asleep for that matter. Nor did he remember how he got to this place. But when he awoke to the sound of a crackling fire, he did not question it.

He was alive and warm and comfortable. Proof enough he was safe. A leathery tongue lapped at his face and Jai reached out to stroke Navi's scarred snout.

She was here, in this cave. So, Rufus was not the only companion that had kept Winter company all this time. He was glad of that.

A scent hit his nose, flooding his mouth with saliva. He sat up, almost unbidden, as if his body had a mind of its own.

They were in a dank cave, no more than a dozen feet deep – more a crack in the mountainside than anything else. Rufus hunched over a small fire, sausages sizzling upon a skillet.

'You,' Jai said.

He'd almost forgotten seeing him.

Rufus avoided his gaze, instead pushing the skillet deeper into the fire.

'Don't worry,' Rufus said, nodding at the cave entrance. 'Smell'll rise, this high up. Only reason that damned direwolf hasn't found us yet.'

Jai scrambled to the open air, sticking his head tentatively out. Below him, he could see the vast expanse of woodland that surrounded the west side of the canyon. To his left, he could see the prison camp. It was shrouded by morning mist, but the west wall was unmistakeable. How Rufus had got Navi up here, he had no idea. The only route to their cave was a narrow goat trail.

'You've been out all night,' Rufus said. 'Raving in Dansk, wouldn't wake no matter what I did, even after I was done healin' you. Surprised tae see you awake.'

Jai sat upon the ground and accepted a proffered sausage. He chewed it slowly, revelling as the fat and juices drizzled on his tongue.

His senses had been heightened permanently, taste included. And he was half-starved to boot. It was, without a doubt, the best sausage Jai had ever eaten.

He looked at his wrists where pink scars had formed. The manacles, he saw, lay beside the fire. They'd been snapped in two.

In that moment, Jai could only wonder at the true strength of the man before him. He'd known he was no low-level soul-bound. But to snap Damantine steel so cleanly . . .

'Was it Frida?' Rufus asked, his voice low and dull. There was shame in his voice. 'Is she alive?'

'She's alive,' Jai said. 'But . . . I dreamed. I saw a life that was not my own.'

Rufus frowned.

'How'd you escape Porticus, lad?' he asked gently. 'Winter's been leadin' us your way since I recovered from that poison. She ran ahead of me last night when I couldn't go further without sleep. Almost lost our way, only I guessed this's where you'd ended up.'

Jai did not want to think of last night. His stomach twisted at the memory. Of the slow, choking death he had felt, up until the very moment of his ascension. But he had to.

Frida had given him the very soul of her beast. Only . . . he was not so sure anymore that she *was* Frida.

'The soulgem from Frida's dragon,' Jai whispered. 'It helped me ascend.'

Rufus nodded slowly.

'That explains the dream. The soulgem o' a beast leaves traces o' itself. Some say even a fragment o' their soul. With that comes memories – theirs, and those o' their soulbound.'

Jai sat in shock, his sleep-addled mind suddenly clearing. Realisation did not hit him hard but rather seeped into his mind, twisting his stomach. How could he have been so stupid?

Frida was no handmaiden. She was the princess of all the Dansk, and heir to the throne of the Northern Tundra.

She had dressed as her servant to visit Jai. She had whispered in her servant's ears at the baths. Swapped places with her handmaiden at the rehearsal, for fear of Jai's warning. The dragon had always been the princess's. Frida . . . was Erica.

He felt betrayed. He had unburdened his soul to her. Told her, in the long nights, of his life in the Sabine court. She had listened and given nothing back. He supposed the knowledge would have done him little good and endangered both her and her people.

He could, at least, forgive her for that. Though that did nothing to numb the sting of it.

And there she was, a de facto queen. Trapped in a backwater prison in the far reaches of the Sabine Empire. She was so close. Just a day's ride from her homeland.

More realisations hit Jai, one after the other. In her grief, she had not mourned just her dragon. She mourned her father. Her family, her friends. Her army. Her *kingdom*.

How she'd had the strength to carry on, he did not know. Did Titus know the girl he held captive was just a handmaiden? Of course he did.

That was why the Gryphon Guard still searched for her. Why Magnus asked about a missing Dansk girl. Jai felt sick, thinking of what the real Frida must have endured at the cruel ruler's hands.

He only hoped Titus's words had been bravado. That she'd been kept safe, as a pawn to trade with whatever was left of the Dansk leadership.

'Aye, that'll do it,' Rufus said, filling the apparently awkward silence. 'The more powerful the beast, the more powerful the gem. That, and how long it's been bonded for. But for someone so new tae cultivatin' . . . colour me impressed.'

Jai shrugged.

'The poison did me good, in the end. And the hanging. No man is more motivated to learn to swim than one who is drowning.'

Rufus was silent at that. Until that moment, Jai had been grateful to him. But now . . . he was angry.

'You did a good job of protecting us, didn't you,' Jai said bitterly. 'You're lucky those guildsmen didn't slit you ear to ear.'

Rufus cleared his throat. Looked down at the skillet and took it off the fire.

'The hemlock . . . it let the booze get me drunk. And I'd drunk enough tae kill a horse. Then with the poison in the stew . . . almost killed me.'

'So why didn't it?' Jai said. 'More's the pity.'

'Cos I've been a drunk for years. Worse than a drunk.'

He spoke with shame in his face, and Jai had to strengthen his resolve. Pity . . . forgiveness . . . trust. He had given all those to Milkar. Where had that gotten him?

'Why'd you come back?' Jai asked.

Rufus closed his eyes.

'You have every right tae hate me, lad. More'n most. But I'll no' let you hate in ignorance. I'll tell you who I am. What I was.'

Jai ignored him, instead taking another heavenly bite of sausage – his ascended tongue and throat able to take them straight from the pan. Whatever Rufus said, it would not shake him. The man had failed them. Broken his word.

'There's no whytblade for you here,' Jai said. 'None there either. Guildsmen took it.'

Rufus shrugged.

'I never needed the blade, lad, I had my own. Never needed tae interfere in your lives neither. Was greed that did it. In truth, I was drinkin' myself to death. Had been tryin' for a few years. Never got the knack for it.'

Jai said nothing. He had not the energy to even think of a reply.

'When I told you I was a Gryphon Guard, I spoke truth. But I was no' just one o' them. I was the first. I once went by Rufinus.'

Jai stared at him.

'Rufinus . . .' he whispered. 'I am sure Leonid once spoke that name.'

Rufus snorted.

'He must've been the only one that did. When . . . it happened . . . none were allowed tae speak it. All I'd done. All my friends had done. Erased, like that. Nameless men.'

He clapped his hands together, making Jai jump.

'I had ten disciples left, when the wars finally came to an end. Men I'd fought beside. Brothers in all but blood. We'd lost so many. Back then, our tower had just been built – the price o' our allegiance. We were happy. Free tae soulbreathe, tae progress down the path. No more fightin' – we had apprentices for that. And then . . . Constantine came o' age.'

Jai had wished to feign indifference, but he could not resist leaning closer. This . . . this was something new.

'He took a liking to my niece. Lila, she was called. A lovely girl, no more'n fifteen years old. What a beauty she would have turned out tae be. She called me Uncle Woof, growin' up. Couldn't pronounce her Rs, back then. I remember that.'

Rufus rubbed at his eyes, almost frustrated at his own emotion.

'Constantine did not wish tae marry her – we knew what he wanted. So we kept her from him as best we could. I even promised tae protect her, the first time she came tae me. But our best was no' enough.'

Tears ran down Rufus's face. Twice, he wiped them away with his sleeve, but it was like holding back the tide.

'She came to my chambers one night. Bloodied, beaten. Her face . . . I could hardly recognise her. She had denied the emperor, and he'd forced himself on her. I was so . . . *angry.*'

He sniffed, staring at his great hands. Twisting them like a chastised child.

'I went tae Leonid along with my closest men. We told him what had happened. Demanded he protect her from him – call him off. Only an emperor could stop another, unless we took the power for ourselves. My men called for it . . . in the heat of it all. But I would never betray Leonid.'

Jai found tears in his own eyes. They came unbidden. Porticus had hardened his heart . . . but not enough, it seemed.

'This was not long after the War o' the Steppe. Leonid had just handed the throne tae his son. He was tired o' the killin'. But he still had power. Enough tae do what was right. Instead . . . I woke tae find a whytblade at my throat. And the others . . .'

There was rage in his eyes.

'Ten brothers died on the tower. The tower they'd fought for all their lives. Their beasts were burned before their eyes, their minds drugged awake so that they would feel every second o' it. And then, in the moment o' their greatest agony, when their beasts gasped their last . . . they were thrown from the top.'

He gripped Jai's hand with sudden urgency.

'Leonid let his son choose our fates. And Constantine did it by turnin' my own blood against me. Offered him the sect in exchange. Lila's own brother. My nephew, Magnus.'

Jai could feel it now. That rage, simmering beneath the surface. He had always been fearful of Rufus. He'd seen the pain there. But not the anger. Not until now.

Now, he understood. It had been so obvious, he almost kicked himself for not seeing it. The two looked so alike. Of all the warriors Jai had met in his life, Magnus and Rufus stood out. Both ruddy faced and barrel chested. They even shared the same jutting chin.

'In the treason trial, Magnus testified against us,' Rufus said, oblivious to Jai's shock. 'Hell, he was the one that captured us, takin' us in our sleep, turnin' the squires against us. He swore we'd plotted against the prince and asked him tae take part. That I had tried tae whore out my own niece to secure my own bloodline upon the throne. That Constantine had turned down her advances and that she had turned violent at his rejection. That she'd deserved that beating. That . . .'

He lost track of his words. In his hand, Jai saw the handle of the skillet bend and crumple, so tightly did the man hold it.

'Leonid let me live. That was what my years of service had bought me. I gave him an empire . . . and he betrayed me. Do you see why I hate him?'

Jai knew Rufus spoke the truth. He knew it in his bones.

'And Magnus?' Jai asked. 'Do you hate him too?'

Rufus sniffed.

'My brother, Magnus's father, was one of the so-called traitor knights. Magnus pointed the finger at his own family. That was what lent such credence tae his words. O' course I hate him. But he was always a cunt. Leonid . . . Leonid was my oldest friend.'

Jai could not help it. He lay a hand on Rufus's wrist, gripping it tight.

'You could not have known.'

Rufus pulled away, wiping his face once more. Rage had taken misery's place. He yanked down his shirt, stabbing a finger at his tattoo.

'After they burned my darling Aquila in front of me, I was a broken man. They pumped me full of hemlock and left me in a poppy den in the Phoenix Empire; told me to never come back. But I came back tae my homeland and joined the Samarions. Took every test until they gave me the tattoo. So that *none* will ever doubt my word again.'

He dissolved into tears once more. Jai realised for the first time that he could not smell the stink of alcohol on the man's breath. Indeed, Rufus looked haggard, and his forehead was beaded with sweat. He had either run out of drink, or had chosen not to. Jai did not feel the need to ask.

'Your tattoo is worthless,' Jai spat. 'You failed Frida. Failed us both. You promised to protect us. Now she rots in a prison. And it was Winter who saved me. Not you. Let that add to the weight of your conscience.'

His words were harsh. Harsher, perhaps, than they had any right to be. After all, it was they who had hired a known drunk. And they too had been poisoned, just as he had.

But he needed Rufus's guilt. He needed a powerful ally, sick and fragile though they might be. It was the only way he was ever going to break Frida out.

'If a Samarion breaks their word, their soul is forfeit,' Rufus said. 'Only through amends can we salvage our afterlife.'

He turned to Jai, his eyes wild and unfocused.

'I am your liegeman now. Yours, and Frida's. Until the both of you deem my debt is paid.'

Jai pondered him a moment. Then gently took the skillet from Rufus's hands.

'Come now,' Jai said. 'Eat. We've a lot to do before nightfall.'

Chapter 94

This plan is madder than the one that got you caught,' Rufus grumbled.

Jai hushed him and peered out into the forest below. Far beneath, there was a clearing. There, a forlorn figure sat upon a log, facing the west.

'You just be ready to jump,' Jai whispered. 'And remember not to kill it. We need it alive.'

Rufus grumbled beneath his breath.

They had spent the day plotting and watching over what they could of Porticus. That, and soulbreathing. Jai's mana was low, though he now had a small reserve, in no small part thanks to Winter. Luckily Rufus had a full core and was able to keep an eye out while Jai soulbreathed within the cave. Winter stayed by his side the entire time, alert as a watchdog, as if Jai was in immediate danger. After last night, she was taking no chances.

It was hard not to explore their renewed connection. Jai wished he had more time. It felt like since she'd hatched they'd hardly had a moment to do so.

Always hunted. Always moving. Tonight, that would change.

Now, Jai could soulbreathe no more, for their target could

arrive any minute. Night was falling quickly and all was silent as a grave.

If the wardens had been sent out to look for him, there had been no sign. More likely they had sent out the direwolf to hunt him down. As a soulbound running full-tilt to the west as far as they knew . . . well, it was the only thing that could catch up to him other than perhaps Beverlai herself. He was counting on it.

'Legion've gone,' Rufus said. 'Right on schedule. Must've left a couple hours ago.'

Jai squinted into the mist, listening. As an ascended soulbound, his enhanced senses cost him no mana. But he could hear nothing – their cave was several miles from Porticus.

'See, the yellowing there,' Rufus said, pointing into the moonlit sky. 'Dust-clouds. They're on the march.'

Jai chewed his lip. If Rufus was right, it was good news. Much of their plan relied on the legion being gone, leaving their route beyond the east wall open. That, and the wardens' complacency at the army's proximity would remain a few days yet. But how could he be sure?

'Don't believe me?' Rufus said. 'Here, listen.'

He yanked his whytblade from his side, and planted it in the rocky ground with a short, swift stab. He pressed his ear to its handle, clicking his finger for Jai to do the same.

Jai did so, Rufus's wiry beard tickling his cheek. He could hear it, ever so faintly. A deep rumbling, like a herd of wild bison.

'Some sounds travel better in the earth,' Rufus said, a wry smile twisting his lips. 'Oh, before I forgot. I've something for you. Keep watch.'

Rufus hurried back into the cave, and returned, to Jai's surprise, with his backpack and sword.

'Frida's whytblade got taken, but that cunt left the rest,' Rufus said. 'Cowardly fucker, came running back all scared-like and took off with the pair o' you over his shoulders. Must've thought a cave-bear was after him. Oh, and your armour and journal's in there for you too.'

If all went as planned, the only blade they would need would be the one in Rufus's hand. If not . . . well the sword would come in handy.

Jai tugged on the backpack, if only to give his back some protection from the biting wind. This high up, they were almost four storeys above the ground, and there were no trees to slow the seemingly endless draughts that haunted this place.

By now, the sun was well and truly set. So they sat . . . and waited to spring their trap.

JAI SMELLED IT BEFORE he heard it. Smelled it on the wind; that animal scent that told him the direwolf was nearby. Far below, their bait remained upon the tree stump. A figure, unawares of what was approaching it.

Neither Rufus or Jai spoke, but an exchanged glance was all they needed to know that it was time. Jai's blade was already unsheathed, and both had dirtied their blades with soil to dampen their shine.

Jai glanced at his core and saw it was almost a tenth full. Enough for a fight, if a short one. He only hoped it would not come to that.

And then, they saw it. It slunk out of the trees, practically crawling upon its belly. Darting from one stump to the next. Hunting.

For the first time Jai realised how fortunate he had been that

Rufus had found him. He might have run on and been hunted down. Even ascended, he was no match for the enormous beast.

Rufus leaned out over the cliff-side, his blade gripped tight in one hand, the rope of Navi's halter in the other. Below, the wolf was but a dozen yards from the figure – a scarecrow, fashioned with Jai's shirt.

Rufus tensed . . . and the wolf leaped.

Jai almost yelled out as the man fell forward, his great frame plummeting like a stone. In the gloom, Jai heard snarling . . . then a simultaneous thud and ear-splitting yelp.

Silence.

For a while Jai peered into the darkness, listening to the sound of rustling below. Then, Rufus's voice.

'It's done, lad! Hurry!'

Chapter 95

J ai crouched in the dirt, his blade held tight against the bound beast's throat. This close, Jai could hardly stand the wet-dog stench of it, yet he could do nothing but press its tied snout into the dirt, if only to muffle its whining.

There was no need for it to make noise. Beverlai would find her bonded partner soon enough, just as Winter had hers.

'Are you sure she'll know to bring Frida?' Rufus hissed.

Jai could not see him, for the big man was hidden in the thick of the forest. If Beverlai did not bring Frida, Rufus would take Beverlai hostage. The woman had no way of knowing that he was there.

'There's nothing else I could want,' Jai hissed back. 'She'll sense her beast's distress and know I've managed to subdue it. Know I'm keeping it alive for a reason.'

Even from where he hid, Jai could hear Rufus muttering beneath his breath.

The big man had been against this plan from the beginning, instead claiming they could take Porticus in a direct assault. But there was every chance Magnus had stayed behind with the scouts. Even Rufus could not take on Magnus *and* the rest of the prison. Or even – though Jai did not say it – Magnus alone, for that matter.

Most pressing of all, Frida did not have time for them to wait for the leader of the Gryphon Guard to leave. By now, she'd be so weak Jai didn't know if she'd even be able to stand. It had to be tonight.

After this, they would find another way to the east. Perhaps return to the Kashmere Road and cut north once they were past the Petrus Mountains. If they were lucky, they could do it.

'This is taking too long,' Rufus whispered. 'It'll be sunrise soon. She must be planning something. If Magnus comes . . .'

'She won't tell Magnus,' Jai snapped, putting as much confidence into his voice as he could muster. 'She'd have to tell him about Frida. Admit she lied to him.'

Even as he said the words, Jai hardly believed them himself. It was the one flaw in his plan – for who was to say Beverlai would not betray Aurelius's secret, or risk Magnus's wrath to save her beast.

The sadist was a fiend, but Jai had seen cruel calculation behind her eyes. Jai hoped the woman would see sense. If Frida disappeared, Aurelius would assume that Jai had broken her out, not Beverlai. Nor could Aurelius make much of a fuss with Magnus and his scouts resting in the prison.

If the cruel gaoler would just think it through . . . she'd come alone.

'Watch your rear,' Rufus whispered. 'She might try to sneak up on you.'

Jai nodded. Winter was a hundred yards behind him, patrolling for that very reason. Navi was with her, if only as another set of eyes. The old girl was exhausted after her climb down the goat path.

A branch cracked, toward the east.

Jai did not speak, for there was no need to. He simply tensed his hand, ready to strike at the first hint of an ambush.

Soon enough, Jai could hear the crackle of leaves underfoot. It sounded like one person, walking with a heavy gait. Then, a silhouette in the gloom.

A woman, carrying a heavy bundle.

Beverlai.

'Took you long enough,' Jai called out. 'I was about to start cutting pieces off. A wolf doesn't need its tail, right?'

It was hard not to twist the blade, in both senses. Not after what Jai had been through.

'Hold, now,' Beverlai said, her voice high and frightened. 'I've brought the girl. That's what you want, isn't it?'

'Step closer,' Jai said, pulling his sword a little higher. 'Show me.'

Beverlai did so, and pulled back the cloth that covered the bundle. In the thin moonlight, Jai could make out Frida's golden hair and the frame of her face. It could be no one else.

Relief flooded through Jai, but he pushed the feeling away. They were not out of the woods yet.

'Put her down,' Jai said. 'And unlock her manacles. I see them there.'

Beverlai remained still.

'You first,' she said. 'Untie my direwolf.'

Jai forced a laugh.

'I let this thing go, it'll rip me to shreds before I've even taken a step. You let my friend free, and then you leave. If you return before morning, I'll slit Ulf's throat. Come back at daybreak tomorrow. You can cut your beast free then.'

Beverlai was silent, then slowly lowered Frida's body to the ground. Jai could hardly believe it. They were almost free. There was a long road ahead, but their ordeal at Porticus was almost over.

.And then, he felt it. The sharp blade pressed into his spine, and the great ham of a hand enveloping his.

'Hello, Jai,' Magnus whispered. 'Fancy seeing you here.'

Chapter 96

There was silence, but for the howling of the wind.

'Before we begin, I want you to know that lady there is the reason you're still breathing,' Magnus said. 'She wants to have some fun with you before I hand you over to Titus. You *and* the girl. Make you watch first.'

Jai let out an involuntary sob as the hand tightened upon his wrist. He felt the bones in his wrists grind and the sword fell from his hand.

'Now,' Magnus said. 'You could run, and I'd have to chase you. But I'll take a hand for that. Then the other. Then something you're fonder of. Won't be needing it without those hands, eh?'

He chuckled at his joke and lifted Jai to his feet by his neck. Higher and higher, until Jai dangled, his feet kicking involuntarily as his throat was crushed by Magnus's meaty fingers.

'You always were a wrong'un, Magnus.'

Rufus's voice drifted from the shadows not far from where they stood. The pressure on Jai's neck lessened and he took a deep, choking breath. His mind was blank. There were no clever words or tricks to free him now. He'd shown his hand . . . and lost.

'Who said that?' Magnus snarled.

Rufus stood in Beverlai's place, his hand contorted in a majicking gesture. Jai heard an intake of breath. He fell in the dirt, suddenly released, and lay like a beached fish, clawing at his crushed throat as he tried to swallow a bite of air.

'Your eyes do not deceive you,' Rufus said, lifting the whytblade. 'Oh, tae see you here, blood o' my blood. Rubbin' shoulders with fetterers, threatenin' the helpless. What a pathetic little cunt you've become.'

Jai stared up, seeing that Magnus's other hand was already twisted in its own gesture. The two men stared at each other. Nephew and uncle. The old buck, and the new.

He tried to crawl towards Rufus, only to feel a boot press him into the earth. Gently . . . like a cat playing with a mouse.

'This is some cheap parlour trick,' Magnus growled. 'You're a dead man.'

'No trick, dear nephew. Just . . . justice.'

Magnus snarled and leaned down so hard Jai thought his back would snap.

'Leonid swore to me. He said he owed you a private death, but he swore to me you were killed.'

Rufus chuckled darkly.

'Leonid broke a lot of promises in his time. Now, here's one from me. And you can believe I'll keep it.'

He yanked back his shirt, revealing the tattoo.

'Titus may have stolen my revenge on him, so you will have tae do. I swear on all that is holy in this godforsaken world that I will kill you. I swear it, on my immortal soul.'

For a moment, Magnus was silent. Then he too chuckled.

'Your soul is as fucked as mine, Rufus. No mark some cunt shat out on your arm will keep you from damnation. Nor will killing me. You judge me for rubbing shoulders with this woman. Why?'

He stabbed a finger at Beverlai, who had staggered to her feet. Her sword was nowhere to be seen, but the woman was already moving. Circling. She had no idea how powerful Rufus was. She thought she had a chance.

'Have you forgotten the thousands you killed for our dear master? Was he not the greatest fetterer of all? Half the fettered in the empire would not be so, were it not for you. For us. Neither of our hands are clean. I just got mine dirtier than most.'

Rufus said nothing, instead grinding down his feet for firmer footing. Magnus laughed at that.

'Let me snap this worm's spine and then we can have at it.'

Rufus turned his hand to point at Frida.

'Kill the boy, I kill the girl. She's worth a kingdom, is she not? Or has your prince not realised yet?'

Jai wheezed a curse under his breath. Rufus was being reckless. Even as Jai glared at him, the big man winked. It was as if he had lost his mind.

Magnus was silent. Then nodded slowly.

'We knew within a few days. The handmaiden broke before our torturers had even started their fun. More's the pity. Had we known she wasn't soulbound, we might have tried . . . something more entertaining.'

Jai attempted to crawl forward until a foot slammed into the ground beside his head, stopping him dead. He lay there as Magnus weighed his life. It would be so easy for the huge warrior to kill him. He could kick Jai's spine through his belly without even breaking a sweat.

'Fine. Beverlai can have him.'

Jai felt a foot hook under his hips and the world spun. Then he was upside down, half a dozen yards away. He struggled to his feet, dazed.

'Here?' Magnus asked.

A blast hurled Magnus back into the forest. Rufus stepped forward, his hand blazing white. His irises glowed, and he turned to Jai with a smile upon his face.

'Don't wait for me. Good luck, lad.'

And then he was gone. Running into the gloom, his whytblade glowing bright.

Jai crouched and located Beverlai. The woman was bladeless, just as he was, with Jai between her and her wolf. She had not realised Jai's blade was lost too. Not until their eyes met.

Beverlai lifted her hand and flexed her fingers. Then she contorted them and pointed at Jai.

'I know you've got some fight in you,' she growled. 'Let's see how much.'

Chapter 97

Jai did not wait to see Beverlai's hand glow, instead sprinting for his discarded blade. A ball of flame whipped by his head and Jai dove aside, rolling in the wet leaves.

Another flared past him, setting fire to the brambles behind. Jai could only roll on, thrusting himself deeper into the thickets as fireballs slammed into the ground around him.

Jai scrambled behind a tree even as flame flattened against its front, nearly lifting it from its roots. He braced himself against it, waiting for the light of Beverlai's hand to fade.

The warden cackled and Jai heard her soothing the direwolf. He peered out to see Beverlai plucking at Rufus's tight knots. She cursed before rummaging around on the forest floor, seeking Jai's sword.

'Come on,' Beverlai hissed. 'Where've you left it. Been a while since Ulf's had a taste of savage.'

In his mind's eye, Jai sensed Winter lying in wait beyond, her little heart nearly beating out of her chest. She awaited his instruction and Jai could tell it took every ounce of her willpower to not attack.

Jai pressed himself against a tree, knowing he had but seconds before the blade was found and the direwolf cut free. If that happened, he was finished.

Winter was his last card to play. Beverlai knew he was soul-bound. Knew he was ascended. But she did not know he was bonded to a nearby beast, let alone a dragon.

Light flared, bright as the sun, then faded. Somewhere beyond, a deep boom rattled the branches, followed by a slap of wind that nearly bowled Jai over and caused the trees to creak.

Then another flash, and another. The very ground shook, so that Jai had to grip the trunk for balance. Whatever Magnus and Rufus were doing, Jai could not imagine their battle would last long either. And he did not trust Rufus to win it.

He needed to end this . . . fast.

Jai had seen some basic gestures in his short time with Rufus, but he had not practised them enough.

A fireball might surprise Beverlai – he knew he could form one, at least.

He contorted his hand and entered the half-trance, forcing mana down his channels. He revelled in how swiftly the mana moved through his body, yet when it reached his hand, it did very little. Fizzled, mere sparks sputtering from his fingertips.

Jai had no time to perfect his finger positioning. Instead, he did the only thing he could. He ordered Winter to attack . . . and dove around the side of the tree.

Beverlai's left hand swung up at the first sign of movement, and Jai saw the old woman was sawing at the wolf's bonds with her right. He ran on, even as Beverlai's eyes began to glow.

Twenty feet. Ten.

A sphere of flame was forming at the tip of Beverlai's finger, swirling like a miniature sun. She screamed out, and Jai hurled himself aside.

The ball flared past his side, setting his shirt aflame. Jai rolled, over and over, as more flame billowed around him. He sensed Winter leap . . . and heard a garbled scream.

Jai was up and running in a heartbeat, ignoring his burning clothes. He charged Beverlai as she stabbed at the snapping, scratching thing wrapped around her head. He hit home, tackling the woman's feet from under her.

The three rolled in the grass, Jai grappling for Beverlai's hands. He found his mark, and Jai wrestled them to the ground, pressing with all his might to keep them from majicking. The blade was somewhere close, but Jai dared not let her hands go.

It comes!

Jai sensed the sudden horror in Winter's mind and dove aside. A grey blur passed over him as furry limbs knocked him off his knees.

Ulf was free.

Jai scrambled for the fallen blade, even as Winter disengaged, lunging for the wolf. Then her mind was aflame with pain and fury, taking Ulf head on in a whirlwind of fur, scales and teeth.

The sword hilt knocked against his palm and Jai spun with the blade, stabbing at Beverlai as the woman wiped the blood from her face.

He hit home, once, twice, before a blind hand swept up. *Light.* Then Jai was hurtling through the air, agony jolting through him as he slammed into a trunk.

Flames spread across his chest, peeling cloth away to roast his skin beneath. Jai ripped away the garment. Turned, and charged again.

Only to be faced with a wall of flame.

Beverlai blazed the space in front of him, an inferno of mana setting the very ground on fire as she tried to clear blood from her vision. Jai raised his wrist to protect his face as the heat battered him.

Beyond, Winter was losing. Already she had broken contact, using the brambles to hide from the slavering direwolf. There was no time.

Jai staggered into the flames, even as they petered out. Beverlai swung her hand from side to side, blinking through crimson-filled eyes. She could not see.

But she could hear, and as Jai took another step he barely side-stepped the streak of flame that shot his way. Weaker, this time. The old woman was almost out of mana.

'Come on, you craven cunt,' Beverlai snarled, swinging her hand from side to side. 'Where are you?'

Her free hand was pressed to where Jai had wounded her shoulder, and Jai watched as the woman's fingers traced a spell there. Healing, the wound sealing before Jai's eyes.

Jai did the only thing he could. He threw the blade with all his might.

The sword slapped lengthways across Beverlai's face, cutting a furrow in her forehead. Reeling, Beverlai blasted a wave of flame.

Jai dove beneath it, taking Beverlai's legs from under her.

Mana roiled in Jai's veins as he pulsed out almost all he had, slamming his fists again and again into her face.

Blood spattered as her nose burst, and then Jai was forced to grapple hand-to-hand once more. Beverlai's fingers were like steel and it was all Jai could do to disrupt their twisting.

Danger!

Jai looked up. Saw Ulf charging at him, Winter limping in pursuit. He had seconds.

The sword! Where was the sword?

Jai reached out, scrabbling in the litter where it had fallen. Found the hilt, even as Ulf leaped. Jai's vision filled with a gaping maw.

A wall of fur slammed into the beast's side.

Navi! The khiro bellowed, rearing and trampling the direwolf as it scrabbled for purchase in the wet soil. It twisted, and lunged, latching onto her snout, savaging her side to side.

Jai lifted his blade, holding it above Beverlai's face. The cruel woman raised her hands, a word half-formed in her mouth. She sobbed, once.

Then Jai plunged his blade down, through her eye socket. Twisted back and forth, screaming hatred into the warden's face.

'Die,' Jai roared, ramming blade through skull, spearing the earth.

Chapter 98

Jai watched as the direwolf collapsed across the clearing, twitching and shaking at its master's death. Navi reared on her back legs. Stomped down once. Twice.

The twitching stopped.

A dull boom echoed through the forest, shaking leaves to float down from the canopy above. It was distant. As if Magnus and Rufus's battlefield spanned over a mile.

Rufus might need his help, but Jai knew well he had no business giving it. He had a responsibility. Frida.

Or Erica . . . Jai's head reeled. He didn't know what to call her.

Jai could make out the princess's figure and looked for movement. She was stirring, but not struggling as he had thought she would be. She looked drunk, or something close to it. Her lips mumbled nonsensically, and she shook and twitched. He would have to carry her. Or at least, Navi would.

'Winter,' Jai croaked.

He had breathed in a great deal of flame and smoke and his throat was choked from it. He felt cooked from both within and without, for his skin was pink and raw where the flames had taken hold. Had he not been ascended, he might well be dead. As it was, his mana was almost spent, the exertion of battle and healing of his burned skin sapping it like a leech.

Winter threw herself into his arms and he clutched her close. She was twice as heavy as he remembered her, yet at the same time felt light as a feather, for he was far stronger now.

For a few heartbeats he let himself calm, her cool scales soothing on his healing chest. Then he struggled to his feet.

Jai patted at his clothes where they were still smoking, even as he ran to Navi. He wrapped her neck in a hug.

'Thank you,' Jai whispered as the three pressed their heads together. 'You saved my life.'

The beast whickered in his ear and nuzzled him with her snout. Jai only wished he could heal her, for the bite there was deep, and dripping blood.

'Winter,' Jai murmured. 'My darling girl. I thank you, too. But I must ask more of you this night.'

The dragon understood his intentions as easily as his words. He did not even need to voice it. She leaped from his arms and limped off to the east. Her body, too, was slowly healing. He could sense it; the mana in her tiny kernel of a core draining fast.

Jai stumbled closer to Frida. He knelt beside her, brushing the hair from her face.

She was so thin, he almost thought they had swapped her with one of the girls from the brothel. Her eyes were sunk into her skull and the skin of her face was paler, such that he could see the spider-lines of her blue veins beneath her skin. Her skin, when he touched it, was dry and thin as rice paper.

It was her. But *less* of her.

'Frida,' Jai whispered. Then: 'Erica.'

She stopped, just for a moment, then continued mumbling.

Dansk, if Jai had to guess. She was not here right now. Not in her mind.

Jai lifted her and placed her gently in Navi's saddle. He shouldered his pack, grateful to it for softening the impact when he had hit the trees.

He could not afford to wait. Jai needed to know if the wardens had heard the sound of battle. If they were coming. Ascended or not, he had barely any mana, and Frida was not exactly able to help. All four of them were injured in some way.

His chest was burned, though not so badly that it inhibited his movement. Frida's, or rather Erica's, delirium meant she would be no help. And Winter . . . she was cut, battered and bruised in a dozen places, with her tail bent and hanging limp at its end.

Jai could not head west now. Not with Magnus in that direction. Nor with a score of horse-riding scouts ready to hunt them as they headed for the Kashmere Road. He was not sure if he and Frida could take twenty trained soldiers, even if they had time to replenish their mana.

He had two choices. The first was to wait to learn whether uncle or nephew survived the battle. Wager on the old veteran and hope they would head west with him as their protector . . . rather than die a cruel death at Magnus's hands.

Or they could escape east through Porticus. Deep into Steppefolk territory, where no small imperial force dared follow. A vast place where they might disappear with enough of a head start.

What else? He was beginning to feel panicked, for the battle had gone silent. He needed to make a choice. Now.

Jai returned to Beverlai's body and yanked his blade free, sheathing it after wiping it on her shirt. Then he retrieved the keys at the woman's hip.

For a moment, Jai stared at Frida. He wished he could ask her what she wanted. He knew, in his heart of hearts, what she would say.

If they headed for the Kashmere Road, or some other mountain pass, it might be many months before they made their way to the Dansk border. And that was if they didn't get caught first. She'd never forgive him if he took the safer, longer path. She wanted to return to her people. To lead them in their darkest hour.

What choice was more insane, when he really thought about it? To walk away when they were so close? Stay in enemy territory, and trust the fates they could outrun whoever came in pursuit?

Or they could attack the prison. Fight or sneak their way through it.

None expected an attack from the west. None expected an attack from a soulbound, weak and injured though he was. And the wardens would be complacent, with the legion so close by. What sentries would stay on duty through this bitterly cold night, watching the clouds of dust the legion threw up in their wake?

Both plans seemed as foolish as each other. To go west spread the risk over many days and might keep them alive a little longer. To go east . . . well, it was one last fight. One more gamble.

Not to mention, he could free the Huddites.

It was Winter that clinched it. By now, the dragon had made it up a tall tree a mile closer to the prison. She saw . . . no threat. Not a sign of life. She was telling him they were safe.

Jai thanked her in his mind and asked her to wait for him by the western wall.

Then he secured Frida into Navi's saddle, even as another blast rocked the trees around him.

'Hang on, Rufus,' Jai whispered.

The khiro nickered at the disturbance and Jai patted the side of her neck to calm her.

'Come on girl,' Jai said. 'Let's go home.'

Chapter 99

J ai crouched in the shadow of Porticus's west wall, his hand
   stroking Navi's soft muzzle to keep her quiet. She was large
   enough that he might clamber upon her back and climb
to the top of the wall. But it would be far easier to sneak
through the gap where it lay unfinished.

Much to his relief, he saw there were no sentinels on the
walls or wandering the grounds. The snow had melted, too –
they would be harder to track once they left this place.

But Jai could *hear* the wardens. He had thought they would
be sleeping, but it seemed the ladies from the brothel had
stayed for yet another night. He could hear them all now,
laughing and singing in the garrison above the east wall's
gatehouse.

In some ways it was a blessing, for he had thought that they
might have heard the sound of battle, distant though it would
have been.

'Winter,' Jai breathed.

The hatchling scrambled to his side, still limping. Jai wished
he knew a spell to heal her. Or even had time to bandage her
many wounds. Instead, he gritted his teeth and began smearing

mud onto her scales, dulling some of the shine. Soon she was almost as dark as her mother had been.

'Wait for my signal,' Jai whispered. 'Go. Now.'

She lowered herself onto her belly and began the slow crawl towards the east gates, hugging the far wall where the poles were. Any warden glancing from the window or walking out for a piss in the latrines might see Jai. But Winter . . . she would be far less noticeable. Just a fox attracted to the stench of corpses.

Jai looked to the horses. Whether the Huddites could ride them, he did not know. But he knew that if they did not take them the scouts might still pursue them into enemy territory before the fear of the Steppefolk turned them back. Might even catch up to them.

Better to solve the problem by freeing the Huddites and letting them take the horses to make good their escape.

But Jai needed to get them out first.

He knew he had a far better chance of escape if he would simply wait for Winter to lift the bar from the eastern gates and ride Navi through at speed. Not to mention that a full prison break would mean every warden in Porticus would come in pursuit.

But he knew he could not leave the prisoners here. Jai had thought he had known misery at the palace. Known suffering.

He had known *nothing*.

And then, Jai saw him.

He had not noticed him before, for the warden had been so still. A single man, sitting upon the ramparts. Facing west.

Facing Jai.

Why this warden had chosen to stay out, Jai did not know. Perhaps Aurelius had forced him to as punishment. Perhaps Jai's escape had precipitated the creation of a new post – a man to constantly watch the prison interior.

Either way . . . Jai could not reach the cells undetected. And if he made a run for it, the wardens would man the walls long before the Huddites had reached the horses.

Without Winter, Jai knew his only card left to play was his mana.

He knew one spell that might help. Balbir's shade spell. It was time to try it once more.

Jai ducked back behind the gap in the west wall and sat cross-legged in the snow. He entered the trance, fully this time.

Within, he saw his core was near empty, though it was so much larger, he realised it was almost as much as if his core had been full before he had ascended. This was the few dregs that had not yet been used up in the battle or in slow-healing his burns in the aftermath. Jai cursed under his breath. He had to move quickly.

Jai took that small reserve and pulsed it to his contorted hand for the second time that night. Again, he felt almost triumphant as the mana reached his fingers.

For a moment, Jai thought he'd succeeded, as mana spurted out . . . but he saw nothing but golden sparks.

'Wrong,' a voice croaked.

Jai spun. Frida was looking at him, hanging upside-down from the saddle.

'Frida!' Jai breathed.

He had not known how scared he had been for her until that moment, for relief flooded him like a drug. For she was still dosed with poison and weak as a lamb in consequence. He had worried she would never wake.

He helped her sit up, for she looked like she had not the strength to stand. She sat slumped, hugging Navi's neck so tight it was as if she feared falling to her death. Her eyes were glazed and her pupils so large they almost hid her iris entirely. Jai had seen that same look before when Leonid took his pain medicine. She was drugged to the gills.

They were running out of time. Already, he could sense Winter was at the gate, waiting to lift the heavy bar that held it closed. He only hoped she had the strength to do so when the time came.

'Show me,' Jai said.

Frida forced a smile with thin, chapped lips and pointed at Jai's fingers.

'Through the fingers . . . not to them.'

It was so simple Jai could have kicked himself. He closed his eyes . . . and pushed *through*.

The effect was immediate. Light flared from his hand, projecting a dull, green glow wherever he pointed them. He could almost feel it against his skin. In fact, he *could* feel it. Numbing him wherever the light touched, as if he had spent the past hour in a cold lake.

He looked at his arm, and saw but a faded shadow in its place. It was working!

'You . . . you're disappearing,' Frida whispered, a drunken smile spreading across her face. 'You're . . .'

Jai did not wait to discuss it further. His mana was well and truly spent and he had no idea how long the charm would last.

Before he could think further, he gave Frida a single, soft kiss on the forehead. And then he ran. Right back into Porticus.

Chapter 100

Jai reached the cell gates in what seemed like no time at all. Adrenaline had lent wings to his feet, though he subsequently wasted a good ten seconds staring at the sentinel, hoping that the disturbance of the gravel had not been noticed.

This was not his own cell, but one of the other two. It was bitterly cold and not a single Huddite was in view, apparently preferring the dubious warmth deeper in the cave.

Jai unlocked the gate as quietly as he could, marvelling at the sight of his hands. Or rather, the lack of. He could see but a shadow. A ghostly half-image of himself.

For a moment, Jai considering calling out. Gathering the men so they were ready for the rush to the horses. But he resisted. He needed to summon them all at once when all the gates were unlocked. And he only had so long before the charm faded.

The next cave was not far, but already the numb feeling that had saturated his body was receding. This spell was far more costly than he had expected. By the time he unlocked the next, it was almost gone. He could see himself. See the shadow he cast.

Jai hurried to the final cell, the one that had once housed

him. He pressed himself to the wall, his eyes fixed on the sentry. The man sat silent, the smallest puff of smoke telling Jai he was smoking a pipe. Jai took full advantage of the distraction, making it to the gates just as the spell sputtered away.

Jai was on his own. The die was cast, and now he could but pray.

'Jai,' a voice whispered.

Jai flattened himself to the mountain, turning his head to the side. There beside him in the darkness . . . was Milkar.

He could see the man was a mess, even in the shadow of the cave. He wore not a thread of clothing and his body was a mass of welts and bruises. Clearly, he was not welcome to sleep with the rest of the men.

'Keep quiet,' Jai whispered. 'Go fetch the others. Quickly.'

Milkar was silent, staring at Jai through the bars of the cave.

'I cannot leave,' he said.

His eyes were vacant. As if the last bit of life had been sapped from him, and only a shell remained.

'My wife . . .'

Jai hushed him harshly and looked deeper into the cave. The Huddites were so deep within he could not even see them. Yet he dared not shout. Any minute, the sentry might spot them.

With trembling hands, Jai slotted the key into the lock.

'My wife is in the garrison,' Milkar hissed. 'We must save her. We must!'

He was loud. Too loud.

'We will,' Jai breathed, trying to soothe him. 'I will.'

'Please,' Milkar uttered, crawling towards him. 'I beg you. You are soulbound. You can—'

'Who are you squealing to now, traitor?' a voice called. 'Do you need a third lesson?'

A figure appeared in the shadows. Hanebal.

'We must take back the prison,' Milkar moaned, snatching at Jai through the bars. 'It's the only way.'

Hanebal stomped into the light, his hand raised threateningly. 'You . . .'

He stopped, seeing Jai's face through the bars.

'Jai—'

'The gates are unlocked,' Jai blurted. 'Gather your men and take the horses. I'll hold the gates open as long as I can.'

He backed away, looking to where Frida and Navi were waiting for him.

'Wait!' Milkar cried.

Jai spun in horror. On the west wall, the sentry stood, scanning the prison. Even in the dark, Jai saw the man start at the sight of him standing in the middle of the prison grounds. Then he was running, headed for the gatehouse.

Below, Winter heaved and Jai heard the steel bar fall to the ground.

'Escape!' Jai bellowed. 'Escape now!'

He ran, ripping the gates wide open as he passed, screaming blue murder to wake the sleeping men within. Navi thundered through the rubble, Frida bouncing on her back. Jai leaped and swung into the saddle, just catching Frida as she almost slipped to the ground.

By now, Huddites were streaming out of the caves, some almost blocking their path. But Jai could not slow Navi even if he had wanted to, and men were barged aside by her thundering passage.

Ahead, wardens were stumbling onto the east wall, many in states of undress. Women screamed.

Jai heard a hiss. Then another, and another.

A crossbow bolt buzzed by, and Jai cursed Milkar with all the breath he could spare. He could only hold on for dear life, listening to the rhythmic snorting of Navi as she galloped full tilt at the gatehouse.

Men screamed now, as the bolts hit home. He could hear horses neighing and Huddites yelling in a language he did not understand.

Beneath him, Navi lowered her head, bellowing as she charged at the doors. Jai braced himself, gripping Frida about the waist. They passed beneath the gatehouse's shadow and Jai instinctively closed his eyes.

He felt the jolt of impact and splinters dusted his face. Then cool air, and the heady scent of churned mud. They were through, galloping through the moonlight.

Jai half-leaped, half-fell from his saddle, drawing his blade. Navi ran on into the night, helped along by a slap on the rump.

Frida . . . she was safe.

Behind, Jai could still hear the wails of wounded men. That, and the thudding and hissing of the crossbows. The noise twisted his stomach, memories of the wedding seizing his mind.

He staggered into the gateway and raised his blade. Footsteps were already echoing down the stairs on either side. Jai had hardly time to call Winter to his side before the first men poured into the gateway.

Jai lunged, skewering one man through the back. He kicked him off the blade, knocking another off his feet. Now the wardens knew an enemy was in their midst.

A spear stabbed at Jai's belly and he sucked in his gut, feeling the kiss of the tip as it slit open his shirt. Winter leaped, scrabbling at the bastard's face. It was the work of two seconds to cut the warden down, Jai's blow slicing him from hip to hip.

More wardens jabbed at him, their helmeted faces inscrutable in the darkness. They drove Jai back, prodding and sweeping with their spears. Winter scampered amid the massed men, causing havoc as she sliced and snapped among the forest of legs. It was enough to allow Jai to cut another man down, before the mass of spears drove him back once more.

Twice, he took a spear tip to the shoulder, then another to his thigh. He backed away, holding his ground between the open doors.

Jai swept up his blade as a warden suddenly broke ranks, knocking the spear tip aimed at his chest. It sliced his cheek to the bone.

A swift stab took the man through the throat, before Jai had to leap back once more. Now, he was out of the gates. Standing in full view in the moonlight.

Wardens stared at Jai as if they had seen a ghost. Winter skidded out, spinning and snarling at Jai's feet. The wardens took a step back.

'You want to fight a soulbound?' Jai screamed, raising a contorted hand. The front ranks peddled the mud with their feet, pushing back as the men behind shoved forward.

And further still . . . the thunder of hooves.

'Come on!' Jai roared, waving his hands. 'I'm right here!'

A horse hurtled into the back ranks, knocking men flying. It made it just a few feet before collapsing with a groan, a spear dangled from its belly.

Hanebal leaped free, even as more cavalry thundered through the gap he had created, knocking wardens aside, trampling the dying horse beneath. Huddites clung to the horses, some two to an animal.

Then, as the last horse thundered through, the wardens' ranks closed, and hands grasped the edges of the great wooden doors.

Hanebal leaped, only for them to slam closed in his face.

Beyond, Jai heard screaming. Men, begging for mercy.

Hanebal battered at the doors, sobbing as the begging turned to screams.

'Come on,' Jai said, pulling at Hanebal. 'There's nothing we can do for them now.'

Hanebal pulled himself free, scrabbling at the doors with his hands.

'Hanebal,' Jai begged. 'We must go.'

The fettered man sobbed, falling to his knees. The sounds from behind the doors were . . . beyond words.

Jai punched out. He crouched, gathering the limp form in his arms.

Below him, Winter chittered, tugging at Jai's trousers with her teeth. Jai turned towards his homeland.

And ran.

Chapter 101

There was no time for conversation when he reached the pitiful remnants of the Huddites. Some thirty men had made it, trotting aimlessly through the last stretch of canyon.

Only half of the men he had freed were present. Many, too, were wounded and hardly able to keep themselves from falling from their horses. Jai was lucky, in a way, for the uninjured Huddites had stopped to render aid, allowing him to catch up.

Now, they galloped on, as fast as their injuries allowed. Navi led the pack, her great legs seemingly tireless as the mud left in the wake of the legion turned to trampled grass. Soon enough, the canyons opened out . . . and they ventured into the Great Steppe for the first time.

It was . . . another world.

No trees. No buildings. No mountains, or even hills.

Just an endless ocean of grass, silver in the moonlight. Stretching out and dancing to the whims of the wind. Somewhere in the recesses of his mind, Jai could just touch the edge of a memory. Of that same sight. Only the grass had seemed taller then.

Behind, there was no pursuit. By now, Aurelius would know Frida was gone and the wardens would have told him of the soulbound Steppeman who had fought them.

Aurelius would not know that Jai had so little mana; he could hardly see his core for the lack of glowing liquid within. He would not risk his men to try and recapture them. Not without Beverlai or Ulf.

Yet they were on borrowed time. The escape had been too loud and taken too long. And now that he was out here, in the cold light of the moon . . . his plan was falling apart.

If Magnus was alive and uninjured, he would come for them whether they were in enemy territory or not. He had borne witness to the great power the leader of the Gryphon Guard wielded. Enough to shake the very forest. Even a warband of twenty Steppefolk would not deter Magnus from his chase. Not with the rightful Queen of the Dansk within his grasp. Without her as his queen . . . Titus could not claim the Dansk throne.

Hell, if Magnus lived, Jai wouldn't be surprised if every gryphon and chamrosh in the empire would soon be heading their way.

They laboured on into the green ocean and Jai cursed the moon above.

It was bright as he had ever seen it, full and heavy enough to bathe silver light across the steppe. He could see too far around them and knew their pursuers would have the same advantage. He imagined Magnus with his great frame, thundering behind them.

His sorry band of escapees moved slowly now. The Huddites were starving, brutalised men. Most were wounded and few had the stamina to do any more than keep atop their horses. Fewer still had the energy to look behind them.

Frida, at least, was slowly recovering from her stupor.

Now she stirred. Looked at Jai through foggy eyes, a soft smile upon her face.

'We are not safe yet,' Jai said, noticing her expression.

Frida eased herself into a sitting position, wincing and clutching her head.

'You saved me. I cannot even begin—'

'You should know,' Jai said. 'The Sabines know who you are. Magnus said as much.'

She closed her eyes and hung her head.

'Is . . . Do you know, is my handmaiden . . . is Frida alive?'

'I do not know. But Magnus said she knew nothing useful. Unless he was lying, your secret . . . the way to bond with dragons. Perhaps it's still safe.'

The girl stayed silent a moment longer. Then she eased herself from the saddle, clutching Navi's neck. She took a few tentative steps.

'Forgive me,' she said.

Erica, he thought.

'I know why you kept your identity secret,' Jai muttered, unable to meet her gaze. 'But now it is known. At least to our enemies. You do not need to lie to me anymore.'

Erica grasped his arm and Jai pulled away. He was not angry at her, not really. He was just not ready to confront it.

'Jai . . . I'm so sorry.'

Jai turned away, staring out over the steppe. It was as if the place calmed him. For despite all they had endured and all they had yet to come, he was unafraid.

'Jai, please.'

Erica pulled on Navi's reins, pulling her to a stop. She turned and faced him, and Jai felt tears come to his eyes unbidden at the sight of her.

She pulled him close. He felt her breath on his mouth, then

his cheek as her fingers traced the scars upon his back. And then she too was sobbing, pressing her face into the charred cloth of his shoulder.

'I should have trusted you,' she breathed. 'I should have from the start.'

'You did it for your family,' Jai said, his chest tightening. 'I . . . I can forgive it. I might have . . .'

'Wait!' a man's voice called behind them. 'We must wait!'

Jai turned Navi, waiting as stragglers caught up to them.

Hanebal took that moment to fall from Navi's back, stumbling in a daze on the long grass. He fell to his knees, tugging and twisting a handful of vegetation. He sniffed it, deep. Jai saw tears in his eyes.

'We have to split up,' a man cried out. 'All of us! They'll track our horses. Follow our hoof prints.'

Men shouted in agreement, one already turning his horse.

Frida croaked, squeezing Jai's waist. 'Half of these men will never make it on their own. They'll bleed out or die of blood poisoning from their wounds.'

Jai was grateful to her for giving him the excuse to keep them together. Selfish though it was, there was strength in numbers. The legion might well have sent out patrols and Jai could not beat one alone.

'Leave now, and half your men will die,' Jai bellowed. 'We must continue in the legion's wake, where the ground is torn. They'll never expect it. It will be as if we vanished.'

'What happens when we run into a patrol, or catch up to them?' a Huddite called back. 'That buys us a few hours at most. And the ground is not all we must worry about. Their wolf will lead them right to us.'

'The wolf is dead,' Jai called out. 'Beverlai, too. How do you think I got the keys?'

Men stared at him, disbelieving. Then Winter leaped onto Jai's shoulder and the staring eyes widened.

'But your man is right,' Jai admitted. 'They will come for us.'

Jai looked down at the torn up ground, where five thousand feet had walked. Amid all this, their hoof prints would be hidden. Even their scent would be obscured by the thousands of legionaries and their pack horses. Enough to fool even a soulbound's senses. But as soon as they turned off . . . Magnus would be able to track them. Even from where he sat, the score of horses gave off a strong stench.

'We've gone far enough,' Jai said. 'Now, our only chance is to disappear. Our horses have served their purpose. We must cut them loose.'

'And what then?' the man said. 'They will see our horses, cropping the grass. Know where we turned off the legion's wake. You've only killed us quicker, you stupid fuck—'

The man reeled as a punch to the belly from Hanebal nearly toppled him from his horse.

Hanebal stabbed a finger at him, and the man fell into silence. Hanebal turned and stared back the way they had come.

'He's right,' he said, so quietly it seemed only Jai could hear. 'Our only hope is to outride them.'

Jai cursed. He knew Magnus could catch up to them whether they kept the horses or not. They could hide, but they could not run.

But . . . there was something they could do. If they could not run or hide . . . perhaps they could misdirect.

'One of us has to lead the horses away,' Jai said. 'Turn off the path, lead them a merry chase. It means . . . it means one of us will be recaptured.'

Hanebal furrowed his brows, then looked down at his hands. 'I am no rider,' he said. 'But if you help me tie the horses' reins together, I'll do it. Perhaps, with luck, they won't catch up to me.'

'No,' Jai said.

He lifted Erica from his saddle, and Huddite hands extended to help. She stared at him, her eyes clouded. Jai leaned out and kissed her forehead.

'Take care of her,' he whispered.

'Jai . . .' she whispered.

Jai smoothed a thumb across her cheek, then gathered himself.

He blinked tears from his eyes and turned them toward the first blush of the rising sun.

'It must be me.'

Epilogue

Jai had cut most of the horses free before daybreak as, one by one, the beasts succumbed to their wounds or exhaustion. None could keep the pace of Navi, nor push as easily through the tall grass that slowed them with every step. The loyal khiro had galloped through the night until their companions were lost to the horizon.

Now, Jai stopped. Dismounted, in the hopes their silhouette would appear to be a wild khiro with no rider. For he had seen something in the distance. A cloud of dust. Shadows, cutting the horizon.

And now . . . drawing closer. Jai fell to his knees, cursing the sky.

The incomers were moving fast. Riders. Jai let his hand fall to his hilt.

He could hear them, whooping in excitement. Wheeling their mounts as they neared, blades extended, surrounding him so quickly as to leave no chance of escape.

Khiroi. Great snorting beasts, with horns rising like prows from their heads. A great, impassable wall of fur.

And upon them . . . Steppefolk.

Men and women, ululating as they raised their curved swords into the sky. A man leaped from his saddle, approaching with his blade drawn. Jai had never seen a man such as he.

His hair was braided so long as to swing behind his legs as he walked. As for his clothing . . . it was all furs and leather, though he went bare chested, with only a simple strip of khiro pelt about his shoulders to keep him warm.

He snarled, spitting words at Jai that he only half-understood.

Jai lifted his chin as the man's blade whipped up, hovering an inch from his neck. The man laughed, apparently impressed by his courage. Then he shrugged and drew the blade back as if to strike.

'Wait!' Jai cried out.

The man's eyes flashed with recognition at the language and he cocked his head.

'Who . . . are you?' he asked.

Jai took a breath and slowly lowered his hands to the ruin of his shirt. He gripped it, and ripped it away, displaying the engraved gorget at his throat. He raised his voice, turning for all to see.

'I am Jai, son of Rohan. Last of his name, rightful heir to the Kidara. And I demand my birthright.'

THE END

Acknowledgements

First and foremost, my heartfelt gratitude goes to my editors, Vicky Leech and David Pomerico, for their unwavering support, patience, and commitment to this novel. The guidance you provided has been indispensable, and I feel fortunate to have had you both by my side throughout this journey.

I also wish to express my thanks to Juliet Mushens, my long-suffering agent. Juliet, your wisdom and belief in my work have made all the difference. I am deeply thankful for your guidance and persistence.

To the broader team at Harper Voyager in both the USA and the UK, that worked tirelessly behind the scenes, I am deeply grateful.

Chloe Gough, Rachel Winterbottom, Kim Young, Natasha Bardon, Hannah Stamp, Robyn Watts, Terrence Caven, Holly MacDonald, Roisin O'Shea, Sian Richefond, Sofia Saghir, Alice Gomer, Harriet Williams, Bethan Moore, Mireya Chiriboga, Gregory Plonowski, Michelle Meredith, Jennifer Eck, Jennifer Chung, Richard Aquan, Lara Baez, Catriona Fida, Bastien Lecouffe-Deharme.

Every book takes a village, and I am profoundly grateful to have had such an incredible team behind me. Your collective talent, dedication, and passion have left an indelible mark on this novel. Thank you all for being a part of this journey, and helping bring this story to life.

About the Author

Taran Matharu is a *New York Times* bestselling author. He was born in London in 1990, where he found a passion for books, writing his first novel at nine years old. Taran started writing *Summoner* at the age of 22 on Wattpad.com, with the story reaching over three million reads in less than six months. After being featured by NBC News, Taran decided to launch his professional writing career and has never looked back. His Summoner series has become a worldwide phenomenon, selling millions of copies in more than 16 languages. *Dragon Rider* is Taran's first adult fantasy.